# STORY OF O
## *Eros, Paris & Surrealism*

## Reese Saxment

BLACK SCAT BOOKS
2024

Black Scat Books
*BlackScatBooks.com*

*To K., with love, delight, champagne and Paris.*

# Table of Contents

Photo courtesy of the Stephen Prince collection. [www.storyofo.info]

# Introduction

*Story of O* by 'Pauline Réage', probably the most celebrated and notorious erotic novel of modern times, was first published in Paris as *Histoire d'O* in 1954 [1]. The identity of Pauline Réage was kept under wraps with surprising effectiveness for forty years, the author only being officially 'unmasked' in 1994 as the distinguished literary critic, editor and translator Dominique Aury (1907-1998) – a name that turned out to be another front – she had originally been christened Anne Desclos [2]. All three names will be used in this book: in the main Dominique Aury, with Anne Desclos for her earlier life, and Pauline Réage when occasion demands. I found the use of Réage for everything to do with *O* or subsequent interviews before she was 'unveiled' made for a bit of a messy read, so I have mostly stuck to Aury. We might however need to be a little cautious attributing to Aury something that was actually said by Aury-as-Réage – they are after all not exactly the same person. Having said all this, I can't promise to be relentlessly consistent about names. I hope the reader will cut me a little slack here!

*Story of O* has been something of a Rorschach ink-blot test ever since it was published. All manner of meanings can be, and have been, read into it. It has been interpreted variously as the pinnacle of erotica, the depths of pornography, a heroically feminist text, a dastardly anti-feminist text, a mystical journey, a psychoanalytic case study, patriarchal propaganda, a subversion of patriarchy, as well as a response to Simone de Beauvoir, Jean-Paul Sartre, Friedrich Nietzsche, and the Marquis de Sade. As one would expect with an ink-blot test, sometimes these critical interpretations tell us more about the hobby-horses of the critics and their own place and time than about the novel itself. Not everything written about *Story of O* does much service to our understanding of the novel, except to provide testament to its enduring fascination.

Pauline Réage made some additional revelations over the years: in 1969 she wrote 'A Girl in Love' ('Une Fille Amoureuse')[3], an account of the creation of the novel, and later gave a few interviews, two of which are particularly significant – to Régine Deforges (twenty-odd years after *O* was published[4]), and to John de St Jorre (twenty-odd years after that[5]). While these are illuminating, they also raise questions of interpretation in their own right. Firstly they date from later decades as the cultural climate was changing and the author was getting older (she was in her sixties when she wrote 'A Girl' and talked with Deforges, and in her eighties when interviewed by St Jorre). Secondly, our author had a pronounced taste for, and a real mastery of, dissimulation and concealment – partly out of self-preservation, partly out of playfulness – and laid false trails with some abandon. A posthumously published interview was entitled *Vocation: clandestine*[6], and Angie David's 2006 biography quite plainly states 'Dominique Aury's greatest passion is secrecy and her whole life is organised around clandestinity'[7]. This is not to devalue the light these later writings and interviews throw on things, but simply to point out that this light may be more than a little slanted on some matters. Nobody, not even authors, even when they are trying to be wholly serious, ever have the final word on a text.

Having said all that, let me now lay out my aims here.

Principally, I want to try to understand *Story of O* in its historic moment. The manuscript was begun (probably) in 1950, completed in 1951 and first presented for publication by Dominique Aury's lover Jean Paulhan later that year. This puts its composition squarely in the period of intense intellectual, literary (and political) ferment of post-Liberation Paris. With the ending of the Occupation during the Second World war, Paris became a hotbed for ideas, with a number of intellectual movements – including a 'cult' of the Marquis de Sade, Existentialism and 'Feminine Humanism' – all flourishing in a context of the increasingly chilly Cold War. Dominique Aury was centrally placed in the literary demi-monde of Paris, and *Story of O* was highly responsive to the ferment of the post-Liberation years, to the extent that it warrants consideration as one of the touch-stone texts of Parisian culture at the time. One knock-on effect of taking this view of *O* is that Anglophone commentaries and criticisms, which have been voluminous and voluble since the novel's publication in the U.S.A. in 1965, are not as central to this account as some readers might expect, and are largely confined to Chapter X.

More specifically I hope to make the case that, without down-playing its relationship with other philosophies and cultural movements of the time, *Story of O* can be best understood in the context of Surrealism. The idea that *O* and Surrealism have connections is not new. From the outset, editions of *O* have featured lithographs and illustrations by surrealist artists [8]; on first publication the most high profile (and enthusiastic) reviews of *O* were by prominent surrealist writers [9]; in 1969 Pauline Réage admitted her debt to surrealism for one of the most striking images in *O* [10], and on occasion other writers have noted associations and correspondences between *O* and Surrealism [11]. Usually it stops there – very few have stepped over the line to assert *Story of O*'s right to citizenship of the surrealist world – the honourable exception being Alyce Mahon who in 2020 identified *O* as a novel 'Breton would happily claim' for the movement [12]. This book is an attempt to delve more deeply into the matter, to explore *O*'s debt to surrealist ideas, notably those of André Breton and Georges Bataille, and to ask the questions: Can *O* be read as a surrealist novel, and does it deserve a place in the surrealist literary canon? Is Professor Mahon justified in her claim that Breton would have embraced *O*, and would he have been right to do so? I don't think it would be much of a spoiler for me to reveal my conclusions here as a pretty emphatic Yes on all counts. [I would of course be the first to admit that *Story of O* is just as much an ink-blot test for me as for anybody else].

I hope this book can be seen as a modest contribution to contemporary surrealist studies' commitment to inclusivity – throwing the net wide to draw into orbit artists and writers not usually associated with the movement, in particular women and those outside of the traditional western heartlands of surrealism [13]. In this case, the new recruit is indeed a woman writer hitherto largely unrecognised by surrealist scholarship, although, rather ironically, she has been found in Paris, the very birthplace of European Surrealism.

Needless to say, I am by no means laying claim to any kind of final conclusions here – if the author doesn't have the last word on her own work, I most certainly don't. Discussing *O* in the context of different intellectual-literary movements gives rise to a variety of interpretations of the novel, not all of which are compatible with each other. Apart from prioritising the surrealist reading, I am not attempting to resolve contradictions arising. To do so would go against the spirit of Surrealism, and anyway readers are perfectly capable of making their own decisions and drawing their own conclusions. In the end I hope this book will be seen as a contribution to a dialogue, perhaps stimulating some lines of enquiry, flagging up some questions, inviting further research, and encouraging responses from others with an interest in this remarkable and truly significant novel.

The book consists of ten chapters and an Afterword:

**1: A Parisian History of *Story of O* – The 1950s** recounts the story of the novel with a Parisian focus – its publication in 1954, reviews and reactions, rumours of authorship, and the legal case it provoked that rumbled on till the end of the decade.

**II: A Parisian History of *Story of O* Continued – The 1960s**

**and After** looks at the follow-up texts by Pauline Réage, 'A Girl in Love' and the novella *Return to the Château* (which may or may not be a chapter suppressed from the original manuscript) [14], before tracing *O* in the 1970s, on screen and in subsequent interviews, the revelation of Réage's true identity in the '90s, and briefly surveying posthumously released material.

**III: Lives and Times: From the Beginnings to the War – 1907-1944** traces the biographies of Anne Desclos (Aury) and Jean Paulhan in their early lives, including her relationships and career, and his involvement in the *Nouvelle Revue Française* (*NRF*), before following their experiences during the Occupation (1940-44), their meeting and their involvement in the Resistance.

**IV: Lives and Times Continued: From Liberation to the End – 1944-1998** traces the Aury-Paulhan story after Liberation in 1944, during the literary renaissance in Paris and the fractious politics of the time as the Cold War set in, the beginnings and development of their affair, *O* in the context of their relationships with significant others, and the story of their later lives.

**V: The Novel in Focus** looks in more detail at the texts of *O* and of Paulhan's preface [15], exploring characters and themes running through the novel, the significance of the title and the author's nom-de-plume, and biographical resonances.

**VI: *O* and the Philosophies of Liberation I – *Érotisme Noir*** begins our exploration of *O*'s place in the intellectual context of post-war Paris, and its relationship with ideas current at the time – focusing on *érotisme noir* and renewed interest in the Marquis de Sade in the 1940s and 50s.

**VII: *O* and the Philosophies of Liberation II – Existentialism and Feminine Humanism** continues our expedition into post-war Paris, focusing here on *O* in the context of Existentialism and the ideas of Nietzsche and Sartre, and the growing interest in women's issues, including the psychoanalytic theories of Marie Bonaparte and others, and the 'Feminine Humanism' of Simone de Beauvoir and Édith Thomas.

**VIII: *O* Among the Surrealists** brings us to the heart of the matter, looking into the relationship between *O* and the surrealists – their enthusiastic reception of *O*, the influence of their ideas on *O* (notably those of André Breton), Paulhan's intimate and long-standing links with the movement, followed by a discussion of *O* as a surrealist novel.

**IX:  *O*, Surrealism and Mysticism** surveys *O*'s relationship with the direction taken by Surrealism after Liberation, towards sexual occultism and the 'politics of Eros' [16], looking into *O*'s role in the rise of women's erotic literature in the 1950s, and its relationship with the contrasting stances on the mystical of Breton and Georges Bataille.

**X: Changing Horizons – *O* Goes International** follows the trail across the Atlantic to the 1966 U.S. publication of *O* [17], press enthusiasm and (radically divergent) feminist responses, and the pendulum swing from the liberal minded 1970s, through the rise of the 'Politics of Prohibition' of erotica in the 1980s, and back again in the 1990s, looking at how Surrealism and *O* fared in these changing times.

**Afterword:  Into the 21st Century** looks at the legacy of *O* in women's erotic fiction in the present century, and reviews the current culture wars where the politics of prohibition has revived, ending with a consideration of the role of a revived Surrealism in defending freedom, imagination and the Politics of Eros, and promoting the legacy of *Story of O*.

A couple of provisos need bearing in mind. The subtitle of the book is 'Eros, Paris and Surrealism', and although each chapter is very much about *Story of O* and/or its author, there will be sections of chapters in which the focus is not specifically on *O* or Aury, but on the other words in the subtitle. Moreover, because of the way the book is structured, we shall on occasion find ourselves revisiting some material and events (and even significant quotes) more than once. Bear with me! This is not me wandering off the point or engaging in lazy repetition, but an attempt to provide context and throw light from different angles, to provide a more nuanced understanding of *Story of O* and the woman who wrote it.

Finally, I will have to apologise here for the book's exclusively western focus. We shall be spending most of our time in Paris, with some visits to the U.S.A., and the odd postcard from the U.K. and locations elsewhere in Europe. No doubt there is much to be said about *Story of O* and its legacies in other countries and continents, but that is beyond my ken, and I would like to invite any who know more of these things to put (metaphorical) pen to paper – I'll be first in line to read all about it.

For referencing purposes I am using the 'Sabine d'Estrée' English language translations of the works attributed to Pauline Réage, originally published in New York by Grove Press, Inc.

*Story of O*, including Paulhan's preface 'Happiness in Slavery' (original text © Jean-Jacques Pauvert 1954; translation © 1965 by Grove Press, Inc.), Ballantine Books (published by arrangement with Grove Press, Inc.), 1973, 13th printing July 1982.

*Return to the Château: Story of O Part II preceded by A Girl in Love* (original text *Retour à Roissy, précédé d'Une Fille Amoureuse* © Jean-Jacques Pauvert 1969; translation © 1971 by Grove Press, Inc.), Corgi Edition 1985, reprinted 1988.

Just for the record, my French language copy of *Histoire d'O* is also a Pauvert 'Livre de Poche', © Jean-Jacques Pauvert 1954, published Dec. 1977.

Translations from French texts, including Régine Deforges' *O m'a dit* (Pauvert 1975; Pauvert 'Livre de Poche' edition 1976) and Angie David's *Dominique Aury* (Léo Scheer 2006) are our own.

I would like to take the opportunity here to acknowledge

the generous assistance and support I received from a number of people while writing this book: Dr. Valerie Costes for illuminations in matters mystical; Maurice Debonnard for the same in matters translational; Linda McAdam and the late Conn Moriarty (CDG) from Surrealerpool for proofing and sleuthing; Slim Smith, editor of *'Patastrophe!* for miscellaneous wizarding; also Tracy Thursfield, John Richardson, John Welson and Surrealism in Wales; Taya King, Darren Thomas and La Sirena; and of course Norman Conquest and everybody at Black Scat Books for their patience and stalwart work in editing and publication.

While every effort has been made to reference and acknowledge sources, there may be omissions or errors; if so, please let us know so we can rectify matters for the next edition.

———————————

[1] Éditions Jean-Jacques Pauvert. English translations were published by Olympia Press in 1954 and 1957, and Grove Press in 1965. The adventures behind these publications will be recounted in subsequent chapters.

[2] Anne Desclos adopted 'Dominique Aury' as a literary pseudonym in 1937, and retained it as her professional name for the rest of her life. She used 'Pauline Réage' exclusively in the context of *Histoire d'O* and related texts and interviews.

[3] Éditions Jean-Jacques Pauvert again – originally published in *Retour à Roissy, précédé d'Une Fille Amoureuse*. Published in English translation as *Return to the Château: Story of O Part II, preceded by A Girl in Love* (Grove Press, 1971).

[4] Published as *O m'a dit: entretiens avec Pauline Réage* (Pauvert, 1975) [literally *O told me: Interviews with Pauline Réage*]. Published in English translation as *Confessions of O* (Viking, 1979).

[5] Published as 'The Unmasking of O', (*New Yorker* August 1st, 1994)

[6] Dominique Aury: *Vocation: clandestine, entretiens avec Nicole Grenier*, (Gallimard, coll. <<L'Infini>>, 1999)

[7] *Dominique Aury* by Angie David (Léo Scheer, 2006) back cover note.

[8] Including Hans Bellmer and Leonor Fini; see chapter VIII

[9] Notably André de Pieyre Mandiargues and Georges Bataille, both in 1955.

[10] In 'A Girl' Réage noted the owl mask in chapter 4 was 'stolen' from Leonor Fini.

[11] Including Susan Sontag (1967), Janis Pallister (1985) and Anna Watz (2023)

[12] Alyce Mahon *The Marquis de Sade and the Avant Garde*, (Princeton University Press, 2020), p. 123.

[13] See for example recent activity by the International Society for the Study of Surrealism (ISSS), est. 2018; *Surrealism Beyond Borders* (exhibition Metropolitan Museum, New York 2021, Tate Modern, London 2022; book by Stephanie D'Alessandro 2021); Anna Watz (ed.) *History of the Surrealist Novel* (2023) etc.

[14] *Retour à Roissy*, published with 'Une Fille Amoureuse' (see note 3 above).

[15] 'Le Bonheur dans l'escalavage' ('Happiness in Slavery', commonly found in UK editions as 'A Slave's Revolt').

[16] The phrase is from Alyce Mahon: *Surrealism and the Politics of Eros 1938-1968* (Thames and Hudson, 2005)

[17] Published as *Story of O* (Grove Press, 1965), translated by Sabine d'Estrée.

# I:  A Parisian History of *Story of O*
## – The 1950s

## PUBLICATION:

In October 1951 the manuscript of a novel was presented to Gaston Gallimard, proprietor of Éditions Gallimard, with a view to publication. The novel recounted the subjection of a young female fashion photographer, referred to only as 'O', to a regime of sexual use, enslavement and erotically sadistic practices to which she submits and comes to adore. The novel was *Histoire d'O* (*Story of O*), written by an unknown and obviously pseudonymous 'Pauline Réage', and was being offered for consideration by Jean Paulhan.

Paulhan was a major figure in Parisian literary circles, and, at 66, was at the height of his influence. He had made his name in the 1920s and '30s as chief editor and then director of the most important literary journal in France (and therefore one of the most prestigious in Europe) the *Nouvelle Revue Française* (*NRF*). Paulhan's status was further enhanced by his role in the Resistance during the German Occupation of 1940-44 where he was a member of several underground groups, co-founded the clandestine CNE (National Committee of Writers [1]), and was a central figure in founding, editing and writing for Resistance publications. While none of this involved the gunplay or sabotage we usually associate with the French Resistance, the literary and intellectual battlefront was an important one, and a risky one. For the Nazi occupiers and their collaborationist allies, control of publishing and the media was a crucial element in their control of France. Subversive literary work during the Occupation was seen by both sides as serious Resistance action, with people being arrested and shot for it. Paulhan was himself arrested once, narrowly evading the Gestapo another time, and some of his colleagues were executed. When Paris was liberated in 1944, Paulhan was recognised as one of the heroes of cultural resistance during the war, and was a significant figure in post-war political struggles in Paris. Resuming his career in the literary world as a senior member of Gallimard's reading committee, he was honoured in 1949 as Commandeur de l'Ordre de la Légion d'Honneur, and later, in 1963, was elected to the Académie Française. In short, Paulhan was a man of considerable stature with real clout in the literary and publishing worlds.

Despite all this, and despite their reputation for publishing challenging books, after long deliberation Gallimard decided *O* was too hot to handle and declined it, the reading committee voting 4 to 1 against, one member telling Gaston Gallimard: 'Gaston, you cannot publish this sort of book' [2]. The subject matter was scandalous enough, but the idea of a female author was pushing things too far. Journalist and philosophical novelist Albert Camus, another member of the Gallimard reading committee and a staunch opponent of censorship, put up a robust defence of the book, but then he was convinced the author of such outrageous erotic imaginings had to be male – 'A woman? Never! This has not been written by a woman!' [3].

Paulhan turned to André Defez of Éditions des Deux Rives (Two Shores) publishing house, and to begin with this looked more promising. A contract to publish was signed and an advance paid to 'Pauline Réage', but Defez then found himself in trouble with the government over a book he had released criticising the French colonial war in Indochina [4]. Understandably reluctant to risk more trouble with a scandalous new book raising the threat of prosecution or even bankruptcy, he apologetically ended the arrangement and gave the manuscript back, generously refusing to accept the refund of his advance [5].

Paulhan then approached another independent publisher, 27 year-old Jean-Jacques Pauvert, whom he had known for more than ten years, since their days in the Resistance when Pauvert had been a teenage courier. Pauvert was an adventurous sort, with an interest in Surrealism [6], and had been achieving notoriety since 1946 publishing the complete works of the Marquis de Sade, with prefaces by many leading writers of the day (including Paulhan), managing to clock up an impressive seventeen prosecutions in the preceding three years as he did so [7] (using his parent's garage address as a front providing him with less cover then he hoped [8]). Since the previous year Pauvert had been aware of Paulhan's preoccupation with an intriguing manuscript, and on finally being handed it one afternoon in December 1953, with a promise from Paulhan of a preface to go with it if he agreed to publish it [9], took it home and read it overnight. In Pauvert's account, he realised straightaway 'It's MY book. Paulhan was right; it is the text I have been looking for for years' [10], and called Paulhan first thing the next morning – 'I woke him and said, "It's marvellous, it'll spark a revolution. So when do we sign the contract?"' [11].

Pauvert did the decent thing by Defez, buying the rights to the contract from him for 100,000 French francs (approx $285, i.e. around $2850/ €2630 today) – the same amount as the Réage advance – and Paulhan let Pauvert in on the secret, that 'Pauline Réage' was in fact Dominique Aury, a mutual acquaintance of them both in the underground literary world during the Occupation. Now 46, Aury was herself on the staff at Gallimard, and had been Paulhan's not-very-secret lover for the last six years. Pauvert later claimed not to have been surprised by this revelation: 'I already knew Dominique Aury as a journalist, writer and translator, and I found the writing (of *O*) to be of the same superb quality as her other work... I recognised her style immediately when I first saw the manuscript' [12].

A contract was formalised between Paulhan and Pauvert for 'Pauline Réage' to receive 12% royalties and Paulhan 3% for his prefacing essay, the understanding being that the two texts were always to be published together. *Histoire d'O* was published in June 1954 by Pauvert under the Sceaux imprint, in a print run of 2000 at a recommended retail price of 1500 French francs (just over $4 at the time). There was in addition a special edition of 600 copies: 470 numbered copies at 1700 FFr, and two collectors' editions: 20 (numbered I-XX) at 17,500 FFr, and 10 (numbered A-J) at 35,000 FFr, with a further 100 unpriced to be given to friends of the publisher and author [13]. Surrealist artist Hans Bellmer provided a red-ink lithograph on the title page of around 200 copies of the special edition (although it is difficult to pin-point which ones as in many cases owners removed the lithograph page for framing or sale). Sales were however less than spectacular, the first printing taking fifteen months to clear [14].

At the same time Pauvert made an agreement (without written contract [15]) with Olympia Press for an English translation – *Story of O* – to be published simultaneously. Olympia shared the same premises as Pauvert at Rue de Nesle in St-Germain, and was run by the incorrigibly dodgy Maurice Girodias with whom Pauvert had a complicated professional relationship. Founded in 1953, Olympia was already in the fore-front of publishing 'dangerous' writers like Samuel Beckett and Henry Miller, and English translations of Sade, Apollinaire and Georges Bataille, not to mention truck-loads of cheap 'dbs' ('dirty books') for bored service-men and sailors. Later, Olympia was to publish J.P. Donleavy's *Ginger Man* and Vladimir Nabokov's *Lolita* (both 1955), Terry Southern's *Candy* (1958) and William Burroughs' *Naked Lunch* (1959). Like Pauvert, Girodias was in endless hot water with the authorities. Having agreed to have *O* translated and published in a print run of 3000, to Pauvert's irritation he promptly overshot by almost the same number again [16]. Later, Girodias was to claim that Pauvert had been nervous about publishing *O*, and had turned to him to steel his nerves for the task [17] – a tale that Pauvert rubbished robustly [18].

**A note on translations:** The first translation into English was by Baird Bryant [19], who was a newcomer to the business, and was given the job when Olympia's experienced hands, Austryn Wainhouse and Alexander Trocchi, were busy with other projects. Unfortunately the Bryant effort was hurried and slapdash and bowdlerised, Pauvert describing it as 'a terrible translation', so bad that Aury wanted it stopped [20]. But Girodias ploughed ahead, Pauvert recalling 'Dominique Aury was furious, Paulhan was beside himself, and then on top of that, Girodias did not pay us. He didn't pay anyone'. Later Girodias commissioned another version, putting seasoned translator Austryn Wainhouse on the case, who made a much better job of it despite not liking it. Admitting 'it seemed to me to be marvellously written with incredible evenness and control', Wainhouse found it 'a very disturbing book', 'striking and unpleasant', generating 'conflicted feelings' in him and leaving him 'divided and upset'. [Right from the start, male responses to *O* have tended towards embarrassment [21]]. As it happened Girodias had no authorisation from Pauvert for a new edition, a minor inconvenience he sought to swerve by releasing it under a different title, a ruse designed to keep the increasingly menacing authorities off his back as well. This illicit re-issue was published in 1957 as *Wisdom of the Lash*, and managed to omit the Paulhan essay, which Girodias attributed to the printer getting drunk and forgetting all about it [22]. Aury, Paulhan and Pauvert were not at all impressed.

**The Novel:** The published version of *O* consisted of four chapters, which we shall only briefly outline here, reserving a more detailed discussion for chapter V.

The first chapter, 'The Lovers of Roissy', establishes itself as a fantasy from the outset with two alternative beginnings, and reads as a dark erotic dream with strong mystical undertones. It recounts the experiences of O being taken by her lover René to a mysterious château at Roissy, where she joins other young women in being subjected to a ritualised regimen of sexual use and punishment by a secret society of men ensconced there, O accepting and even glorying in her treatment as a testament to her love for René. The subsequent chapters provide more of a narrative storyline and introduce additional characters. In chapter two, 'Sir Stephen', O's life and career, her Parisian apartment and photography studio are featured, along with O's favourite fashion model Jacqueline, and the Englishman Sir Stephen, who is introduced as René's older (sort of) brother. René gives O to Sir Stephen, who with his harsh discipline progressively becomes O's new object of worship. The third chapter, 'Anne-Marie and the Rings', recounts O's seduction of Jacqueline, and her sojourn in the house of one Anne-Marie at Samois, where she is trained further with the lash, taught to whip other girls, is seduced by Anne-Marie, and finally mutilated with iron rings through her labia and branded as the property of Sir Stephen. The final chapter, 'The Owl', is set in a holiday villa in Cannes, where O continues to serve Sir Stephen, realises she is no longer in love with René (who is now becoming obsessed with Jacqueline), flirts with Jacqueline's 15 year-old sister Natalie, and is finally paraded in an owl mask (and not a lot else) at the soirée of another of Sir Stephen's friends, the Commander, where she stuns the guests by her uncanny presence.

The novel ends with a brief one-paragraph epilogue offering an alternative ending, where O, faced with abandonment, requests and is permitted to die. Thus the novel's ending is symmetrical with the opening where two alternate beginnings were provided.

**Paulhan's Preface**: Published with *Histoire d'O* under the title 'Le Bonheur dans l'esclavage' ('Happiness in Slavery') [23], Paulhan's substantial essay covered a lot of ground, taking pot-shots at a range of philosophical targets, and making some quite breathtaking (and not necessarily entirely serious [24]) allegations about women and their purported needs. It was also an affirmation of the role of the female protagonist, O, as the driving force of the narrative, and a strong confirmation that the author was a woman. Paulhan disingenuously denied any knowledge of her identity, although his confidence that the novel was an 'ardent love letter' (Preface p. xxxii) hinted that he knew more than he was letting on. Paulhan saw the novel as 'erotic' and 'dangerous', but urged a reading of it in mystical rather than sado-masochistic terms, and presented it as a work of real literary significance, which, coming from a man of his stature in the Parisian world of books, was praise indeed. Again, we shall take a closer look at this preface in chapter V.

**The Game:** If we pause for a moment to ask what exactly Aury and Paulhan were up to here, it is hard not to suspect they were playing a kind of game. Paulhan had already said in his preface that the novel was a love letter (without admitting he knew to whom), and later Pauline Réage was to describe *O* as a seductive manoeuvre, to keep a potentially wayward lover enthralled, 'like Scheherazade' [25], and confirming it was indeed 'une lettre d'amour' to Paulhan [26]. So most certainly a personal love game, but Aury's playful evasions during the successive interviews amount to games of hide-and-seek with the public (with the co-operation of her interlocutors, who faithfully kept the secret of her identity until she was ready to divulge), and the scale of the game might be larger still. The title of the 1999 publication of an interview (with Nicole Grenier in 1988) was *Vocation: Clandestine* – suggesting secrecy and evasion as cardinal traits of Aury and her life. This view was supported and developed by Angie David in her 2006 biography: 'Erotic literature is the way to live clandestine experiences after the war. For characters like Dominique Aury and Jean Paulhan, who love the danger, the duplicity, the contradictions (of Resistance life) during the war –, it is necessary to reconstruct the conditions of a clandestine life'; 'The presence of eroticism in the 1950s corresponds to a passion for clandestinity among intellectuals. They form a secret community, like the resistance fighters during the war. The elitism of such a way of life accentuates its condemnation by civil and political society'; 'the clandestine is a vocation for her (Aury), but also a game' [27].

This throws a different complexion over the subsequent dramas around *O* – especially those involving public outrage or legal action – after all, what could the French authorities do to Aury, Paulhan and Pauvert compared to the Gestapo during the Occupation? [Although in fact the French legal system did have another trick up its sleeve – it could drag legal fuss out over years and bore everyone]. The suggestion is that Aury and her friends were people whose engagement with danger during the war left them with a taste for excitement that was not being satisfied during peace-time. They needed adventure, and thrills, and the clandestine game of *Story of O* provided that – for David, *O* was not written out of commitment or revolt but 'out of play, out of a taste for risk' [28]. And part of the fun, as we shall see, was weaving a complex net of stories about *O*, dropping hints and half truths, leaving clues, creating false leads, setting traps for the unwary. One of the aims of this book is to try to unpick some of these fabulations, but I have no doubt there is still a long way to go.

We might also consider the possibility that the content of *O* is also to be seen in terms of excitement and fun. It has been discussed at length in terms of its mystical qualities, as we shall see, and this is an important angle. But much discourse and criticism, especially when it gets worked up over *O*'s gender politics, might be missing something vital – that this is an erotic book, and the erotic is fundamentally about heightened pleasure. Consensual sado-masochism is sexually thrilling for both parties. It does not denigrate the importance of *O* as literature to suggest that some criticism is off-target because it reads *O* too 'seriously'. We shall have similar points to make about reading the Marquis de Sade in chapter VI.

## REACTIONS

**Press and Public:** Initial reaction to *O* in France was muted and contradictory, although the Olympia translation fared better when smuggled into the U.S.A. In France the attention was on Simone de Beauvoir's *Les Mandarins*, which won the prestigious Prix Goncourt, and even more so on the debut novel of 18 year-old Françoise Sagan, *Bonjour Tristesse* (the title adopted from a surrealist poem by Paul Éluard [29]). This won the 'triple crown of French publishing that summer – critical acclaim, a scandalous reputation, and huge sales' [30], winning the Prix des Critiques – with the assistance of one Dominique Aury [31]. By contrast, *O* was greeted with what Réage later called 'a curious muffled scandal' [32], attracting gossip behind closed doors, tactical silence in the newspapers, and poor sales (mostly to *Nouvelle Revue Française* subscribers, some of whom sent employees to buy it [33]). Réage recalled 'Everyone talked about it in private, but the press was silent' [34] (although in fairness the press did have other things on its mind, with the fiasco at Dien Bien Phu in May and the rapid unravelling of the French empire in Indochina). In fact the press blackout was not total. The Sunday weekly, *Dimanche Matin*, published a review by Claude Elsen in September 1954 entitled 'L'Amour Fou' ('Mad Love' – a reference to André Breton's 1937 surrealist text), which praised the 'delirium' of *O* and claimed a lineage for it dating back to the medieval romance Tristan and Iseult. But apart from Elsen (and a review in *Carrefour* in January 1955) [35], and despite Paulhan's efforts to drum up interest [36], in a climate of threatened and actual prosecutions of 'obscene' books, newspapers were wary of publicising and bookshops wary of displaying and selling (except under the counter at inflated prices) a book that might itself be banned at any moment [37]. When a survey conducted by *L'Express* in 1955 on the landmark books of the time deliberately omitted *O* from its list [38], Paulhan wrote to the paper arguing that *O* was 'one of the most important books of the last years' [39], but his piece was spiked.

Literary reviews were however more open and positive. André Berry, in Albert Camus' journal *Combat* in March 1955, admired the 'sombre and powerful images, precise tableaux, subtle observations', and 'dignity' of the eroticism of *O* [40], and Aimé Patri in *Preuves* in October 1955, described *O* as 'An erotic noir novel composed in the manner of the works of the Marquis de Sade, but with more literary skill and less frenzy', praising its 'supreme skill' in 'evoking the worst horrors in a perfectly icy tone' [41]. The loudest and most enthusiastic chorus came from reviewers with Surrealist connections, including Jean-Louis Bédouin (who sneaked a preview in February 1954), Georges Bataille (May 1955), André Pieyre de Mandiargues (June 1955) and Nora Mitrani (1956-57). In Pauvert's view, the contributions of Mandiargues and Bataille were of particular importance, being actual articles to celebrate the appearance of *O* [42]. We shall look at these texts and the relationship between *O* and the Surrealists in more detail in Chapter VIII.

There were some sour notes too. In October 1954, Camus' colleague and friend Maurice Nadeau found *O* too controlled and lacking in the Sadean 'delirium' he thought the subject matter deserved, complaining '(t)he most "daring" descriptions use the language of the salon'. However, unlike Camus, he was willing to take seriously the possibility that 'a woman of letters hides ... behind that pseudonym', and, rather perceptively, noted a drop in quality after the first eighty pages [43]. The most outright condemnation came from the highly celebrated Catholic writer François Mauriac, who derisively retitled the novel *Les Mémoires d'une belle* (*The Memoirs of a Prostitute*), thus, Réage pointed out, managing to be 'wrong on two scores': 'they are not memoirs, and I am not a courtesan' [44]; (we might add a third score, that Mauriac thought

Paulhan had written it [45]). According to Aury, Mauriac 'really didn't understand anything' [46]. In November 1954 Mauriac launched a broadside in *L'Express* against *O* (without naming it) as exemplifying 'literary mores that make me vomit' [47]. Paulhan wrote to him in March 1955 inviting him to actually read the book and offering to send him a copy, an offer Mauriac declined, 'I do not want to read this book', which he designated 'immoral'. In summer 1958 matters flared up again when Mauriac's article in *L'Express* was republished in an anthology [48], and Paulhan retaliated in a letter challenging the 'violence' of Mauriac's repeated 'calumny' against *O*, questioning the honesty of reviewing a novel he had not read, and insisting on the mystical dimensions of the novel to which the 'reviewer' was clearly oblivious. Mauriac responded by reiterating his 'disgust and exasperation at the primacy of sexuality in literature', dismissing readers of *O* as 'fools', widening the discussion to encompass Sade whom he found 'unreadable', and concluding 'I am tempted to judge this generation on the status it grants to Sade' [which comes as a bit of a surprise given that he had published an essay on Sade by Paulhan in July 1945 in his review, *La Table Ronde* [49]]. Paulhan's offer to send Mauriac his preface to *O* to peruse, with the assurance that it was 'perfectly decent', went unheeded, but Mauriac had another go at *O* in *Le Figaro Littéraire* in February 1963 dismissing it as 'atrocious' and 'intolerable' [50].

Predictably enough, the Catholic Church and the Communist Party both condemned *O* as well, the former damning it as immoral and putting it on the Vatican proscribed list (along with works by Sartre, Simone de Beauvoir and other contemporaries), the latter dismissing it as petit-bourgeois irrelevance to the historic class struggle [51].

Later, Réage spoke of reactions she encountered personally, from people speaking in front of her without knowing she was the writer, 'I am really used to people telling me, indirectly, you have written a filthy story, this is vile, this is disgusting, you have dishonoured women, you have dishonoured your-self, besides it's badly written, it's badly put together, it's badly thought through, and the rest.' She 'even received a letter from a woman who cursed the womb that had borne me, a biblical insult par excellence.' None of this bothered her much, except the implication that the book had been written just to make money 'But it isn't true, it wasn't to make money. I did not expect that' [52], and anyway, for a long time there was no money.

Among the Anglophone literary community in Paris, *O* created a bit of a stir. George Plimpton, editor of *The Paris Review*, was flattered to be suspected of authorship ('It wasn't me, but it's a rumour I prefer not to scotch' [53]), while Alexander Trocchi of *Merlin* magazine (by now more or less run by Olympia) hailed it as a masterpiece, recommending it to Jane Lougee (a young woman of independent means who had been funding *Merlin*) in an attempt to seduce her, offering himself as her Sir Stephen, and going on to seek funds to set up a real-life Roissy, with himself presiding. Here he ran into two snags. The first was that Jane Lougee, astonishingly enough, wasn't interested, the other was that Austryn Wainhouse's estimate of the Roissy venture's costs came out north of $100,000 [equivalent to around $1 million today]. The idea was dropped [54].

**The Authorities**: *O* managed to elude major uproar until January 1955 when it won the prestigious Prix des Deux Magots – a book prize established in 1933 as an alternative to the more academic and conventional Prix Goncourt. The presentation of the award was photographed by the press with heavily veiled 'Pauline Réage' (possibly Aury, more likely a stand-in) flanked by two previous prize winners, Raymond Queneau (ex-surrealist and member of the Gallimard reading committee), and Albert Simonin (author of the influential crime novel *Touchez pas au Grisbi!* [55]). All this drew the attention of the government censorship body, the Commission du Livre, who decreed:

"The Commission, having listened to M...'s report and having discussed it.

Deems that the book published by Jean-Jacques Pauvert describes the adventures of a young woman who, to please her lover, subjects herself to all of his erotic whims and all abuses.

Deems that this book, blatantly and deliberately immoral, where scenes of debauchery involving two or more characters alternate with scenes of sexual cruelty, harbours a disgusting and contemptible ideology, and is thus an outrage to good morals.

Is of the view that there is a case for legal proceedings" [56].

The Commission swung into action straightaway, and by April 1955 had reached its conclusions: the novel would not be banned, but would have restrictions imposed on it – it should not be sold to under-18s, and there should be no advertising or public display of the book [57]. These restrictions remained in place for the next twenty years.

However, no sooner had the Commission du Livre closed its file, than Senator Pernot, representing 'family values' and the interests of the League of Large Families, launched his own case for 'contempt of good morals' against *O*. Needless to say he had not read the novel himself, as he openly admitted, but the word of a friend that it was 'unsafe' was enough for him to raise the matter with the Minister of Justice in July 1955 with a view to action [58].

The Brigade Mondaine (vice squad) were soon on the case, interrogating Pauvert, Paulhan and Girodias about the identity of the author of this scandalous book – Pauvert and Paulhan both being represented by Maurice Garçon, Gallimard lawyer and a formidable defender of freedom of speech. Pauvert played a clever hand, indicating that he thought he knew, but were he to air his suspicions to the police – especially since some names in the frame were of high ranking ladies (citing Mme. Lucie Faure, wife of the Minister for Finance and Economic Affairs, as an example) – there was danger of a dreadful fuss for everyone (including, by implication, the Brigade Mondaine) if he turned out to be mistaken [59]. Girodias, true to form, took the opportunity to confuse everyone by saying that though he did not know who wrote the book (which was probably true enough), he did know who Pauvert thought was responsible, but that Pauvert was barking up the wrong tree [60].

Paulhan had his own angle to play. In his 1954 preface to the novel, he had denied all knowledge of the author's identity, but now, in his testimony to the Brigade Mondaine (dated August 5th, 1955) he admitted he did know her [61]: "Around three years ago, Mme Pauline Réage (a pseudonym) paid me a visit at the *Nouvelle Revue Française* where I am director and submitted a thick manuscript titled *Histoire d'O*.' [Straightaway, in this opening sentence, Paulhan was being wayward with the details: first, he had in fact received the manuscript four years before, taking it to Gallimard in October 1951; second, the *NRF* did not actually exist at that time, having closed in 1944 and not being re-launched until 1953. Both facts would have been easy for the police to check. It is possible these were genuine slips of memory, but it is more likely that Paulhan was teasing the doziness of the vice squad]. Anyway, to continue with his testimony: 'I receive eight to ten manuscripts a day, but this one struck me immediately, both by its literary quality, and, if I may say so, for a subject so perfectly risqué, by its restraint and decency.

I had the sense I was in the presence of an important work as much for its form as for its tone, pertaining more to the mystical than the erotic, and that could be to our time what the *Letters of a Portuguese Nun* or *Dangerous Liaisons* were to theirs [62]. That's what I said to Mme Réage when she came back to see me.'

Paulhan went on to give an account of his experiences with Gallimard, Defez and Pauvert to get the book published, his contribution of a preface which 'highlights the philosophical and mystical sides of the work', which he then suggested was now 'somewhat at odds with the contents of the book', with 'M. Pauvert, in agreement with Mme Réage, having removed from the book the whole of the third part where the heroine is faced with her decline without telling me at the time.' [The idea that the published text was actually incomplete, an idea that might have started as one of Paulhan's jokes, was to become a saga in its own right, as we shall discuss in the next chapter].

He continued, 'I do not think that this is a book for everyone, any more than *Dangerous Liaisons* or *Letters of a Portuguese Nun*, however, I believe that, if one reads it carefully, it is clearly not in any manner comparable to a pornographic production. If it presents any danger it is rather by the violence of the passion one finds depicted, and by the endless dreaming it seems to be immersed in.'

With regard to the provenance of the novel, Paulhan denied any hand in it as writer or editor, pointing out the difference in writing style as proof against his authorship, before confirming that *O* was Mme. Réage's first novel, adding that the author, 'coming from an academic family she was afraid to scandalise, has always refused until now to reveal her real name.' He went on to say 'I have promised her as I have done with other authors not to reveal her name. Nonetheless, given that I have the opportunity to see her regularly, I will inform her of the statement I am making now, and in the event she decides to make herself known, I would invite her to get in touch with you.'

Claude Elsen rallied to the cause again in *Dimanche-Matin* on 28 August 1955 with a piece entitled 'Ubu Censeur' (a reference to Alfred Jarry's brutal, ignorant and dictatorial anti-hero Père Ubu [63], here enthroned as censor), pointing out that one of the main laws justifying the action against *O* was from the Ministry of Public Health in 1939, designed for the benefit of 'French Family and Births' and 'the protection of the race', and ratified by Marshall Pétain, giving it impeccable collaborationist and pro-fascist credentials. Elsen concluded that the idea that *O* posed a threat to youth, the family, the birth rate and 'the race' was ludicrous [64].

The legal threat did not go away, however, in part because the case of *O* was caught up in the turbulent political climate of the times. Since the autumn of 1954 the nationalist campaign for Algerian independence had been hotting up, with terrorist attacks and military reprisals ramping up the levels of violence; the French electorate was worryingly divided, and the authorities responded with draconian censorship of publishing and the press. By 1957 things were looking grim for *O* and those associated with it, and Paulhan drew up a list of witnesses for the defence, including Albert Camus, in readiness for the climactic legal battle. Meanwhile, Réage, according to her own later account, had been left quite unperturbed. 'The police were rather generous.' she said, 'I learned at the time they had discovered my name, address, date of birth and everything on my identity. They never mentioned it. I can't help seeing in that a kind of Ancien Régime elegance, a sort of courtesy towards an unknown and insignificant woman simply because she was a woman.... But of course they turned against Jean Paulhan and Jean-Jacques Pauvert, and I have felt guilty to let them alone take all the risks...' [65]. Apart from her completely misleading description of herself as 'unknown and insignificant', she was also glossing over the fact that the police did get on her trail, interviewing her at her home and leaving her unsure if charges for 'insulting good morals' were to follow. The added complication was that she lived with her mother and she saw the police arriving, so Aury had to throw her off the scent by telling her the visit had been a case of mistaken identity [66]. In fact her mother seemed to have been quite skilled at denial in her own right – another time a friend told Aury, in front of her mother, that she was suspected in some circles as the author of *O*, and when the friend left, Aury recounted 'I thought there would be a showdown with her.

But she just turned to me and said "Would you like another cup of tea?"' [67].

**Rumours of Authorship**: While *O* did not attract the attention it deserved as a novel on publication, receiving instead a tiresome amount of fuss from the authorities, the mysterious identity of the author kicked the rumour-mill into over-drive – who was this 'Pauline Réage', and above all, what sex was s/he?

The commonly accepted story is that the writing of *O* was a secret between Aury and Paulhan, with Pauvert let in on it when he agreed to publish, and Girodias only catching on later. However, it seems a number of Aury's women friends were in the know from the start – including Odette Poulain, Odile de Lalain, Élizabeth Porquerol and Édith Thomas (some of whom we shall meet again).

Outside of that select group, where the secret was kept close, theories abounded. Albert Camus was far from being alone assuming such work must have come from the pen of a man, and various writers all found themselves in the frame as possible contenders, including André Pieyre de Mandiargues (surrealist writer of erotica [68]), André Malraux, Henry de Montherlant, Raymond Queneau, George Plimpton and Paulhan himself [69]. In fact Paulhan was prime suspect, despite his denials and his perfectly legitimate point that his writing bore no resemblance to that of the novel – 'This is obvious if you compare my style to that of Mme Réage' [70], a view supported by Pauvert, who confirmed that Paulhan's style was completely different [71]. But the fact remained that Paulhan was directly linked to the book (having written the accompanying preface), and to the author (whom he had admitted knowing in his 1955 statement). Moreover, it had been noted that 'Pauline Réage' was a near anagram of *égérie Paulhan* [72] ('Paulhan's inspiration'? Or 'muse' [73]?). [More recently it has been suggested that Georges Bataille might have inadvertently fanned suspicions about Paulhan. Bataille had written an essay (under his own name) to accompany the publication of the novella *Madame Edwarda* by 'Pierre Angelique' – an author who was later revealed to be none other than Bataille himself. This might have raised the possibility that Paulhan was pulling the same stunt with O [74].]

The possibility of a female author was not entirely excluded, however. Some women's names were mooted, including surrealist artist Leonor Fini and author Louise de Vilmorin [75], and Mme. Lucie Faure [76]. Within a couple of years all sorts of people of both sexes were boasting of authorship to their friends [77]. Aury's own name cropped up on occasion [78], and she was occasionally asked directly, to which, in her own account, she would always reply 'This is the question I never answer' [79], although in truth she was perfectly capable of bare-faced lying, recounting how one day in 1955, after lunch with Paulhan and novelist Jules Supervielle, the latter challenged Aury with a direct 'It appears you have written a very fine novel,' to which she replied, 'Me? No, I don't write novels' [80].

**The Official Reaction Concluded:** In the end the threatened prosecution never materialised. Within a few years the story was floating around in the U.S.A. that ministerial action had put a block on legal action against O – a source in 1963 naming André Malraux, de Gaulle's Minister for Cultural Affairs (and one of the suspects as author of O in the 1950s) as the man responsible [81]. In her 1994 St Jorre interview, Aury gave some confirmation of this, citing a reshuffle of government ministers (by no means an uncommon occurrence at the time) as changing the game. Her gynaecologist (also a personal friend) was living with a man (unnamed) who just happened to have been appointed Minister of Justice. Paulhan had urged Aury to make use of that connection, and she managed to get herself invited over for lunch. Nothing was said about the book, but afterwards, when Aury thanked the Minister to take her leave, he insisted on walking her to her car, kissed her hand and said 'Madame, I was very pleased to meet you'. Aury recalled 'That's all. The next day, he issued a decree ending all the proceedings against '*Story of O*'. Under French law, when a minister does that no-one can ever resume legal action. That was the end of it' [82]. In her 1988 interview with Nicole Grenier (published in 1999), Aury had recounted the same story, but here she named names. She identified the friend in question as Odette Poulain (who had already bought the novel and to whom Aury explained everything), and the government minister – the 'garde des Sceaux' (Keeper of the Seals, i.e. Minister for Justice) – as Édouard Corniglion-Molinier [83]. A colourful character, Corniglion had been a pilot in the First World War, an adventurer, flying over the Yemen in 1934 with Malraux in search of the realm of the queen of Sheba; he had also been a film producer – one of his productions being the film version of Malraux' great 1937 novel of the Spanish Civil War, *L'Espoir* [84]. He saw active service as a pilot with the French air force in 1940, and subsequently with the Free French, before getting into politics after the war as a Gaullist and then a Left Republican. Corniglion held the ministerial post between June and November 1957 [85], which sets the time window for Aury's meeting with him. In addition, Aury revealed that she did not actually get to speak directly to Corniglion at all during the lunch, but was appreciative of his exemplary and 'perfectly 18th century' discretion, in wanting to see what the author of *O* was like and taking her measure without saying anything, thus avoiding, in Aury's own words, making her 'feel awkward or... have to thank him' [86].

Inevitably, Pauvert gave a different explanation, attributing the end of the legal affair to the skill of Maître Garçon in challenging the credibility of the laws under which the action was taking place, and winning the case on legal grounds [87]. In fact, charming though her story is, Aury's lunch with the Minister cannot have been the pivotal moment she claimed, as the case continued to drag on. In January 1958 Pauvert was summonsed for 'having committed the outrageous offence against public morality by publishing, selling, offering and distributing, or delivering for distribution copies of the book *Histoire d'O* ... and that Jean Paulhan had become accomplice to the outrageous offence against common decency (...) committed by Jean-Jacques Pauvert by having knowingly aided or abetted the latter...' [88]. At which point it all went suddenly off the boil, and the case against *Histoire d'O* fizzled out (unlike *Lady Chatterley's Lover* which came to court in London in 1960, to the ultimate embarrassment of the prosecution). No charges were brought and *O* was not suppressed in France, although some English language copies were confiscated from Olympia, along with copies of Nabokov's *Lolita* and other books (perhaps justifying Girodias' defensive measure of republishing *O* under a different title [89]). Finally, on October 29th 1959 Maurice Garçon could declare the case closed.

So what happened? Clearly Aury's lunch date did not settle the matter – at least not as decisively as she claimed – so perhaps we should accept Pauvert's rather unromantic account of Maître Garçon's legal adroitness. There is however another possibility. In May 1958 in Algeria, the army and hard-line European colonists reacted to the looming possibility of Algerian independence by staging a coup in Algiers. This raised the threat of military insurrection in France itself, which terrified the government sufficiently to invite General de Gaulle (who had been off the political scene for five years) to come back and rescue the situation. This he did in October 1958, with a clean sweep that installed a new constitution, replacing the parliamentary Fourth Republic with a new more centralised Fifth Republic, staffed by a whole raft of new faces (including Malraux). Taking on emergency presidential powers at the beginning of 1959, he proceeded to organise for Algerian independence – running the gauntlet of assassination attempts by ex-military groups incensed at his 'betrayal' [90]. Algeria finally attained its independence in 1962. Without ruling out the possibility that Corniglion had nudged official attitudes in a new direction, or denigrating the legal brilliance of Garçon, it is highly likely that the authorities, faced with a military coup in Algeria, major constitutional crisis and complete overhaul of government, simply found other things more important than endless fuss over a risqué novel.

---

[1] Comité National des Écrivains

[2] Angie David *Dominique Aury* Éditions Léo Scheer 2006, p. 11 , citing Dominique Aury: *Vocation: Clandestine, entretiens avec Nicole Grenier* Éditions Gallimard. Coll << L'Infini >> 1999. The man in question was Jean Dutourd.

[3] *Ibid*, p. 12 , citing Aury, 1999, quoting Camus.

[4] *Le Trafic de piastres* by René Despuech.

[5] John de St Jorre : *The Good Ship Venus, The Erotic Voyages of the Olympia Press* (1994) Pimlico 1995 p. 216

[6] John Calder: *The Garden of Eros* (2013) Alma Books 2014 p. 124

[7] Geraldine Bedell: 'I wrote the Story of O' *The Observer* 25 July 2004

[8] Amy Wyngaard: 'Sade, Reage and Transcending the Obscene' Bradford K. Mudge (ed.) *The Cambridge Companion to Erotic Literature*. Cambridge University Press 2017 pp. 210-223

[9] James Campbell: *Paris Interzone* Secker and Warburg 1994 p. 167

[10] David 2006, p. 11 citing Pauvert, *La Traversée du livre, Memoires I*, (Éditions Viviane Hamy, 2004) p.196

[11] Cited in Bedell 2004

[12] Cited in John de St Jorre 'The Unmasking of O' *The New Yorker* August 1st 1994, p. 46

[13] I am indebted to Conn Moriarty for his sleuthing work here. According to official exchange rates in 1954, $1 was worth around 350 FFr. RRP in dollars for the standard trade paperback and the collectors' editions were close to the exchange rate, but RRP for the numbered edition of 470 was inflated fourfold from just under $5 to $20. In reality, many copies of all editions went for higher prices in any currency. To get a rough idea of today's values, $1 in 1954 had around the same purchasing power of around $10 (c. €9) today. (The-financialnews. com) [See also David 2006, p. 14, footnote 13]

[14] Régine Deforges *O m'a dit* (1975), Éditions Jean-Jacques Pauvert 1976 p. 12, citing Pauvert.

[15] St Jorre 1995, p. 217

[16] Amy Wyngaard: 'The End of Pornography: The Story of Story of O' MLN 2015 Sept; 130(4) 980-997. Johns Hopkins University Press.

According to St Jorre 1995 p. 220, the agreed print run was 2000 but Girodias printed 5000.

[17] Calder 2014, p.127 citing Girodias *Une Journée sur la terre II: Les Jardins d'Eros* (Éditions de la Différence, 1990)

[18] St Jorre 1995, p.217

[19] Campbell 1994, p. 167; St Jorre 1995, p. 218. According to Calder 2014, p. 128, Bryant's wife Denny was implicated as well.

[20] St Jorre 1995, p. 218; subsequent quotes in this paragraph are from here, pp. 217 & 220.

[21] Carol Cosman: 'Story of O' (*Women's Studies: An Interdisciplinary Journal* 1974: 2 25-36)

[22] St Jorre 1995 p. 221

[23] The preface was first published in the *Disque Vert* review for Jan-Feb 1954, cited David 2006, p. 46. Calder 2014, p. 127, suggests that *Le Bonheur dans l'esclavage* was the original proposed title of the novel, but Pauvert recommended the less inflammatory *Histoire d'O,* leaving the original title to Paulhan's preface.

[24] David 2006, p. 31-32 ''this preface is intended to be funny, and is, said Dominique Aury "provocative".

[25] Deforges 1975 p. 100-101

[26] St Jorre 1994, p. 50

[27] David 2006, pp. 38, 44, 547

[28] *Ibid.* p. 38

[29] 'La Vie immédiate' (1932)

[30] St Jorre 1994, p.42

[31] David 2006 p. 115

[32] Cited in Deforges 1975, p. 13

[33] David 2006, pp. 14, 12

[34] Réage cited in Deforges 1975, p. 13

[35] 'Mystère d'O', 26 Jan 1955, cited Wyngaard 2015

[36] David 2006, p. 14

[37] Deforges 1975, p. 13-14

[38] David 2006, p. 14. David attributes this to an act of jealousy and spite by one Françoise Giroud at *L'Express*, using a 'feminist pretext' against a novel she has 'always hated' to silence others' voices, David p. 51.

[39] Réage quoted in Deforges 1975, p. 13

[40] André Berry, 'Chambre rouge et chambre des supplices', *Combat*, 14 March 1955, Fonds Jean Paulhan IMEC, cited in Alyce Mahon: *The Marquis de Sade and the Avant Garde*, Princeton University Press 2020, p. 151, and note 140, p. 252.

[41] Aimé Patrie 'L'eau et le feu', *Preuves* No. 56, Oct 1955, cited in David 2006, p.42

[42] Michel Surya: *Georges Bataille An Intellectual Biography* (1992) Verso 2002, p. 568, note 14

[43] Maurice Nadeau, Reading note on *Histoire d'O, Les Lettres Nouvelles*, Oct. 1954, cited David 2006, p. 13

⁴⁴ Réage: 'A Girl' 1969/ 1971 p. 19

⁴⁵ John Taylor *TLS* 5 April 2002  review: François Mauriac & Jean Paulhan *Correspondence 1925-1967*, ed. John E, Flower, Paris: Claire Paulhan.

⁴⁶ Aury, 1999 p. 106, cited in David 2006, p. 44

⁴⁷ This and the following quotes are all from the Paulhan-Mauriac *Correspondences 1925-1967*, ed. John E. Flower, Éditions Claire Paulhan, 2001, all cited in David 2006, pp. 45-46.

⁴⁸ *Bloc-notes,* Flammarion, June 1958

⁴⁹ *Le Marquis de Sade et sa accomplice*, cited in David 2006 p. 45/ Mahon 2020 p. 132

⁵⁰ Cited in Mahon 2020, p. 150

⁵¹ Mahon 2020 p. 158.

⁵² All Réage quotes in this paragraph are cited in Deforges 1975, p. 102-103

⁵³ Cited in St Jorre 1994, p. 43

⁵⁴ Calder 2014, pp 56-58

⁵⁵ *Don't touch the Loot!* (1953), which pioneered a new style of crime writing, deploying realistic underworld argot. Adapted for screen (script co-written by Simonin, directed by Jacques Becker) in 1954, starring Jean Gabin, Lino Venturi and Jeanne Moreau.

⁵⁶ Cited in Deforges 1975, p. 16. Having read this out to 'Réage', Deforges laughingly commented, 'It's a beautiful text is it not?'

⁵⁷ David 2006, p. 18

⁵⁸ *Ibid.*p. 16; Pernot was interviewed by Daniel Dreuil in *Combat*

⁵⁹ *Ibid* p. 15 footnote 16 citing Pauvert, Jean-Jacques 2004 p. 215 : 'Yes, he said, I think I know the author. (...) I wouldn't want to tell you anything because I could be wrong. Names of course have been circulated. Well known names. One could mention, for example, Madame Lucie Faure (...) You see the danger that I would be in, and would put respectable people in, if I named just one person, and only on suspicion. >> .

⁶⁰ Campbell 1995, p. 175

⁶¹ The text of Paulhan's deposition is quoted in Deforges 1975, p. 8-11, all quotes are from there. The complete text is in Appendix 1.

⁶² *Lettres de la Religieuse Portuguaise* (Gabriel-Joseph de la Vergne, Comte de Guilleragues, 1669) and *Les Liaisons Dangereuses* (Choderlos de Laclos, 1782)

⁶³ Ubu made his first appearance in *Ubu Roi/ King Ubu,* first performed in Paris in 1896, creating a first-class riot, prompting W.B. Yeats to conclude 'After us the savage god', and providing a fore-warning of a whole string of posturing, thuggish dictators since then – including Mussolini, Franco (according to Picasso, 1937), Stalin, Idi Amin etc. (Hitler didn't quite fit the Ubu mould but managed something even worse). So far the 21st century has seen a remarkable efflorescence of Ubus plaguing the world stage.

⁶⁴ David 2006, p. 17

[65] Réage, cited in Deforges 1975, p. 11-12

[66] St Jorre 1995, p. 218

[67] *Ibid.*, p. 219-220; St Jorre 1994, p. 47. Réage gave a slightly expanded account to Deforges 1975 (pp. 22-23) :'There is a silence. Then my mother's voice, very calm: "She has never told us this." Another silence. Once the fellow was gone, my mother asked me if I wanted more tea.'

[68] Having just written (under the name Pierre Morion) *L'Anglais décrit dans le Château Fermé* (literally: *The Englishman Described in his Closed Castle*, (Pauvert 1953) which recounts the adventures of M. de Montcul aka Sir Horatio Mountarse. Cited in Mahon 2020 p. 252 footnote 136.

[69] See for example: 'Un secret bien gardé'/ 'A well-kept secret,' *Dimanche-Matin*, 1955, dossier de presse *Histoire d'O*, IMEC, cited in David 2006, p. 13

[70] In his 1955 testimony, cited in Deforges 1975, p. 10

[71] Cited in St Jorre 1994, p. 46

[72] David 2006, p. 36, footnote 81

[73] Mahon 2020, p. 132

[74] Susan Sontag: 'The Pornographic Imagination' (*Styles of Radical Will*, Martin Secker & Warburg 1967), republished in Georges Bataille: *The Story of the Eye*, Penguin (1979) 1982, p. 95. In fact Sontag's account doesn't quite stand up. According to Surya (2002 p. 545, note 8), *Madame Edwarda* was first published in 1941 by Éditions du Solitaire (although back-dated to 1937) and the Bataille essay did not accompany it until a 1956 republication by Pauvert. Only in 1966 was Bataille officially outed as author of the novella, in a subsequent Pauvert edition (illustrated by Hans Bellmer). However, the authorship of *Madame Edwarda* would almost certainly have been known among the Paris literary in-crowd long before 1966, and the idea of practical jokes with misleading articles to muddy authorship waters was in the air [Nabokov played games with bogus introductions and the like in *Lolita* (1955) and *Pale Fire* (1962), although did not disguise his authorship of the novels]. Sontag might have been onto something, but it is quite possible that Bataille's little *drôlerie* might have been a response to the misattribution of Réage's work to Paulhan.

[75] Referred to by Aury in a letter to Edith Thomas, 3rd August 1954, cited in David p. 432 note 97

[76] Calder 2013, p. 129 cites Pauvert claiming the police were pressurising him to name her, which contradicts the account of Pauvert's statement to the Brigade Mondaine cited in David 2006, p. 15, note 16. Possibly Pauvert having a quiet joke of his own?

[77] Pauvert, cited in St Jorre 1994, p.47.

[78] David 2006, p. 432, note 98: In letter to Édith Thomas, 25 Sept. 1954 Aury cited Paulhan, Mandiargues and herself as people of interest to *Carrefour* – with Mandiargues as chief suspect (another of her little variants on the truth, perhaps, as that honour belonged to Paulhan).

[79] *Ibid.*, p.32 citing Aury: 1999 p. 104

[80] *Ibid.*, p.19 citing .Aury 1999 p. 107

[81] Sabine Destré 'A Note on the *Story of O*' *Evergreen Review* 7, p. 32. Cited Wyngaard 2017, p. 217

[82] Aury, cited in St Jorre 1994, p. 47; St Jorre 1995 pp. 219-220

[83] Aury 1999, p. 115, cited in David 2006, p.20

[84] Literally *Hope* (translated as *Days of Hope* or *Man's Hope*); the film version was released in 1940 as *Espoir, sierra de Teruel*

[85] https://rulers.org/frgovt2.html

[86] Aury,  1999 p. 117, cited in David 2006, p. 21

[87] Pauvert's version, cited in Mahon 2020, p.251, note 98

[88] Cited by David 2006, p.18

[89] St Jorre 1994, p. 47

[90] Providing the inspiration for Frederick Forsyth's *The Day of the Jackal* (1971)

# II: A Parisian History of *O* Continued – The 1960s and After

## THE 1960s

By the 1960s the true identity of Pauline Réage was starting to become known in exclusive French circles, both literary and political. Aury's son, Philippe d'Argila remembered one event where General de Gaulle startled his wife by greeting Aury with 'Ah, the writer of *Story of O*!'[1], and Aury recalled that when Paulhan was up for consideration for membership of the Académie Française in 1963, copies of *O* were laid out on the seats by someone trying to scupper his chances. This tactic backfired rather impressively – '"He was elected and we made a good sale. Forty books!"'[2]. However, as late as 1968 Aury's authorship came as news to Paulhan's daughter-in-law Jacqueline. At Paulhan's funeral, Jacqueline remembered, 'There was a very big bouquet of flowers with no name attached.... I was standing next to Dominique Aury, whom of course I knew well, and I remarked, "I suppose they must be from Pauline Réage." Dominique turned to me and said, "Mais Jacqueline, Pauline Réage, c'est moi"'[3]. Philippe d'Argila claimed he didn't find out till 1974 when people came round to discuss the film adaptation. He was in his mid-forties by then, and was not at all shocked: 'I already knew her as a writer, and it is a very good book'[4].

Further editions of *Histoire d'O* were published in Paris during the 1960s, all by or with permission of Pauvert, several being illustrated by surrealist artist Leonor Fini – one in 1962 with sixteen full page lithographs being particularly celebrated [5]. In 1965 a new translation of *Story of O* was published in New York by Barney Rosset of Grove Press. This edition raised the profile of *O* internationally and greatly increased sales, and it became for a while 'the best-selling and most widely read contemporary French novel outside France' [6], striking a chord with the sexual liberation of the 1960s and 70s, but antagonising some emergent U.S. feminist groups who found cause to adopt an apoplectically hostile stance towards it (we will discuss all this further in chapter X). *O* has never been out of print and has been translated into more than twenty different languages.

**The 'Suppressed' Chapter and the Enigma of the Epilogue:** The 1960s was also the decade when the saga of *O* took a mysterious turn. In the early '60s an extra sentence was inserted into the epilogue, suggesting yet another proposed ending; and in 1969 a sequel was published, touted as the lost final chapter of *O* that had been 'suppressed' in 1954.

Hints that something odd was afoot were first dropped at the moment of *O*'s original release, and it was perhaps predictable that it was Paulhan who started the hare running. In his 1954 preface to *O*, he made a string of cryptic remarks about the ending of the story. The published edition of the novel had ended with O in her owl mask attending the Commander's soirée, where at dawn Sir Stephen and the Commander 'possessed her one after the other' (*O* p.203). This was followed by the epilogue: 'There exists a second ending to the story of O, according to which O, seeing that Sir Stephen was about to leave her, said she would prefer to die. Sir Stephen gave his consent.' (*O* p.204) [7].

Paulhan began by stating his perplexity that the novel that 'began with such promise', should 'turn out so badly', where O 'remains in that kind of brothel to which she was led by love' and 'rather likes it' (Preface p. xxvi) [a statement that perplexes us as well, as it bears no relation to either the finale of the text or the epilogue]. He then went on, 'I too was surprised by the end. And nothing you can say will convince me this is the real end. That in reality (so to speak) your heroine convinces Sir Stephen to consent to her death,' [thus deftly contradicting what he had just said, by acknowledging the published epilogue *was* the given end, while at the same time denying its legitimacy as the 'real' ending]. He then concluded, 'But obviously there are things that have been left unsaid...' going on to suggest that Réage 'might one day want to write a sequel to O's adventures'. These gnomic remarks are, no doubt intentionally, difficult to interpret, but would seem to amount to a case that the given epilogue was not the 'real end', and that there was another ending, where O winds up living in a brothel – an ending that Paulhan on the one hand implied he had seen (and not liked), while on the other hand suggesting it was yet to be written, but was on the cards as a sequel at a later date.

The following year, Pieyre de Mandiargues, in his review of June 1955, gave the screw another turn, with the allegation that the published version of *O* was literally not the whole story, and that along with the four published chapters of the novel, 'a fifth one may have been suppressed' [8]. A few weeks later Paulhan broadly corroborated Mandiargues in his statement to the vice squad (August 1955) that there had originally been a 'third part' of the novel 'where the heroine is faced with her decline' [9], that had been withdrawn by Jean-Jacques Pauvert and Pauline Réage before publication without his knowledge [10].

In the 1960s published texts of *O* began to reflect these rumours. From 1962, Pauvert's French editions adopted an additional sentence into the epilogue, 'In a final chapter, which has been suppressed, O returned to Roissy, where she was abandoned by Sir Stephen,' with the original paragraph about Sir Stephen consenting to O's wish to die following on afterwards (*O* p. 204) [11]. This additional sentence created an imbalance in the novel, providing three endings in place of the original two, upsetting the equilibrium with the two alternate beginnings, but it was however consistent with Paulhan's and Mandiargues' assertions that the published text was not complete and a section had been omitted. The 1966 Grove Press version also featured this insert into the epilogue, as have all legitimate U.S. editions since then. Editions in the U.K. (and U.S. pirates), derived from the Olympia/ Wainhouse translation, generally do not [12].

Then in 1969 a new volume was published, containing what purported to be the missing final chapter from *O*.

## *STORY OF O* PART II

The death of Jean Paulhan in October 1968 at the age of 83 seems to have been the trigger for Pauvert to publish a second volume by 'Pauline Réage'. This comprised two new texts, a third-person account of the composition of *O*, entitled 'Une fille amoureuse' ('A Girl in Love'), and a short novella entitled *Retour à Roissy* (literally *Return to Roissy* but rendered as *Return to the Château*). This novella was presented as the lost chapter, 'suppressed' in 1954.

**'A Girl in Love':** Here Réage gave a fascinating and beautifully composed if somewhat romanticised account of the writing of *O*, beginning, 'One day a girl in love said to the man she loved: "I could also write the kind of stories you like..."' ('A Girl' p.9). Describing their clandestine affair, their 'places of refuge' – by the river, in parks, rented rooms – a fugitive love, each having to go home before the night was over – he to his wife, she alone (p. 10), she went on to recount how one night she began to write, in an almost entranced ecstasy of inspiration: 'The girl was writing the way you speak in the dark when you've held back the words of love too long and they flow at last.' (p. 11). She showed him her work, but with trepidation, 'what if the phantasms that it revealed were to outrage her love or, worse, bore him or, worse yet, strike him as being ridiculous?' But he approved of what he read, asking her '"What happens after that? Do you know?"' to which she responded, 'She knew' (p. 13), and she continued to write, in fits and starts, reading to him as they parked 'on some bleak but busy street' on afternoon trysts (she always drove), but it was difficult, and she 'had to stop, break off, once or more than once, because it is possible silently to imagine the worst, the most burning detail, but not read out loud what was dreamt in the course of interminable nights' (p. 14).

But 'one day the story did stop. Before *O*, there was nothing further than that death toward which she was vaguely racing with all her might could do, that death which is granted her in two lines.' At this point she mentioned Paulhan, but only to say that she had promised not to reveal how the manuscript came into his possession, just as she promised 'not to reveal the name of Pauline Réage' (p. 14), who is, she revealed, an aspect of herself. For '... nothing is more fallacious and shifting than an identity...' and perhaps 'in each of our lives we are the meeting place of several souls?'. Moving into a narrative mode where she quotes Pauline Réage as though she is another, she wrote, 'Who am I, finally,' said Pauline Réage, 'if not the long silent part of someone, the secret and nocturnal part which has never betrayed itself in public by any thought, word, or deed, but communicates through the subterranean depths of the imaginary with dreams as old as the world itself?' (pp. 14-15). She then asked herself 'Whence came to me those oft-repeated reveries, those slow musings just before falling asleep, always the same ones, in which the purest and wildest love always sanctioned, or rather always demanded, the most frightful surrender', replete with chains and whips, noting how these 'strange dreams', 'the delirium and the delights of the impossible' 'oddly lightened... the days that followed'. How, rather than trying to use reverie to plan or organise her life, she learned how 'one could without fear build and furnish clandestine castles, on the condition that you people them with girls in love, prostituted by love, and triumphant in their chains', anticipating Sade's castles that she was not to discover until after her own fantasies had built her own castles from 'strands of this immemorial network of forbidden dreams' (pp. 15-16).

Again quoting Réage-as-Other, she continued, '"What intrigued and excited him, I mean the man for whom I was writing this story" she went on, "was the relationship it might have with my own life,"' and talked about the origins and inspirations of some of the other characters – René and Jacqueline (who between them broke her teenage heart), Sir Stephen (a stranger she had glimpsed one time in a bar in Paris) and Anne-Marie (who may have been inspired by 'a friend') [we shall have more to say on these in chapter V]. She also took a moment to comment tartly on 'a major writer' (left unnamed but evidently Mauriac) and his insulting claim that *O* was the memoirs of a courtesan. She went on to identify Roissy-en-France as 'glimpsed during a brief excursion one spring, scarcely more than a place-name on a map', and admitting the influence of Leonor Fini's owl masks on the final scene of *O* (pp 19-20). 'A Girl in Love' confirmed that the writer of *O* was a woman and that *O* was indeed an act of love by the author to her lover. [The text did not identify the lover, but the linking of the names Pauline Réage and Jean Paulhan in the same sentence provided a hint to the observant that Paulhan might have played a bigger role in this story than merely arranging its publication.]

***Return to the Château:*** The narrative of the sequel picks up directly after the soirée that ended the original novel, with O feeling anxious that Sir Stephen's attitude towards her is changing. René only features fleetingly in a passing reference (*Return* p. 25) that implies that he will take Jacqueline to Roissy (which is not confirmed), while Natalie, distraught that Sir Stephen's deference to her mother's decision that she go back to school means she will be denied her visit to Roissy, is compensated with 'seduction' by O and then Sir Stephen, and packed off out of the story.

A sense of mystery is introduced as O wonders what Sir Stephen actually does for a living (apart from owning a castle in Scotland), but he reveals nothing, and orders her to provide sexual services to some strangers, including an unsavoury Fleming called Carl. Sir Stephen sends O to Roissy where Anne-Marie takes charge of her, and it is revealed that Roissy is in reality an expensive and exclusive gentlemen's club and brothel, where the girls have identity cards and are prostituted commercially, and are paid for their services. It is also revealed that Anne-Marie is a doctor, with the (seemingly magical) powers to protect the girls from pregnancy, inconvenient periods, and venereal diseases. O's treatment at the hands of various customers are recounted, and O is distressed to hear that Sir Stephen has been there and did not come to see her, but he does send her a message telling her to treat Carl well to encourage him to keep coming back.

O does as she is bid, and Carl gives her expensive jewels and tells her he wants to take her away to Africa (he owned mines in the Belgian Congo, *Return* p. 114) and then America. O is horrified and plans to escape, but then news comes that Carl has been found shot dead in the forest of Fontainebleau (presumably near Anne-Marie's fiefdom at Samois?). O and the police suspect Sir Stephen, who has now gone to ground. Anne-Marie does not believe this, and it comes out that Carl had been double-dealing some shady business partners. The novella ends here, with Anne-Marie telling O she is free to leave, with her jewels, '"But if your prefer," Anne-Marie went on, "you can stay on here."' (*Return* p. 137).

The story recounted in this sequel was consistent with the new sentence inserted into the epilogue to French editions of *O* earlier in the 1960s, and also with Paulhan's reference to an ending with O remaining in the 'brothel to which she was led by love' (Preface p. xxvi), all of which would support the idea that *Return* was indeed the 'suppressed' chapter Mandiargues and Paulhan spoke of in 1955.

Predictably enough, accounts of how this alleged editorial amputation took place vary. Paulhan's story in 1955, as we have seen, was that Pauvert and Aury decided to pull it without his knowledge [13]. This was flatly denied by Pauvert, who claimed in 1994 that 'Paulhan and I agreed the book was very beautiful, very classic without the last chapter which was more like something out of a spy novel. So we told (Aury) we would like to leave it out. She was not pleased but she said, all right, do what you want. So, we took it out' [14]. In his 2004 memoirs Pauvert reiterated the same line: 'A point which has always remained the object of a controversy between Paulhan, Pauline Réage and me. I remember very clearly – and Pauline Réage too – that it was Jean Paulhan who, in agreement with me, had removed from the book this third part, a long chapter entitled "Retour à Roissy", which we will meet again' [15]. Dominique Aury had her own take on it, insisting she 'had not wanted it published at all' [16]. In the view of Aury's biographer, it was Paulhan who suppressed it, going on to lie to the Brigade Mondaine about it, and 'never ceas(ing) to confuse the issue' [17]. The fact that it only saw the light of day after Paulhan's death would lend weight to the idea that he was the main obstacle to its publication, his claim to the contrary being presumably just another one of his little jokes.

**Publishing *Retour à Roissy*:** If the story of the supposed suppression of *Return* in 1954 is convoluted, the story behind its eventual publication fifteen years later is equally tangled, ably assisted by Aury's shifting attitudes towards it. In 1971 when the U.S. Grove Press edition, *Return to the Château, Preceded by A Girl in Love*, came out, it was presented as a continuation of *Story of O* ('part of the same dream'), but somebody, under the initials 'P.R.' (generally accepted to have been Réage), put in a forthright disclaimer: 'The pages that follow are a sequel to *Story of O*. They deliberately suggest the degradation of that work, and cannot under any circumstances be integrated into it' (*Return* p. 21). In 1974 Réage presented a case for *Return*'s publication: 'I wanted to break [O's] world of fantasy, to see what was happening, to see if the story was becoming real... It was a good way to show that the realisation of a fantasy can only be disappointing' [18], restating in her 1988 interview 'I wrote this ending on purpose... to destroy some kind of dream', while recognising it as 'intolerable... the lowest porn, the most mundane crime story... deliberately sordid' [19]. By the 1990s she was roundly condemning *Return* as 'very poor' [20], '... extremely bad, abominable. It was a mistake. 'Story of O' was pure dream, pure fantasy. 'Retour à Roissy' was reality, with all its banality, harshness and sordidness. It was the other side of the dream... It was a degradation into reality... prostitution, money, force etc. It was *une mauvaise fabrication*, as we say. It should be suppressed' [21].

The question *why* it was eventually published predictably throws up different possible answers. Aury claimed that Pauvert had wanted to publish *Return* to refloat his ailing publishing house (threats of litigation by Girodias presumably won't have helped here), to which she replied 'No, you won't publish it alone. I'll give you a little story about how *Histoire d'O* was written – 'Une Fille Amoureuse' – and then you can publish both of them together' [22], and went on to write this 'little story' sitting beside Paulhan's death-bed in hospital in Neuilly through the summer of 1968. Pauvert recalled it differently. His version was that he asked Aury to write 'A Girl'– 'There was no question at that time of publishing *Retour à Roissy*', but 'one day, she said she couldn't do it (i.e. write 'A Girl') any more. Paulhan was dead and she couldn't continue' [23]; at this point Pauvert suggested publishing *Return* alongside it to make a sellable volume, and Aury agreed. This has been read as the exploitation of Aury for financial gain, just as O is commercially exploited in *Return* [24], but a less cynical interpretation is provided by Aury's son, Philippe d'Argila: 'I think she published the sequel to please Pauvert, to thank him for all that he had done' [25]. Another possibility has been mooted, that maybe she didn't really care any more. According to Jacqueline Paulhan, after Jean died, Aury put together a book of recollections of him, and 'after that, she kind of gave up her interest in the world. She pulled back from the world and lost her short-term memory' [26], (although having said that she comes over as sharp enough in interviews until the last year of her life, nearly thirty years later).

In the end it is not clear which of Aury or Pauvert was lobbying most strongly for 'A Girl', and how enthusiastic either of them were to publish *Return*, nor how financial need motivated either or both of them. As it happened, sales were poor, either due to 'a new wave of Puritanism... sweeping France' after the 1968 events [27], or more likely due to the sheer awfulness of the piece, which never rises above banal mediocrity. In general, critics and commentators, while admiring 'A Girl', have gone along with Aury's 1994 view that *Return* is something much inferior to *O,* and deserving little heed. That seems fair enough to this writer.

On top of all this it is open to question whether *Return* really is the chapter written by Réage and allegedly 'suppressed' in 1954. Many commentators accept it as such [28], but the evidence is not at all clear. Réage's reference in 'A Girl' to O's goal 'racing' towards 'that death which is granted her in two lines' (p. 14), suggests the original epilogue was the true ending of the novel. In an interview in 1974 she discussed *Return* as a valid sequel (see p. 60) [29], but in her long book-length interview with Régine Deforges she made no reference to it at all [the only mention of it in the entire conversation being a single comment by Deforges that *Return* was the 'withdrawn' part of *O* Paulhan had talked about in his 1955 deposition] [30]. Réage ignored it altogether, concentrating instead on emphasising that the real ending was O's wish to die [31]. In 1988 she referred to death as '(a) way of freeing oneself from existence', saying 'O makes this choice, it pleases her. Thank God, we kill her at the end' [32] – the alternative being the 'intolerable' ending given in *Return* (see above). In the 1994 interview with John St Jorre, Aury hedged her bets, claiming that she didn't know how to end the novel 'so I left it open' [33]. Overall, the case seems to stack up that the ending given in the original epilogue, the death of O, was the ending Réage intended, with *Return* as an alternative she may or may not have written, at the time of *O* or later, and about which she (at least later) felt less than enthusiastic.

Angie David, in her biography of Aury, emphatically denies the legitimacy of *Return* in Aury's eyes. It is 'not the real end, according to her... not the end of which Dominique speaks', 'not the last deleted chapter, but a commission from the publisher, which she considers completely worthless' [34]. Instead, David emphasises that '(t)he only real end is the one (Aury) recognizes, the death of O'. However, although 'Dominique has chosen this ending... Paulhan refuses it', asking her 'not to kill O, an end he considers too violent, too realistic'. David goes on, '(t)hen he removes the last chapter, where O is abandoned at Roissy'. All of this suggests the death of O was indeed Réage's preferred outcome, but that *Return* did exist as an alternative ending by 1954, and Paulhan didn't like either of them. Interestingly, David implies that the ending where O died might have been developed beyond a mere epilogue: 'the last chapter not included is the end that Dominique Aury always alludes to, as if no other existed – that of the (epilogue) of the original edition: the death of O', but '(t)hat ending ultimately never existed, or maybe only in manuscript', going on to ask that when Paulhan mentions a possible sequel in his preface (p. xxvi), 'is he referring to the real ending, which no one has ever read – O's death – or what will actually be released?'.

The intriguing possibility emerges that Réage might have actually drafted (or even written), a final chapter where O meets her death – 'the last chapter not included', 'which no-one has ever read', existing 'only in manuscript' – of which the only trace surviving in the final novel is the original epilogue. As for *Return*, that might have been Réage's work, or someone else's. It might be the last section of *O*, spiked by Paulhan in 1954 before seeing the light of day fifteen years later, but the statements of Paulhan, Mandiargues and Pauvert don't unequivocally confirm that (and we have grounds for caution in dealing with their testimony anyway), so it might have been composed at a later date. My own intuition, for what it's worth, is that it isn't Réage's, but a concoction by hand(s) unknown, presumably chez Pauvert, and probably later – maybe only just before its 1969 publication. If there really was a genuine 'suppressed' chapter, was it perhaps Réage's draft of the death of O?

But if Réage did write a chapter where O died, questions arise: What happened? Why was *Return* published in 1969 in preference to it? And how long before forged versions of Réage's chapter start turning up?

In chapter V we shall have more to say about *Return*, and particularly about 'A Girl'.

## THE 1970s

In 1971 the U.S. edition *Return to the Château, Preceded by A Girl in Love* was published by Grove Press (translated of course by Sabine d'Estrée), but the event that triggered the next chapter in the story was the translation of *O* to the big screen. The context here was provided by liberalisation of censorship laws regarding 'hard-core pornography'. In the U.S.A. such laws were effectively abolished in 1970, opening the door to a wave of 'porn' films, the most notorious being Gerard Damanio's *Deep Throat* in 1972. In 1975 new legislation in France permitted 'hard-core', and young directors from the generation of the May 1968 *événements* seized the opportunity to strike what they considered to be a blow for freedom of expression, civil liberty and to *épater les bourgeois*. For the next two years explicit sex films were prominent, even dominant, among the fare on offer in French cinemas – both home grown and imported from the U.S.A. and elsewhere. It was these developments that provided the moment for *Story of O* to move from page to screen.

**Cinema and O:** The first cinematic reference to *O* was a playful allusion in the title of the François Truffaut/ Jean-Luc Godard short film *Une Histoire d'Eau* (*A Story of Water*) shot during the freak floods in and around Paris in 1958 [35]. In 1960 Kenneth Anger began a film adaptation of *O*, but with his protagonist being the daughter of the Finance Minister and the discovery that the funding came from a kidnap ransom, Anger wisely walked away [36].

By the mid 1970s however the climate was ripe for direct screen adaptations of *O*, the most significant being Just Jaeckin's *Histoire d'O*, a Franco-Canadian/West German production in 1975 featuring Corinne Cléry, Udo Kier and Anthony Steele [37]. This was a respectful if 'generally reckoned to be a rather pallid version' [38], Jaeckin's background as a fashion photographer for *Elle* and *Vogue* giving his piece of *haute couture* art-house erotica an ambience reminiscent of a high-end skin-cream commercial. The film eschewed any hint of the 'hard core' of the time, being 'exquisite to look at' but perhaps '*too* painterly to capture the almost religious fervour of the source novel' [39]. The narrative was edited for 1970s tastes – the 15 year-old Natalie was tactfully air-brushed out, O is presented as proud and shame-free, and in the final scene is shown taking a dominant role, persuading Sir Stephen to let her turn the tables by stubbing his cigar out on his hand, a scene presumably intended as a concession to growing feminist concerns about gender and power relations. Obtaining release in 1975 in France, the U.S.A. and elsewhere, Jaeckin's mild example of self-consciously cinematic soft-core was still sufficiently alarming to British conservatism for it to be denied certification and release for another quarter of a century [40].

Samm Deighan (2012) has linked Jaeckin's *Histoire d'O* to Luis Buñuel's *Belle de Jour* (1967) as examples of art-house erotica that present the secret sex lives of women [41]. In both cases, the woman in question is from a bourgeois milieu – Séverine in *Belle de Jour* (portrayed by Catherine Deneuve) is the affluent wife of an accomplished young doctor, O in Jaeckin's film (as in the novel) a successful fashion photographer. Each woman has a need to 'push the boundaries' and shatter the conventions of 'normal' life in order to achieve gratification; both do it by entering a world of sado-masochistic fantasy and ritual. Although both films are directed by men, and the women are sexually objectified in both, it is female desire that drives the narratives, and the protagonists 'manage to subvert masculine control and bourgeois values with their sexually masochistic performance. These experiences are dramatically life changing for both women, and they each gain a degree of agency over their lives by bringing their masochistic fantasies to life' [42]. It is the 'anarchistic, anti-bourgeois subtext' of these films that proves them to be neither anti-feminist nor sexually exploitative [43]. In fact it is likely that links between *Belle de Jour* and *O* may go deeper. Buñuel's film is based on a 1928 novel of the same name by Joseph Kessel, but in many ways echoes Pauline Réage's novel more closely, and may represent the first actual influence of *O* in cinema (we will return to this in chapter VIII). Interviewed for the 2005 DVD release [44], Jaeckin showed a sensitivity to the politics of art-house erotica, clearly walking on egg-shells, bending over backwards to reassure the viewer that his film was not reality – not to be tried in real life, but to be enjoyed in the mind – nor was it pornography, which 'shows everything... like a clinic... It's what I hate'. Repeatedly using the word 'fantasy', Jaeckin insisted he was trying 'to understand what she (the author) wants to say', without making any judgements, and to do it with 'eroticism', which is something beautiful, from the imagination, 'like a phantasm', the absolute opposite of pornography – all the while insisting 'I am not a pornographer, I am a dreamer'.

Aury apparently found the script reasonable, but not the direction or acting, and dismissed the film as 'abominable' (a sentiment shared by Pauvert, who thought it a 'stupid film') [45] – Aury's attitude presumably being less than sweetened by being 'screwed financially' over screen rights [46]. Still, in this writer's opinion, Jaeckin's *Story of O*, despite its cheesiness, is in a superior league to his previous effort, the brutal and thumpingly unerotic Emmanuelle (1974).

**The 1970s Interviews:** For all its faults Jaeckin's film, while still under production, stimulated renewed interest and increased sales for the novel [47]. On the back of this Pauline Réage gave two interviews, a fairly perfunctory one to Jacqueline Demornex, the other, a much longer and more significant encounter, to journalist and publisher Régine Deforges. Both interviewers agreed to respect Aury's desire to keep her identity concealed.

**Jacqueline Demornex:** In this brief interview, published in *Elle* magazine, September 2nd 1974 [48], Demornex memorably described her first impressions of Pauline Réage: 'She is sitting there; silent. How could I dare talk to her of eroticism, of sadism, of *O*? Pauline Réage has the air of a nun. Navy blue suit, flat shoes, no make-up at all... She is intimidating' [49]. In the interview, Réage dropped some hints from her personal life, admitting to have suffered betrayal by a lover in her youth [in 'A Girl' she had implicated a René and a Jacqueline in her teenage heart-break (p. 17-18) – we discuss this further in chapter V], creating a mystery for the biography sleuths with her confession that she had been in love three times, and articulating what was to become her oft-stated view that '(t)o be no longer loved... is the worst of punishments. Death is preferable' [50].

Réage also provided justification for *O*, such books being cathartic for the reader, for a novel only troubles a person if it connects with something already deep within them. Sensitive to emerging anxieties about O's submissiveness, Réage gave reassurance that O always had the right to refuse [which is not strictly true in the first chapter], and should not be seen as the victim of coercion, going on to say 'I think that in all true passion, there is a quest for the absolute that can only be attained through a feeling of abandon, of a total dispossession of the self... Passion is a serious matter' [51]. It was in this interview that Réage provided the explanation for *Return* as a deliberate attempt to break the fantasy of *O*, a view she later rescinded (as discussed above p. 54) [52].

**Régine Deforges:** In contrast to the Demornex interview, the interview with Régine Deforges, published in 1975, was much longer, philosophical and wide ranging. Deforges was 40 at the time, and in 1967 had been the first woman in France to launch her own publishing house, L'Or du Temps. [Referencing André Breton's epitaph in 1966, 'Je cherche l'or du temps' ('I search for the gold of time/ the times'), the phrase is also a homophone for *l'hors du temps* ('outside of/beyond time/ the times')]. Specialising in erotica, for which Deforges was an enthusiastic advocate (becoming known as the *Papesse de l'érotisme*), L'Or du Temps published Apollinaire, Restif de la Bretonne, Théophile Gautier and the surrealist Pieyre de Mandiargues, and attracted enough legal trouble and expenses to have to close in 1972 – the final straw being some scurrilous political pamphlets and the republication of Louis Aragon's 1928 surrealist novel *Le Con d'Irène* (*Irene's Cunt*) [53]. Régine Deforges was also Pauvert's partner – they'd been together since 1958, and had a daughter – and the interview was set up by Pauvert in what was effectively his second attempt, after 'A Girl', to get Aury to tell her story [54]. The two women hit it off extremely well, and began a close friendship which inspired Deforges to try her own hand at writing erotic novels [55].

The interview was more of a conversation, with Deforges sharing the stage with Réage, presenting herself as 'a scandal maker', 'a young woman who has published erotic books, who has posed naked for popular magazines!' aware of how the public sees her as 'a sort of literary pin-up, champion of sexual freedom which she evidently practises twenty-four hours a day' (p. 6), and happily expounding her own views on jealousy and other topics as they talked. However, she did not hog the limelight, and successfully drew Réage, who began the interview by insisting this would be her last (p. 5), to discuss (sometimes rather elliptically) not just her novel and its history, but also literature and morality in general, along with 'her childhood, her youth, men, women, the war, eroticism and love' [56].

Réage described how, aged 14 or 15, she had discovered erotic classics (by Crebillon fils, Boccaccio and so on) in her father's library and how her father, rather than discourage her interest, decided it better she learn the facts of life, and arranged, via one of her older female friends, for his daughter to meet with a young male cousin who showed her his equipment (without touching her) (p.19-20). But it was Gothic medieval novels by Walter Scott and Anne Radcliffe that really fuelled Réage's teenage fantasies of underground caves and imprisoned girls (p.125), along with a delight in secrecy and clandestine affiliations that was to last all her life. Secret societies offer something to everyone – 'In childhood for comradeship, friendships; when one is adult, for love, secret love; during war, for acts of resistance. ... But everything that touches secrecy can be fascinating' (p.77), – secrecy and the erotic being closely entwined: 'there is an almost intoxicating bitter-sweetness in seeing the man one loves in a crowd at a party, and he dares not meet your eyes, nor yours his. And you tell yourself: a moment ago he was holding me in his arms, and only he knows, and only I know.' (p.78). She reiterated that O was a gift, a letter, to the man she loved, a seduction to keep the affair going, 'Like Scheherazade' (p. 100-101), but also that without him the book would never have been written – her desire to write it having been ignited by meeting someone who would appreciate it, an accomplice (p. 100, 106). As for the actual writing, 'the first sixty pages just flowed... Afterwards I tried to build a story, but the first sixty pages came by themselves' (p. 208). She confirmed it was Paulhan's idea to release the book – she had not thought it publishable, but had made no objection (p. 108). For Deforges, *O* was indeed, as Paulhan had said in his 1955 statement, the *Dangerous Liaisons* or the *Portuguese Letters* of our time (p. 104).

Both women defended the moral integrity of the work. If O is effectively prostituted in the novel, that caused neither woman any unease. In Deforges' view, 'money is sexy' (p.68), and that 'for a woman, from time to time, it is not unpleasant to be a piece of merchandise, an object of barter,' (p.69), and she queried 'But why can't we solicit? Someone who sells tomatoes says: come and look at my fine tomatoes. A girl could say: come and see my beautiful breasts or my lovely eyes.' (p.71). For her part, Réage stated 'Flesh for money, I have never found that shocking, personally' (p.70), and admitted that if a man had ever paid her for love, 'I imagine it would have given me the greatest pleasure' (p.69).

As for *O* being pornographic and an offence to decency, both women took a robust view. For Réage 'concentration camps offend good morals, so does the atomic bomb, and torture – life itself offends good morals', there was nothing offensive about erotic books (p.17), Deforges supporting her on the senselessness of a society finding the selling of 'obscene' books worse than the selling of guns (p.71). In Réage's view, it was 'absolutely scandalous' that pornographic literature is banned – in her view it was not the readers of pornography who commit crimes, it is the ones who don't (p. 193). After all, 'tortures and violence in *Histoire d'O* are entirely of the same order as fights in crime novels... it's just make-believe, it isn't real. It belongs to the realm of dreams... the tortures of erotic novels, and the fights, injuries and brutalities of crime novels, are the same thing.' (p.139). Being told by 'a famous doctor' that '"People who write that [sort of thing] are very ill"' thoroughly amused her, 'because I did not feel mentally ill, nor by the way particularly perverted.' (p.22).

Addressing the question of O's motivation, the interview entered deep waters, with Réage confirming that 'O seeks to be destroyed, and the deepest destruction is humiliation' (p.36), and Deforges raising the question of 'the danger that one seeks when one is a young woman wandering alone at night in the Paris streets, that desire for the male and rape buried in the unconscious of our civilised minds' (p.91), and wondering of her interviewee whether she might have ever found herself following the path of desire to her own destruc-tion, to which Réage replied she understood the allure (p.111-112). But Réage was at pains to point out that, along with the 'pity, and sympathy' she felt for O, she recognised that she was 'very courageous' (p.140), and both resourceful and strong, agreeing with Deforges that O 'dominates by an excessive submission', saying 'She uses the only weapon left to her. She is not left any other. But I believe it is a formidable weapon, as long as it lasts,' and going on to ask whether in fact 'O does not use René and Sir Stephen and all this ceremonious and weighty organization of castle-prison, of forced debauchery, irons and chains, to obtain the fulfillment of her dream, that is to say, her destruction, her death. Is it not, secretly, her requirement that governs them? She wins, in the end...' (p.205-206). But in Réage's view, death is not the worst fate – that is separation: to be separated from those one loves. One is in hell. I do not know if there is a heaven, but I know in any case there is a hell. It's separation' (p.40), and she was willing to countenance unfaithfulness so long as the loved one does not leave: 'I find that, when one loves someone what is unbearable is that he leaves you, that he deserts you; the fact that he is interested in someone else is not that serious providing that he does not leave you, that he does not desert you, providing that he comes back, that he still loves you, that he does not abandon you' (p.48). But if being abandoned is the worst of fates, to abandon oneself in love is a glorious destiny. To be engulfed in love, as O was, is 'very cruel', and a negation of freedom, 'she was not free, since she loved someone, one is not free when one loves,' (p.141), but when Deforges pointed out how often she used the word 'abandon', Réage responded: 'Because I think that it is an ideal, the absolute trust in what we love, the total embracing of one's fate, the acceptance, if you prefer, of both oneself and of others' (p.80). It is in this context that O's desire for death can be understood, as a poetic expression of the ultimate apotheosis of engulfment in love.

As far as feminism was concerned, Réage dismissed the M.L.F. (Mouvement de Libération des Femmes) for the excesses of their actions, while insisting 'I have never been a member of a feminist movement, but I have always been a feminist.' (p.59). Later in the interview she talked about Mme. de Merteuil in *Dangerous Liaisons*, and her ability to use herself as an object to enjoy pleasure, and as an instrument to wield power, and endorsed her contempt for Cécile, who was indeed 'despicable', for her 'lack of character' (p. 203).

The interview ended on a melancholy note. For Réage, *O* was 'a fairy tale for another world, a world where some part of me lived for a long time, a world that no longer exists except between the covers of a book. It is the book of a stranger who I am astonished probably used to be me. I wrote it for someone who is dead today, and I will die soon... The images, the dreams have left me... the days and nights rush at full speed towards a great silence', and she concluded with telling Deforges how she was looking forward to disappearing into that silence (p.220-221).

**1970s Reactions:** As if to make up for the less than friendly reception it had offered the novel in the 1950s, *L'Express* was inspired by the release of the film to give *O* extensive coverage in two editions in September 1975, reprinting Paulhan's preface [57] along with extracts from the Deforges interview, an article by Madeleine Chapsal arguing for *O*'s relevance to contemporary France [58], and a full-frontal nude photo of Corinne Cléry on the front cover. *L'Express* reinforced the views of Réage and Deforges that it is war that is obscene, not sex, and that the liberation and expression of women's sexuality is in itself feminist progress.

Predictably there was a backlash against the film and its publicity, with feminist activists from the M.L.F. attacking the premises of *L'Express*, writing graffiti on the walls and shouting *'Pas d'argent sur notre corps!'* ('Our bodies are not for sale!/ Don't make money from our bodies!') [59], with the Archbishop of Paris, conservatives and the Communist Party all rallying to the cause and calling for sanctions [60]. The government responded, establishing an X certificate classification for 'pornographic' films, with a hefty 33% tax imposed, and the old censorship system being replaced by a visa system instituted for films before release [61]. This put an end to the mid 1970s erotica free-for-all in French cinema, but sales of *O* peaked, so Pauvert was happy – 'we never sold so many copies. 1974 was the year of *Story of O*' [62].

## THE 1980s AND 90s:

As it happened, Aury's wistful prognostication in the Deforges interview of her imminent end was a little premature – she still had more than twenty years left to her. Much of that time she stayed out of the lime-light, although she gave a couple of interviews in the 1980s (including to Nicole Grenier in 1988, where her delight in secrecy and the clandestine emerged as a major theme), on the understanding that nothing would be released or published until after her death. Then, in the early 1990s, by now well into her eighties, she opened up to a couple of researchers: North American scholar Dorothy Kaufmann who wanted to interview Dominique Aury about her relationship with historian, writer and political activist Édith Thomas, for whom Aury had written a 'moving' obituary in 1970; and British journalist John de St Jorre, who wanted to interview Pauline Réage as part of his research for a book on Maurice Girodias, who had died in 1990.

**Dorothy Kaufmann:** During a series of conversations between 1990 and 1995 with this 'petite, charming, and austerely elegant woman', who was friendly and welcoming, but also 'elusive and enigmatic', Kaufmann was evidently taken somewhat aback by some of Aury's revelations [63]. Firstly, 'almost in passing', her confession regarding Édith Thomas that "'we had a brief love affair, she and I'", and also, when describing the fracas with the censors over *O*, Aury more or less openly admitted she was the author, something she seemed to assume Kaufmann already knew. Aury gave Kaufmann a copy of *Retour à Roissy* – not, as was made clear, for the novella, which Aury dismissed as 'very poor', but for 'Une fille amoureuse', which Kaufmann found 'astonishingly beautiful' and which Aury described as 'the only true story I ever wrote'. Aury signed the copy she gave Kaufmann with the name 'Pauline Réage'. Kaufmann, 'respecting French codes of discretion', never directly discussed Aury's authorship of *O* with her, nor did she reveal it publicly, only publishing her account of the interviews in 1998, when the cat was out of the bag. We shall look in more detail at this in later chapters.

**John de St Jorre:** In this interview, appearing in *The New Yorker* in 1994 [64], Dominique Aury, now aged 86, agreed to speak about *O* under her own name, finally revealing the true identity of the mysterious author of this 'rather beautiful book' in which 'religious references abound...' 'permeated with mystical and sacrificial imagery... the first explicitly erotic novel to be written by a woman and published in the modern era'. Described by St Jorre as a 'calm, clearheaded woman who answered my questions easily and with dry humor', Aury was 'a small, neat, handsome woman with gray hair and gray-blue eyes...', her 'smooth firm hands and open sandals enhanced a suggestion of youth', 'her voice... vibrant and her eyes... clear.' Listing her professional achievements and awards, including the Légion d'Honneur, St Jorre identified her as 'a highly skilled and much respected woman of letters', as well as Jean Paulhan's war-time Resistance comrade, editorial assistant and then lover from 1947 until his death in 1968. In the interview Aury talked about her clandestine relationship with Paulhan – she living with her mother, he with his wife (who suffered from Parkinson's disease) – and the writing of the novel, where she confirmed the accuracy of her 1969 account, 'A Girl in Love' as 'pure truth' [65]. She had written the novel for Paulhan, and had done so for a number of reasons. First as a gift to his Sadean tastes (as she said in 'A Girl' p.9); second, as *une enterprise de séduction* to maintain his interest in her – 'By the early 1950s, she felt that he was slipping away' [66] – "What could I do? I couldn't paint, I couldn't write poetry. What could I do to make him sit up?.... I wasn't young, I wasn't pretty... it was necessary to find other weapons"; and finally to prove to him that women could write erotica, something Paulhan had not hitherto believed – Aury recounting the conversation: '"I'm sure you can't do that kind of thing," he said. "You think so?" I said. "Well I can try"' [67], and she wove her own fantasies in with the Sadean motifs. [This third reason, with Aury rising successfully to a challenge, is the one that finds most favour with recent Anglophone commentators, although the 'Scheherazade' motive should not be dismissed – after all, in the legend, Scheherazade not only saves her own life, she also gains control through her wit and knowledge, wins the sultan and becomes queen [68]].

The strategy worked – he was 'ensnared' ('her word' [69]). "The first sixty pages flowed out of me... They wrote themselves. Why was it like that? Probably because I had been dreaming…" she said, and so impressed was Paulhan that he urged her to write more – "'Have you got any more?" he would ask. "Do you have the next chapter? Keep at it." [70], which she did, but 'after the explosive beginning, the writing slowed… not because she found it difficult but because she tried to give the story more of a structure' [71]. She continued writing for three months over the summer of 1951, sending the pages by post, and reading it to him in the autumn when they met up again. But 'one day I found I couldn't go on and that was all. Paulhan said it was all right. "You can stop now," he said' [72], but she realised 'I didn't know how to end it, so I left it open. Why not?' [73], adding, 'I am not a novelist, you know' [74].

Aury had harboured 'no thoughts – or intention – of publication' [75] but Paulhan took charge, had the manuscript typed, asked her to let him find a publisher, to which she agreed provided her anonymity was protected, and wrote his preface. Aury insisted Paulhan had no hand in the writing of the book – his role being entirely motivational, and despite him making comments in the margins of the typed manuscript, and being suspected of 'doing some heavy editing', Aury insisted he made only one change, suggesting that she remove the word '*sacrificiel*' [76] (which according Geraldine Bedell, in a book dedicated to sacrifice, must be 'some kind of in-joke' [77]).

It has been suggested that Aury's acceptance of Paulhan's wish to have the book published parallels O's submission to the will of her lovers in the novel – as Bedell goes on, 'It is impossible not to wonder whether there is a faint echo, in Dominique Aury's consenting to finish and publish the book, of O's progressive self-annihilation' [78] – but the prospect of publication certainly did not dismay her. According to one friend, 'like all writers, Aury wanted to be published and was flattered by Paulhan's conviction that what she was doing was good' [79], and in a later interview Aury showed that she really had cared about publication, revealing that the rejection by Gallimard still rankled with her: 'Gaston Gallimard said "We can't publish books like this," though he had published Jean Genet, which was much nastier' [80].

In the end, Aury confirmed Paulhan's claim in his 1954 preface that *O* was 'the most ardent love letter a man could ever receive' [Preface p. xxxii), averring *'C'était une lettre d'amour*... Nothing else' [81], all the scandal being 'Much ado about nothing...' [82]. But there was a final twist, St Jorre discovered he was 'in for a double surprise', that the author 'wore more than one veil': Pauline Réage and Dominique Aury were both pseudonyms, behind which was 'yet another persona, her true identity,' but, St Jorre wrote, 'she asked me not to publish it... and this I agreed to' [83].

**Dominique Aury's Secrets**:  The question *how* Dominique Aury managed to keep her secret for so long is commonly explained in terms of the sheer unlikelihood of such a demure, genteel lady with such conservative dress-sense harbouring such an imagination – 'It seemed inconceivable that a woman with such a drab exterior could explore a sexual compulsion that drove her protagonist toward oblivion,' as one commentator rather bluntly put it [84]. In fact more people were in on the secret than is commonly assumed, but a sense of 'decency', a word employed by Paulhan, Deforges and others to describe *O*, seems to have prevailed in French literary circles, so that those in the know kept quiet, and turned a blind eye to any hints or evidence entering public awareness.

Like much else in this story, the reason *why* Aury wanted to keep her identity concealed for so long and then finally decide to unveil is open to different accounts [85]. Perhaps she was protecting her family, or Gallimard's reputation, or her position there [86]. Aury's own account, in a subsequent television interview, was that she wanted to wait for her parents to die, and then to wait a little longer: '"When you learn that it was written by a very old lady it loses some of its scandal"'. St Jorre's professionalism would perhaps have reassured Aury that he would not write about her 'in a sensationalist way', or maybe, as her son Philippe d'Argila suggested, she did not actually intend to 'confess' but St Jorre's skill as a journalist won her over – 'He's a good journalist. I'm not sure she followed too precisely what he said. I don't think she meant to tell him at that time'. Régine Deforges disagreed, believing it was intentional: 'She didn't like lying, and she was relieved' to unburden herself. [Deforges' claim that Aury was averse to untruth is of course exquisitely comical].

There is however another possibility. Around 1990 Aury was short of money and asked Pauvert to organise for her the sale of the manuscript of *O* (a dozen or so school exercise books, hand-written in pencil). A Swiss collector of erotica who had recently bought the original manuscript of de Sade's *Cent Vingt Journées de Sodom* was interested, and ended up buying the exercise books, 'the type-script with Paulhan's editing suggestions and comments' (which rather contradicts the insistence of both Paulhan and Aury that Paulhan had made no editing interventions), 'some correspondence between the author and Paulhan concerning the publication of the book', plus letters from Pauvert and Aury giving their accounts of the story of the book. Aury claimed they made 'several hundred thousand francs', Pauvert recalled 'well under $100,000' [87] (given the exchange rate at the time of around 5 FFr to the dollar, it is actually possible to square up Aury's and Pauvert's stories for once). Financial considerations may well have been significant in Aury's decision to draw the publicity of finally unveiling herself.

In fact the revelation that Pauline Réage was Dominique Aury should not have come as a huge surprise to anyone who had been paying close attention over the years. For a start, Réage wrote in the very distinctive style of Aury, whose work was well known in literary circles. Pauvert claimed he 'recognised her style immediately' when Paulhan gave him the manuscript [88], and soon after publication, surrealist poet and Sade biographer Gilbert Lely compared Réage's and Aury's writing styles and wrote to Aury, 'You can tell me whatever you want, it is you who has written it' [89]. Others subsequently tried the same experiment with the same result [90].

Moreover, rumours that Réage was Aury had been circulating for years. According to Aury's own letters to Édith Thomas, her name was in the running by August 1954 [91]. In 1955, *France-Soir* had speculated on possible candidates for authorship, referring to 'several young writers (who show promise!)... and notably... Dominique Aury' [92], and by the late 1960s the French press had obtained a photographic copy of a cheque made out by Pauvert to Aury which had 'settled her identity' among Paris critics [93]. In 1971 Kenneth Tynan, compiling an anthology of sexual fantasies (that in the end never appeared), invited Aury 'the reputed author of *L'Histoire d'O* (sic)' to contribute. She declined on the grounds that the author '"to whom you are addressing your request through me – if I understand rightly – is altogether out of this creative world... If she tried again, she would write trash. Better not."' [94] (a reply that might be read in the light of the *Return to the Château* fiasco in 1969). In an article on *O* from 1984, it was stated 'it is now generally assumed that it was written by the French literary critic Dominique Aury' [95], in 1990 *Le Monde* named Aury as author of 'the sulphurous erotic novel *Histoire d'O*' [96], and during one of Pauvert's bankruptcies in 1992 [97], a creditor saw in the accounts that 'Dominique Aury' (who had never been published under that name by Pauvert), was owed *une somme fabuleuse* [98].

John de St Jorre, while himself convinced of Aury's sole authorship, nevertheless recorded some alternative views [99]. One was that of Clifford Scheiner (connoisseur of erotica in New York) who believed it was group effort, with Aury, Paulhan, Pauvert and possibly others all having a hand in it, populating the novel with real people and real events (he even claimed to detect Girodias and Leonor Fini turning up as visitors to Roissy – presumably in *Return*). Another was Richard Seaver,

U.S. publisher and translator who in the 1950s worked in Paris with Merlin Press – translating Beckett amongst others – before working at Grove Press in New York. Seaver told St Jorre, 'Look, it's more complicated, more mysterious than you think. You have to ask yourself: "Is Dominique Aury telling you the whole truth?"' giving as an example of her evasiveness her tactical omission of Paulhan's philandering in 'A Girl'. [Doubts about Aury's veracity sounded ungracious at the time, but as Aury's appetite for the clandestine has become better known, perhaps give us less of a jolt now]. Seaver also questioned the authenticity of the hand-written exercise books as the original manuscript, wondering if they might not have been concocted after *O* was published, and again suggested *O* was the product of other hands as well as Aury's – even implying some input from the shadowy 'Sabine d'Estrée', suggesting she 'and the author are linked... Someone else, apart from Dominique Aury, was involved in writing *Story of O*.'

Pauvert dismissed all this, accusing Scheiner of being a myth-making conspiracy theorist, and Seaver of being out of touch [100]. Pauvert's account was that he saw the exercise books, and could confirm they were in Aury's hand, but more conclusively, the style of writing in *O* was very much hers. Paulhan had already pointed out the difference between his writing and that of Réage in 1955 [101], a view Pauvert emphatically endorsed, adamant that it was Aury and only Aury, having instantly recognised her hand when he saw the manuscript: 'She is a great writer and absolutely uncopyable... Paulhan said he could not write like that... his own style was quite different, very dry, ironic, he could not change it' ' [102]. [Having said this, it is worth remembering that Pauvert was just as capable of tactical misinformation as anyone in this story, so his testimony should also be treated with caution. Aury repeatedly admitted she found it hard to proceed beyond the first sixty pages, and the involvement of additional helping hands in later chapters is not impossible, although should not be assumed.]

**Régine Deforges (encore):** In 1995, *O m'a dit* was reissued [103] with a new introduction by Régine Deforges, in which she celebrated the 'relationship of infinite tenderness, made of profound affection and respect... the softest of friendships' [104] she enjoyed with the now 88 year old Aury, who had agreed to the 1975 interview 'to please me', but declined to be interviewed further: '"But my child, I have told everything and I am so tired"'. Deforges reports, 'I did not insist.' She did however wonder about the currency of *O* by the 1990s, observing that 'cinema has not done justice to the book,' that 'the great film of *O* and her love is yet to be realised, ' she asked 'perhaps it is too late?', perhaps times have changed, for now, 'when we evoke *Histoire d'O* and *O m'a dit*, we feel that a long time has gone by, that women and men, overfed by television and films with forcefully realistic images, can no longer be moved by *O*.' Deforges concluded: '*O m'a dit* is a sincere book, where neither Pauline nor I have cheated. It still looks like us.'

**Pola Rapaport:** Despite declining to be interviewed further by Deforges, Aury did grant another interview, in 1998, to Pola Rapaport for a documentary film. Rapaport had read her older sister's copy of *O* at the age of 13 (the same age Aury had been when she read *Dangerous Liaisons*), and, although professing no taste for S&M herself, nevertheless admitted that *O* 'catches people's imaginations,' finding the book 'fascinating and erotic and repellent all at the same time: it's unfiltered and unique' [105].

Rapaport interviewed Aury herself, and was able to incorporate footage of Aury from the 1960s and an interview from 1986 as well, on the understanding that the documentary would not be shown until after Aury's death. In the 1986 interview, Aury remembered Paulhan as 'tall, broad-shouldered, somewhat heavy-set, with a Roman-like face, and something both smiling and sarcastic in his expression,' observing 'Existence filled him with wonder, both the admirable and the horrible aspects of experience, equally so. The atrocious fascinated him. The enchanting enchanted him' [106]. She reiterated to Rapaport what she had told St Jorre, 'I wrote it alone, for him, to interest him, to please him, to occupy him. I wasn't young, nor particularly pretty. I needed something which might interest a man like him' [107]. In her interview with Rapaport, Aury was finally showing signs of losing some of her mental acuteness – knowing she was born in 1907, Aury guessed she must be 70 or 80 and was sweetly surprised to hear she was 90 ('Oh, good... good for me'), before summarising her tale: 'I had a lover who I loved very much for whom I wrote *Histoire d'O*... Jean Paulhan. He was sixty, sixty five or something like that and I was around forty and I was very much in love with him.... I had a husband who was a mistake, with whom I had a child who was not a mistake. Otherwise nothing except Jean Paulhan. I lived with him for fifteen years, eleven years. I don't remember,' but after his death in 1968, 'The last part of being alive, of my life being alive. After that, I didn't. I stopped everything' [108]. [A moving valediction, but even here Dominique Aury showed that she had not lost her ability to gently nudge people off the scent when it suited her].

**The End:** Dominique Aury retired to her room in the house in Boussise she had lived in for more than thirty five years, and died there in on April 27th 1998, five months before her 91st birthday, surrounded by her cats and dogs [109]. There were obituaries in several papers, including *Le Monde* and *Libèration*, Régine Deforges writing the one in *L'Humanité*. In June 1999 a homage to Aury in the *NRF* (where she had worked since 1953), celebrated her 'extraordinary passion for literature' while evading any reference to 'Pauline Réage' or *O* [110]. The same year Nicole Grenier's 1988 interview with Aury was published (by Gallimard, in a series edited by Philippe Sollers) with Aury given as the author. And finally her last secret, disclosed to St Jorre and certainly known to Paulhan among (possibly many) others, doubtless including Pauvert and Deforges, could be revealed in the public domain, that her original name had been Anne Desclos, a name she had locked away in the late 1930s [111]. In fact this was another revelation that had been hiding in plain sight for some years. The *Dictionnaire Biographique* for 1980 gave Dominique Aury's real name as Anne Desclos, so after the St Jorre 'revelation' in 1994, the Réage = Aury = Desclos equation should have been a straightforward deduction [112]. If anyone did make the connection, they evidently drew the proverbial veil of discretion over it.

In 2004, the fiftieth anniversary of the publication of *Histoire d'O* was commemorated by Geraldine Bedell's article 'I Wrote the Story of O' and Pola Rapaport's film *Writer of O*. With the opening credits featuring a sequence of titles that hit all the targets: SEX, LOVE, SURRENDER, LITERATURE, FEMINISM, CENSORSHIP, LIBERATION, *Writer of O* consisted of Rapaport's own reminiscences of reading *O*, her interview with Aury , footage from the 1960s and 1986, interviews with Pauvert, St Jorre, Deforges and Barney Rosset, and dramatised re-enactments of scenes from *O*, from the life of Aury and Paulhan, and from the 1975 Deforges interview, with Rapaport reading from 'A Girl in Love'. The film was praised for providing 'an engaging, informative, and provocative view of an important chapter in the history of women's sexual freedom, and an archival record of an unsung feminist heroine' [113], and the dramatisations of *O* were commended in *Sight and Sound* as 'erotic without being leering or exploitative, and also gently disturbing, somehow capturing the soulful clarity of the original text and making plain Aury's correlation between the exposure of O's loving self sacrifice and the vulnerability of prayer' [114].

That same year the French government announced that *Histoire d'O* was to be included in 'a list of national triumphs to be celebrated in 2004' [115], and another mystery promptly presented itself. An exhibition 'La Bibliothèque Gérard Nordmann' was staged at the Martin Bodmer Foundation, Geneva, which displayed the original manuscript of *Histoire d'O* as one of the prime exhibits – the accompanying catalogue being entitled *Éros invaincu* (*Eros Unconquered*) [116]. Evidently Nordmann was the unnamed Swiss collector of erotica referred to by St Jorre to whom Aury (according to Pauvert) had sold the manuscript and her correspondence with Paulhan about *O* (see above, p. 70). But the Geneva exhibition made no mention of the correspondence. Angie David, at work on her magisterial biography of Dominique Aury, recognising how invaluable it would be for her researches, was immediately on the case to track it down. But the correspondence was not among Aury's collection of letters at Boussise, nor was it in the Jacques Doucet library (where Aury had claimed in the 1970s she had deposited it [117]), nor did Nordmann's widow admit to any knowledge of it. However, David's publisher, Léo Scheer, then received a tip-off from Pauvert that there was 'no point' searching for it, Pauvert being (in David's words) 'the only one authorised to establish a critical edition of *Histoire d'O*, and research around the secrets of the novel is therefore useless'. David concluded from this that Pauvert had kept the correspondence all along, possibly not even telling Aury that it was being diverted from the Nordmann deal. If so, what was he planning on doing with it? Apparently not a lot. In the eight years between the publication of David's biography and Pauvert's death, nothing came to light. This might be explicable if there was a confidentiality clause of secrecy till after the death of Aury's son (Aury claimed there was one with the apparently phantom Doucet library 'collection'), but Philippe died in 2020, aged 90, and as far as I know, there has still been no sign of it (assuming it actually exists, of course...).

Pauvert was 88 when he died in September 2014. As for other major players in this story, Barney Rosset was 89 when he died in 2012, Régine Deforges 78 at her death in April 2014, and at the time of writing, John de St Jorre is still batting, at

87 not out. An interest in erotica does not seem to be bad for the health. Only Maurice Girodias let the side down, dying in 1990 at a mere 71.

---

[1] Bedell 2004
[2] Aury cited in St Jorre 1994, p. 47
[3] Bedell 2004
[4] Bedell 2004
[5] La Compagnie des Bibliophiles. Le Cercle du Livre précieux. Cited Peter Webb: *Sphinx – The Life and Art of Leonor Fini* Vendome Press 2009 p. 293.
[6] St Jorre 1994, p. 42
[7] The literal translation is: 'There exists a second ending to the story of O. It is that, seeing herself on the point of being left by Sir Stephen, she preferred to die. He consented.'
[8] André Pieyre de Mandiargues *"Histoire d'O", Critique,* June 1955, cited in David, 2006, p. 12 footnote 7
[9] Cited in Deforges 1975 p. 9
[10] There is apparently a reference in a letter from Pauvert to Paulhan, early August 1954, that 'The complete edition will soon appear, and everyone will forget the abridged version...', going on to say he would like to see 'the proofs of the last chapter.' (https://jean-paulhan-sljp.fr/). I am grateful to Stephen Prince for this information which he provided via intermediaries Jan 2022.
[11] Information provided by Conn Moriarty; David 2006, p. 27 refers to the extra sentence in the 1966 reprint and the Livre de Poche editions.
[12] It has also caused a fair bit of confusion with some commentators believing it has been present in French editions since 1954, but omitted from the Olympia/Wainhouse translation, along with the Paulhan preface, before being reinstated by Grove Press.
[13] Paulhan deposition cited Deforges 1975, p. 9
[14] St Jorre 1995, p. 224
[15] Pauvert 2004, p. 216, cited in David 2006, p. 27-28
[16] St Jorre 1995, p. 224
[17] David 2006, p. 28
[18] interview with Jacqueline Demornex, cited in St Jorre 1995 pp. 224-226.
[19] Aury 1999 p. 108 cited David p. 28
[20] Cited in Dorothy Kaufmann: 'The Story of Two Women: Dominique Aury and Édith Thomas' *Signs* vol. 23, no. 4 Summer 1998 p. 8
[21] Quote combined from St Jorre 1994, pp. 47-48, and St Jorre 1995, p. 224.
[22] Aury cited in St Jorre 1995, p. 224

23  Pauvert cited in St Jorre 1995 p. 224.
24  'the medium had become the message when the novelist quite literally became a prostitute, the ultimate in participation' Jan B. Gordon: "The Story of O' and the Strategy of Pornography' (*Western Humanities Review*; Winter 1971; 25, 1), p. 32, footnote
25  Bedell 2004
26  Jacqueline Paulhan cited in Bedell 2004
27  St Jorre 1995, p 225.
28  Including St Jorre 1994 and Mahon 2020 p. 137.
29  With Jacqueline Demornex,
30  Deforges 1975, p. 10
31  Deforges 1975 p. 15
32  Aury, 1999, p. 108 cited David 2006 p. 28
33  Cited in St Jorre 1995, p 224
34  All quotes in this paragraph are from David 2006 pp. 28-30
35  Les Films de la Pléiade, first screened 1961.
36  See David 2006 p. 50 for a fuller account.
37  Bedell 2004
38  Black 1999
39  Andy Black – 'The Story of O' , (*Necronomicon* Book 3, Noir, 1999)
40  The year 2000, according to IMDB. The film was released by Arrow Films on VHS and later DVD as *The Story of O* [sic]
41  Samm Deighan: 'Female Pleasure and Performance' in Karen Ritzenhof & Karen Randell,  *Screening the Dark Side of Love: From Eurohorror to American Cinema*. (Palgrave Macmillan 2012)
42  Ibid p. 133
43  Ibid p. 143
44  'Interview with the Director, The Story of O', DVD, Arrow Films 2005
45  cited in St Jorre 1995 p. 225
46  David 2006, p. 50
47  Which was republished in different versions, including a graphic novel by Guido Crepax, (Franco Marco Ricci, Milan 1975)
48  Issue no. 1498
49  cited in Deforges 1975, p. 5-6
50  cited in St Jorre 1995, p. 226
51  cited in St Jorre 1995, p. 227
52  St Jorre 1994, p. 47-48; St Jorre 1995: p. 226
53  *Daily Telegraph* obituary of Régine Deforges, 19th June 2014
54  David 2006 p. 56
55  Her first being the semi-autobiographical lesbian story *Le Cahier volé* (*The Stolen Diary,* 1978), her best known *La Bicyclette bleue* (1981)
56  *O m'a dit* 1975, back cover.
57  Retitled 'O et l'equilibre mystérieux de la violence' – Mahon 2020 p.255, note 235
58  'Le Choc d'Histoire d'O' cited in Mahon 2020, p. 176
59  David 2006, p. 50

60  *Ibid*

61  *Ibid*, p. 50-51

62  cited in St Jorre 1995 p. 225

63  Kaufmann 1998. All quotes in this paragraph are from pp. 886 and 895.

64  An expanded version appears as chapter 8 '*Une Lettre d'Amour, the True Story of Story of O*' in his book on Girodias and Olympia Press 1994 (1995). Unless otherwise stated, all material and quotes in this section are from St Jorre 1994, pp. 42-44.

65  St Jorre 1995, p. 237

66  *Ibid,* p.212

67  Cited in St Jorre 1994, p. 43, compare Réage 'A Girl' 1969/ 1971 p. 9

68  Mahon 2020, p. 141

69  St Jorre 1995 p. 211

70  Cited in St Jorre 1994, p. 45, compare Réage 1969/ 1971, p. 13

71  *Ibid*, p. 45

72  Cited in *Ibid* p.46

73  Cited in *ibid*, p. 47;  this again implies that the enigmatic post-script to *O* was the original ending and *Return* was added later.

74  Cited in St Jorre 1995, p 224

75  *Ibid* p. 211; a view confirmed by Deforges in interview with Bedell 2004

76  St Jorre 1994, p. 46.

77  Bedell 2004

78  *Ibid*

79  Elizabeth Porquerol, cited in Bedell 2004

80  Television interview in 1994, cited in Bedell 2004

81  Cited in St Jorre 1994, p. 51; 1995 p. 231

82  Cited in *Ibid* p. 50; 1995 p. 231

83  *Ibid*, p. 44

84  Carmela Cuiraru : 'Pauline Réage and Dominique Aury' in *Nom de Plume: A (Secret) History of Pseudonyms,* (Harper Collins 2011), reprinted as 'The Story of the Story of O', *Guernica* 15 June 2011

85  Which are reported in Bedell 2004, from which the material in this paragraph is taken.

86  See also David 2006 p. 189

87  St Jorre 1995 p. 230

88  Cited in St Jorre 1994, p. 46

89  David 2006, p. 19, citing Aury 1999, p. 107

90  Owen Holloway cited in St Jorre 1995, p. 232, and James Campbell, cited Campbell 1994, pp 174, 176-7.

91  David 2006 p 432 note 98

92  *France-Soir*, 1955, dossier de presse *Histoire d'O*, IMEC. Cited in David 2006, p. 13

93  Gordon 1971

94  Kathleen Tynan: *Kenneth Tynan* (Methuen 1988) p. 295

[95] Nathaniel Brown and Rebecca Blevins Faery: 'The Total "O": Dream or Nightmare?' *Mosaic*; Spring 1984; 17, 2

[96] 'Les Infortunes de Gallimard', *Le Monde* 23 Nov. 1990, cited in Kaufmann 1998, p. 883, footnote 1

[97] Referred to by Guy Debord in a letter from May 1992.

[98] Campbell 1994 p. 177/ TLS 8 May 1998 / This raises the interesting question of where all that money went – Rex Roberts: 'Writer of O' *Film International Journal*, vol. 108, Issue 6, 22 Feb 2007.

[99] St Jorre 1995 pp. 232-234

[100] *Ibid*, p. 238

[101] Paulhan's testimony to the Brigade Mondaine Aug. 5th 1955.

[102] St Jorre 1995, pp. 233, 238

[103] Fonds Pauvert

[104] All quotes in this paragraph are from Deforges 1995 cited by Sisyphus47 2013 (3) in https://ofglassandpaper.com/2013/05/08/writerswednesday-o-ma-ditavant-propos/

[105] Bedell 2004

[106] *Ibid*

[107] Cited in Rapaport 2004; Bedell 2004

[108] Cited in Maya Gallus, dir. *Erotica: A Journey into Female Sexuality* Sienna Films, Canada, 1997) Pola Rapaport dir. *Writer of O* Zeitgeist Films 2004; Bedell 2004

[109] David p. 189

[110] *Ibid* p. 190, note 143

[111] Kaufmann 1998 might have been the first.

[112] I am grateful to Conn Moriarty for this little nugget.

[113] Mia de Bethune: 'Writer of O' (Review) *Art Therapy: Journal of the American Art Therapy Association*, 26(A) pp. 191 –195, 2009

[114] Tim Lucas: 'Writer of O' *Sight and Sound* July 2006, p. 87

[115] Bedell 2004 p. 1

[116] All the material in this paragraph is from David 2006 p. 547-548

[117] This was the same collection to which André Breton donated his unpublished letters and papers in 1965, Polizzotti 2009 p. 552

# III: Lives and Times: From the Beginnings to the War – 1907-1944

Although the focus of this book is on the novel rather than on the author, it is worth taking a little time to look into the biographies of Aury and Paulhan – paying particular attention to the highly politicised times of the Second World War and Liberation as the context for their relationship with each other, and the writing of *Story of O* [1].

## BEFORE 1940

**Anne Desclos**: The woman who was to write *Story of O* was born on 23rd September 1907 in Rochefort-sur-Mer, in the Nouvelle-Aquitaine region on the west coast of France, to a Catholic mother, Angèle Louise (née Auricoste), and a Protestant father, Victor Auguste Desclos. Christened Anne Cécile, the baby was raised by her Breton paternal grandmother in Avranches on the northern coast, on the border of Brittany, where she imbibed Celtic culture. In later interviews, Aury took clear positions with regard to her parents. Her mother she depicted unsympathetically as one whose disgust at bodies, sexuality, pregnancy and breast-feeding led her to more or less abandon her daughter ('She didn't like men... She didn't like women, either. She hated flesh' [2]). By contrast, she always expressed admiration and adoration for her father, Auguste, a comparatively exotic figure, literary and bilingual, who held dual French and English nationality, having been born to French parents in London and living there till he was 15 [3]. Auguste served as an interpreter for the British air force in the

First World War, moved in educational (and later diplomatic) circles, had a keen eye for the ladies, and was an intellectual, emotional and sensual presence in his daughter's world [4]. In reality, Aury's relationship with her parents were more nuanced.

After a solitary, bookish and religious childhood, and early schooldays in Clermont de l'Oise (where by her own account she was a bit of a tomboy, leading the gang and getting into fights [5]), the family moved to Paris in 1919 for Auguste to take up a teaching post, and Anne had her secondary education at the Lycée Fénelon. Attracted by the mysteries of Catholic liturgy, and the teachings of the 17th century mystic after whom her school was named, Anne nevertheless claimed she was never in fact baptised Catholic [6]. Along with school, she received another, equally if not more significant education among her father's books – Shakespeare (her favourite, whom she read in English), the Bible (in particular the King James translation – again in English), Baudelaire, Proust, and erotica which she was devouring by her early teens (with Auguste's liberal-minded approval), *Dangerous Liaisons, Letters of a Portuguese Nun* and Boccaccio's *Decameron* [7].

Anne gained her qualification in English from the Sorbonne in 1929 and started work in teacher training at the University of Columbia in Paris. She also married, and for a husband chose a man who was almost the complete opposite of her father, a journalist called Raymond d'Argila, who was not just politically extremely right wing, but temperamental and violent as well. In 1930 they had a son Philippe, but by 1933 d'Argila's brutality had prompted Anne to leave him. She took Philippe to return to her parents, living with them for the next three decades. She also sued d'Argila for divorce, which was a messy business, with Anne suffering ill-health (she had recurring migraines all her life), before it was finally settled in 1935, with Anne winning custody of Philippe. Jettisoning her married name, she adopted her mother's surname [8], which, along with her choice of husband, suggests her relationship with Auguste was not as ideal as she later claimed. If it was some kind of rebellion, it was not over yet, as Anne was to remain in right-wing circles for some years.

In later years Aury insisted her personal life was thoroughly uneventful – apart from the 'mistake' of a husband long before, 'that's all. Otherwise nobody except Jean Paulhan' [9], her sexual life being restricted to fantasies of being a prostitute or a nun – 'I did not have the temperament, nor the true desires, physical, I mean to say, everything happened in my head' [10]. As is so often the case in Aury's life, the truth was considerably more colourful, and these claims about her private life were among the most flagrantly misleading she ever made.

In 1933 she began a relationship with Thierry Maulnier (real name Jacques Talagrand), one of a group of young right-wing journalists she met through d'Argila, along with Maurice Blanchot, and Robert Brasillach – this latter being, like Maulnier, a supporter of Charles Maurras' nationalist Action Française. The affair with Maulnier was clandestine to begin with (adultery would weaken Anne's claim to custody of her child if the ever-threatening d'Argila found out), and was to be a relationship of intensity and great significance [11].

To set the scene: France had suffered disproportionately in the First World War (losing nearly one and a half million dead, 7% of its population) [12], economic recovery was slow, and the 1929 Wall Street Crash hit hard. The 1930s was a decade of recession and political unsteadiness, governments collapsed in quick succession, and a sense of crisis took hold, with radicals of both left and right talking insurrection. To begin with,

the demarcation lines between them were not crystal clear
– both sides rejected capitalism and democracy, although
Marxists tended to talk in terms of class and economics, while
the right (a mix of nationalists, fascists, royalists, hard-line
Catholics and the like) were more prone to go on about nation
(sometimes 'race') and 'spiritual' rebirths. In 1932 the *NRF*
published an edition on the 'New Spirit of the 1930s' covering
communist and far-right 'new order' opinion together.

In 1933 Stalin began to fully assert himself in the Soviet
Union and over international Communism, Hitler came to
power in Germany, and political polarisation in Paris hard-
ened. In February 1934 there were large scale demonstrations in Paris by left and right (Anne Desclos marching on
both sides on different days [13]), excitement over imminent
revolution ran high, reaching a bloody climax when far-right
anti-Semites clashed head-on with the left, leaving 1500 casu-
alties, including 16 dead [14].

A left-leaning Popular Front managed to form a government in 1936, which created a degree of optimism among
working-class voters, but it was all but paralysed by right-
wing opposition, and France could do little more than watch
as international fascism became more confident and assertive. Mussolini's 1935 invasion of Ethiopia, Hitler's unop-
posed annexation of the Rhineland in 1936, the capitulation
of Paris and London to Hitler's demands for Czech territory
at Munich in September 1938, and Franco's victory in the
Spanish Civil War in April 1939 boosted the right, incensed the
left, and demoralised the majority into a slough of defeatism
and denial.

Maulnier was thrilled. Along with Brasillach and other
'fascistically-minded intellectuals' [15], he was anti-capitalist,
anti-communist, anti-liberal, anti-democratic and obsessed
with the 'crisis of civilisation', applauded Mussolini's and
Franco's victories, praised the Munich 'settlement' and hailed

the Nazis as the great bulwark against communism. Brasillach was to follow his political trajectory through to thorough nazification, while Maulnier remained a French nationalist. Although impressed by the dramatic spectacle, romance and rhetoric of fascism, Maulnier did not believe Italian or German totalitarianism could be imported into France, and in his immersion in French cultural history – admiring Racine and classical literature (and loathing psychoanalysis and Surrealism) – he acknowledged the legacies of both monarchy and the French Revolution in the making of France, and believed in the 'universal values' French culture embodied [16]. He was anti-Semitic, buying into the belief that the Jews were the master-minds behind international capitalism (a belief with depressingly wide currency on the left as well), but did not share Catholic dogmas about Jews as 'Christ-killers' or Nazi ravings about Jews as a 'degenerate' or evil 'race'. Maurice Blanchot, the third member of Aury's circle with a taste for this 'aesthetic... highly spiritual "literary fascism"' [17], shared most of Maulnier's views but was not involved in Action Française, and took a more anti-German line, damning what he saw as France's corrupt parliamentary democracy and failure to stand up to Germany's expansionist policies. He condemned Hitler's 'barbarous persecution of the Jews' in Paul Lévy's *Le Rempart* in 1933 [18], while at the same time peppering his articles in other journals with anti-Semitic slurs. [There is still debate over whether Blanchot was serious in his liaison with fascism, or whether his game was more a matter of shock tactics and anti-establishment provocation [19]].

The affair between Anne and Maulnier seems to have had a complicated beginning, correspondence between them making reference to tangled relations with a 'Jacqueline' and a 'René' (names of significance in *O*, of course). The story is convoluted and obscure, but seems to indicate that both had been engaged in some degree of romantic involvement with Anne, until René (evidently a renowned seducer) and Jacqueline set up with each other when Anne and Maulnier got together [20]. [Additional spicier hints are dropped in correspondence between Anne and Maulnier of 'unmentionable relationships', even 'debaucheries' with others [21], including in August 1934 cryptic references to a mysterious assignation at the Louvre with Anne, René, a certain Claudine and one Milleret, which a lawyer acting for d'Argila (presumably out to dig dirt on Anne's character in the divorce and custody battle) was trying to investigate.... Make of that what you will]. In the event the divorce was granted in 1934 and finalised the following year [22].

In January 1936 Maulnier, with Brassilach and Blanchot and others, launched *Combat* (not to be confused with the Resistance journal of the same name, founded in 1941) which lasted until the following year – Maulnier adopting for it the nom de plume 'Dominique Bertin'. In January 1937 he launched *L'Insurgé*, again with Blanchot. This only lasted until October, but was significant as the publication where Anne started her literary career, contributing articles on art (her own tastes basically classical, but also encompassing Turner and the Impressionists) and literature (Shakespeare remaining her especial favourite). Apart from condemning the Popular Front for lionising Zola and the French Revolution, she avoided political comment, and there is no evidence of her expressing or holding any pro-fascist or anti-Jewish opinion (she 'always rejected' and 'was appalled by' anti-Semitism [23]). She seems however to have been shaken as well as excited by the 1934 events, developing by the late '30s a marked dislike of mass politics. This was a view she felt she shared with Shakespeare – referencing *Coriolanus* as evidence that 'one of the things (he) hated most' was 'the mob' [24] – a view that would have rendered both fascism and communism deeply unappealing to her. She was to hold that view for the rest of her life. It was at *L'Insurgé* that she adopted the name 'Dominique

Aury'. Speculation on this name suggests that 'Dominique', being a gender neutral name (Maulnier was using it as well), 'had the advantage of obfuscation' [25], while 'Aury' presumably derived from her mother's maiden name, Auricoste, the surname Anne had been using since her divorce. The initials D.A. were the reverse of those of her father (and also her own original name) [26]. Maulnier still called her 'Annette', but from 1937 her public and professional name was Dominique Aury.

When *L'Insurgé* folded in October, Aury's circle started to pull in different directions. Blanchot largely retreated into the literary world (he had been involved with *Journal des débats* since 1931), Maulnier continued with the French nationalist *Action Française*, and Brasillach edited *Je suis partout* (*I am Everywhere*) which was well on the way towards open fascism and virulent anti-Semitism. Relations between Blanchot and Brasillach ruptured, and Anne hovered in a position somewhere between Maulnier and Blanchot (both of whom were personally dear to her [27]).

Meanwhile, since 1935, Auguste Desclos had been working with L'Office des Universités et Écoles Française, where he encountered one Jean Paulhan, by then, at fifty or so, the leading light of the prestigious *Nouvelle Revue Française*. Auguste told his daughter of his new acquaintance, and introduced her to some of his writings, and it is likely that Anne and Paulhan met in passing at the office at some point [28]. In 1938 Gallimard published Maulnier's *Au-delà du nationalisme* (*Beyond Nationalism*), and with the threat of war looming, Maulnier, now convinced the Axis powers were the principal enemy, rallied to the national cause and joined up when mobilised. That autumn he and Anne began working on an *Introduction à la poésie française* – the idea being most likely Anne's, although Maulnier and Gallimard (possibly even Paulhan? [29]) may have had a hand in it. The anthology was published in September 1939, with Maulnier named as editor and Dominique Aury as assistant. In subsequent printings Aury's name was dropped, which naturally upset her but seemed of little concern to Maulnier. Justice eventually prevailed and her name was reinstated in May 1940 [30]. On publication the anthology caught a wave of French cultural enthusiasm just as war was declared, earning the praise of André Breton and the attention of Paulhan.

**Jean Paulhan**: Born in 1884 to a Protestant family in Nîmes, Paulhan spent four years in his twenties as a college lecturer in Madagascar where he researched local proverbs and lived the colonial life (complete with 'native' mistress), adopting some rather imperialist attitudes that never fully left him [31]. He married Salomé Prusak (Sala) in 1911 and over the next seven years had a daughter and two sons [32].

During the First World War Paulhan served as an officer in the Zouaves, was wounded in battle and awarded the Croix de Guerre. In Paris he networked in the literary and arts scene, coming under the influence of Apollinaire, the central pivot of the Parisian art world (with whom he shared an admiration for Sade). He also met André Breton, who praised his translations of Malagasy poetry, and introduced him to Paul Éluard (we shall trace Paulhan's relationship with the Surrealists in chapter VIII). Paulhan tried his hand as a novelist (and was considered for the Prix Goncourt) in works addressing initiation, the imminence of death and the possibility of 'rebirth', his style being compressed, reminiscent of fable or dream, with a Kafkaesque texture [33]. But his principal role was as an enabler, stepping in to fill at least some of the gap left by the early death of Apollinaire in 1918 (victim of the 'flu epidemic after being weakened by a shrapnel head-wound received during the war), and achieving such a central position that in 1919 Éluard described him as the *éminence grise* behind the Parisian avant-garde [34]. In 1918 he began an affair with Germaine Dauptaine, and in 1920 both were recruited to work at the *Nouvelle Revue Française* [35].

This review had been launched in 1909 under the directorship of novelist André Gide, with Gaston Gallimard and Jean Schlumberger in editorial roles, and was committed to a liberal-minded editorial policy, prioritising the 'autonomy of aesthetic values' over political sides, even in the wake of the divisive Dreyfus affair [36]. In 1911 the *NRF* spawned Éditions Gallimard, which was to become 'the most astonishing concentration of a country's literary talent in the history of publishing' [37]. After closing during the First World War, the *NRF* re-opened in 1919 with Jacques Rivière as its director. It retained its 'openness, its non-conformism, its Protestant sensibility' [38], along with the commercial canniness to court a wide audience, giving itself a broad remit to cover a range of writers from traditionalists to modernists like James Joyce and T.S. Eliot. By 1920 it was already the leading French review, 'one of the prime cultural institutions of the radical Third Republic, if not the most important' [39], the 'unchallenged centre of Parisian literary activity' [40], providing a model for Modernist reviews internationally, including Eliot's *Criterion*, launched in 1922 [41].

As the director's health declined, Paulhan found himself taking an increasingly responsible role, and when Rivière died in 1925 Paulhan effectively took over his role, in which capacity he introduced Kafka's work to France and fostered the career of that most Sadean of surrealists, Antonin Artaud. Paulhan was officially appointed director in 1935, and in his hands the review's star continued to rise. There, and at Gallimard, where he had a senior editorial position, he continued to publish avant-garde texts, including Breton's *L'Amour Fou* (*Mad Love*) and Artaud's *Théâtre et son Double* (both 1937), and sponsored Jean-Paul Sartre's literary break-through with *La Nausée* (1938), organising press campaigns and offering him a regular column in the *NRF* [42]. In 1933 Paulhan divorced

Sala and married Germaine [43] (by odd coincidence the same year that Anne Desclos left her husband).

During the political stand-offs between left and right in the 1930s Paulhan led the *NRF* to an anti-fascist position, while remaining firmly independent of communism. Disliking the growing polarisation of French political culture as prohibiting debate and fostering extremism, Paulhan published writers from across the spectrum from left-wing through liberal to conservative (making overtures to Maulnier to contribute in 1930), recognising that all were part of French culture and had the right to be heard. As such, the *NRF* bill of fare was exceptionally rich and varied [44], which predictably attracted fire from the Communists who condemned it as bourgeois and uncommitted, the Church and conservatives who found it contaminated by the legacies of 'obscene' and 'debauched' writers like Rimbaud and Lautréamont [45], and fascists like Brasillach who in 1938 dismissed it as 'anarchic and scholarly' [46], a slur that no doubt delighted Paulhan.

## 1940-1944 – THE WAR YEARS

**Invasion and Occupation:** After the declaration of war in September 1939, and the seven months of the *drôle de guerre* ('Phoney War'), in April 1940 hostilities in western Europe began in earnest with German armies rapidly invading Denmark, Norway, the Netherlands, Luxembourg and Belgium, before coming up against France, the strongest military power in the region. And France caved in completely in five weeks. Among the factors mooted for this disaster – the unexpected effectiveness of the German *blitzkrieg* (up-ending the lesson of the First World War that the advantage lay with the defenders), French administrative unpreparedness [47], military incompetence [48], lack of unity between mutually mistrustful Allies and so on – the calamitous state of French morale needs to be considered.

The widespread defeatism and demoralisation of the French public in the 1930s was compounded by division and confusion. The right was split between nationalists ready to fight for their country and fascists welcoming the Germans as deliverance from what they saw as the 'decadence, corruption and chaos' of the Third Republic. The left was equally split, between pacifist socialists on the one hand and a tough-minded Communist party (PCF – Partie communiste français) on the other, well-organised, influential – but almost completely paralysed. In August 1939 the PCF newspaper *L'Humanité* had been calling for 'Union of the French Nation Against Hitlerian Aggression' [49], but they were already wrong-footed by history. Two days earlier the Third Reich and the Soviet Union had signed a 'non-aggression pact' and Moscow now demanded loyal Communist parties embrace its new ally. Suppressed by the French government as an agent of a hostile power in September 1939, the PCF had gone underground, and with the invasion in 1940 *L'Humanité* reversed its earlier policy and called on PCF members and supporters to fraternise with the Nazis [50]. The result was a serious crisis of conscience and loyalty among French communists, confusion, disunity and a lack of decisive conviction amongst everybody else, and swift and catastrophic defeat.

Early June saw the evacuation from Dunkirk and by the 14th the Nazis had occupied Paris. Marshall Philippe Pétain, much-decorated 84 year-old veteran of the First World War, broadcast for an 'honourable peace'. An 'armistice' (i.e. surrender) was signed on June 22nd and by July 10th Petain was made *Chef de l'État Français* (Head of the French State) [51]. This 'state' was divided into two zones. The Occupied Zone (the north and west, including Paris and the Channel and Atlantic coastlines) was controlled directly by the Germans and run by French collaborating officials answerable nominally to Pétain, but in reality working directly (and over-enthusiastically) for the German authorities. Curfews and severe rationing were imposed, and collaborating officials unquestioningly implemented Nazi anti-Semitic policies, while financially reimbursing the Germans for the honour of being occupied. The unoccupied 'Free' Zone (central and southern France, including the Mediterranean coast), was run directly by Pétain from his administrative centre in Vichy, with Pierre Laval as chief minister and Charles Maurras (of Action Française) in a senior role. Here a 'National Revolution' was launched, backed by the church, fostering traditional values, rural life and big families, and replacing the French Republican 'Liberty, Equality, Fraternity' (*Liberté, Egalité, Fraternité*) with its own 'Work, Family, Homeland' (*Travail, Famille, Patrie*). The Vichy regime was strongly Catholic, Anglophobic, anti-Semitic, anti-Masonic and anti-Communist. But even among Vichy supporters there was divergence of opinion. Some, like Laval, envisioned a 'new order' of a Germanised Europe, in which France played a subordinate role; others, like Maurras, favoured a national regeneration of an independent France. While the Nazi-Soviet pact held, the Germans officially tolerated the Communists (although mutual mistrust led to the PCF wisely remaining underground [52]). By contrast, Vichy's open hostility to Communism created the bizarre situation where Pétain's officials thought the Nazis took too soft a line [53], and communists were more likely to join resistance against the French regime in the south than against the German occupiers in the north. Vichy anti-Semitism led to bans, census-taking, regulation and arrest of Jews that went well beyond the requirements of the Nuremberg Laws [54]. Vichy laid claim to a degree of independence, and the adoption of an *attentiste* (wait-and-see) 'neutrality', but in reality it was a client state of the Third Reich, committed since October 1940 to full collaboration. However its nominal independence did create a certain amount of wriggle room for a nascent resistance to slip through the fingers of police control, moving back and forth between the zones, taking advantage of liaison failures between the border authorities where bureaucratic incompetence and sometimes wilful non-co-operation kept windows usefully open.

**Dominique Aury's Circle and the Onset of War:** With the outbreak of the war the young men of Aury's acquaintance took divergent paths. Thierry Maulnier and Robert Brasillach were mobilised into the French army and after the 1940 'armistice' both rallied to Vichy France and Marshall Pétain's 'National Revolution'. From here Brasillach shifted further to the hard right and committed himself unreservedly to Nazism, in 1941 re-launching *Je suis partout* (which had been shut down just before the invasion) in an even more virulently anti-Semitic manifestation. Maurice Blanchot took a different tack, condemning the 'armistice' from the outset and gravitating to the Resistance (although never writing for the clandestine press). He became close friends with ex-Surrealist poet and Resistance leader René Char, helped find safe haven for the family of Jewish philosopher Emmanuel Levinas, and was targeted by fascist papers (including *Je suis partout*) as a Jewish sympathiser [55]. Later in 1941 he gravitated to Bataille's group and its fascination for dark eroticism. Maulnier meanwhile moved to Vichy, where Aury, unwilling to leave her son and family in Paris, declined to join him. In October 1940 he began a relationship with an actress, Marcelle Tassencourt, admitting the fact to Aury in July 1941, who did her best to accept it. Maulnier continued to write for *Action Française*, an official paper of Vichy, but kept a distance from *Je suis partout* while remaining cordial with Brasillach (which Aury refused to do, snubbing him when she and Maulnier met him in Paris in late 1941). In spring 1942 the affair between Aury and Maulnier finally ended. Aury was distraught at being abandoned (which remained to her the worst of all possible fates), and her biographer, Angie David, suggests that in fact Maulnier was the great love of her life [56], which certainly up-ends the usual reading of Aury's story. Certainly the end of the affair with Maulnier was a major and traumatic event for her, but even as the relationship was declining, Aury was beginning to re-orientate her life, gravitating to the Resistance, her motivation being patriotic rather than ideological [57].

**The Free French and the Resistance – The Cultural Front:** On June 18th 1940 General Charles de Gaulle issued a radio proclamation from exile in London in which he rejected the legitimacy of Pétain's 'honourable peace', urged the French people to resist, and set up the Free French as the true expression of French national identity and political will.

Resistance in France was initially small-scale and piecemeal, consisting of largely unco-ordinated actions of a mixed bag of groups and individuals – patriots, republicans, monarchists, Gaullists, socialists, surrealists, some communists and so on – and took many forms throughout the war, including sabotaging the Nazi war effort, concealing Jews and rescuing Allied airmen. But there was another battlefront that also mattered: the struggle for culture – particularly literary culture. Although not well appreciated outside of France, this struggle was important and the stakes were high. Both sides recognised that whether France submitted to occupation or fought back depended on its state of morale, and this depended in turn on how far its cultural status could maintain or even assert itself as distinctively and independently French. So long as the French continued to believe their writers 'embod(ied) civilisation itself' [58], there was a real danger to the occupying forces that France would not lie defeated for very long.

As a result, for leading figures in the Nazi Occupation it was a priority to destroy the French 'cultural superiority complex' [59] and ensure French acceptance of the supremacy of Germany, not just militarily, but intellectually and culturally as well. The willing collaboration of writers like the leading novelist and author of notorious anti-Semitic tracts Louis-Ferdinand Céline, was immensely valuable here. However, the crusade to culturally degrade France was not all plain sailing. For a start, some educated Germans, including several of senior rank, could not shake off their own admiration for French culture. Secondly, it made good practical sense not to antagonise French sensitivities over-much – pressing the humiliation of French culture too far could easily backfire, alienating people and pushing even potential collaborators towards resistance to protect their heritage. Finally, it was good propaganda to recruit significant French writers, artists and intellectuals, including dissident ones if possible, to write for official (i.e. collaborationist) publishers [60].

The result was some ambivalence in German attitudes towards French culture. Even the German ambassador Otto Abetz seemed in two minds, on the one hand pushing for the French to acknowledge the cultural triumph of Germany [61] while on the other trying to encourage subversive writers to publish in the collaborationist press – hoping to recruit them into collaborating in their own right, preventing them from becoming literary martyrs, while at the same time keeping a watchful eye on them [62]. [In some cases German ambivalence tipped over into reverse collaboration. Count Franz Wolff Metternich, appointed head of 'Art Protection' for the occupying forces in August 1940, came to such a degree of 'understanding' with Jacques Jaujard, director of the Louvre, that he was eventually sacked for speaking out against the requisition of French art by his own side [63]].

For the French literary world, the most significant German official was Lt. Gerhard Heller, who took up his post as head of the literary section of the Propaganda Unit in Paris in November 1940. A Nazi party member since 1934, he was thoroughly committed to anti-Semitic policies excluding Jews from public life [although in his post-war memoirs he claimed he had been filled 'with horror' at the Holocaust

[64]. At the same time he took literature seriously, harboured a long-standing admiration for the *NRF* and Paulhan, and favoured a light touch in the regulation of French publishing. Rather than draconian supervision, he preferred to encourage publishers to play along by offering them considerable powers of self-censorship, his policy being to keep the temperature down by encouraging the French to believe the Occupation was benign. In his memoirs, he took pride in relating that during his stint in Paris, the publication rate went up, and more books were published there than in either the U.K. or the U.S.A. [65].

Gaston Gallimard accepted a deal that if the Germans kept their hands off his publishing house, he would agree to run it on their terms. He contributed to the 'Otto List' of proscribed books, published in autumn 1940 (named for Otto Abetz but actually compiled by collaborating publishers), which included Freud, Thomas Mann, Stefan Zweig, Louis Aragon – and Adolf Hitler. [This ban on *Mon Combat* (i.e. *Mein Kampf*) has been dismissed as mere supine collaboration by self-censoring publishers to stop the French discovering how much Hitler hated them [66], but since the French edition had already edited out the Francophobic rants [67], the ban may have had a more subversive edge]. Gallimard also joined the round-table of Franco-German intellectuals meeting regularly to foster international cultural 'co-operation'. This of course made him a collaborator, but it gave him leeway to smuggle into print works the Nazis would not have permitted if they were directly in charge. For General de Gaulle, it was imperative that French writers remain in print, and in 1943 he was discussing with André Gide the possibility of launching a Free French literary review – 'perhaps only a French soldier-politician could attach such importance to "culture"' [68]. That same year in a speech made in Algiers, de Gaulle praised writers, both in exile and those still in France, for their work in stiffening resistance, counter-acting the humiliation of defeat, Occupation and collaboration, fighting 'the great spiritual and moral battles of the war' [69] and keeping the flag of French literary culture flying with pride. The honour of France itself depended to a significant extent on how successfully French literary culture continued to flourish.

**Paulhan and Aury During Occupation 1940-42:** Nobody understood this better than Jean Paulhan, who from the outset took a leading role in cultural and intellectual resistance, working to set up underground publishing outfits, and using noms de guerre like Jean Guérin and M. Desarènes (named for the street he had just moved to Rue des Arènes in the Latin Quarter) [70]. All the while he was aware that his effectiveness as a *résistant* lay in keeping channels open with the other side – with colleagues who were collaborators, and even with the Occupiers themselves – in order to exploit contradictions between them. This required some manoeuvring.

When in autumn 1940 Otto Abetz, acting on his (alleged) opinion that there were 'three great powers in France: communism, the big banks and the *Nouvelle Revue Française*' [71], made clear his intention to co-opt the *NRF,* the editorial team voted to close it down. Abetz over-ruled them, and Gaston Gallimard complied, allowing the Germans to take over the review as the price for leaving the Gallimard publishing house alone. Paulhan resigned as *NRF* director, and Abetz appointed in his place senior staff member (and enthusiastic pro-Nazi [72]) Pierre Drieu La Rochelle. Having been a leftist in the 1920s, married to a Jewish woman, hobnobbing with the Surrealists, close friend to Aragon, and on the staff of the *NRF* (it was Breton who had introduced him to Paulhan [73]), Drieu shifted increasingly to the right through the 1930s. In April 1940, while still working at the *NRF,* he set up a rival journal, *La Revue Française des idées et des oeuvres*, with Thierry Maulnier, for which Blanchot wrote on Lautréamont and Aury contributed translations of John Donne. This only lasted for two issues, and in October Drieu leaped at the chance to run the *NRF,* to enforce a doctrinaire Nazi line in publication, and stamp on 'the cluster of Jews, pederasts, Surrealists, little pawns of the Freemasons' he imagined had been running it up till then [74]. The first collaborationist issue of the *NRF* came out in December.

Despite having officially resigned, Paulhan still kept an office at the *NRF*, where, trading on his respected status and experience (even if suspected of harbouring subversive sympathies), he managed to bend Drieu's ear on occasion in matters of publication. Paulhan also retained his position as literary editor at Gallimard, and from here worked to foster a working relationship with Lt. Heller, exploiting the German's preference for the 'light touch' in censorship. Effectively playing Heller and Drieu off against each other, Paulhan gained scope for getting dissident writers into print, while causing Heller anxiety that he, the German officer, might be accused of 'decadence' by the French collaborator [75].

At the same time Paulhan was active in resistance and clandestine publication. In June 1940 he set up the first resistance group of intellectuals, Les Amis d'Alain-Fournier [76]. Soon after the Musée de l'Homme group was established (with Samuel Beckett as a member), with which Paulhan's group merged. Paulhan edited the group's paper *Résistance*, the first underground publication during the Occupation, hiding the duplicating machine in his Gallimard office. The first issue was December 1940, coinciding with Drieu's first collaborationist edition of the *NRF*.

In March 1941 Paulhan joined the Socialisme et Liberté group set up by Jean-Paul Sartre when he returned to Paris from POW camp, dedicated to 'resistance through words', and engaged in the surreptitious distribution of anti-collaborationist poems in public places [77] (failing to gain traction, this group dissolved in October). Also in March André Breton managed to take his family out of France to New York [78], a route taken by several other leading Surrealists including Max Ernst and Marcel Duchamp. The contrast between Sartre's engagement and Breton's escape fuelled the view that Surrealism lost its bottle and fled, deservedly forfeiting its cachet in the Parisian cultural world. Major figures from Breton's circle who remained (Aragon, Éluard, Tzara), abandoned Surrealism for Communism, reinforcing the idea that Surrealism as a movement had fizzled out [79]. This helped clear the way for Sartre and his 'Existentialist' group to take centre stage after Liberation, although in fact Surrealism was not inactive during the war.

In 1941 a surrealist resistance group centred around Noël Arnaud [80] set up a clandestine press, La Main à Plume (The Hand with a Pen/ The Hand That Writes – a quote from Rimbaud). The Main à Plume group were in contact with Breton, and with Magritte and Picasso (who provided funds), and associated briefly with Éluard, publishing his *Liberté* (copies of which were dropped across France by Allied aircraft, making it perhaps the most influential resistance poem of the war). Along with their resistance publications, La Main à Plume were not above sectarian squabbling, their pamphlet 'Nom de Dieu!' being an attack on Bataille, dismissing his occult quasi-mystical ramblings in favour of direct action [81]. With the Communists mobilising in the Resistance in 1942, La Main à Plume, loyal to Breton, stuck to their surrealist guns as poets, repudiating the 'committed' political poetry promoted by the PCF and exemplified by 'counterfeiters' like Éluard and Aragon [82]. As activists, however, they worked alongside the Communists, and, unusually for an underground literary group, engaged in armed resistance. Eight of their members were killed during the war, and another, Jacques Hérold, was commended for his bravery during the Liberation [83]. Working with the Communists caused tensions with Gérard de Sède and others, and the group split in 1944, some of them regrouping around Breton when he returned to Paris after the war [84]. Breton himself worked with the French language section of Voice of America, broadcasting to Occupied Europe, his voice being an 'inspiration', described as 'resound(ing) like an encouraging call' in France [85].

In May the Musée de l'Homme group was exposed and rounded up. Beckett escaped but other members, including Paulhan, were arrested. The founding members Anatole Lewitsky and Boris Vildé were executed and other members were deported, but Paulhan was released after intervention by Drieu. [It would seem that Drieu also moved to protect Gallimard, Malraux and even Aragon at various points [86], asking Heller to protect them, although exactly why he did so remains open to question [87]]. On his release, Paulhan resumed his resistance activities. Along with his wife Germaine (diagnosed with Parkinson's disease in 1940 [88] but still defiantly active), and a colleague Jacques Décour, Paulhan set up a new paper *Lettres françaises,* first issue July 1941 [89].

In June 1941, Hitler launched Operation Barbarossa, the invasion of the Soviet Union, and the war entered new dimensions of horror and brutality. Anti-Semitism in the Third Reich and occupied territories intensified. On July 31st Heydrich was appointed to organise the 'Final Solution' to the 'Jewish question', by September the wearing of the yellow star was made mandatory for Jews, and the following month the purpose-built extermination camp Auschwitz II (Birkenau) was established in Poland. In France, *Au Pilori* had published its 'DEATH to the Jew' tirade in March, Brasillach's *Je suis partout* joined the anti-Semitic chorus and in the autumn 'The Jew in France' exhibition was followed by a spate of bombings of synagogues by 'hooligan' elements (with official sanction) [90]. At the same time, war between Nazi Germany and the Soviet Union released the Communist movement from its limbo, and enabled it to mobilise against the Nazis. In France, as elsewhere, the Communists provided a ready-made national organisation which raised the Resistance game to a different league [91] (although their tardiness in getting involved was to leave a significant legacy after the war). French society became progressively more polarised, with public opinion starting to harden against occupation, and various expressions of civilian non-co-operation developing [one colourful example making its mark by 1942 being the 'Zazou' sub-culture of jazz-fuelled teenage dandies making a career of irritating the authorities [92]].

While Brasillach, Drieu and other collaborating writers happily visited Germany for a 'Congress of European Writers' on a junket sponsored by Goebbels, Paulhan, along with Germaine, Décour and some colleagues, set up the clandestine CNE (Comité National des Écrivains/ National Committee of Writers), which met in the *NRF* offices (right under Drieu's nose). This was to become a highly successful focal point for literary resistance to the Occupation, recruiting over the next couple of years a broad membership including communists Claude Morgan and Louis Aragon, soon-to-be communist Édith Thomas, Catholic François Mauriac, ex-surrealist Raymond Queneau, and over the next couple of years Camus, Elsa Triolet (Aragon's die-hard communist wife) and Sartre [93].

But not everything was about politics and resistance. In 1941, Paulhan's magnum opus, the culmination of fifteen years of work – *Les Fleurs du Tarbes* (*The Flowers of Tarbes*) – was published. Since the mid 1920s Paulhan had been concerned that many writers were wasting their energies 'inventing, rather than exercising, language' [94], and now he formalised his theory, contrasting two modes of writing – that of 'Terror', and that of 'Rhetoric'. In the 'Terror' mode, characteristic of Romantics and Modernists, writers take a Cartesian view that thought is superior to word, and struggle to 're-invent' language, subordinating it to thinking in their pursuit of authenticity and originality. As a result, they tend to tyrannise the reader with their 'vision' – for Paulhan, the literary 'terrorist' was by definition a 'misologue', one who hates discussion or argument. In the 'Rhetoric' mode, writers use the existing language, including traditional literary devices, proverbs and even clichés, in order to communicate and achieve common understanding [95]. Paulhan wanted 'to stem the evolution of the Terror which attacks, in addition to literature, the foundation of common language, which amounts... to wanting to undermine the very basis of the democratic system' [96]. [Paulhan's prioritising of communication and understanding was to find an echo with Camus and Sartre, see chapter VI. Overall his reasoning sailed close to that of Bertrand Russell (1946) [97] who saw Romanticism as the ancestor of both Fascism and Communism.]

Paulhan's book received favourable reviews, including one from Maurice Blanchot. This might have been a bit of mutual back-scratching, as Blanchot's novel *Thomas l'Obscur* had been published, with help from Paulhan, by Gallimard that year, but Paulhan was touched, and a friendship was born. It has been suggested that the female protagonist of Blanchot's novel was based on Anne Desclos [98], and by strange coincidence, the woman herself (now Dominique Aury) contacted Paulhan out of the blue in October 1941 with a plan for another poetry collection, this time an anthology of French devotional verse from medieval times to the present. Paulhan agreed to edit, and was sufficiently taken by Aury's qualities to recommend her to Drieu as executive secretary at the *NRF* in December. Drieu rejected her, apparently convinced that the job was too intellectually demanding for a mere woman [99], but did accept Paulhan's suggestion of Blanchot for the job early the following year.

Aury was by this time gravitating to the Resistance, looking for a new life, attracted to the clandestinity, danger and obedience to command demanded of her as a *résistant* [100]. She was perhaps also at this stage ready to reconnect with her father. She had first come across Paulhan through her father in the mid '30s, and the resemblance between the two men was striking – in age, humour, charm, literariness, broad-mind-edness, Protestantism, erotic tastes, love of women, and a 'capacity for happiness' she found unique to those two [101]. Later she was to idealise and idolise both of them. As a *résistant*, Aury was meeting new people, including the teenage Pauvert [102], and was distributing underground literature, including *Lettres françaises*, and by early 1942 was finding Paulhan sufficiently *sympathique* to slip him a copy of the latest issue of the paper, unaware that he had edited it [103]. Aury and Paulhan worked together on the anthology through 1942, laying the basis for their later relationship.

**Paulhan and Aury During Occupation 1942-44:** Meanwhile, the European conflict broadened into a truly world war with Japan's attack on Pearl Harbour and South East Asia in December 1941 embroiling the Allies in a new Eastern arena of conflict, and provoking the U.S.A. to mobilise. In January 1942 the Wannsee conference in Berlin fully activated the 'Final Solution' and the Shoah (Holocaust) moved to maximum intensity. Collaborationist France reached its own moral nadir in July with the Paris police rounding up 13,000 Jews (4,000 of them children), locking them up in the Vélodrome d'Hiver ('Vel d'Hiv', the winter cycling stadium) before handing them over to the Nazis for deportation to the Auschwitz gas chambers [104].

On the cultural front, a new German diktat that all published works had to be officially registered with the occupying authorities provided a boost to the clandestine press, in which Paulhan was of course ubiquitous. At the same time his machinations with the collaborationist press were working well. He oversaw the rule-bending at Gallimard that was to enable the publication of Sartre, Beauvoir, Camus, Queneau and even Aragon (who was on the Otto List of banned writers that Gaston Gallimard had helped compile). At the *NRF* Paulhan managed to wangle publication of pieces from a range of left-wing, *résistant* and surrealist writers, including Paul Éluard, as well as tributes to 'decadent' writer James Joyce and Jewish philosopher Henri Bergson [105]. Paulhan's priorities were firstly to ensure dissident writers were published, in both 'official' and underground presses, sending a message that even the collaborationist press could be colonised by *résistants*; second to offset political polarisation, exploiting differences among collaborators and occupiers in a bid to undermine their unity; and finally to keep the *NRF* going [106]. The *NRF* had been his life's work, and he never lost his faith that one day he could rescue it and resurrect it to its former glory.

But his double game was a dangerous one. Not only was he perpetually under threat of exposure as a *résistant*, he was also engaging in activities that could, after the war, lay him open to charges of collaboration – recruiting writers for Gallimard and the *NRF* (making those who agreed technically collaborators too), and making his own contributions to officially sanctioned publications. From 1942 he was even attending the salon of American fascist-sympathiser Florence Gould where he socialised over cocktails with high ranking Nazi officials [107]. Others were doing much the same – François Mauriac was attending the Gould salon, and Marguerite Duras concealed her work as a PCF operative behind a screen of hobnobbing professionally with Drieu and Heller.

Others had different views. Sartre had initially been against any concession to collaboration – berating Beauvoir on his return to Paris for buying on the black market and signing a document confirming she was not Jewish in order to keep her teaching job [over time he adapted to the pragmatic and murky world of dodging and dealing of occupied Paris and by November 1943 he was willing to pull strings to arrange a well-paid job for Beauvoir with a collaborationist radio station]. Others were more adamant: prestigious writers like Paul Valéry and André Gide rejected invitations to contribute to the collaborationist *NRF*, while *résistant* writers Tristan Tzara, René Char and novelist Édith Thomas flatly refused to co-operate with Paulhan's or anybody else's plans to get them published by the 'official' press [108].

In May 1942 the clandestine literary resistance received a serious set-back when Jacques Décour, co-founder of *Lettres françaises* and the CNE and close friend of Paulhan, was arrested, tortured and shot. The CNE disbanded, but Claude Morgan, Édith Thomas and Paulhan reconvened it the following month [109]. The reconstituted CNE took over and re-launched *Les Lettres françaises* in September 1942 with Morgan at the helm [110]. [This went on to become 'the most influential organ of (French) intellectual resistance during the war' [111], with a circulation of 12,000 by autumn 1943]. Also in autumn 1942 clandestine publishing house Éditions de Minuit released its first novel. Set up initially by Jean Bruller (aka 'Vercors') and Pierre de Lescue, but with Paulhan soon involved and indispensible, Minuit was less concerned with propaganda than with quality literature expressing the richness of French culture. Nevertheless, it retained its connection with the lived experience of the times, and its first publication, Vercors' *Le Silence de la Mer*, made a powerful statement against adapting to the Occupation and falling for the charms of apparently civilised occupiers [112]. Vercors' specific aim was to repudiate the image of the 'good German' fostered by the writings of Wermacht officer and author Ernst Jünger, who was stationed in Paris and working for Abetz at the time [113], but his novel could also be construed as a comment on Paulhan's relationship with Heller (whose co-operation had recently permitted Gallimard to publish Camus' *L'Etranger*). Whether Paulhan registered this or not, he ensured Vercors' novel was widely distributed in France, London and New York [114].

But there were signs that things were beginning to turn. In the summer of 1942 the German invasion of the Soviet Union bogged down at Stalingrad, and in October American troops landed in North Africa where the local Vichy commanders surrendered Morocco and Algeria to them and came over to the Allies [115]. This prompted the Germans to move in and take direct control of Vichy, reducing Pétain to a mere figure-head, and shoring up Pierre Laval as chief of an even more collaborationist French government. [Maulnier's protest was to stop writing for *Action Française* although he did not go so far as to join the Resistance]. In early 1943 the Milice (Militia) was founded under Laval's authority, and worked full-throttle with the Nazis to fight the Resistance and Free French and round up Jews for mass murder. France was effectively in a state of civil war [116]. Not everything went the way the Nazis intended, however. In Toulon the Vichy fleet scuttled itself rather than fall into German hands, and Laval's ramping up the quotas of French workers to be sent as forced labour to Germany backfired as many went AWOL to swell the ranks of the Resistance [117].

Meanwhile General de Gaulle felt his position as leader of French forces among the Allies under threat. One challenge came from senior generals who had come across from Vichy, who were more experienced and a lot more biddable than he was (he being a notoriously fractious individual). The other came from the prominence of the Communists in the Resistance – their status being greatly enhanced by the successes of the Red Army on the Eastern Front that year, destroying whole German armies at Stalingrad and Kursk. In May 1943 de Gaulle sent Jean Moulin to France to set up a National Council of Resistance [Conseil national de la Résistance – CNR]. Despite tensions, the different Resistance organisations, Communist, Gaullist and others, did manage to co-ordinate, and even though Moulin was soon arrested, tortured and executed, the CNR held. The effectiveness of the Resistance was increased, and de Gaulle's leadership position of both the Free French and the Resistance was confirmed.

Under Paulhan's guidance, Dominique Aury's book, *Anthologie de la poésie religieuse français* (*Anthology of French Religious Verse)* was published by Gallimard in March 1943, with Aury named as editor. In fact Gallimard hadn't been keen on the project, but Paulhan had prevailed [118] (eight years later Paulhan's attempt at a repeat performance with *Story of O* was to have less success). Blanchot was by now in the Resistance, along with his friend Bernard Milleret [who was Aury's occasional landlord, and a keen 'admirer' – and presumably the Milleret with whom Anne and Maulnier had shared that mysterious tryst at the Louvre in 1934 (see p. 86)]. Blanchot ran the literature section for the journal *Jeune France* (which had been an official Vichy publication), for which Aury wrote articles. Now a published name, Aury would have been entitled to attend CNE meetings if she had wished, but she chose not to.

The biggest literary splash in 1943 was made by Sartre and Beauvoir. Sartre's play *Les Mouches* (*The Flies* – a reference to informants [119]) was performed in Paris in June with a nod from Heller. Making open reference to 'liberté' it was hailed by *Les Lettres françaises*, defended by Paulhan against Mauriac's sour and 'perfectly unjust' judgement of it [120] and condemned in Berlin for its 'defiance'. It also provided the moment for the meeting of Sartre and Camus. In August Sartre's magnum opus *Being and Nothingness* (*L'Être et le Néant*) and Beauvoir's novel *L'Invitée* (*She Came to Stay*) were published by Gallimard. Paulhan had sponsored the first (although was less taken with the literary quality of the second), and Existentialism had arrived. That autumn Sartre and Beauvoir started making the acquaintance of Picasso and other significant figures in the Paris scene, including Leiris and Queneau. In summer 1943 Paulhan and Gaston Gallimard had managed to close down the *NRF* to rescue it from further collaborationist contamination, both anticipating (wrongly as it turned out) that they would be able to revive it as soon as the war was over, but in November the CNE had published its first list of literary collaborators to be brought to book, and Gaston Gallimard was on that list.

By early 1944, as the sense that the war was entering its end-game began to percolate through, collaborators began to turn evasive or go to ground, Sartre's *Huis Clos* (*No Exit*) was a success, and the Existentialist group – Sartre, Beauvoir, Camus and Maurice Merleau-Ponty – began to position themselves for a leading role in the new cultural scene when liberation came – although not without a certain wistfulness, as Sartre put it: 'we were never freer than during the German occupation... every free thought was a victory' [121]. There would be challenges and difficult choices ahead. Paulhan was particularly aware of this. Not everyone understood the complexities and contra-dictions of the literary world during Occupation, and it was going to require some handling to rescue people like Gaston Gallimard after the war. In the meantime Paulhan continued with his activities, in clandestine publication, manipulating the 'official' publishers, and working with Heller, nudging him to intervene for detainees or turn a blind eye to illicit activities – which caused Heller some trouble when the French writer Céline publically accused him of 'collaborating' with Galli-mard and being 'private secretary of the *résistant* Paulhan' [122]. In May 1944, however, Paulhan reaped some personal benefit from his efforts in maintaining contacts. Elise Jouhandeau (wife of collaborationist writer Marcel, a friend of Paulhan) denounced Paulhan to the Gestapo as a Jew – seemingly in a jealous pique. Heller managed to tip Paulhan off about his imminent arrest in time for him to escape over the rooftops (no mean feat for a hefty man of nearly sixty). Crossing Paris, he took refuge in the apartment of a fellow writer who, despite being a collaborator, could be trusted to hide him [123].

[1] I am of course much indebted to Angie David's 2006 biography of Dominique Aury here, especially Part II

[2] Cited in Bedell 2004

[3] St Jorre 1995, p.212

[4] Deforges 1975 p. 28

[5] *Ibid* p. 29

[6] *Ibid* pp. 30-31

[7] *Ibid*, p. 18, 203

[8] David 2006 p. 239

[9] Cited in Cited in Gallus 1997

[10] Cited in Deforges 1975 p. 25

[11] Which Angie David explores in detail in Part II of her 2006 biography.

[12] Peter Watson, Peter: *The French Mind* Simon & Schuster 2022 p. 520

[13] David 2006, 217

[14] Andrew Hussey *Paris, The Secret History* (2006), Penguin 2007 p. 344

[15] Zeev Sternhell cited in Ian Pindar 'A Sort of Defeated Tenderness' *TLS* 1 May 1998

[16] David 2006 210

[17] Mahon 2020 p. 139 note 88.

[18] Leslie Hill *TLS* letters 8 May 1998

[19] See, for example, Jeffrey Mehlman *Legacies of Anti-Semitism in France* (1983) for the prosecution, and Leslie Hill *TLS* letters 8 May 1998 for the defence.

[20] David 2006 pp. 317-318

[21] *Ibid* p. 320: 'relations inavouables', 'libertinages'

[22] *Ibid* p. 222

[23] *Ibid* 231, 299; Mahon 2020, p. 139: 'Aury shared (Mauliner's) nationalism but never expressed any anti-Semitic or protofascist position'.

[24] Deforges 1975 p. 196

[25] St Jorre 1994, p. 44

[26] Kaufmann 1998 p 899

[27] David 2006 p. 237

[28] *Ibid* pp. 71-72

[29] *Ibid* p. 71

[30] *Ibid* p. 257

[31] Mahon 2020 p. 143

[32] gw.geneanet.org / David 2006 p. 179

[33] *Le Guerrier appliqué* (1917) and *La Guérison Sévère* (1918, pub 1925), Mark Hutchinson: 'Among the Misologues' *TLS* 17/10/1997

[34] Cornick 2008, p. 18

[35] David 2006 p. 24

[36] Patrick McCarthy 'On the Left Bank' *TLS* 5 June 1998.

[37] David H. Walker 'On the Public Stage' *TLS* 27 November 1998

[38] Cornick 2004, p. 46

[39] Cornick 2008, p. 12/ 'frequently cited as the most prestigious literary and cultural review in 20th century France' Cornick 2004, p. 37

[40] Walker 1998

[41] Cornick 2008, p.9

[42] Annie Cohen-Solal: *Sartre, A Life* (1985), Heinemann 1987 pp. 112-116

[43] David 2006 p. 24

[44] The *NRF* has been described as a garden of opposites: 'romantic impulses side by side with positivistic ones, irrationality side by side with intellectualism, the dionysian principle and the apollonian, avant-garde trends and more classical ones, nihilism and constructivism, chaos and order, revolutionary tenets side by side with more conservative ones' W. Gobbers, 'Modernism, Modernity, Avant-Garde: A Bilingual Introduction' 1995, cited in Cornick 2008 p. 26.

[45] René Johannet in *La Revue des deux mondes* 1928, cited in Cornick 2008, p.12

[46] In *La Revue Universelle* 15 June 1938, cited in Cornick 2004

[47] there was, for example, no ministry for munitions or plans for rationing – Alfred Cobban: *A History of Modern France Vol 3 1871-1962* Pelican 1978 p. 175

[48] 'traditionalism, ignorance, arrogance and paralysis' Marc Bloch *Strange Defeat* (1946), – cited in Agnès Poirier: *Left Bank* Bloomsbury 2018, p. 16

[49] August 26th 1939 cited in Cobban 1978 p. 174

[50] *L'Humanité* (August 1940); *Ibid* p. 190

[51] *Ibid* p. 182

[52] *Ibid* p. 190

[53] I am indebted for much of the information in this paragraph to Caroline Perret: 'Taking an Intellectual Stance Between Communist Resistance and Fascist Collaboration: Jean Paulhan and the *Épuration* Process in France at the End of WWII' 2018 In: Grinchenko G., Narvselius E. (eds) *Traitors, Collaborators and Deserters in Contemporary European Politics of Memory.* Palgrave Macmillan Memory Studies.

[54] Daniel Solomon *Legend of Innocence* The Tablet, June 28th 2022

[55] Leslie Hill, letters, *TLS* 4 June 1999; Emmanuel Levinas stated he 'never saw an anti-semite' in Blanchot (David 2006 p. 326)

[56] David 2006, p.299-300

[57] Kaufmann 1998 p. 890 cites Aury: "What idiocy to bring a moral judgement to bear on political ideas. One can die for people or for things, but not for an idea. An idea is always malevolent once it is put into practice"

[58] Swiss writer Herbert Lüthy cited in Martyn Cornick and Christopher Flood: 'Reconciling France: Jean Paulhan and the "Nouvelle Revue Française," 1953' *South Central Review*, Winter, 2000, Vol. 17, No. 4, p. 29

[59] Watson 2022, pp. 566, 573

[60] Perret 2018

[61]  Watson 2022, p. 566

[62]  Hussey 2007 pp. 370-371

[63]  Poirier 2018 pp. 25-26

[64]  A claim that was entirely predictable, but may have been sincere. Gerhard Heller: *In an Occupied Country, Nazi Cultural Policy in France – Memories 1940-44*, Kiepenheuer & Witsch, Cologne, 1982, p. 200, cited in 'second.wiki – Gerhard Heller'

[65]  Watson 2022 p. 573

[66]  Frederic Spotts *The Shameful Peace* Yale University Press 2010, cited Watson 2022 p. 568

[67]  Hussey 2007, p. 347

[68]  Alan Sheridan 'Gide's Wartime Political Stance', *TLS* 16 Jan 1998

[69]  De Gaulle, cited in Cornick & Flood 2000, p. 30

[70]  Cornick 2004; David 2006, p. 285

[71]  A quote cited (or possibly coined) by Paulhan in interview with Dominique Aury in *Gavroche* 8 February 1945, cited Cornick 2008, p. 15; also in Poirier 2018 p. 31;  also Arbaizer 1981 cited in Perret 2018.

[72]  Bernard-Henri Lévy:  *Adventures on the Freedom Road* (1991) The Harvill Press 1995 p. 155

[73]  John Flower 'Letters of an Odd Couple' *TLS* 27 Sept. 2019

[74]  Lévy 1991/ 1995 p. 161

[75]  *Ibid* p.157.

[76]  Alain-Fournier was a writer who took up arms in the First World War. Author of the novel *Le Grand Meaulnes* (1913), he was killed in action within a few days of the outbreak of hostilities in September 1914, aged 27.  The name of the group is probably a coded reference to 'Alain' (pseudonym of Emile-Auguste Chartier, 'guru of the liberal-Radical Intelligentsia' in France whose 1926 work, 'The Citizen Against the Authorities' was an inspiration (Cornick and Flood 2000, p. 35).

[77]  Bakewell, Sarah: *At the Existentialist Café* Chatto & Windus 2016 p. 144

[78]  Courtesy of Varian Fry and the Emergency Relief Committee (funded from the U.S. and backed by Eleanor Rooseveldt).

[79]  A view promoted by Maurice Nadeau *Histoire du Surréalisme* (1944/1965) Pelican 1973

[80]  Later including Jacques Hérold, Victor Brauner, Christian Dotremont and others.

[81]  Published by Sans nom ni lieu in 1943

[82]  Polizzotti 2009 p. 460

[83]  Alyce Mahon *Surrealism and the Politics of Eros 1938-1968*, Thames and Hudson 2005 p. 104

[84]  De Sède was to achieve notoriety later with his book *Le Trésor Maudit* (*The Cursed Treasure*, 1968) which set the whole 'mystery of Rennes-le-Château'/ 'Priory of Sion' bandwagon rolling, inspiring Baigent, Leigh and Lincoln's *The Holy Blood and the Holy Grail* (1982) [which Dan Brown drew on in his *The Da Vinci Code* (2003)].

[85]  André Thirion, cited by Polizzotti 2009 p. 459

86 Perret 2018;  David 2006 p. 93, note 57

87 Did he genuinely doubt that they could be *résistants* (Flower 2019)? Did he retain some loyalty for old colleagues, or some belief in a camaraderie of writers above and beyond politics? Did he like to wield a little power of his own, or earn the gratitude of those he helped? Was there a frisson in tweaking the authorities? Was he trying to salve some guilt in his own conscience, or perhaps taking out insurance in case things went pear-shaped for him in the future? It is an open game – anyone can play.

88 David 2006 p. 74

89 www.revueslitteraires.com/articles.php?lng=fr&pg=2876

90 Hussey 2007 p. 360

91 Cobban 1978 p. 190

92 Hussey 2007 pp 365-66

93 Perret 2018

94 Letter to Gide 1925

95 Hutchinson 1997

96 François Demont: 'Le dadaïsme et le surréalisme chez Paulhan : pour une appréhension des discours et des dynamiques littéraires' *Littérature* 2020/4 (no. 200) p. 32

97 Russell *History of Western Philosophy* George Allen and Unwin (1946)

98 David 2006 p. 375

99 *Ibid.*, p. 71

100 *Ibid.* p. 303

101 *Ibid.* p. 197

102 St Jorre 1994 p. 46

103 David. p. 74; St Jorre 1994, p. 44

104 Daniel Solomon 'Legend of Innocence' *The Tablet*, June 28th 2022

105 Poirier 2018 pp 31-32

106 David 2006, p. 85

107 Watson 2022 p. 570

108 David 2006 p. 428

109 Dorothy Kaufmann: 'Resistance and Survival – Edith Thomas: Simone de Beauvoir's Shadow Sister' *Simone de Beauvoir Studies* vol 12, 1995  p. 34

110 This seems to be the explanation for so many sources citing September 1942 as the launching of the paper: www.gallica/bnf.fr; www.humanite.fr

111   Kaufmann 1998, p. 888
112   www.leseditionsdeminuit.fr/unepagehistorique
113   Hussey 2007 p. 370
114   Poirier 2018 p. 37
115   Cobban 1978 p. 192
116   *Ibid.* p. 194
117   *Ibid.* p. 193
118   St Jorre 1994, p. 44
119   Watson 2022 p. 567
120   Paulhan letter to Jean Fautrier, 23 June 1943 ; Presses universal de Rennes 2005
121   'La République du silence', *Les Lettres françaises*, 1944, Poirier 2018 p. 61
122   Poirier 2018  p. 57
123   David 2006 p. 93

# IV:  Lives and Times Continued: From Liberation to the End – 1944-1998

## THE LATE 1940s

**Liberation and Épuration – 1944-45**:  Paris was liberated two months after D-Day. As Allied troops approached in mid August 1944, staff at the fascist press and radio stations went to ground and high-profile collaborators like Céline fled. A general strike was called (which the Paris police tactically joined), barricades went up on the 19th and the Resistance uprising began. Fighting was severe, with over 6000 fatalities that week, but on August 24th General Leclerc's 2nd Armoured Division of Free French, backed by the U.S. 4th Infantry Division, reached Paris, and by the next day were in control of the city. The German military governor of Paris, General Dieter von Choltitz, wisely (for his own neck) disobeyed Hitler's orders to dynamite the city (which might have been impossible for him to do by then anyway), and surrendered to Leclerc and communist Resistance leaders. The following day General de Gaulle asserted his position as commander of the Free French and the Resistance by leading the parade down the Champs Elysées to a ceremony in Nôtre Dame before enthusiastic crowds (who were still in serious danger from Nazi snipers).

Paris was delirious at Liberation, in what Simone de Beauvoir called an 'orgy of fraternity' [1], but that mood did not last long. The war and Occupation had bequeathed a legacy that was not easily left behind, and almost immediately the backlog of tensions and conflicts reached boiling point, continuing to seethe for some years to come.

General de Gaulle knuckled straight down to business to consolidate his position, declaring himself head of a Provisional Government and proceeding to neutralise any possible opposition to his leadership. He outmanoeuvred ex-Vichy generals who had the ear of the Americans and an eye on power, and disarmed and disbanded the Resistance, taking some of its leaders into his government while telling the rest to join the Free French or go home. By October 1944 he had direct control over all French armed forces, had marginalised any independent potential power-bases, Communist and ex-Vichy, and had won official recognition from the Allies for his Provisional Government.

At ground level, however, de Gaulle did not call all the shots, and from the outset there was a backlash against collaborators by *résistants* and vengeful civilians that the authorities could not control. Spontaneous in origin, fuelled by grievances building up during the Occupation, exacerbated by anger at what was widely seen as de Gaulle's high-handedness and ingratitude to the Resistance, and fanned by the PCF, the *épuration* (purge/purification) of late 1944 and early 1945 saw summary justice against those accused of collaboration, leading to an estimated 10,000 executions [2]. How far the *épuration* represented justice was, however, a moot point. The demand for vengeance simplified the pragmatic complexities of life under Occupation, and although proportionately fewer were killed in France than in Belgium or the Netherlands, the fact that some were condemned on less than rock-solid evidence or were victims of feuds and personal grudges made for an ugly situation. In addition, many thousands of women, accused of 'horizontal collaboration', were publicly humiliated, heads shaved, often tarred and feathered, and paraded through the streets in carnivalesque displays of collective persecution. Photographs of shaven-headed women ('les tondues') still provide the most readily recognisable images of the reprisals [3].

Those in positions of authority were in two minds over the question of purgation and penance. On the one hand, it was understood that peace and reconciliation were necessary for France's future, while on the other there was a widespread feeling that some kind of ritual cleansing was needed to exorcise the dark shadow of defeat and degrees of collaboration that had been France's day-to-day experience under Occupation. General de Gaulle called for expiation to enable France to climb from the 'abyss' to regain her self-respect and pride (not to mention her international status), and Camus wrote 'a country that fails its purge is about to fail its renovation' [4], although François Mauriac felt that while purging was a 'necessary evil', it could easily become a 'running sore' [5]. The uncontrolled violence of the *épurations* was however of great concern to de Gaulle and the Allies, and the Paris literary world was deeply uneasy.

Aware that writers, journalists and radio commentators, the 'most visible face of collaboration' [6], were being singled out for condemnation, the ex-*résistant* press tried to bring some order to things. In September 1944 the CNE, now at last able to meet in public, published a manifesto in the first legally published *Lettres françaises* calling for unity along with 'fair/righteous punishment' of collaborators and 'traitors' (signed by a broad spectrum of literary luminaries including Paulhan, Sartre, Camus, Malraux, Mauriac, Paul Valèry, Éluard, Queneau and Aragon). It also published a blacklist of a dozen collaborationist writers – including Brasillach, Céline, Drieu and Charles Maurras – who stood accused of subverting French thinking and engaging in 'pure treason' [7]. The problem was that 'fair punishment' meant different things to different people, and words like 'traitor' and 'treason' raised the spectre of the death penalty, which was by no means universally acceptable to signatories of the *Lettres françaises* manifesto.

The fault-line, unsurprisingly, lay between the Communists and more or less everyone else. Despite fears in some quarters, France had not been on Stalin's shopping list for Communist take-over, and the PCF did not pose any real threat to de Gaulle's leadership, but it could still contest de Gaulle's authority among the people, citing their commitment to the Resistance and the scale of their sacrifice – calling themselves the 'party of the 75,000 shot' [8] – as giving them the right to demand revenge against collaborators and 'traitors'. Louis Aragon, effectively cultural commissar of the PCF, took a hard Stalinist line, but there was increasingly vocal opposition to what was effectively becoming a blood sport. Simone de Beauvoir deplored the 'medieval sadism' of the treatment of collaborationist women [9], and even signatories of the CNE manifesto spoke out — Camus and Mauriac expressed serious reservations, but it was Jean Paulhan who, after initially supporting black-listing, stuck his neck out to challenge Stalinist-sponsored purges.

For Paulhan, literature mattered more than politics, and purging writers for their political beliefs was a waste of talent. The PCF were wrong that all writing had political significance – for him, literature and polemics were distinct; writers had a 'right to error', but no writer had the right to denounce another [10]. [Paulhan's line here echoed the Marquis de Sade, for whom the sanctimonious inquisitors who persecute heretics are worse than the people they condemn, and Oscar Wilde, that books are to be judged on the quality of the writing, not on their moral stance]. For Paulhan, writers were not responsible for what other people did in their name, and the scale of the guilt of collaborationist writers was small beer compared to that of industrialists, generals and others who directly engaged in the crimes of Occupation and Vichy [11]. Here Paulhan found himself in direct conflict with Vercors, for whom writers were *more* guilty as their influence was wider. For Paulhan, to blame writers for what others did 'under their influence' was to deny those others their own agency and responsibility in their actions (an example of 'Bad faith', to use an existentialist term). And this led to what was really the nub of the argument: that the PCF was engaged in a grotesque act of Bad Faith of its own, trying to deflect attention away from its own collaboration in 1940-41 by cracking down on the fraternisation of others, exaggerating its sacrifice during the war [12] and hypocritically accusing others of treason when it was itself obeying the orders of a foreign power [13]. For Paulhan, the self-righteous posturing of the PCF was a smoke-screen for denouncing, slandering, blacklisting and boycotting any writers who criticised their motives or in any way objected to their line. Paulhan was on collision course with the Stalinists, and his success defending Gaston Gallimard from charges of collaboration brought by Aragon, and defending himself against accusations levelled by other members of the CNE (his own exemplary record in the Resistance speaking eloquently for itself), did nothing to defuse the situation [14].

By early 1945 de Gaulle's government, with the backing of the Allies, was asserting legal process over the excesses of the *épuration*. De Gaulle's stratagem was to insist that the 'true' France had always been *résistant* [15], at heart at least (a view that Michael Curtiz' 1942 film *Casablanca* helped propagate internationally), which both justified his own position as true leader of all the French, and repudiated any legitimacy or legality to Vichy. It also portrayed the majority of the French as wait-and-see *attentistes*, spiritually pro-resistance, and guilty of nothing worse than doing whatever they had to do to get on with their lives – a view Sartre shared [16]. Consequently there was neither feasibility nor justice in trying to hunt down and punish every pragmatic act of quasi-collaboration by every citizen of France.

High profile collaborators were a different matter, and these needed to be arrested and arraigned, but when in the dock, Pétainists put their own spin on things, insisting that

Vichy had been committed to protecting the French people, including French Jews, while de Gaulle had led the fight for the honour and name of France. This 'Shield and Sword' defence (despite flying in the face of all the evidence [17]), provided a useful myth for reconciliation, and gained traction with de Gaulle and some intellectuals (notably Sartre's colleague, Jewish philosopher Raymond Aron [18]). It also provided a window through which active Vichy supporters – including Thierry Maulnier – could escape prosecution. This, along with the dropping of charges against most of the big names under investigation – Arletty, Coco Chanel, Maurice Chevalier, Colette, Jean Cocteau – raised unease that de Gaulle's government was being too lenient. In the end around 40,000 prison sentences and 50,000 sentences of 'national degradation' [19] were handed down by French law courts between 1944 and 1951, when a general amnesty was declared. There were also 7,037 death sentences, of which nearly 90% were commuted. Marshall Pétain and Charles Maurras were among the beneficiaries of this clemency (Maurras still managing to complain he was the victim of the revenge of Dreyfus). Pierre Laval's sentence stood, and he faced the firing squad in October 1945.

A contentious case was Robert Brasillach. Named on the CNE's first blacklist, Brasillach was arrested in September 1944 and put on trial for treason in January 1945. Paulhan, along with Camus, Paul Valèry, Cocteau, Colette and others campaigned for clemency for him, not that they were defending his Nazi propagandising, anti-Semitic vitriol and war-time demands for summary execution of *résistants*, but they all stood against the condemnation of writers. The case against Brasillach amounted to the charge that even if he did not have blood on his hands, there was 'blood on his pen' [20], and the defence that writers are not responsible for what others do in their name was weakened here by Brasillach's policy of publishing the whereabouts of Jews and suspected *résistants* in his paper. Beauvoir for one had no sympathy for him and opposed the clemency campaign [21] (Aury's position is uncertain [22]). In the end de Gaulle over-ruled Paulhan, Camus and their friends, and Brasillach was shot in February 1945, but he was the last writer to be executed. Drieu La Rochelle evaded the legal process. His status as a writer had led to offers of help as Liberation approached [23] – Lt. Heller could arrange exit papers, Malraux could set up a new identity if he joined the Resistance – but Drieu refused everything, went to ground, and committed suicide in March 1945. By then the popular enthusiasm for *épuration* was evaporating and writers were no longer in danger for their lives, but CNE/PCF blacklisting continued.

**Literary Renaissance – 1944-47:** With the end of the war in Europe in May 1945, de Gaulle pressed ahead with his campaign to reassert the international prestige of France, and achieved some impressive successes on the political front – winning a place for France among the fraternity of victorious Allies, a slice of Occupied Germany and a permanent seat on the Security Council of the fledgling United Nations. But he understood that France's claims to recognition as a power needed backup from its cultural eminence, which had historically underpinned its standing as a nation, both internally and internationally. That meant that culture, particularly literary culture – the 'Republic of Letters' – had a crucial role in 'legitimis(ing) the restoration of France to international standing' [24]. In other words, France's return to the top table of world politics required a literary renaissance at home. On this point there was a strong consensus supporting him. The Parisian intelligentsia – writers, publishers and editors (those whom Beauvoir was to term the 'mandarins' in her 1954 novel of that name), rallied to the cause, and journals and reviews proliferated – in 1947 Sartre was to write '(p)erhaps never since the eighteenth century (has) so much been expected of the writer' [25].

The war-time clandestine journals were openly available by autumn 1944. The PCF ran several, including *Ce Soir* (edited by Aragon) and *L'Humanité,* and in September launched a new weekly for women, *Femmes françaises*. The CNE ran the first legal publication of *Les Lettres françaises* in September 1944. Édith Thomas was an old hand as a contributor, Dominique Aury a new recruit; Bernard Milleret provided illustrations. Edited by communist Claude Morgan, it was not yet a PCF mouthpiece, but was on their list for a take-over. There were also independent Resistance papers like *Combat* (no relation to Maulnier's right-wing journal of the 1930s), founded in 1941 and edited by Albert Camus from 1943-47.

Conservative papers like *Carrefours* were still in business, publishing articles by Maulnier and Blanchot. Further left, Algerian writer Jean Amrouche, under the patronage of André Gide, in 1945 launched *L'Arche*, published by Éditions Charlot, to which Camus (himself born to French settlers in Algeria) contributed [26]. Amrouche invited Paulhan to join in, but Paulhan was not comfortable with its political flavour and declined.

Gallimard wanted to relaunch the *NRF* with Paulhan back at the helm, but it was proscribed by the CNE for its war-time collaboration, so Paulhan was obliged to formally liquidate it in November 1944. Gallimard sponsored replacements instead. The first and most important of these was *Les Temps Modernes* (named after the 1936 Chaplin film), which started organising in September 1944 around a central team of Sartre, Beauvoir, Maurice Merleau-Ponty, Raymond Aron and Paulhan, with some input from Camus. It launched its first issue in October 1945 (by which time Paulhan, uneasy with the weight it gave to political commitment, had pulled out) [27]. In spring 1946 Gallimard sponsored another journal, *Les Cahiers de Pléiade*, which Paulhan edited. Dominique Aury joined the staff, Jean Fautrier provided art-work and soon after Blanchot was contributing. Other papers may have imagined themselves as superseding and replacing the *NRF*, but Paulhan was under no illusions, for him the space left by the *NRF* would only ever be filled by the resurrection of the *NRF*. Also in 1946 Maurice Girodias provided the impetus for another new journal, *Critique,* which, under Bataille's editorship and with Blanchot and Raymond Aron on board, achieved both status and longevity [28].

These reviews and journals took different political positions. The Communist papers peddled a hard Stalinist line, and by 1946 *Les Lettres françaises* was gravitating that way. Sartre agreed that writers should be politically committed towards the left (the tradition of the *intellectuel engagé* since Zola defended Dreyfus in the 1890s), and *Les Temps Modernes* was strongly political. Merleau-Ponty was pro-Communist anyway, and Sartre had an ambiguous attitude to the PCF (although they kept him under fire as a rival – in Stalinist eyes independent thought was a bourgeois luxury). *L'Arche* was responsive to the increasing demands from Algeria for independence. Camus and Paulhan both stood against injustice but were less attracted to doctrinaire ideologies. In Camus' *Combat* Georges Bataille wrote to condemn the reductive effect of political dogmas and prejudice [29], and his own *Critique* was open to a wide range of content and opinion [30]. At *Cahiers de la Pléiade* Paulhan continued to insist that the prime concern of writers should be writing, not polemics – as Aury put it, for Paulhan, 'no cause was more sacred than that of literature' [31]. To this end Paulhan published a range of writers, including ex-collaborators, true to his belief in a writers' fraternity beyond politics. There was also a political pragmatism here – Paulhan saw a need for reconciliation [32], and was doing his bit to deter extremism by respecting degrees of opinion across the spectrum, encouraging moderate leftists to keep their distance from communism, and conservatives to steer clear of the far right (which was keeping its head down for now, but had not gone away).

In autumn 1945 Sartre and his group reinforced their cultural status in Paris: along with *Les Temps Modernes* Gallimard also published the first two volumes of Sartre's *Les Chemins de la Liberté* (*The Roads to Freedom*) [33], as well as Beauvoir's *Le Sang des autres (The Blood of Others)*, which added to the key texts of Existentialism. Aury interviewed Beauvoir for her article 'What is Existentialism?' for *Les Lettres françaises,* while Sartre's and Beauvoir's texts were of course roundly condemned by both the Communist Party and the Church, acting as usual in strange concert with each other.

In October 1945 a general election, the first in France where women had the vote, brought in a government where nobody had a commanding presence, and in Paris two new terms were being heard: 'The Third Way' – a position between the state authority of de Gaulle and the Stalinism of the PCF, and 'Humanism' – a philosophy of human dignity, morality, rights and justice that drew support from a wide range of writers and thinkers. Camus called for the former in *Combat* in October, and at the end of that month Sartre gave his lecture confirming that Existentialism was a Humanism [34] in a venue so crowded that women fainted – the drama of the event ensuring Sartre's superstar status. The Existentialist brand went international with Sartre's lecture tour of the U.S.A. in December. The Parisian cultural scene received a boost when Breton returned from the U.S. in April 1946 and re-launched Surrealism, with a string of short-lived periodicals. Georges Bataille and his circle had already been reviving an interest in de Sade and *érotisme noir*, and Breton's revitalised Surrealism had strong points of contact here (as indeed did Existentialism). We shall look at this in more detail in later chapters. Paulhan and Breton re-established contact, but despite the revival of Surrealism, it was Sartre's group that held sway over Parisian youth. It was new, libertarian, could claim an 'authenticity' in having been *résistant* (something they denied to the Surrealists, conveniently ignoring La Main à Plume), and offered a future beyond the wretched mess of *épuration* [35]. Beauvoir had first been asked if she was 'an existentialist' in spring 1944, and soon after Paulhan was predicting that Sartre was 'becoming the spiritual leader for thousands of young people' [36]. In May 1947, an excitable press exposé of 'How the Troglodytes of Saint-Germain-des-Prés Live', featured a Gothic-flavoured picture of aspiring film director Roger Vadim illuminating a cobweb-haired Juliette Greco with a candle, and described the 'gigantic orgies of the filthy young existentialists', 'drinking, dancing and loving their lives away in cellars' [37]. This put the new generation and their jazz club haunts, like Le Tabou, firmly on the map. By 1949 Miles Davis was there, bringing some of the best American jazz to Paris and engaging in an affair with Greco. A new era of youth culture was dawning.

**Polarisation – 1946:** At the beginning of 1946 de Gaulle, unwilling to play coalition games in a hung government, resigned from politics (gambling on being able to return in an unassailable presidential capacity at some later time), and the PCF took the opportunity to reinforce their claim to the banner of the Resistance by organising an exhibition of *résistant* art in which only proper communist social realism was permitted (to the disgust of many, including Simone de Beauvoir).

At the same time, Arthur Koestler's 1940 novel *Darkness at Noon*, lifting the lid on the horrors of the Stalinist show trials of the 1930s, was published in France and was taken up by Camus and others. Koestler himself came to Paris in October 1946, and there was uproar. Welcomed by the Sartre circle (before distressing Beauvoir with the violence of his bedroom behaviour), Koestler precipitated a gloves-off ideological struggle with the Communists in what was effectively an opening salvo in the Cold War – Koestler insisting that the PCF, with its adherence to the Moscow line during the Nazi-Soviet pact, had sabotaged the war effort in 1940; moreover, it was now a Trojan Horse for Moscow, with the power to paralyse

France at Stalin's behest, and it was necessary for France to prepare itself for a new Resistance against Communist take-over [38]. These views had a mixed reception in France, where although many were dubious about the Communists, there was widespread suspicion of the U.S.A. and anti-communism as well [39]. Koestler was not pro-American in fact, favouring instead a West European federation as a counterweight to both Moscow and Washington, but his strident anti-communism was off-putting to many. Nonetheless he may have affected the result of a referendum on a new constitution where the PCF suffered a serious set-back. The Communists of course went into over-drive to attack him – blaming him for their defeat and vilifying him as an anti-French traitor/ Trotskyist/ bourgeois counter-revolutionary/ CIA stooge and so on. Sartre allowed Merleau-Ponty to attack Koestler in *Les Tempes Modernes*, Camus defended him in *Combat*, and the friendship between Camus and Sartre was seriously strained.

By November 1946, Paulhan and Aragon were at logger-heads. Paulhan had continued including works by ex-collaborators like Jouhandreau in *Pléiade* while Aragon demanded a total ban on blacklisted writers. Paulhan refused to back down, but he did resign from the CNE, as did some sympathetic colleagues, including Dominique Aury and Jean Schlumberger.

**Dominique Aury and Liberation – 1944-47:** During all this turbulence and turmoil, Aury hit her stride both professionally and personally. Recognising her potential, Paulhan helped further her career by putting in a word for her with colleagues and contacts in the literary world. In November 1944 he recommended her to *Femmes françaises* and in 1945 to Jean Amrouche at *L'Arche.* Aury joined the reading committees of Éditions Charlot (with Camus and Blanchot) and Guilde de Livres in Lausanne, and in April 1946 Paulhan employed her at *Cahiers de Pléiade* – her first contact with a Gallimard project. In addition, Aury became increasingly involved in selection committees for literary prizes. She was also taking advantage of the sexual freedom characterising the literary world in Paris at the time, celebrated in Beauvoir's novel *Les Mandarins* (1954) whose characters, 'especially its women, are uninhibited and sometimes predatory' [40]. Aury became the mistress of Jean Amrouche for some months, 'as well as, it was said, that of Albert Camus'[41], probably had flings with Blanchot and Milleret, and a 'brief and violent' sexual encounter with Arthur Koestler [42]. In July she interviewed Paulhan when he won a literary prize from the Académie Française, but resisted his amorous overtures. Nothing daunted, Paulhan began a relationship with poet Édith Boissonnas that was to last for many years.

The most significant of Aury's romantic entanglements in the mid 1940s was with Édith Thomas [43]. Journalist, novelist and historian, Thomas' first book, a novel called *La Mort de Marie* had been published in 1934 by Gallimard, where she met Paulhan [44]. During the political disturbances of that year, as Aury's circle turned to the right, Thomas went left, although her attraction to communist ideals was tempered by her detestation of Stalinist dogma – 'their hardness, their narrowness, their lack of critical thinking' [45] – a view that the Moscow show trials and the Nazi-Soviet pact did nothing to ameliorate. She supported the republic in the Spanish Civil War and reported from the battle-front in 1936 and 1938, soon after being diagnosed with pulmonary TB (to add to the TB of the bones she had been suffering from since 1931) [46]. This led to her spending two years convalescing near Bordeaux, restless at her inability to take action over the invasion and Occupation. In 1941, however, she was in Paris, where her committed anti-fascism led her toward the Resistance. She played a major role in reconstituting the CNE with Paulhan and Claude Morgan in 1942 after the execution of Jacques Décour, hosting their meetings in her apartment from 1943, and contributing to *Les Lettres françaises* [47]. Morgan was a communist, and Thomas found Paulhan's playful character and delight in word-play and paradox irritating, but they managed to work together effectively. Overcoming her scruples, Thomas finally joined the PCF in September 1942 – 'it seemed to me that the time of total commitment, of unquestioning obedience, had arrived' [48]. She had short stories and poems published by Minuit (one of her poems being cited by de Gaulle in his 1943 speech about literature and Resistance [49]), in early 1944 wrote about the maquis *résistance* in the Cévennes, and in September accepted the editorship of the new PCF women's journal, *Femmes françaises*. In November she asked Paulhan for recommendations for a literary columnist and he introduced her to Dominique Aury. The two women hit it off immediately, and Aury wrote book reviews and articles on women's rights, but neither was happy with the paper – Thomas disliked the lack of editorial independence and the Party's socially conservative 'family values' line on the role of women [50], and Aury disliked the Party line on everything. In January 1945 they both quit. Thomas resigned – the PCF forcing her to redraft her resignation letter to cite health reasons rather than any political criticism. Aury cannily got herself fired so she could collect unemployment insurance [51]. The differences between the two women were stark: one was a 'spinsterish' communist who saw American capitalism as a greater danger than Soviet Communism, and was committed to politically engaged literature (before Sartre climbed on board); the other was a sexually liberated more-or-less Gaullist who shared neither of these views. What they did have in common was an acceptance that at least some victims of the *épurations* deserved what they got, and a dislike of Aragon's dictatorial manner and the 'Bad Faith' of the PCF [52].

Despite all the differences, a friendship was born. In February 1946 Aury was favourably reviewing Thomas' 1945 novels *Le Champ Libre* and *Études des Femmes* [53], admiring the independence of the female characters [54]. In the first, a substantially autobiographical novel, the protagonist is named 'Anne', which was one of Thomas' war-time pseud-onyms (the fact that Anne was Aury's real name was probably coincidental). The significance of a 'Dominique' in the second novel is less likely to be accidental, which suggests Thomas might have already been developing an 'awareness' of Aury. By autumn Aury was helping Thomas with her research for biographies of heroic women from history.

Then things took a turn. In her diary on October 27th 1946, Thomas wrote: 'This morning D. (Dominique) said to me: "Edith, I've drawn you into a trap." She was pale, ill, agitated. "I love you the way a man loves a woman." What to do? My God (who doesn't exist), what to do? I feel friendship, respect, deep affection for her. We agree on what is essential; we experience things, people, books in the same way. I love her delicacy, her intelligence, her exceptional quality of being. If she were a man, I would be infinitely happy about her love for me. If I were a man, I would love her. But she is a woman and I am a woman. What to do?' [55]. That same day Dominique sent Édith a letter 'to tell you I love you, and to kiss you,' confessing 'I do not know how to control myself any more... I have never loved a woman the way I love you,' admitting her 'admiration, respect and this combatant camaraderie based on tenderness and which is so powerful in time of war. To have held you in my arms even for a second this morning made me wobble... I kiss both your hands...' [56]. The next day Édith was acknowledging 'I love her (as much as I can love a woman)', and within a few days Aury had her way, in later years cheerfully depicting herself as a predator, flattering Thomas that she had given up a male lover for her [57] (a passing reference in a letter of August 1947 to a 'B in the past' might suggest this was Bernard Milleret? [58]) – 'I was the bad boy in our story, it's true. I enjoyed the role' [59]. Thomas was completely conquered and fell heavily, her journal reporting the violence of her passion – 'I'm burning... I'm thirsty... I'm hungry... Will you be my orchard, my water spring? Or will you be like fire, consuming everything...?' [60], but her love was plagued by anxieties – over her own frumpiness, over whether Aury ('a born huntress' [61]) was making hay elsewhere, and also Aury's secretive nature, discreet to the point of prevarication, which contrasted sharply with Thomas' own forthright honesty. By August 1947 Thomas was waxing 'mystical' about her love for Aury – delirious and committed to complete abandonment in love [62] – 'You're my illness, my love, I am ill of never having enough of you' [63], but Aury had started talking about Paulhan, and Thomas wrote 'I am convinced Paulhan is beginning to love D., and since she admires and loves him, my love will not weigh very much in that balance. Thinking about that, I cried for two hours', but Thomas knew she could not accept simultaneous love affairs the way Aury could, 'I would rather lose D. than share her. I feel as jealous as a tiger. It is awful to love another the way I love her. My friend, my love, my lover, *my* mistress' [64].

That same month, Éditions Charlot, which financed *L'Arche*, went into a tailspin. Amroche approached Paulhan and Aury for funds – unsuccessfully as it happened. Paulhan's reluctance came from a mixture of professional (and personal) rivalry, along with doubts about the financial integrity of the set-up. Aury may have shared his suspicions, and most likely couldn't afford it anyway, but with Charlot in trouble, she faced redundancy. However, Thomas reassured her that Paulhan would not let her fall.

Thomas was right about that, and about the threat of a developing romance as well. Paulhan did look out for Aury professionally, and the two of them did begin an affair that same August. Clandestine, of course, to keep it from colleagues at Gallimard, Paulhan's family – and also from Aury's ex-husband d'Argila who was on the prowl again, this time accusing her of failing to provide adequately for Philippe's education. Aury's own account dates her interest in Paulhan back five years earlier. Working with him on her anthology of devotional verse throughout 1942, she found herself taken by this 'towering literary figure, handsome in an imperious way, with features that most readily expressed amusement and disdain' [65], his charm, humour and intelligence, his evident growing awareness of her, not to mention his resemblance to her father on a number of scores (as we noted on p. 102), including being 'quite a ladies' man' [66]. Aury was smitten. As she put it later: 'It was slow, but it went very—efficiently. It wasn't the first time someone had taken an interest in me [67], and I was just a bit intrigued. At first, I thought it was a caprice. But, no, it was better than that. He was a wonderful person' [68]. Germaine was now seriously ill, and Paulhan made it clear his responsibilities of care made it impossible to leave her. His marriage to Germaine lasted the rest of his life, as did his affair with Aury.

Consummating her relations with Paulhan spelled the end of the affair with Édith Thomas, who could not countenance shared love – but Aury would not allow a complete split, and successfully rescued a friendship between them. In a curious re-play of the Maulnier-Desclos affair, this time it was Aury who was the heart-breaker, but she refused to inflict on Thomas the cruellest fate, abandonment, condemning her to 'pain and anguish'. Aury claimed she phoned Thomas 'every day of her life until her death' [69].

**Paulhan and the Cold War – Round One 1947-50**: In 1947, the Cold War really kicked into gear. In France an attempted new dawn, putting the Third Republic behind it and founding a Fourth Republic, immediately fell into crisis, with inflation, strikes and rationing, and fifteen cabinets in seven years. A power-grab by the PCF had put the Communists in effective control of the CNE and *Les Lettres françaises,* disenfranchising non-communist *résistants*. Paulhan decided to hit back. The moment he chose was when the PCF tried to set themselves up as standard bearers for national pride by co-opting (amongst others) 19th-century symbolist poet Arthur Rimbaud as a patriotic/ communist icon. Paulhan wrote an article for *Le*

*Figaro* mischievously reminding everyone that back in 1927 there had been an official attempt to designate Rimbaud as a 'patriotic' figure (which he certainly wasn't), which had been rubbished by the Surrealists in a text drawn up by none other than Louis Aragon. As Aragon and the PCF leaders seethed, Paulhan appeared to offer an olive branch, releasing an anthology of war-poetry, co-edited with Aury, *La Patrie se fait tous les jours*[70], featuring work by the whole range of *résistant* writers, including Aragon, Éluard, Vercors and other communists, along with Beauvoir, Camus, Sartre, Mauriac, Malraux and Gide, as well as Édith Thomas, Aury and Paulhan himself. No surrealists were willing to be included, as they opposed 'committed' poetry as a contradiction in terms.

The PCF/CNE were not so easily placated, however, and continued to harass Paulhan for persisting in publishing blacklisted writers in *Pléiade*. But Paulhan was primed and ready, and in April published his first 'Letter to the Members of the CNE' (four more appearing at interludes until September), attacking their hypocrisy in blacklisting and banning authors when so many of them, Aragon included, had been only too happy to be published in the 'official' (i.e. collaborationist) press during the Occupation – often through the good offices of Paulhan. The PCF were furious – attacking Paulhan, and also Sartre, whom they saw as a threat (one side-effect of this being a reconciliation between Sartre and Camus). They published a list of 'enemy intellectuals' (which, interestingly did not include Paulhan or Breton[71]), and officially adopted the 'Zhdanov doctrine' emanating from Moscow, that only positivist, socialist realist and morally symbolic art was legitimate and progressive[72]. In November they went on the offensive against a book entitled *I Chose Freedom*, published in the U.S. in 1946 and written by one Victor Kravchenko, who had defected from the U.S.S.R. while on a trade mission. Kravchenko's exposé of the horrors of the Soviet gulags became an international best-seller, and the PCF/CNE condemned it in

*Les Lettres françaises* as a U.S. intelligence fabrication [73]. That same month Paulhan and Aury published a new anthology, *Poètes d'aujourd'hui* (*Poets of Today*) which was more of a provocation to the CNE, featuring a number of blacklisted writers. Aragon, incensed, refused permission for any of his work to be included, and prevailed on Éluard to pull out as well. His subsequent denial that he had arm-twisted Éluard provoked Dominique Aury to a highly out-of-character confrontation with him, bawling him out in public as a liar [74].

Meanwhile fear of Moscow seized the U.S.A., which responded with the carrot of the Marshall Plan of financial aid to western Europe to forestall the spread of Communism, and the stick of the H.U.A.C. (House Un-American Actvities Committee) hearings to root out communist 'subversion' at home. In France, de Gaulle tried to set up his own 'Third Way' between Washington and Moscow with his RPF (Rassemblement du peuple françaises/ Assembly of the French People), which temporarily won wide support, from among others Malraux and Aron, but Malraux was already siding with Koestler on the dangers of PCF sabotage and Soviet invasion, and the RPF (and Gaullism) shifted to the right. De Gaulle always had a fractious relationship with the U.S., and wished to keep channels with Moscow open, but his political sympathies were not neutral, and in Paris, space for a Third Way remained vacant. By the end of the year, things were turning against the PCF – its opposition to Marshall Aid was unpopular, and the derailing of a train by communist militants in December, which killed 16 people, led to widespread disillusion with the endless strikes and their PCF backing.

In February 1948, the Humanist intelligentsia in Paris finally tried to organise themselves into a Third Way political party, the pro-European RDR (Rassemblement démocratique révolutionnaire/ Democratic Revolutionary Assembly). Sartre played a leading role, committing much time and money to the cause, and the RDR attracted the support of

Breton, Beauvoir, Camus, Merleau-Ponty, Richard Wright and Aron amongst others. The RDR's stance was against capitalism and Stalinism, in favour of a pan-European unity of progressive-minded people from across the classes – opposing de Gaulle's rhetoric of state authority and the prestige and greatness of France with a language of human dignity, solidarity and justice that owed much to Camus [75]. Paulhan co-operated with them [76] – although he may not have been completely comfortable with their anti-Gaullist rhetoric [77], but then Breton was not as fervently hostile to de Gaulle as some of his friends would have liked either [78]. Bataille also apparently wanted to join, but Sartre (who was never entirely convinced of his sanity) seems to have 'prevented him from doing so' [79].

Paulhan also joined with Sartre, Camus and Breton (and the rest of his Surrealist group) in supporting U.S. veteran Garry Davies' demand before the United Nations in 1949 to repudiate national identity and be recognised as a citizen of the world. But polarisation in Paris had already gone too far. The RDR foundered in autumn 1949 as it became evident that the membership was fatally divided between those who would, when push came to shove, side with Moscow, and those who would side with Washington. Politically, the 'Third Way' was a failure, but culturally and intellectually it remained a force to be reckoned with for another twenty years or more, providing a context for Aury and *O*.

In 1948 another new journal, *La Table Ronde*, was launched by Catholic *résistant* François Mauriac, in partnership with Thierry Maulnier (who had been mostly keeping his head down since Liberation and concentrating on writing plays). This paper was conservative, but eschewed overtly doctrinaire politics. Paulhan and Mauriac were old comrades, but Paulhan's amicable relations with *La Table Ronde* managed to incense the CNE even further, and they retaliated by taking his name off the mast-head of *Les Lettres françaises* (the paper he had co-founded).

Meanwhile, the Cold War just got colder. In 1948 Moscow denounced Tito and had Hungarian communist Rajk shot in 1949 after a rigged trial, just as Mao established a Communist regime in Beijing. In Paris, Kravchenko won a libel case against *Les Lettres françaises*, which tainted the PCF with dishonesty for its attempt to deny the horrors of the Soviet gulags, and strengthened Koestler's case against Communism. Meanwhile Malraux, suspicious that Sartre was secretly pro-Moscow, pressurised Gallimard to stop bankrolling *Les Temps Modernes,* so Sartre took his review to Éditions Julien. In 1950 the Korean War began, fear of nuclear cataclysm peaked, and the McCarthy witch-hunts began in the U.S.A. (climaxing in 1954). That year, 1950, also saw the campaign to lobby the Communist Czech government against the show trial of historian and surrealist Záviš Kalandra. Paulhan and Aury joined with Breton, Sartre, Beauvoir, Camus and others in this campaign, which was opposed by the PCF. Breton appealed to Éluard for support, but he, by now a die-hard Stalinist, refused to sign. In his view the mere fact that Kalandra had been charged in the first place was ample proof of his guilt, and it was inconceivable that his confession had been forced. Kalandra was shot for his 'crimes' [80]. By 1951 however, Sartre and *Les Temps Modernes* were confirming Malraux' suspicions that they did see Communism as the lesser of two evils in the Cold War, and in this brave new Manichaean world, with Washington supporting any tin-pot dictators in the developing world as anti-communist 'friends of the Free World,' the only politically progressive route was support for Moscow. Camus attacked Sartre as an apologist for state violence and terror, willing to turn a blind eye to immense human suffering for some abstract 'greater good'; Sartre, insulted by Camus' *L'Homme révolté* (*The Rebel*, 1951) that damned communist insurrection as dehumanising, retaliated that Camus was merely an intellectual counter-revolutionary, aloof and bourgeois. Their friendship did not survive. [Interestingly, Camus' book precipitated another divorce as well. Like Sartre, Breton and his group also disliked the book for its negative attitude towards revolt, Benjamin Péret dismissing Camus as a 'Sunday rebel'. However, the anarchist group Breton had been co-operating with at the time disagreed, and that put paid to that relationship too [81]].

**Dominique Aury 1947-50**: These were turbulent years for Aury and her circle on the personal front. Living with her parents, her teenage son Philippe and her maternal grandmother, Aury not only had to support them all, but had to contend with a raft of problems. A difficult relationship with her intrusive and jealous mother, the needs of her son, compounded by harassment from d'Argila that she wasn't providing well enough for the boy, on top of which Paulhan was still seeing Édith Boissonnas, and Édith Thomas was distressed by trials and tribulations of her own. Not surprisingly, Aury's health took a turn for the worse, with severe stress and migraines, and acute appendicitis at the end of 1947 (in strange synchrony with Thomas who suffered the same thing at the same time).

Édith Thomas' problems were political and personal. She had left the CNE in 1947, and had been busy writing biographies – one on Jeanne d'Arc (trying to rescue her from becoming a right-wing political icon), and in 1948 one on 19th century feminist and socialist Pauline Roland (which Paulhan tried to get published, but Gallimard refused, and it languished till 1956 [82]). In 1949 her relationship with the PCF, which had been rocky since 1945, went into terminal crisis. Disgusted by their belief that 'the ends justify the means', and their acceptance of the Zhdanov doctrine and Moscow's behaviour towards Tito and Rajk, Thomas resigned from the Party [83]. She wrote an article for *Combat* explaining why, and PCF leader Maurice Thorez personally retaliated by condemning her as one of the 'weaker elements', 'afraid of the struggle' (an extraordinary allegation against one who had done and risked so much for the CNE during the Occupation) [84]. Thomas was devastated and isolated, effectively boycotted, with Aury being one of the few to stand by her. But Thomas was also jealous of her friend's relationship with Paulhan, which made life awkward for Aury, and with the Aury-Paulhan affair going public in 1950, things were made no easier for Thomas. The affair was understandably not easy for the now-bedridden Germaine either – Aury apparently experiencing more guilt over this than Paulhan [85], whose commitment to ensuring Germaine was cared for seems to have been enough to assuage his conscience. Moreover, Thomas thoroughly disapproved of Aury's new habit of spending her summer holidays at Florence Gould's luxurious holiday residence in Juan-le-Pins, outraged not just at Aury's apparently amoral fascination for opulence, but also that she was willing to be friends with such a notorious ex-collaborator as Gould.

But there were new developments too – Aury was impressed by Simone de Beauvoir's 1949 analysis of women and their place in society, *Le Deuxième Sexe* (*The Second Sex*), continued her translations of Anglophone writers, including Koestler and Waugh, made the acquaintance of surrealist writer Pieyre de Mandiargues, and won praise from Georges Bataille for her translation of James Hogg's 1824 book *Confessions of a Justified Sinner*. At the same time, Paulhan (now a member of the Légion d'Honneur) was exploring the further shores of the erotic. He had been fostering the career of the painter Jean Fautrier, who had exhibited with Picasso, Derain and Chagall in the 1920s, had illustrated books (including Bataille's *Madame Edwarda* in 1941 [86]) but whose career had stalled. Paulhan organised an exhibition of his work in 1943, and started employing him as illustrator at *Pléiade*. Fautrier was one of the exponents of 'Taschisme' (a movement akin to American Abstract Expressionism) and was married to a much younger woman, Jeanne (aka Jeanine) Aeply. Jeanne had left her previous husband and child when she was 21, and two years later (in 1944) married the 46 year old Fautrier. Sexually submissive to him, and periodically on the receiving end of his violence, she, like her husband, enjoyed multiple relationships outside of marriage. Paulhan seems to have accompanied Fautrier to 'libertine' evenings, whose flavour seems to have been more about sexual license than sado-masochism, but pleasingly clandestine nonetheless. Paulhan may have been a participant, but being quite a lot older than the others present, was more likely to have remained an observer [87]. Aury had met Fautrier and Aeply by 1947, but four-way games between them seem unlikely as Aury and Paulhan were not 'swingers' – Aury's erotic fancies lay closer to prostitution than orgy [88]. Moreover, neither woman liked the other's man any more than the men liked the other's woman.

Paulhan had a long-standing interest in Sadean sexuality, and wrote articles about it after Liberation. He also started fostering the career of a new young writer, Alain Robbe-Grillet, arranging in 1949 for the publication of his first novel, *Un Régicide,* (by Minuit, after Gallimard refused it), forming a friendship with him that owed much to shared literary values (for Robbe-Grillet, 'the only possible commitment, for the writer, is literature' [89]), and a common interest in Sadean erotica.

It was in this context that Aury, on holiday at Florence Gould's place Juan-le-Pins in the summer of 1950, working on an article on *Dangerous Liaisons'* female protagonist, Mme. de Merteuil, began collecting her thoughts for *Story of O* [90]. Written (mostly) the following year, *O* was to become the terrain where various currents in Aury's life met and cross-fertilised – her fascination for devotional poetry and mystical sacrifice, her sexual and emotional pleasure, her awareness of Paulhan's erotic tastes, her taste for luxury, her worries about Édith Thomas, her anxieties over Édith Boissonnas, possible influence from the relationship between Aeply and Fautrier, and her experience of the range of intellectual and literary currents flourishing in Paris at the time, including *érotisme noir,* Existentialism, Feminine Humanism and Surrealism. We shall discuss all this in more detail in the next chapters.

## THE 1950s AND AFTER

**Paulhan and the Cold War – Round Two 1952-53:** Paulhan's rather Protestant taste for fighting the good fight, fuelled by a natural belligerence in his character, not to mention a penchant for mischievous devilry, led him to go on the offensive against the PCF/CNE again in 1952 with another devastating broadside – his 'Letter to the Directors of the Resistance' – targeting Aragon, Vercors, Morgan and Éluard. The letter was published by Minuit (having been rejected by Gallimard – around the same time as it rejected *O* )[91], and denounced the continued persecutions and purges of collaborating writers as injustices perpetrated by the machinations of the PCF, which wasted the talents of the victims. It also challenged the integrity of those who would condemn writers for collaborating with the Germans whilst themselves collaborating with the Soviets [92], and accused the *résistants* of betraying their principles by becoming executioners [93] (a vocabulary echoing that of Camus' *Neither Victims nor Executioners* in *Combat,* 1946). In *Les Lettres françaises* in February 1952 Elsa Triolet, Aragon's wife and fellow-communist, condemned Paulhan as the 'successor to Drieu La Rochelle' [94], but his letter had hit home. Aury was in full agreement with Paulhan over the letter (although typically kept her head down) [95], but ironically, despite her own struggles with the PCF and her agreement with the burden of Paulhan's 1947 letters, Édith Thomas took serious umbrage, interpreting this latest letter as an attack on the integrity of the *résistants* themselves [96]. The PCF retaliated by accusing Paulhan of pandering to the collaborationist press during the Occupation by trying to recruit *résistant* writers, and cited testimony from Thomas in 1941 as evidence against him. Paulhan was delighted at having provoked the PCF, but annoyed that Thomas had allowed her name to be used in this way, and downright furious when she stuck to her guns over her decision. Relations between them broke down – it being unclear which of them was the main instigator of the split, although jealousy between them was mutual [97]. Aury's prime loyalty was to Paulhan, but despite his demands she refused to abandon her friendship with Thomas, although she kept it secret from him for two years. Even so, Thomas always felt Aury had sided with Paulhan, though Aury continued to hope for reconciliation between them.

In January 1953 Paulhan and Gallimard (having closed *Pléiade* the previous spring), with the backing of the venerable André Gide, finally managed to relaunch the *New NRF* to wide press coverage and accolades, attracting contributions from Malraux, Blanchot, Mandiargues, Jouhandreau and Bataille amongst others. Aury was taken on in a senior position, which she was to hold for decades, writing on Colette, Dylan Thomas, Woolf, Nabokov and others, the *NNRF* being another string to her bow as editor, translator, critic and literary prize panellist. It would be hard to over-state her significance to the Parisian Republic of Letters. Committing itself to 'authentic' writing rather then popular, media-friendly pap, the *NNRF* adopted no political or literary doctrines, and resisted all pressures to conform from the authorities, political parties, the press and mass culture, while being quite unfazed by accusations of elitism [98]. The return of the *NRF* (it resumed its original title in 1955) and the breadth of its remit provoked a rather pointed comment from Sartre in March 1953 that *he* would never accept the work of ex-collaborators in *Les Temps Modernes* [99], and some mudslinging from Mauriac. Sensing a threat to the sales and influence of *La Table Ronde,* he accused the revived *NRF* of being still tainted by its collaborationist past under Drieu [100] – Mauriac's dyspepsia towards *O* being very likely a side-effect of his rage over the resurrection of the *NRF* [see pp. 28-29]. The *NRF* went on to develop the careers of Alain

Robbe-Grillet, Nathalie Sarraute, Pieyre de Mandiargues and others, and took up its old role of spreading French culture abroad, as welcomed by, among others, Philip Toynbee in London. It is still in publication today.

**After 1953 – Later Life:** As the 1950s got under way, France entered a period of growth, even a degree of political stability. De Gaulle retired from politics to write his memoirs (and continue to bide his time), France withdrew from its colonial ambitions in Vietnam in 1954 (leaving it to the U.S. to move in and suffer a long defeat over the next twenty years). The new challenge to what was left of the French overseas empire was the heating-up of the campaign for Algerian independence, which precipitated the 1958 crisis that gave de Gaulle the chance he had been waiting for to take power in a new Presidential Fifth Republic (see p. 38) – a political return that provoked little opposition from Aury or Paulhan.

Paulhan was by now a grandfather – his son Frédéric and daughter-in-law Jacqueline (with whom Aury developed a friendship) had been living with him and Germaine in Rue des Arènes since 1945 and had children of their own – Jean (born 1951) and Claire ( born 1955). The long-drawn out fight between Paulhan and the PCF/CNE had petered out by 1955. Stalin was dead and even Moscow was starting to distance itself from his legacy (to the chagrin of the die-hard French Communists). However, the Soviets had not lost their capacity to lose friends and sympathisers, their invasion of Hungary in 1956 further tarnishing the reputation of them and their creed. In France, the PCF found its power and influence waning.

Overall life had settled into a less frantic gear for Dominique Aury. From 1950 she had been working as an editor and reader at Gallimard, where she translated English language writers including F. Scott Fitzgerald and Henry Miller, and joined the staff of the *NNRF* when it re-launched in 1953. She was made Chevalier de l'Ordre de la Légion d'Honneur and was awarded the Grand Prix de la Critique Littérature in 1958 for her *Lectures pour tous* (*Readings/Stories for Everyone*) [101]. From the mid-1950s she was in a correspondence with Blanchot sufficiently affectionate to raise the question of clandestine romantic relations between them [102]; if so, this might have been during the time of the correspondence, but was perhaps most likely in the mid 1940s when the two of them were working together and Aury was treating herself to a bit of a wild time. There was however a shadow on Aury's horizon: Paulhan was still seeing Édith Boissonnas, which probably lay behind her admission in later interviews that in the early 1950s she felt Paulhan was 'slipping away', which in turn provided the motivation to write *O* [103]. If *O* was a device to re-seduce Paulhan, it worked, but it did not succeed in driving Boissonnas off the scene. In 1954, the year *O* was published, Paulhan and Boissonnas were experimenting with mescaline together (just after Aldous Huxley published his adventures with it in his *The Doors of Perception*), and in 1959 the two of them went on a trip to Japan, accompanied by Fautrier and Jeanne Aeply, and without Aury [104]. Whether Aury saw this as a snub, or whether she was unable to go for family reasons and 'understood' Paulhan taking alternative company is not clear. But she was amiable enough with her rival to attend, with Paulhan and Odile de Lalain, a ceremony in 1967 where Boissonnas received an award for her poetry [105].

It was however Fautrier and Aeply who were to provide the major drama of the end of the decade [106]. Between 1958 and 1962 letters between Dominique Aury and Aeply reveal the latter's marriage going badly on the rocks, her desire to write, her sexual libertinism, her struggle with alcohol and tranquillisers, and Fautrier's repeated psychological and physical violence to her (to which she seems to have had a mixed reaction). Aeply's letters indicate a demanding, even neurotic, emotional dependence on Aury, along with a sensual intimacy that strongly suggests a (clandestine, of course) sexual affair with her. Fautrier blamed Aury for encouraging his wife to leave him, while Paulhan found Aeply manipulative in her relentless, and in his view, rather unhinged, burdening of Aury. Dominique Aury's own attitude was rather complex – on the one hand encouraging and providing support for a friend in need, while at the same time enjoying the opportunity to exercise her seductive powers. Like Édith Thomas, Aeply was unfamiliar with lesbian sex, although unlike Édith, she was highly experienced with men. Certainly, again like Thomas, Aeply found Aury emotionally evasive and unwilling to open herself up, about which Aeply complained incessantly. Aeply finally left Fautrier in 1962, and he died of cancer two years later (which Paulhan believed was connected). Aury stayed in touch with Aeply, despite Paulhan's discouragement, although she did distance herself somewhat, and she went on to have a career as a novelist – Aury reading her manuscripts, and Paulhan (despite his dislike of her) trying to get her published. Aeply later joined Philippe Sollers' *Tel Quel* journal, and in 1965, thanks to Paulhan, landed a job at Gallimard.

In 1960 Paulhan put himself in bad odour with many of his old friends by refusing to sign the 'Manifesto of the 121'. This was a show of strength by Parisian intellectuals against French imperialism in Algeria, calling on French conscripts to desert, organised by Blanchot and surrealist Jean Schuster, signed by (amongst others), fellow surrealists including Breton (who, when legal action threatened, claimed full responsibility for it) [107], along with Sartre and Beauvoir, Guy Debord, Maurice Nadeau, Alain Robbe-Grillet, Françoise Sagan, François Truffaut and Vercors [108], and was almost as divisive as the Dreyfus case [109]. Now 75, it seemed that Paulhan was sliding towards a conservative dotage, although he had never been exactly 'progressive' on imperial matters, as his account of the Barbadian slave revolt in his preface to *O* would indicate. Blanchot never forgave him. However, Paulhan was not the only leading figure not to sign – Camus didn't either, nor did Aury (Maulnier, predictably, actively campaigned against it). De Gaulle's refusal to prosecute Sartre over his public campaign against French involvement in Algeria ('One does not arrest Voltaire') reinforced the status of public intellectuals in France, but by then de Gaulle was already realising that Algerian independence was inevitable, and that the Manifesto in fact served his purposes. Whether Sartre felt there was any actual tacit understanding with de Gaulle, he did in 1962 share with him the unpleasantly interesting experience of being targeted for assassination by the paramilitary pro-colonialist OAS [110]. He and de Gaulle both survived. When de Gaulle eventually put the Algerian question to a referendum, Paulhan voted in favour of independence [111].

In 1961 Aury at last had a house of her own, in Boussise-sur-Bertrand (near Melun, on the way to Fontainebleau), which she might have bought with royalties from *O*, although her story was that Paulhan had wanted to give her a gift, perhaps travel or a house, from the proceeds of the sale of paintings from his collection, and she chose a house [112]. The following year her father Auguste died (the same year Albert Camus was killed in a car-crash). In 1963 Aury joined the jury for Prix Femina [113]; Paulhan was inducted into the Académie Française, and retired from publishing to concentrate on his writing, staying with Aury at weekends, but his health was deteriorating. Aury wrote to him daily, signing herself 'Anne'– proof that her original name had never fallen into total abeyance, in one letter in February 1963 calling on her heart to martyr itself for his health [114]. By 1965 Paulhan, now seriously ill, was living with Aury at last (Germaine being cared for by their son Frédéric and daughter-in-law Jacqueline), while Aury and Blanchot ran the *NRF*. In 1967 Aury invited Édith Thomas to visit her in Boussise where she and Paulhan were at last reconciled. Breton had died in 1966 and the cultural movement of the 'Third Way' reached a climax in the Maydays of 1968 – celebrating Breton and radicalising Blanchot to the far left, prompting him to resign from the *NRF*, which he found too open-minded [115]. That year Paulhan was hospitalised in Clinique Hartman, Neuilly, where Aury visited daily [116] and wrote 'A Girl in Love'. Paulhan's son Frédéric asked Aury to make the decision when to switch off the life support for his father, which she did on October 9th 1968 [117].

The following year de Gaulle finally retired, and in 1970 Aury's mother Louise died, as did Édith Thomas (of viral hepatitis), Paulhan's widow Germaine following two years after that. Thomas' last novel, *Jeu d'échecs* (*Chess* [118]), published in 1970, gave a lightly fictionalised account of her love with Aury, centred around two women: the narrator, Aude, who is seduced by the androgynous artist Claude (whose description resembles Aury [119]), both with a history in the Resistance, the one out of political commitment, the other out of the love of adventure [120]. Claude is presented as working on illustrations to *Alice's Adventures in Wonderland* (a novel much beloved of Aury, and, incidentally, the surrealists), and the work is dedicated to D.A., 'who knows the story, with my constant affection' [121]. Jeanne Aeply produced two works in this period, both of which resonated with Aury. *Une fille à marier* (*A Girl to Marry*, 1969), was apparently written at the same time as Aury's 'A Girl in Love', and similarities (in title and theme) suggest some collusion between the two writers and the two pieces. In 1972 Aeply's follow-up, *Eros Zéro*, echoed *O*, not just in its title, but in its depiction of a Roissy-style secret place, 'Paradise', where women remove their underwear to gain entry, and in its depiction of the theme of abandonment and annulment. On republication in 1997, reverberations of *O* persisted, with Pauvert providing a preface claiming he did not know the author, but that she was 'apparently' the wife of a painter admired by Bataille and Paulhan, and her book had received the approval of 'Pauline Réage' [122].

Sartre, Beauvoir and Maulnier all died in the 1980s, and Jeanne Aeply stopped visiting Aury [123], who lived on, quietly working at Gallimard, remaining there (part-time) into her eighties [124], still influential in the literary prize world (arranging for Régine Deforges to join the jury for Prix Femina in 1985 [125]), and with occasional forays into the media limelight as outlined in chapter II, until her own decline and death in 1998 [126].

----

[1] Cited in Poirier 2018 p. 108

[2] Julian Jackson *Charles de Gaulle* Cardinal 1990 p. 29.

[3] One knock-on of this was an upsurge in anti-sex piety that led to the closure of the brothels in 1946

[4] Cited in Poirier 2018 p. 84

[5] Cited in Mahon 2020 p. 250 note 37

[6] Kelly, Michael et al., '3. Crises of Modernisation' in Forbes, Jill and Kelly, Michael (ed.) *French Cultural Studies* Oxford University Press  1995 p. 101

[7] Cited in Perret 2017

[8] *Parti de 75000 fusillé* (Poirier 2018 p. 84)

[9] Cited Poirier 2018 p.79.

[10] Paulhan to Éluard Oct 44, cited in Perret 2017

[11] Cornick and Flood 2000 p. 31

[12] Stéphane Simonet *Atlas de la Libération de France* (2004), estimates 25,000 French civilians executed, deported or otherwise killed (cited Poirier 2018 p. 337). This would include *résistants* from all groups, not just the PCF, which seriously undermines the PCF's claim to be the party of 75,000 martyrs – although the scale of the PCF's exaggeration was not fully realised at the time.

[13] David 2006 p. 318

[14] Perret 2017

[15] Ibid

[16] In his 'What is a Collaborator?' (1948) he argued that only a section of the bourgeoisie had collaborated, the working class and peasantry being free of such a taint.

[17] Robert Paxton *Vichy France: Old Guard and New Order* (1972), Paxton and Michael Morris *Vichy France and the Jews* (1981) cited in Solomon, Daniel: 'Legend of Innocence' *The Tablet*, June 28th 2022: The French population struggled on a poorer diet than many others in Occupied Europe, many were sent as forced labour to Germany. France was almost unique in voluntarily handing over Jews from unoccupied territories, and the 75% survival rate of French Jews owed less to Vichy or French collaborationist benevolence than to Nazi resources being overstretched.

[18] Aron *Histoire de Vichy* (1954), cited in Solomon, 2022

[19] Kelly et al. in Forbes and Kelly (ed.) 1995 p. 100

[20] Pindar 1998

[21] Hussey 2007 p. 85

[22] Aury took a harder line than Paulhan against collaborationist writers (David 2006 p. 90). She had broken with Brasillach by 1941, but she had known him in her youth... However, sentimentality does not seem to have been a cardinal trait in her.

[23] Lévy 1995 pp. 161-162

[24] Cornick and Flood 2000, p. 27-28

[25] *What is Literature?* Routledge 1993, pp. 185-186, cited in Mahon 2020 p. 125, p. 249 note 1

[26] Mahon 2020 p. 140

[27] *Les Temps Modernes* split from Gallimard in 1948, but proved to be much more than a stop-gap, remaining in publication till 2019

[28] Surya 2002, pp. 368-69; published by Éditions de Minuit since 1950, *Critique* was edited by Bataille until his death in 1962, and is still going.

[29] Perret 2017

[30] Surya 2002 p. 369

[31] Cited in Mahon 2020 p. 250 note 40

[32] Cornick and Flood 2000, p. 28

[33] Vol 1: *L'Age de Raison* (*The Age of Reason*) and vol 2: *Le Sursis* (*The Reprieve*); the third volume, *La Mort dans l'Âme* (literally *Death in the Soul* but translated as *Iron in the Soul*) followed in 1949.

[34] Published as *L'Existentialisme est un humanisme*, 1946

[35] Hussey 2007 p. 388

[36] Cohen-Solal 1987 pp. 222-223

[37] *Samedi Soir*, 3 May 1947, cited in Hussey 2007 p. 389; Poirier 2018 p. 204

[38] Cornick, Martyn: 2015 'The New Resistance? French Intellectual Realignments after the Liberation: the Case of Armand Petitjean' *Journal of War & Culture Studies*, 17526272, Aug 2015, Vol. 8, Issue 3

[39] McCarthy 1998.

[40] Review from *The Guardian* (back cover of Fontana edition 1966). Despite her denials of anything autobiographical in her novel, shadows of real people are detectable in the characters, including Beauvoir herself (in 'Dr. Anne Dubreuilh'), Sartre, Camus and Nelson Algren. 'Scriassine' clearly owes much to Koestler, and, interestingly, he is presented sympathetically as intelligent, subtle (though manipulative), but admirable in his moral implacability against Stalinism. Scriassine charms Anne, but there is misogyny and violence in their encounter in the bedroom, although afterwards, Anne 'hold(s) nothing against him'. *The Mandarins*, Collins Fontana 1960 pp. 42, 43, 96-102.

[41] David 2006 p.80

[42] Poirier 2018, p. 324

[43] Dorothy Kaufmann 1998 deserves the credit for bringing the Édith Thomas story to light.

[44] David 2006 424

[45] Thomas 1934 cited in Kaufmann 1998 p.887

46 Kaufmann 1998 p. 888
47 Ibid p. 887-888
48 Cited in ibid p. 888
49 Kaufmann 1995 p. 34
50 David 2006 p. 41
51 Kaufman 1998 p. 890-891
52 David 2006 p. 396
53 Literally *The Open Field* and *Women's Studies.*
54 David 2006 p. 399
55 cited Kaufmann 1998 p. 892; David 2006 p. p. 401.
56 Aury 27 October 1946, cited Poirier 2018 p. 141
57 Poirier 2018 p. 142; David 2006 p. 402
58 David 2006 p. 407
59 Kaufmann 1998 p. 892
60 Thomas' journal 2 November 1946, cited Poirier 2018 p. 142
61 Poirier 2018 p. 142
62 David 2006 p. 405
63 Cited Poirier 2018 p. 209
64 Thomas journal 1st Aug 1947, cited David 2006 p. 407; Kaufmann 1998 p. 893
65 Bedell 2004
66 Jacqueline Paulhan, cited in Bedell 2004
67 One of the great understatements.
68 St Jorre 1994, p. 44
69 Aury cited in Kaufmann 1998 p. 886
70 Translating roughly as *The Motherland is built day by day*; Editions de Minuit Feb. 1947. The title takes back possession of La Patrie from Vichy slogans, implying a renewal of the country through Resistance and Liberation and (perhaps) progressive politics, and repudiating the fantasy of the eternal mythical homeland propagated by right wing ideologies. My thanks to Maurice Debonnard for unpicking this one with me.
71 Raising the question whether old friendships and loyalties were playing a role. Aragon had after all one time been good friends with both Breton and Paulhan.
72 Poirier 2018 p. 212
73 Poirier 2018 p. 294-296; Watson 2022 p. 589
74 David 2006 p. 100
75 Julian Jackson *Charles de Gaulle* Cardinal 1990 p. 30
76 Durozoi 2002 p. 488
77 David 2006 p. 361 considers that by the late 1950s Paulhan and Aury were Gaullists.
78 Polizzotti 2009 p. 514
79 Surya 2002 p. 399, 564 note 5
80 Durozoi 2002 p. 465
81 Ibid p. 529
82 David 2006 p. 424

83 Kaufman 1998 p. 888
84 Ibid p. 889/ 901
85 David 2006 p. 119
86 Ibid p. 42
87 Ibid p. 476
88 Ibid p. 522; see Deforges 1976 pp. 68-71
89 Cited in Kelly et al., in Forbes and Kelly (ed.) 1995 p. 165
90 David 2006 p. 64
91 Mahon 2020 p. 132:
92 Hutchinson: 1997
93 Perret 2018
94 Elsa Triolet, "Jean Paulhan, successeur de Drieu la Rochelle," *Les Lettres Françaises* 7 February 1952 Cited in Cornick and Flood 2000 p. 44 note 55.
95 Kaufmann 1998 p. 886
96 Ibid p. 886; The fact Paulhan had convened his planning meeting with Camus, Malraux, Mauriac and Sartre and others the previous December in her apartment understandably didn't please her much either.
97 For Kaufmann (1998 p. 886) and Mahon (2020, p. 146), it was Thomas taking umbrage that broke the relationship; David (2006 p. 146-7) argues it was Paulhan's anger that did it; see also David p. 428
98 Cornick and Flood 2000
99 Ibid. p. 43, note 42
100 Ibid. p. 36
101 David 2006 p. 168
102 Ibid p.363; see also F. Nourissier 'La Secrete', *Le Figaro*, 31 March 2006
103 See for example St Jorre 1995 p. 212
104 David 2006 pp. 184
105 Ibid.
106 This story is a major discovery by Angie David 2006 – unless otherwise stated, the material in this paragraph comes from her biography, pp. 539, 493-4, 374.
107 Also Michel Leiris, Gérard Legrand, André Masson, Jean Louis Bedouin, Robert Benayoun and Mandiargues
108 Other notables included Pierre Boulez, Marguerite Duras, Alain Resnais, Nathalie Sarraute, Simone Signoret
109 McCarthy 1998
110 Organisation armée secrète – a terrorist group violently opposed to Algerian independence.
111 David 2006 p. 361
112 St Jorre 1995 p. 230; David 2006 pp 40, 175 refers to both versions.
113 David 2006 p. 165
114 David 2006 p. 182
115 Ibid p. 375

[116] Aury told St Jorre that she slept there for four months – St Jorre 1994, p. 48.

[117] David 2006 p. 176

[118] Literally 'Game of Defeats'

[119] Kaufmann 1998 p. 886

[120] Ibid p. 890

[121] David 2006 p. 408

[122] Ibid p. 542

[123] Ibid p. 544

[124] St Jorre 1994, p. 44

[125] David 2006 p. 57

[126] David 2006 p. 189 –190 gives a tragic account of Aury's sad and lonely end, staying in her room, not eating, surrounded by 'dozens of cats and dogs', in a squalor of 'filth' and 'dust' (la saleté, la poussière).

# V: The Novel in Focus

Having given a brief summary of the novel in the first chapter, it is now worth discussing *Story of O* and the accompanying preface 'Happiness in Slavery' in more detail.

## THE NOVEL

As published, the novel consists of four chapters:

**i) 'The Lovers of Roissy' ('Les Amants de Roissy')**: more of an atmosphere piece than a narrative, this chapter reads like an almost hallucinatory fantasy, a sense reinforced by the estranging device of two alternative beginnings, both of which describe O being taken by her lover René to the château of Roissy. Here O is subjected to the rituals of an arcane society of men, where women are entirely subordinated to the men's sexual demands. Bluntly informed 'You are here to serve your masters' (*O* p.15), O is penetrated in every orifice by seemingly everyone, and bound and whipped repeatedly (although not by René).

It is emphasised to her that this is not about sexual enjoyment – 'you have to get past the pleasure stage, until you reach the stage of tears' (10) – and René tells O that he will make demands beyond her capacity to consent – 'your submission will be obtained in spite of you' (33). The real purpose of all this is her 'enlightenment', to teach her she is not free, and is 'totally dedicated to something outside yourself' (17). This 'something' is René, whom she is to be trained to revere as a deity, receiving his spend in her mouth 'as a god is received' (19), and through being prostituted by him learns to treat other men 'as though they were so many reflections of him', 'thus he will possess her as a god possesses his creatures' (32).

Religious and devotional references and imagery abound: O kneels 'as nuns are wont to do' (10), and finds it 'sacrilege' whenever René does cunnilingus on her, as she feels it is she who should be kneeling (30). Her experience is explicitly sacrificial: 'if torture was the price she had to pay to keep her lover's love, then she only hoped he was pleased she had endured it' (27), but the heart of O's training is the transformative power of spiritual ecstasy expressed in erotic terms. Relentlessly violated by the men of the fraternity and the valets, she is utterly degraded, and relishes it, feeling herself 'literally to be the repository of impurity, the sink mentioned in the Scriptures' (44), but there is 'so much sweetness mingled with the terror in her ... her terror itself seemed so sweet' (23). The 'blessed darkness' and 'blessed chains that bore her away from herself' (47) 'freed her from herself' (39), and through penetration and punishment 'she lost herself in the delirious absence from herself which restored her to love and, perhaps, brought her to the edge of death' (39). The parts of her body being 'most constantly offended' become the most 'beautiful' and 'ennobled', and she feels she herself has been 'ennobled and gained in dignity through being prostituted', and is 'illuminated' by it all, attaining the 'serenity' one sees 'in the eyes of hermits' (44). Finally René comes to take her home, but before she leaves she is given an iron and gold ring to wear on her finger, the signet bearing a Celtic three-spoked sun-wheel (50), which identifies her as a woman initiate of Roissy, and available to any man who recognises its significance.

**ii) 'Sir Stephen'**: in this, the longest chapter, the novel widens its cast and performance space, and deepens its introspective rumination. O's life as a fashion photographer in Paris and the apartment she shares with René are depicted, and the references to O as devotee of her lover-as-deity continue: she kneels 'in the manner of Carmelites', and, being forced to keep her legs open, she feels an 'internal prostration, a sacred submission, as though a god, not he, had spoken' (57), for 'never had she felt herself so totally committed to a will which was not her own, more totally a slave, and more content to be so' (60).

Additional characters are introduced, notably O's glamorous, ambitious and egotistical fashion model Jacqueline, and the older 'Englishman' (a Scot in fact), Sir Stephen H., who explains that although he and René are not true relatives, 'in a way, we are brothers' (73). René takes O to meet Sir Stephen with the purpose of giving her to him. O's progressive subjection to Sir Stephen while René withdraws gradually into the background provides the main theme of the chapter.

A new flavour begins to pervade the chapter, that of homo-eroticism. O takes a growing interest in Jacqueline, and positions herself to seduce her, while it becomes evident that René's relationship with Sir Stephen is, on an emotional level, not merely fraternal – with the older man as alter-ego, love object and father figure, all of which we discuss below.

Much of the chapter concerns O's examination of her motivations and desires. Sir Stephen degrades and insults her: she feels 'vanquished, undone and humiliated' (80) by his penetration; he tells her 'you are easy', that she longs for all the men that desire her, that 'you love René but you desire me, amongst others' (86), and, slapping her face, tells her 'you'll obey me without loving me, and without my loving you' (88). Yet he always asks for her to consent to what he is going to do to her (122 etc.), and O realises quite early on that she wants him to love her (82).

Despite the growing power of Sir Stephen over her, O continues to worship René, considering herself 'fortunate to count enough in his eyes for him to derive pleasure from offending her, as believers give thanks to God for humbling them' (84). She realises her love for him has robbed her of her freedom, but she exults in this – 'She was no longer free? Yes!

Thank God she was no longer free', for that way she is 'lost in happiness' (94). But there is a down-side – if he is ever indifferent to her, she is plunged into despair, and this despair is linked to a sense of guilt – 'for she was guilty. Those who love God and by Him are abandoned in the dark of night, are guilty, because they have been abandoned'. René is punishing her for a sin that only she and Sir Stephen know, 'her wantonness' (95), a sin that is redeemed by being whipped and 'sanctified' by her prostitution (96, 108), allowing her to prove her love and thus bring her joy. She wonders if Stephen is right that 'she actually enjoyed her abasement?', but if so, 'the baser she was the more merciful was René to consent to make O the instrument of his pleasure' (96). O's Catholicism is emphasised as she recalls a sign she saw in Wales once: 'It is a fearful thing to fall into the hands of the living God!'. O does not subscribe to such Puritan sentiment, for her, the terror is in being cast out of those hands (96) and she concludes with the prayer, 'Oh let the miracle continue, let me still be touched by your grace. René don't leave me!' (97).

If O's love for René has stripped her of her freedom, it has also stripped her of her old powers to tempt and seduce (93), and she has more mixed feelings about this. Having been seduced as a teenager by an older female friend, Marion, O went on to have quite a predatory history of her own, although she has come to understand the relationship between sex and power, realising that 'what she took – or mistook – for desire was actually nothing more than the thirst for conquest' (94). This thirst she slaked in the past tempting both sexes, but predominantly women, 'courting' girls when she was at school (98), loving the freedom of the hunt and her control over seduction, taking active pleasure in seeing and touching [she won't be naked in front of women, and prefers caressing to being caressed] (99), delighting in the sight of women surrendering, recognising that a girl presenting her naked body is giving a gift (100) – a gift O will not give to other women. O is modest about her looks, seeing other women as more beautiful, but by seeing herself in a mirror she can see a 'kind of reflection of theirs' (100).

O can still assert over Jacqueline when René is there (98), but he is 'leaving her free, and ... she loathed her freedom', which is 'worse than any chains' (103). Yes, she could take Jacqueline at any point and pin her against the wall 'the way a butterfly is impaled', but she feels now more like a captive animal that serves the hunter, no longer a predator in her own right (103).

At the same time she recognises René's power is waning as he subordinates himself to Stephen, serving the older man's desires more than his own (104), even his own passion being a by-product of Stephen's interest in O (108), and O understands that the 'kind of equality' between herself and René 'eliminated in her any feeling of obedience, the awareness of her submission' (111). Submitting herself to Sir Stephen's 'habits and rites' (73), O realises she wants him to feel 'more than desire' for her (90), and comes to regard the wounds he inflicts as 'the mark of a god upon her' (109). She wants to use terms 'slave' and 'lord' (112), but she does not submit to Stephen in everything – she cannot masturbate when he commands her, fearing that she would earn his or René's disgust if she did so (87-88), and she resists his request to groom Jacqueline for Roissy (123).

**iii) 'Anne-Marie and the Rings' ('Anne-Marie et les Anneaux')**: changing gear again, this chapter has less interiority and more narrative drive, and introduces the theme of female worlds presided over by female power. Jacqueline inhabits a family circle of elderly Russian women, which is depicted as grubby and stultifyingly oppressive. O rescues Jacqueline by offering her a home in her own flat, where she finally gets round to seducing her, and starts to acclimatise herself to the idea that she can groom Jacqueline for Roissy – 'and what if she were to be reduced to what I have been reduced to, is that really so terrible?' (135).

O has meanwhile been serving Sir Stephen's demands (sometimes in front of his enigmatic Black house-keeper Norah), and is then introduced by him to Anne-Marie who presides over her own Sapphic domain, a 'totally feminine universe' (157), at Samois, in Fontainebleau forest, where O is to feel 'her condition as a woman' 'heightened and intensified' by exclusive contact with other women.

In contrast to the miserable matriarchy of Jacqueline's family, Samois is elegant and luxurious and sexual and excessive, and a place of further transformation. On arrival O is subjected by Anne-Marie to a sort of marriage service [1] where she is asked 'Do you consent, O, to bear the rings and monogram with which Sir Stephen desires that you be marked...?', to which she replies 'I do', and Sir Stephen kisses her, murmuring 'Are you mine, O, are you really mine?' (53). At Samois, young women are punished savagely at Anne-Marie's command, confirming O's belief that 'the female of the species was as cruel as, and more implacable than, the male' (156). O finds the suffering of other girls lovely, and comes to comprehend better her own attitude to torture – how she likes the idea of it, feels such pain when it is inflicted that she would do anything for it to stop, but afterwards feels happy it took place (156). Whipped and seduced by Anne-Marie, O is rendered 'more open, more profoundly enslaved, than she had ever thought was possible' (157), and is introduced to the 'terrible feeling of pleasure' in whipping another girl (162). Finally her labia are pierced to carry iron rings, and she is branded the property of Sir Stephen, and feels exalted by her mutilation, deriving 'a feeling of inordinate pride' (167) from her marks of possession.

Reunited with Sir Stephen, O enjoys assignations with him around Paris, enjoying being frequently mistaken for his niece or daughter (169), and he sets up a display of whips in her room that resembles the martyrdom of St Catherine or the

Crucifixion (171). Sir Stephen demonstrates his ownership of her by making her available to other men, and O gets him to punish her ferociously to scare off a young man who has fallen for her and wants to rescue her (173-74).

**iv) 'The Owl' ('La Chouette')**: in this, the shortest chapter, the narrative continues with emotional temperatures rising at a holiday villa in Cannes. O, proud of the rings in her vulva (178) and now completely devoted to Sir Stephen's will, makes love to Jacqueline for his voyeuristic pleasure. Meanwhile René has been falling helplessly in love with Jacqueline who makes herself sexually available to him but remains emotionally aloof. O realises she is not in love with Jacqueline but 'with girls in general', which is like 'loving her own image' (195), but Jacqueline's fifteen year-old sister Natalie is smitten with her and what she has heard of Roissy, and wants to replace Jacqueline as O's female lover. O tells her she is too young, which Natalie angrily disputes, but Sir Stephen resolves the issue by insisting Natalie must remain untouched until the autumn when, to the girl's delight, he promises she will be taken to Roissy and given to O there. Meanwhile O sees René weakened by his love for Jacqueline, and although no longer in love with him herself, and happy to be freed of that love (186), she is upset at Jacqueline's uncaring attitude to him, seeing her as callously stripping him of his strength and care-free ways and effectively enslaving him, and the two women have a violent row (190-191).

Sir Stephen then introduces O to the physically repulsive Commander ('Commandant'), whose grotesque size stimulates in her the conflicting desires to escape from and be taken by him. The story culminates with O, on a leash held by Natalie, being taken by Sir Stephen to a soirée at the Commander's where she is paraded naked, her face covered by an owl mask – appropriate for her sense of herself now, not so much a hunter in her own right but a bird of prey trained to bring her kills to her master – 'she was apt at hunting, a naturally trained bird of prey who would beat the game and always bring it back to the hunter' (196). The company are astonished by her sheer strangeness 'as though she were a real owl', (202); 'was she then of stone or wax, or rather some creature from another world...?' (203), and at dawn, when all the guests have gone, O is 'possessed' in turn by Sir Stephen and the Commander.

Post-script: The novel ends with an epilogue presenting an alternate ending, echoing the alternative beginnings in chapter one: 'There exists a second ending to the story of O, according to which O, seeing that Sir Stephen was about to leave her, said she would prefer to die. Sir Stephen gave her his consent.' [204]. Since the early 1960s, as we discussed in chapter II, French and licensed American editions have incorporated an additional sentence at the beginning of the epilogue: 'In a final chapter, which has been suppressed, O returned to Roissy, where she was abandoned by Sir Stephen'.

## COMMENTARY

***Story of O*: A Novel of Parts?** We discussed in chapter II the knotty question of whether *Return to the Château* really was a 'suppressed' chapter from *O*, published fifteen years later as a sequel. Here we address a different question – did the original novel, as published in 1954, in fact consist of two parts?

It was Maurice Nadeau, in his (rather critical) 1954 review, who first drew attention to a marked difference in quality between 'the first eighty pages' and the rest of the work [2] (see pp. 62, 67), with the first part commanding a higher status. This was a view Pauline Réage was to endorse. In 'A Girl' (1969), she spoke of the erotic fantasy she wrote in a state of inspired ecstasy to please her lover, and her subsequent development of the piece at his urging (pp. 11-14). In *O m'a dit* (1975) Régine Deforges made the point that 'Many people have said: "This book is in two parts"', to which Réage replied, 'People have good reason to think there are two parts,' going on to explain (twice) that the first sixty pages more or less wrote themselves – a spontaneous effusion of pent-up fantasies – while the rest was 'invented, thought through, constructed' [3] (we shall have more to say about these 'first sixty pages' in later chapters). Interviewed by St Jorre in 1994, Aury confirmed this and recounted how Paulhan urged her to write more. In St Jorre's words, 'after the explosive beginning, the writing slowed... not because she found it difficult but because she tried to give the story more of a structure' [4], a view Bedell (2004) shared: 'The erotic charge seems less intense... overall the novel loses energy [5]. It is the initial inspired piece of writing, the 'explosive beginning' that we find in 'The Lovers of Roissy'. The subsequent narrative, encompassing O's life in Paris, her job and apartment, Sir Stephen, Jacqueline, Anne-Marie and so on is a more consciously thought-out development of that text, although not without interest in its own right. This later elaboration may have involved contributions from others (as discussed in chapter II, pp. 71-72), but there is no compelling evidence for this.

Like everything else in this tale, details of the where and when of the writing are not crystal clear. In 'A Girl', Réage talks of beginning *O* in late spring one (unspecified) year, with the rest being written, at her lover's urging, through late summer on holiday by the sea, and into the autumn back in Paris (pp. 11-14). This is usually taken to be 1951, the year the manuscript was offered to Gallimard. However, there is correspondence between Aury and Édith Thomas dating to October 1950 where Aury referred to some apparently experimental writing that she describes as her 'strange enterprise', 'an astonishing exercise in style' of which she is 'terribly afraid', to which Thomas replied 'How much I would love to read your manuscript, my dear!' (something Aury did not permit)[6]. This might be taken as evidence that *O* was already underway, in the aftermath of Aury's essay on Mme de Merteuil in summer 1950 (see p. 138) [7]. Aury (as Réage) spoke to Deforges of her love for erotica and Gothic in her adolescence [8], and letters from Thierry Maulnier in summer 1938 refer to stories that Anne Desclos had been making up, of which he wanted to hear more [9]. It is perfectly possible that re-reading *Dangerous Liaisons* for her article on Merteuil inspired her to put pen to paper in 1950, and the description she gave of her writing in the October 1950 correspondence with Édith Thomas might suggest it was 'the first sixty pages' that came out of her then, the Roissy fantasy that she may well have felt too erotically intense to let Thomas see. If so, then it would be the later chapters she was writing in the summer and autumn of 1951, at her parents' house in Paris, then the family holiday home in Launoy (Seine en Marne) and/or Florence Gould's in Juan-le-Pins, and finally back in Paris [10].

How far 'The Lovers of Roissy' retains some distinctive identity, with the later chapters representing, to some degree, a change of tack, will be considered again later.

**Locations in *O*:** Roissy is of course the best known location in *O*, although it only features in chapter I, 'The Lovers of Roissy' (and of course in the 'sequel', *Return to the Château*). Today, the real geographical Roissy is under Charles de Gaulle airport, but Réage's own account plays down any real significance to the place, suggesting (in 'A Girl', p. 19) that she came across Roissy-en-France during a 'brief randonnée one spring', and it registered as 'scarcely more than a place-name on a map'. Randonnée has been translated as 'excursion' [11], but the implication is 'hike' or some other wandering off the beaten track, suggesting an experience from her younger years, probably in the company of Maulnier.

O lives on Île St-Louis, an island in the Seine. Once a rather bohemian location — Baudelaire lived there in the 1840s, and Zola placed his artist's studio there in *L'Oeuvre* (*The Masterpiece*, 1885) - by the 1950s it was on the up. O's apartment is under the eaves of an old house looking south on Quai de Béthune, from where she would be able to see

Nôtre Dame on Île de la Cité to her right, and where, if she was still there in the late 1960s, she would have been just up the road from President Pompidou's town house. Her studio is on Rue Royale which runs between Madeleine and Place de la Concorde: O is evidently a *very* fashionable fashion photographer. Sir Stephen lives in Rue de Poitiers, off Rue de l'Université, not far from what is now Musée d'Orsay – exactly where we would expect a man of his wealth and status to reside. The site of Anne-Marie's matriarchal version of Roissy is given as 'Samois' (i.e. Samois-sur-Seine) near Fontainebleau.

These locations provide a geographical structure for the *Story of O*, as O moves through her experiences. Although we do not hear about her apartment until after her adventures at Roissy, in terms of narrative chronology it predates Roissy in O's life, so we can if we wish trace her journey from her apartment, through Roissy, Sir Stephen's apartment and Samois to the climax in Cannes. How we read these way-stations will depend on how we interpret the arc of O's story. [Kaja Silverman 1984 sees the locations as a succession of Sadean enclosures through which O progresses on a journey of degradation, her body inscribed by punishments as she is broken down and reconstituted. In her apartment, her life is pain-free (René never punishes her), but unfocused and hedonistic; at Roissy she is subjected to a 'scopic regime' of make-up and mirrors and whip-marks upon her body, where she is rendered an object to be looked at and 'read' by male power, without the right to look back; at Sir Stephen's she is obliged to give her consent and co-operate in her treatment, as she is remade as a subject who actively submits to the desires of others, while confessing the wantonness of her own, thus legitimising her punishment; then at Samois she is made to express gratitude for her mutilation, as she is objectified into property and ultimately, at a final location near Cannes, into a dehumanised masked statue on her final trajectory to death [12]. Interesting though this account is, its exclusive focus on woman-as-victim marginalises both the agency of O as a character and Pauline Réage as author. It would be interesting to plot alternative accounts of O's voyage through these locations].

**The Characters: 'O':** In 'A Girl' (p. 16), Pauline Réage reported the fascination of 'the person for whom (she) was writing' that *Story of O* might have autobiographical resonances. Réage denied any clear reflection of herself in O – who was 'an idea, a figment, a sorrow, a negation of destiny' (p. 17) – but admitted other characters (and places) had some basis in her past. This hasn't stopped plenty of people from conflating O with her creator, including Pieyre de Mandiargues in his review, Régine Deforges and John de St Jorre in the titles of their interviews, Dorothy Kaufmann and others. In her 1975 interview with Deforges, Réage flatly denied that the novel reflected any personal experiences, especially of a sexual nature, admitting the extremities of her imaginings: 'the wildest love... the most frightful surrender... childish images of whips and chains...' but insisting they had no basis in actual experience – although she was willing to admit she liked physical danger, that risking her life pleased her, 'yes, very much so' [13] (a valuable quality for a member of the Resistance). Despite the richness of her imaginings, including telling herself she thought she 'had the vocation' for 'soliciting, prostitution' Réage insisted that 'everything happened in my head' [14].

This might not be strictly the case. Descriptions of lesbian sex are 'obviously strongly felt' [15], and there is correspondence here with Aury's own erotic life. And her affair with Thierry Maulnier seems to have left its mark [16]. We are not told O's age (except that she is about the same age as René, *O* p. 111), but she seems youngish – closer to the age Aury was when she was with Maulnier than with Paulhan [17]. The references to the parks and the taxi waiting for René and O in the opening page of 'The Lovers' are likely to be recollections of her time with Maulnier – public haunts and taxis were not so much part of her life with Paulhan, where all was clandestine and Aury had a car. Letters to Maulnier in the 1930s echo the language of *O*, making reference to the writer's suffering and sacrifice, and Maulnier's abandonment of her in 1942 is almost certainly the trauma that haunted Aury (and O) — compounded perhaps by the loss of the mysterious 'René' in 1933, and by the time of 'A Girl' in 1969, by a much greater abandonment — Paulhan's death. Moreover, Aury had encountered sexualised violence: from her husband Raymond d'Argila (whom she divorced for his brutality) and later from Arthur Koestler, a notorious aficionado of rocky-road sex, for whom female consent was of no import. Overall it is quite possible that O's 'adventures' may owe something to Aury's (to some degree therapeutic?) reimagining of some of her own experiences. None of this would justify one-to-one identification of O and Réage/ Aury, although points of similarity (and difference) are to be expected. It has been noted that 'Clearly, submission to higher authority held an enormous attraction for (her)' [18], and Aury admitted she liked obedience, schedules and orders [19], all of which feature strongly in the regime at Roissy. Moreover, O's 'manipulative, playful and ruthless' [20] seduction of women resonates with her author (although her vanity 'to the point of narcissism' [21] rather less so).

Other sources for O have been cited. In 1994 Aury claimed that O was initially named Odile, a name taken from 'one of the North African group that came to Paris after the Liberation, and was very much in love with Albert Camus at one time... We worked together and she later married a Royal Air Force pilot and went to England. She knew all about the name and was enchanted. But after a few pages I decided I just couldn't do all those things to poor Odile, so I just kept the first letter' [22] [Odile has subsequently been identified as Aury's friend Odile de Lalain [23], and evidently one of the women who knew about O]. It has been suggested that O may owe something to Jeanne Aeply, a victim of Jean Fautrier's violence who 'delights in feeling physical pain' [24], although his brutal abusiveness to her bore no relation to the aesthetically-poised ritual cruelties of the Roissy brotherhood and Sir Stephen. More convincing is the influence of Colette Peignot, the 'saint of the abyss' in Georges Bataille's secret society Acéphale in the 1930s [25]. Réage may well have drawn on Colette for O's character, and used her name for one of Anne-Marie's girls at Samois. We shall discuss Colette Peignot's significance to O further in chapter IX.

**René and Jacqueline**: Bearing in mind that 'O's story is a work of the imagination brought into being by a woman who circulates, as creator, through all her characters' [26], it is nevertheless fair to ask how far other characters have origins in people Aury knew, and in 'A Girl' (pp. 17-19) Réage gave an account of some of these.

René 'was the remembrance, no, the vestige of an adolescent love, rather the hope of a love that never happened'. Anne Desclos' school-friend Jacqueline had loved him, 'And before she loved him, she had loved me. She had in fact been responsible for being the first to break my heart.' As fifteen-year-olds, Jacqueline had developed a crush on Anne, which was not reciprocated until it was too late, and Anne found she had lost them both. Later correspondence between Anne Desclos and Maulnier confirms the existence of René and Jacqueline, and some kind of romantic tangle between them and Anne, which ended with René and Jacqueline running off together (see p. 85). The correspondence however places this in September 1933, ten years or so after the date suggested in 'A Girl'. This might contradict 'A Girl', or might suggest Jacqueline and René were indeed people from Anne's teens with whom she stayed in touch, and with whom amorous relations remained complicated. Whatever the case, René still managed to be around the following year for the mysterious 'ceremony' in the Louvre [27].

In 'A Girl', Aury maintained the 'Jacqueline' in the novel only owed her appearance and hair to the real Jacqueline of her teens, while the character owed more to a chic, pampered and 'overbearing' actress Réage had lunched with once. This was very likely Marcelle Tassencourt, the actress for whom Maulnier abandoned Aury, whom Aury referred to in a 1941 letter as having seen her one time in all her finery [28]. This seems to receive support in the Deforges interview where Réage talked of a girl she 'had dealings with once' who 'took my place in the heart of a boy I loved', and who was 'an extraordinary beauty' who 'knew how to dress' (in contrast to Réage who described herself as poor and dowdy, although consoled by the idea that she 'worried' her rival), and of whom there was 'an echo... in *Histoire d'O*' [29] — presumably another reference to Marcelle Tassencourt in the guise of Jacqueline. This suggests Réage was playing a doubling-up game: conflating the 'real' Jacqueline with Marcelle into the character of Jacqueline in *O*, and the 'real' René and Maulnier into the character of René. If so, then the possibility arises that Réage was trying to reassure herself that Maulnier had only abandoned her because he had become the dupe of a seductive vamp – although she still wanted to symbolically punish him by making René suffer from Jacqueline's cold heartedness (a fate she liked to imagine for Maulnier from Marcelle?). Imaginary score-settling was certainly on the menu. In 'A Girl' (p. 18), Réage reported concerning Jacqueline, 'And I took my revenge by shipping her off to Roissy'. In fact this fate is not at all clear from the novels as we have them — the last we see of Jacqueline in *O* is at dinner in Cannes with O, Sir Stephen, Natalie and René, (*O* p. 198), and on the first page of *Return* it is 'intimated' that René will take her there (*Return* p. 25), but we hear no more about her. The significance of this is that it might be a further hint that *Return* is not the 'real' follow-up to *O*, and it is in the true sequel (that has not come to light), that Jacqueline goes to Roissy. The presence of Jacqueline's younger sister Natalie raises the possibility of further identifications – one sister seduced by O but ultimately rebellious and fractious with her, the other eager to submit to Roissy and both promised to and devoted to O – being extensions of the same person as well.

To add to the complexity of 'René', Réage considered how far he was based on her: 'Is René what I might have become if I had been a man? Devoted to another, to the point of yielding everything to him, without ever finding it anachronistic, this vassal-to-lord relationship? I'm afraid the answer is yes.' For that matter, we might want to consider how far Jacqueline in *O* is an 'extension of O herself', with a trajectory from (some degree of) liberty to entrapment by O [30]. The pile-up of possible identifications is almost endless.

**Sir Stephen**: In 'A Girl' (p. 18), Réage said Sir Stephen owed something to a man her 'current lover', a man 'under thirty', had pointed out to her in a bar near the Champs Elysées one time: 'Fifty years old probably, an Englishman certainly', he was 'half-seated on a stool at the mahogany bar, silent, self-composed with that air of some gray-eyed prince that fascinates both men and women,' her lover 'pointed him out to me and said "I don't understand why women don't prefer men like him to boys under thirty."' This encounter provided a 'silent, unilateral rapport between him and my companion, between him and me' which 'reappeared out of the blue ten years later' in her story. Ten years before the writing of *O* would be 1940/41 when seeing an Englishman relaxing in a Parisian bar would have been a little surprising, but we can safely assume the 'current lover' referred to was Maulnier and he turned thirty in late 1939, so we can allow Réage a little leeway here with her dating. The claim that the 'silent, unilateral rapport' between the three of them was revisited in Aury's novel hints strongly that just as Sir Stephen owed something to the mysterious Englishman, so O was indeed to an extent an echo of Aury/Desclos, and that René was to a degree a fictional incarnation of Maulnier.

Sir Stephen must certainly owe something to Paulhan as well, and again the O-as-Aury connection is strengthened by both Paulhan and Aury recognising the novel as a 'love-letter' from her to him [31]. It also seems highly likely that the joyous account in *O* (pp.168-9) of Sir Stephen and O together wandering the streets of the Latin Quarter is an idealised fantasy version of her own experience with Paulhan, who lived in Rue des Arènes with his wife, making such outings unlikely in reality. The sleazy hotel they adjourn to (*O* p.169) is perhaps a more accurate depiction of their secret trysts.

**Sir Stephen and René:** The relationship between René and Sir Stephen has attracted considerable discussion. They are described as 'in a way... brothers' (*O* p. 73) – another sibling pair echoing Jacqueline and Natalie. Commentators usually interpret their relationship as 'step-brothers' or 'half-brothers' [32], but neither of these terms is quite accurate. Stephen explains to O that he was the son of his father's first wife, but his father then remarried and it was the second wife who raised Stephen as a boy. This woman later divorced Stephen's father and re-married, and from this new union René was born (*O* pp. 72-73). We are not told at what point Stephen and René actually met. They may perhaps be best described as *frères de lait* ('milk-brothers').

There are however several more layers to their relationship. On one level they can be seen as extensions or different aspects of the same man – Sir Stephen as René's more dominant alter-ego. O is told Sir Stephen is 'another form of your lover: you will still have only one master' (*O* p. 73), creating a trajectory where the gentler younger avatar, René, surrenders O to the older one, Sir Stephen, 'the stern master he himself was unable to be' (*O* p. 105). If there is a reference to Aury's real life here, perhaps she was dressing the wound she received from René/Maulnier, with their loss being Paulhan's gain. If René is a stepping-stone to Sir Stephen, then the next step would seem to be the Commander – taking O from romantic lover to dominating master to a massive figure who inspires in her both fear and the desire to be crushed (*O*, p. 194) [33].

There is in addition a pronounced homo-erotic dimension to the men's relationship. O realises that Stephen is a love object for René, and the sexual subtext of that love is made quite explicit. O notes that René loves Stephen 'in that passionate way boys love their elders' (*O*, p. 90), and that 'if Sir Stephen had liked boys... O did not doubt that René, who was not so inclined, still would have readily granted to Sir Stephen both the slightest and most demanding of his requests. But Sir Stephen only liked women', going on to recognise that 'through the medium of her body, shared between them, they attained something more mysterious and perhaps more acute, something more intense than an amorous communion...' (*O*, p. 105). Though avowing the heterosexuality of both men, O certainly considers the possibility of bisexuality in them — after all, Stephen only uses her orally and anally —'as he would have a boy' (*O*, p. 168). Questioned by Deforges: 'In René's and Sir Stephen's case do you see a homosexual relationship?', Réage replied, 'Yes, not effective, but real,' agreeing that 'René is submissive to Sir Stephen' and explaining it in terms of 'Anglo-Saxon "hero-worship", which dictates one always admires the older man.' [34]

Furthermore, several commentators have detected oedipal dynamics between the two men as well, noting René's father-fixation for Sir Stephen [35], despite there being only ten years between them (*O* p. 73), and pointing out that *O* illustrates Freud's oedipal theory that the essence of male domination is competition between men with woman as the prize [36]. Aury rejected this, explaining to Deforges that the 'hero-worship' she saw between René and Sir Stephen was 'no father-son relationship at all, it's older-younger brothers, war comradeship, almost a military relationship' [37].

**Réage/ Aury, Sir Stephen and René**: Aury may have denied anything oedipal between Sir Stephen and René, but readily admitted oedipal dynamics between Sir Stephen and O, extrapolating to Deforges on women's desire for older men, like the Englishman in the Paris bar. Sir Stephen 'links to a desire for one's father. He is a father figure', that 'one always looks for a father', and in the novel O delights in being mistaken for Sir Stephen's niece or daughter when out with him (*O*, p. 169). This is consistent with Aury working through her feelings towards an adoration for her literature- and woman-loving father, Auguste (and distance from her cold fish of a mother), and her love for Paulhan as a quasi-oedipal passion (see pp. 102, 131). Responding to Deforges' question: 'So, one has practically always sought to make love to one's father?' Aury replied 'Ah yes, surely, and at the same time without doing it,' going on, at Deforges' prompting, to admit the attractions of the idea of incest, and how much she loved and admired her father, who kissed her and held her in his arms, acknowledging 'some sensuality' between them, for he was 'a man who adored women, who was with women very kind and generous... He was marvellous' [38]. Sir Stephen's nationality is interesting here – his 'Englishness' has no resonance with Paulhan, but does with Auguste, who was raised in London (see p. 81), and perhaps with Maulnier, who studied there.

Aury's hint that René can also be read as an avatar of herself throws another light on interpretations of the René/ Sir Stephen relationship, and generates even more complex interplay all round. O and René do indeed parallel one another, both being 'feminised' in Sir Stephen's presence, both progressively giving up agency and even identity as the story progresses – the novel is explicit about their 'equality' (111). This would make them in effect siblings, but the symbolic family configuration also has resemblance to the parenting of O by Sir Stephen as father-figure, and René as his 'wife' – a nurturing mother-figure to O [39], but characterised by 'discursive impotence', unable to direct the meaning and development of the narrative [40], more willing to suffer than to hurt. This reinforces the homoerotic undercurrent between him and Sir Stephen, and also reinforces the identification between René and O, and greatly increases the scope for 'queer' readings, as the lesbian predation described in O's history, her seduction of Jacqueline (and implied future seduction of Natalie), meet an echo in the homoerotic dynamic of René and Sir Stephen, with Aury herself, in reality bisexual, manifesting as both male and female characters in 'queer' relationships in her fiction.

The fact that Paulhan had been made a Commandeur of the Légion d'Honneur in 1949 suggests that the Commander in 'The Owl' can also be read as an avatar of Paulhan. While this might throw a softer light on the final page where O is taken sexually by both the Commandant and Sir Stephen, 'one after the other' (*O* p. 203), the emphasis on the Commandant's grotesque physical appearance – 'an enormous man, a giant of a creature... his head shaved and his vast belly swelling beneath his open shirt..' (*O* p. 192) – raises some intriguing questions of its own. Either some ambiguity towards Paulhan, some vestige of hostility from Aury's earlier relationship with Auguste, or an indulgence of an erotic excitement to be found in the disgusting, which takes us into the realms of Sade, George Bataille and Salvador Dalí, for whom disgust is a reaction to what we most desire, as we shall discuss in chapter IX.

**Anne-Marie**: 'Anne-Marie, I don't know at all,' Aury claimed ('A Girl' p. 19), although she then went on to say 'One of my woman friends (whom I respect, and I am slow to respect) might well be Anne-Marie were it not for the fact that she is the epitome of purity and honor', suggesting that the character's 'rigor and her resolve, her free and easy manner, and straightforward unequivocal way in which she exercised her profession' might indeed come from this friend. Later she was to confirm to Dorothy Kaufmann what the latter was already starting to suspect, that her account of Anne-Marie in *O* was 'alluding to Édith Thomas'[41].

Kaufmann suggested there are references to Thomas in *O*. Anne-Marie's apartment is located in the same area as Thomas', near the Observatoire, and there seems to be a reciprocal game of homage going on in the women's novels. In Thomas' *Études de femmes* (1945), one of the three main female characters is 'Dominique' (which we may take as a nod to Aury), the other two are 'Claire' and 'Yvonne'. In *O*, Anne-Marie has three young women staying with her at Samois, 'Colette' (who may be named for Acéphale's 'saint of the abyss'? see p. 334), and 'Claire' and 'Yvonne', One suspects Aury is returning the compliment [42].

The triangular relationship of O, Anne-Marie and Sir Stephen echoes Aury, Édith and Paulhan, with Anne-Marie/Édith loving O/Aury but playing a supporting role to the bond between Sir Stephen/Paulhan and the protagonist. But the Édith/Anne-Marie association becomes perplexing with the character's compliance with a male-dominated world [43], and her role in punishing and mutilating women. One possible reading is that Anne-Marie (named for St Anne and her daughter, the Virgin Mary) runs what is effectively a convent where women are prepared for the masters, but learn complicity with one another's submission in a Sapphic sorority where they experience exaltation in suffering, erotic delight, love and tenderness with their sisters [44]. However we read it, this triangle in *O* must have taken on the hues of a lost world by the time it was published, with the breakdown in relations between Thomas and Paulhan.

In the actual writing of *O*, Aury always described her motives in terms of her relationship with Paulhan, playing Scheherezade to keep his interest, but it may also have been a move in her relationship with Thomas. Telling Thomas in late 1950 about her 'strange enterprise', yet refusing to let her see the manuscript (see p. 159) would have piqued Thomas' jealousy over Aury's intimacy with Paulhan, and was perhaps a message to a still overly-attached Édith that Aury had an intimacy with Paulhan from which she was excluded. And perhaps this blew up in everyone's face when Thomas was incensed enough by Paulhan's 'Letter to the Leaders of the

Resistance' (while *O* was being mooted for publication) to help the CNE hit back against him, which ruptured relations between them altogether (see pp. 139-140). When *O* came out, Thomas was apparently 'horrified, scandalised' by it [45], to an extent which seems to have surprised Aury, who doubtless knew that Thomas shared her own 'dark fantasy of self immolation' [46] (as we shall discuss in chapter VII), and she could only, rather lamely reply, 'But I know you like Fénelon'. The question arises whether Aury actually expected Thomas to take a more positive view of *O*, even to accept it as a text of mystical love (as Paulhan and the surrealists did), or was she deliberately shocking her to precipitate some degree of a crisis, to put the brakes on Édith's emotional entanglement with her? Aury's emphasis on how hard she worked to keep her friendship with Thomas from fading, and to protect her from 'her pain and anguish' [47] (see p. 131) might be taken as a sign of guilt. Not just over leaving Édith for Paulhan in 1947, but perhaps also for the crisis in the relationship in 1952, which may have owed as much to Aury's doings as to Paulhan's politics. The complete split between Thomas and Paulhan may have been more than Aury bargained for, but it would appear that she managed the matter quite effectively, keeping both Paulhan's love and Thomas' friendship, and even finally reconciling them in 1967.

**Titles and Names: The Author:** Another question that invites consideration is why 'Pauline Réage'? In 'A Girl' Réage explained that 'Pauline' was borrowed from 'two famous profligates, Pauline Borghese and Pauline Roland' (p.11) – the former being a spirited and independently-minded sister to Napoleon, the other a 19th century French socialist and feminist – the implication being that Pauline Réage combined qualities from both women. Édith Thomas greatly admired Roland, and was working on a biography of her as Aury wrote *O* [48], and Kaufmann (1998) sees in Aury's adoption of the name 'Pauline' a 'hidden tribute' to Thomas. Other possibilities have been mooted, however. 'Pauline' may carry the meaning 'pertaining to St Paul', whose epistles in the New Testament repeatedly assert that it is God's will that woman accept her subordination to man [49], a doctrine Réage might be signalling she accepts [50], or is rebelling against [51].

In 'A Girl' (p. 11) Aury claimed 'Réage' was from a place she found in a real estate register, apparently from the area where her father had once owned a house [52]. Again, other theories have been proposed: perhaps there is an echo of réagir – to 'react', maybe reacting to St Paul (positively or negatively, depending on how one wishes to interpret Aury's values), or even suggesting 'reactionary', as in repudiating progressive politics, liberty and democracy [53] (which may gain credence from Aury's links with right-wing nationalists in the 1930s, although by 1950 she had long since left those circles). Anagrammatic games with Paulhan's name have also been suggested (see p. 35) which Aury flatly denied [54].

**The Novel's Title:** *Histoire d'O* was preceded by literary texts featuring a female character named 'O' in the title — Kleist's *Marquise von O* (1808), and Nabokov's *Mademoiselle O* (1936) — and Aury was probably aware of them, but this doesn't seem to be a particularly revealing observation. It is more interesting and fruitful to look into the wording of the title. *Histoire* has multiple layers of possible meaning. When presented with the definite article (*l'histoire*) it translates as 'story' or 'history' so *L'Histoire d'O* (an erroneous title used by a surprising number of commentators [55]), would translate clearly as *The Story of O*. But the actual title does not use the definite article, and without it the word *histoire* becomes highly elastic. It can imply 'just a little story', 'nothing but a story' or 'just one of those stories' [56], but it can also carry other connotations, including 'business' (as in *c'est une drôle d'histoire* = it's a funny business), or 'fib', or 'fuss' (as in *faire toute une histoire* = cause a lot of fuss); it can refer to a relationship or to a dispute in a relationship, or can indicate whimsicality (*histoire de rire* = just for a laugh) [57]. The meaning of *d'O* is also highly versatile, encompassing 'of O', 'about O' etc. The possible permutations of the title in translation are considerable: it can certainly be *Story of O*, or *Something about O*, but it can also translate as *O's Business*, *Fibs* or *Fuss About O* and so on. Take your pick.

**The Protagonist's Name:** Great play has been made of the significance of 'O' as a name. Some commentators emphasise it as an anonymity, the zero that stands for no individual identity, indicating anyone, with *Histoire d'O* as the history of every woman [58]. Others wax lyrical with symbolic metaphors (some more ineffable than intelligible). It has been seen variously as a shorthand for the essence of woman, referencing a nothing [59]; an impersonality (like 'K' in Kafka's *The Trial*), an object, a sexual symbol, a zero, 'the complete form, the circle that encloses the world... the vanishing point, back to the womb... – death' [60];  as the initial letter of open, ouvert, orifice [61]; or referencing anonymity, the omphalos (navel), the Caballist O representing the alchemical oeuvre (the sphere, the earthly orbit, the female principle, the full moon), Obedience and Orifices that she no longer owns but which must be Open to the phallic deity [62]. Links with the 'female sexual function' have been made [63], some, like Andrea Dworkin (1974), insisting on a literal, reductionist view of 'O' as the brutal representation of the hole between the character's legs, all that there is to define her, all that she is in this novel [64].

Aury herself rejected symbolic readings of *O*, insisting it was merely the surviving initial of the character's original name Odile, taking a particularly strong stance against those who would identify it crudely with the female sex organ — 'it has nothing to do with erotic symbolism or the shape of the female sex' [65]. She named her protagonist O 'to ensure anonymity, to emphasise the private fantasy world, not to symbolise the shape of the female sex or issue any universal feminist message' [66].

As is often the case with Aury, there is scope for taking her claims with a pinch of salt, as the idea that 'O' connotes 'nothingness' pervades the novel and remains persuasive. In Shakespeare 'nothing' was, among other things, a common euphemism for the vagina ('no-thing'). Perhaps the best example of this being the title of his comedy *Much Ado About Nothing* (c. 1598), a title that would itself be a perfectly legitimate, even highly apposite, translation of *Histoire d'O*. Aury, an accomplished literary professional fluent in English (and daughter of a lecturer in English literature), would most certainly have known this – which would make her description to St Jorre of the fuss over the scandal of *Story of O* as 'much ado about nothing' [67] a wry literary joke rather than a mere turn of phrase.

In Shakespearean usage, the letter 'O' was freighted with significance, referring to the stage itself — the 'wooden O' in the prologue to *Henry V* (where incidentally the walls of the theatre are referred to as a 'girdle'), and since 'all the world's a stage' (*As You Like It,* II, 7), by extension the Earth itself, an identification reinforced by the name of Shakespeare's theatre, 'The Globe' [68].

**Paulhan's Preface – 'Happiness in Slavery' ('Le Bonheur dans l'escalavages'):**
*Story of O*, on its publication in 1954, was accompanied by Jean Paulhan's essay 'Happiness in Slavery' which has generated controversy and exerted considerable influence in its own right. Part review, part philosophical exercise (of varying degrees of comprehensibility), it has set the scene for much subsequent criticism and commentary of the novel, and has left a complex legacy.

It is divided into an introduction, three substantive parts, and a conclusion.

**'A Revolt in Barbados' ('Une révolte à la Barbade'):**
Wrong-footing his readers from the outset, Paulhan begins

with an account of an alleged incident in Barbados in 1838 when recently freed ex-slaves presented their palindromic ex-master, Glenelg, with a notebook of grievances about freedom, and demanded to be taken back into slavery, with a grisly outcome for Glenelg and his family when he refused [69].

From here Paulhan launches a broadside against freedom as a source of conflict and oppression, alleging 'the only freedoms that we really appreciate are those which cast other people into... (a)... state of servitude' (xxii) and the 'all-consuming passion for freedom... never fails to lead to conflicts and wars that are no less consuming' – and never-ending, as 'the slave, according to... one dialectic, is in turn destined to become the master', and so it goes on. In contrast with the violence of the demand for freedom, Paulhan extols the bliss of 'the surrender of oneself to the will of others (as often happens with lovers and mystics),' and ridding oneself of 'selfish pleasures, interests and personal complexes,' a sacrifice which is 'in no wise a joyless act, nor one lacking in grandeur.'

The 1838 book of grievances, being 'an apologia for slavery', would be seen as 'heretical' today, when 'it would be considered a dangerous book' (xxii), but with *O* we have to deal with 'another kind of dangerous book. To be more specific: with an erotic book' (xxiii).

**I – 'Decisive as a Letter' ('Décisif comme une lettre'):** What makes *O* dangerous for readers is that it changes, even 'marks' them (the word used in *O* for the protagonist's whippings and mutilations), but the danger it poses to reviewers is to trip them up. Such novels take time to understand, making first reviews look 'a bit simple-minded', but Paulhan is game and willing to engage, even though he claims he doesn't know 'what to make of it, or what it all means', advancing 'through *O* with a strange feeling, as though I am moving through a fairy tale,' which are, he acknowledges, 'the erotic novels of children' (xxiii).

Taking the plunge, he asserts that, along with the danger,

the novel has two other salient features: one is 'decency' – 'if there is one word that comes to mind when I think of *O*, that word is decency' (xxiv), a word he cannot and will not try to justify; the other is the 'indefinable, always pure and violent spirit, endless and unadulterated' that blows through its pages, a 'decisive' spirit, unperturbed by 'moans or horrors, ecstasy or nausea'.

Ordinarily he prefers reticence in a writer, but has to acknowledge that *O* 'is managed like some brilliant feat' – 'a speech... a letter rather than a secret diary', although the mystery of who is writing, and why, remain. 'But to whom is the letter addressed? Whom is the speech trying to convince? Whom can I ask?' before declaring (quite disingenuously) 'I don't even know who you are.' (xxiv)

He is however willing to affirm 'that you are a woman I have little doubt,' citing as evidence the author's attention to details of dress, and that O, on 'the day when René abandons her to even more torments... still manages to have enough presence of mind to notice her lover's slippers are frayed and notes she will have to buy him another pair' (xxiv-xxv). In Paulhan's view, 'this is something a man would never have thought of, or at least would never have dared express.'

But there is more to O than this 'feminine' sensibility, she has a heroism to her, she is a figure who 'in her own way... expresses a virile ideal. Virile, or at least masculine,' and (in without doubt the most controversial and provocative passage of his essay) Paulhan eulogises this heroism (in both author and O conflated) in the willingness to reveal the 'truth' about women. 'At last a woman who admits it! Who admits what? Something that women have always refused till now to admit (and today more than ever before). Something that men have always reproached them with: that they never cease obeying their nature, the call of their blood, that everything in them, even their minds, is sex. That they have constantly to be nourished, constantly washed and made up, constantly beaten.

That all they need is a good master, one that is not too lax or kind: for the moment we show any kind of tenderness they draw upon it, turning all the zest, joy and character at their command to make others love them. In short, that we must, when we go to see them, take a whip along.'

He goes on, 'Rare is the man who has not dreamed of possessing Justine. But so far as I know, no woman has ever dreamed of being Justine. I mean, dreamed aloud, with this same pride at being grieved and in tears, with this consuming violence, with this voracious capacity for suffering, and this amazing will, stretched to the breaking point, and even beyond. Woman you may be, but descended from a knight or a crusader. As though yours was a dual personality, or the person for whom your letter was intended was so constantly present that you borrowed his taste, and his voice. But what kind of woman, and who are you?' (xxv) – Is the author a dreamer, who listens to her heart, or a woman of the world 'who knows whereof she speaks' (xxvi)?

As for the inconclusive ending to the novel, Paulhan is puzzled, even anxious, that a story that began with such 'sobriety, in a climate of asceticism and chastisement' 'should turn out so badly', with O remaining in the 'brothel to which she was led by love', and coming to like it (xxvi)...

**II – 'A Ruthless Decency' ('Une décence impitoyable')**: ... but he cannot accept that the ending in the post-script where O asks Sir Stephen to consent to her death is 'the real end'... No, the author is leaving room for a sequel...

Erotic books are dangerous, 'yet what if the role of the erotic (or of dangerous books if you prefer) was to inform and instruct us?' (xxvii). Having earlier refused to explain or justify his use of the term 'decency' (xxiv), he now goes on to do just that, describing 'decency' as a female quality in erotic literature, but having less to do with propriety than with a searing honesty that exposes the body in all its abjectness – 'A decency into whose hands it is dangerous to fall. For, to satisfy it, nothing less than the hands tied behind the back will do, than the knees spread apart and the bodies spread-eagled, than sweat and tears.' (xxviii)

This decency, honesty, eroticism and danger takes us into the realm of terror. 'I seem to be saying frightful things. Perhaps I am, but in that case terror is our daily bread – and perhaps dangerous books are those which restore us to our natural state of danger.' For love and its declarations, to commit to another for life, if we really weigh them up and attend to them, are terrifying. 'And what mistress, if she were to measure for a moment the meaning of her words: "Before I met you I never loved anyone else... I have never experienced real emotion before I knew you?" would not be equally terror stricken at the words slipping past her lips?  Or these, more sagacious – sagacious? –: "I should like to punish myself for having been happy before I met you!" There she is, trapped by her own words. There she is, so to speak, getting what she asked for.'

It is O's needs and desires that drive the narrative, René and Sir Stephen merely service her. There are plenty of tortures in *O*, 'Almost as many tortures as there are prayers in the lives of ascetics in the desert,' but they are not 'inflicted joyfully' – 'René refuses to inflict any, and although Sir Stephen consents to them, it is as though he is performing a duty. So far as we can tell, they do not enjoy themselves. There is nothing sadistic about them. It all happens as though it was O alone who, from the outset, demanded to be chastised...' (xxviii)

But if the men are not sadists, neither is O a mere masochist, and Paulhan launches into a lengthy repudiation of 'masochism' as a way of understanding O – dismissing the word as a mere semantic trick that may or may not have any meaning at all, but which certainly does not explain O. But after emphatically rejecting the idea that O is motivated by anything so mundane as sexual pleasure, he goes on, 'All we have to do now is to listen to her' (xxx)...

**III – 'Strange Love Letter' ('Curieuse lettre d'amour'): ...**

and here he climbs into the driving seat with 'Réage' to fanta-sise about the secret message of O to her lover, hearing her voice talking of 'the fiery wellsprings of the blood'. Needing more than the mere happiness her lover brings, she demands that he become her god, and a cruel one at that. Yes, he makes her 'healthy and happy and a thousand times more alive', but she needs more, to be kept in a cage and half starved. 'Anything that brings me closer to illness and the edge of death makes me more faithful. It is only when you make me suffer that I feel safe and secure. You should never have agreed to be a god for me if you were afraid of assuming the duties of a god, and we all know they are not as tender as all that. You have already seen me cry, now you must learn to relish my tears... It is all too true that when you come to call on us, you should bring a whip along', even a cat o'nine tails (xxx).

Paulhan continues ventriloquising the author's voice – 'What constantly betrays you is my imagination, my vague dreams', urging her lover to 'rid' her, 'deliver' her from them, so she won't even be able 'to dream of being unfaithful'. 'But first make sure you brand me with your mark' – the riding crop, or chain, or rings through her labia, to 'let the whole world know I am yours,' for 'as long as I am beaten and ravished on your behalf, I am nought but the thought of you, the desire of you, the obsession of you. That, I believe, is what you wanted. Well, I love you, and that is what I want too.'

For only when she ceases to be her own mistress, when her body is no longer her own, then she becomes 'a creature from another world', and when she has lost all knowledge of herself, then the caresses of other men, her lover's 'envoys', whom she cannot tell apart from each other, will mean nothing – [which reassures Paulhan, for whom 'what bothered (him) for a long time was the prostitution' (xxxi)] – and Paulhan goes on to consider whether myths and folksongs have truth when they talk of sacred prostitution and dying for love? – concluding with the oft-quoted line, 'Without any doubt, *Story of O* is the most ardent love letter any man has ever received' (xxxii).

Paulhan now takes aim against the fashionable trend of the time for free love and casual relationships. Transient affairs are not wrong in themselves, but they are not love, for real love is not free. 'Love implies dependence – not only in its pleasure but in its very existence and what precedes its existence: in our very desire to exist...' (xxxiii) – dependence on the lover's body, mind and soul. 'As for freedom... any man or any woman who has been through that experience will rather be inclined to rant and rave against freedom, in the vilest, most horrible language possible.' He concludes, 'No, there is no dearth of abominations in *Story of O*. But it sometimes seems to me that it is an idea, or a complex of ideas, an opinion rather than a young woman that we see subjected to these tortures.' (xxxiii)

**'The Truth About the Revolt'** (**'La vérité sur la révolte'**): Paulhan now takes a detour to discuss in general terms how the nature and expression of power has shifted. Once there were tyrannies and direct cruelties (of parents over children, husband over wife, teacher over pupil, slavery and public execution), now these have been replaced by the indifference of bureaucracy and mechanised war – 'The only tortures we inflict today are anonymous and therefore undeserved ones' (xxxiv). In Paulhan's view, there is in cruelty 'a mysterious equilibrium of violence for which we have lost all taste, and even our understanding of the term,' and revels he is 'not displeased that it is a woman who has found them again,' indeed, he is 'not even surprised.'

He confesses he finds women 'marvellous', attributing to them an enviable connection with the state of childhood, and a mysterious understanding of sewing, cooking, interior decorating, animals, and 'those half-mad creatures we allow among us – children'. For Paulhan, women do not suffer from much individuality – 'it would appear that to each woman is given the capacity to be all women... at once,' and whereas men accept each other as they are, 'there is not a woman alive who isn't interested in changing the man she loves, and at the same time changing themselves' (xxxv).

Coming full circle, Paulhan finds the truth is 'that Glenelg's slaves were in love with their master, that they could not bear to be without him', and it is this 'same truth which, after all, lends *Story of O* its resolute quality, its incredible decency, and that strong, fanatic wind that never ceases to blow.' (xxxvi)

## COMMENTARY

Paulhan's essay is a very strange mix. It demonstrates his erudition, directly referencing Sade's *Justine* (1791), Hegel's 'master-slave dialectic' [70], and Nietzsche's aphorism 'Are you approaching women? Do not forget your whip!' [71], while anticipating Michel Foucault's views on the changing face of power from the directly physical to the 'knowledge-power' of bureaucracy [72]. It is also an opinion piece, giving Paulhan a free hand to lay into some of the philosophies most influential at the time – notably the Existentialist cult of freedom which gets a good bashing twice, but he also takes a (completely hypocritical) swipe at the 'free love' that flourished in the Liberation years (and deployed existentialist freedom as an alibi), and at psychoanalysis with its indulgence of 'personal complexes'.

In addition, Paulhan uses his essay to stir a few things up. For a start his cryptic comments on the ending (xxvi) started the hare of 'suppressed' chapter/ sequel running (as discussed in chapter II). Moreover his preface is a vehicle for some outright provocation. He makes dubious if not down-right bizarre assertions about colonial slavery and the love slaves supposedly felt for their masters, and allows himself some broad and Rousseauan generalisations about the differences between the sexes and the nature of women. In particular, he claims *O* as a confession of the fundamental desires of women, which can only be described as masochistic, arising from their obsession with their sex, a confession that can be taken as eternally true of their very nature [73]. [Talk of fundamental differences between the sexes has never rested easily with Anglophone feminism (although some discourses make such differences implicitly), but has had more of a cachet in French circles, where 'differénce' feminism has flourished, notably among those writers associated with Psych et Po since the 1970s, whom we shall discuss in chapter X].

Although Paulhan's account of femininity comes over as outlandishly misogynistic, with his claims that women need to be 'nourished, constantly washed and made up, constantly beaten' (xxv) and so on, one wonders exactly how serious he is in all this. For example, when he cites as 'evidence' for female authorship that only a woman could possibly have thought of depicting O, faced with another round of whipping, still having 'enough presence of mind' to notice René needs new slippers (xxiv-xxv), it is hard not to detect a whiff of dry humour behind the sheer bathos of this observation. For Aury's biographer, Angie David, Paulhan's preface 'is meant to be funny' [74].

In his essay Paulhan indulges his customary love of contradiction and paradox. Having insisted that this is an erotic novel, expressive of innate and eternal feminine sexuality (which is essentially, from his description, masochistic), he then downplays these very points. He rejects that mere sado-masochistic high-jinks are in play here, denies that René and Sir Stephen derive any pleasure from what they do (xxviii), and enthusiastically refuses any role for mere 'masochism' in O's motivation. Paulhan's rejection of the term can be explained by the contested nature of 'masochism'. In psychiatry it is a pathological condition, in Existentialism a maladaptive life-stratagem, in psychoanalysis a part of an individual's psycho-sexual make-up (and not necessarily a negative one), while for BDSM aficionados a source of erotic delight. By eschewing the word 'masochism', Paulhan is trying to keep O out of the hands of psychiatry with its limiting labels about 'sexual deviations' [75].

Meanwhile Paulhan highlights sexual desire, the purported universal male desire to 'possess a Justine' (xxv) and the uniqueness of O wanting to be Justine. Moreover he identifies the novel as 'an ardent love letter' (xxxii) from a woman to her god-like lover, which is, under the circumstances, the ultimate flattering accolade for him (and close to being an open admission that despite his denials, he knows full well who wrote it) – to which he replies with this preface, which amounts to a love-letter back to Réage (whom he has conflated with O) [76].

Having said that, he then wants to insist – and this is the central thrust of his essay – that, as is strongly suggested in the novel, *O* is fundamentally a mystical parable. This idea has been highly influential on later commentators and critics [77], and takes us into the orbit of writers associated with Surrealism, notably Georges Bataille. Along with the stress on *O* as a mystical text, Paulhan's other significant legacy is his emphasis on the agency of women in the novel. O and her demands are the driving force of the narrative, but more than that, Paulhan hails the author of this 'dangerous' book of strange 'decency' as a heroic figure, a woman colonising the hitherto male preserve of erotic writing, rediscovering the erotic glories of cruelty first explored by Sade, and very much a writer to be reckoned with, author of a novel that demands to be taken as serious literature.

Dominique Aury's later comments on the Preface fell a little short of laudatory, saying it was 'provocative', but 'did not correspond so much to the book' [78], and admitting later that 'even she couldn't make head or tail of it' [79]. As with so much else of Aury's testimony, as with that of Paulhan, this may or may not be really the case.

1  Brown and Faery 1984
2  Nadeau 1954, cited David 2006, p. 13
3  Deforges 1975, pp. 126-127
4  St Jorre 1994, p. 45
5  Bedell 2004  p.2
6  David 2006 pp 430-431 citing letters by Aury 5 October, Thomas 10 October 1950 (Fonds Édith Thomas, Archives Nationales)
7  David 2006 pp. 64-66, 430
8  Deforges 1975 p. 124-125
9  David 2006 p. 323
10  David 2006 p. 26
11  Sabine d'Estree translation, 'A Girl' 1969/1971 p. 19
12  Kaja Silverman: 'Histoire d'O: The Construction of a Female Subject' in Carol S. Vance (ed.) *Pleasure and Danger, Exploring Female Sexuality* Routledge and Keegan Paul 1984
13  Deforges, 1975 p. 108, 44
14  Deforges 1975 p. 25
15  Bedell 2004
16  David 2006 pp. 299, 312-317
17  Anne Desclos was with Maulnier when she was aged between 25 to 34, and one suspects most people would imagine O as mid to late twenties. Corinne Cléry was 25 when she played the part in Just Jaeckin's 1975 film – Udo Kier(René)  was 31, and Anthony Steele (Sir Stephen) was 55. However, the connection Réage made between Sir Stephen and the fifty-year old Englishman she had seen in the Paris bar raises a complication. In O we are told in O that Sir Stephen is only ten years older than René, and by implication O. If Réage was seeing herself in O to any extent, which seems likely, perhaps she was imagining her as simultaneously her younger self when she was with Maulnier, and as her current self (aged 43-44) when she wrote her novel.
18  Bedell 2004
19  Deforges 1975 p. 42
20  St Jorre 1995, p. 45
21  Anne Young : 'Subversive Complicity: A Story of O(r)' *Literature Interpretation Theory*, 24:4, 2013
22  cited in St Jorre 1995, pp 45-46
23  David 2006 p, 171; also known as Odile de Laléne Laprade [see storyofoblog.wordpress.com/23/09/07]
24  David 2006 p. 537, 539
25  See Surya 1992/ 2002 pp. 196-208; also David 2006 pp 345-346
26  Kaufmann 1998 p. 902
27  cited David 2006 pp. 317, 319 from Talagrand correspondence
28  David 2006 p. 322
29  Deforges 1975 p. 153
30  Brown and Faery 1984

31  St Jorre 1995, p. 231
32  E.g. Wyngarde 2017, p. 214; Deforges 1975 p. 15
33  Brown and Faery 1984 p. 203
34  Deforges 1975 p. 119
35  Marcus 1978 p. 198
36  Benjamin 1980 p. 159
37  Deforges 1975 p. 119
38  ibid 1975 p. 27-28
39  Michelle A. Massé 1992 *In the name of Love: Women, Masochism and the Gothic* Cornell U.P. pp. 128-129; this 'family' dynamic features in Anne Rice's *Interview with the Vampire* (1976).
40  Silverman 1984 p. 338
41  Kaufmann 1998 p. 896
42  ibid 1998 p. 896
43  Brown and Faerie 1984
44  Schullenberger 2005 p. 267
45  Kaufmann 1998 p. 897
46  ibid 1998 p. 885
47  ibid 1998 p. 886
48  ibid 1998 p. 895: Thomas' book was *Pauline Roland: Socialisme et feminisme au XIXe siecle* (1956)
49  Ephesians 5: 22-24/ I Corinthians 11: 3, 7-9/ I Corinthians 14: 34-36/ I Timothy 2: 11-12. (Brown and Faerie 1984)
50  Marcus 1978 pp. 204-205
51  Brown and Faerie 1984 p. 197
52  St Jorre 1994, p. 44
53  Marcus 1978 p. 204
54  St Jorre 1994 p, 44
55  Including Millett 1970, Gordon 1971, Brownmiller 1975, Marcus 1978, Benjamin 1980, Kaplan 1991, Huston 1992, Kustritz 2008, Musser 2015.
Paulhan in his Preface [VIII, XI, XXI, XXIII, XXVII] and Deforges in her interview (p. 211) also use the definite article but clearly indicate it is *not* part of the title.
56  Brown and Faery 1984 p. 192
57  *Collins Roberts French Dictionary*, Dictionnaires Le Robert, Harper Collins, 5th edition 1998
58  Brown and Faery 1984 p. 192
59  Sontag 1967 p. 102
60  Marcus 1978 p. 204
61  Benjamin 1980 p. 156
62  Janis L Pallister 'The Anti-Castle in the Works of "Pauline Réage"' *The Journal of Midwest Modern Language Association* Vol 18 No. 2 Autumn 1985 Loyola University, Chicago
63  Brown and Faery 1984 p. 192
64  Dworkin 1974 'Woman as Victim: "Story of O"' *Feminist Studies* 2.1 p. 108.

⁶⁵ cited St Jorre 1994, p. 46

⁶⁶ Mahon 2020, p. 177 #240

⁶⁷ Cited in St Jorre 1994 p. 50

⁶⁸ Some of these associations are revisited in the title of Gustav Courbet's 1866 painting of a woman's naked pudenda, *L'Origine du Monde* (*The Origin of the World*), which was for some time in the possession of Jacques Lacan and Sylvie Bataille.

⁶⁹ It is possible this is the revolt referenced in Jean Rhys' *Wide Sargasso Sea* (1966)

⁷⁰ Hegel, G.W.F.: *Phenomenology of Spirit* (1807)

⁷¹ Nietzsche, Friedrich: *Of Old and Young Women* in *Thus Spoke Zarathustra* (1883-85); trans. R.J. Hollingdale, Penguin Classics 1961/1985, p. 93

⁷² For example: Foucault *Power/Knowledge: Selected Interviews and Other Writings 1972-1977* Colin Gordon et al (ed.) Harvester Press 1980

⁷³ Silverman 1984 p. 320

⁷⁴ David 2006 p. 31

⁷⁵ Sontag 1967 pp. 113-114 insists O's ardour takes her beyond mere psychiatry.

⁷⁶ Massé 1992

⁷⁷ Schullenberger 2005 for example sees *O* as best understood as a text of secular religion

⁷⁸ Aury 1999 p. 113 cited in David 2006, p. 32

⁷⁹ St Jorre, cited in Bedell 2004

# Gallery

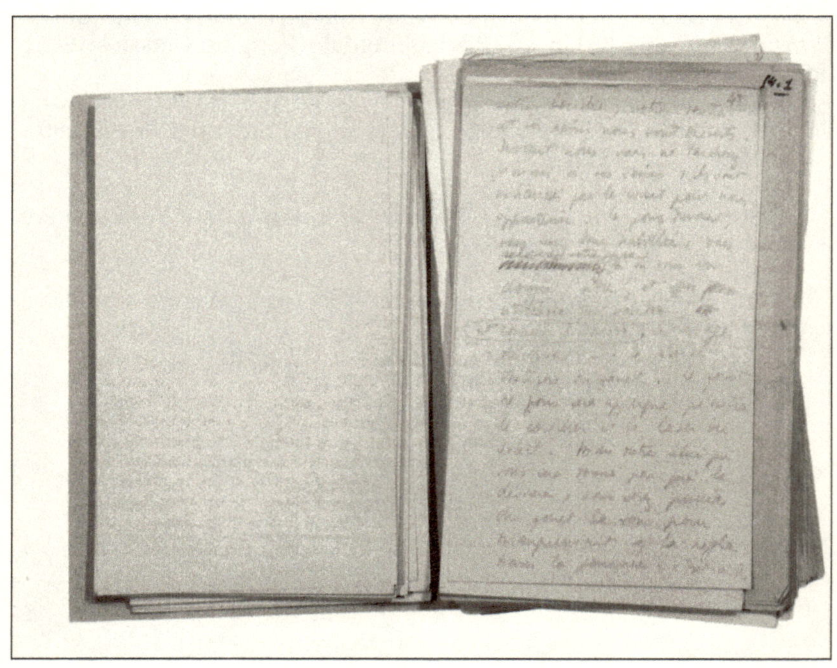

The original, handwritten manuscript of *Story of O.*

Dominique Aury (1954), at the time *Story of O* was published.

Jean Paulhan

O's apartment, Quai de Béthune, Île Saint-Louis (4th arr.).

Sir Stephen's Paris apartment, Rue de Poitiers, (7th arr.).

*Histoire d'O,* illustration by Leonor Fini

The owl mask 'stolen' from Leonor Fini, illustration by Linda McAdam.

André Breton, 1924 – the year he wrote the *Surrealist Manifesto.*

Jean-Paul Sartre and Simone de Beauvoir

*The Robing of the Bride* (1940), *(La Toilette de la mariée)* by Max Ernst

*Au Rendez-vous des amis* (1922) by Max Ernst

Seated from left to right: René Crevel, Max Ernst, Dostoyevsky, Théodore Fraenkel, Jean Paulhan, Benjamin Péret, Johannes T. Baargeld, Robert Desnos. Standing: Philippe Soupault, Jean Arp, Max Morise, Raphael, Paul Éluard, Louis Aragon, André Breton, Giorgio de Chirico, Gala Éluard

Régine Deforges

# VI: *O* and the Philosophies of Liberation I – *Érotisme Noir*

## INTRODUCTION

Among the range of thinkers and writers who gravitated to Humanism and the political 'Third Way' after Liberation, three main groupings stand out. First, Existentialism, centred around Jean-Paul Sartre, Simone de Beauvoir and Albert Camus. This had been making its mark as a discernible movement since 1943 and was firmly established in the ascendant by 1945. Second, Surrealism, re-grouping with several of the old faces and many new ones when André Breton returned to Paris in April 1946, and holding its first post-war exhibition the following year. Finally Feminine Humanism [1], a looser network comprising Beauvoir again, Édith Thomas – and Dominique Aury – who by 1949, along with psychoanalysts like Marie Bonaparte, was putting women's issues firmly on the philosophical and political map. All of these movements were Humanistic in that it was the human condition rather than the will of any god that interested them (although Surrealism and Feminine Humanism understood that the mystical was part of our nature and our world as well). In addition, they were all searching for a political 'Third Way', independent of the established positions and movements of the time. They opposed fascism, conservatism and the power of the Church; they took a critical, often oppositional stance to state power and American political influence, and they rejected Stalinist communism. Mostly they leaned to the non-aligned left. Breton, after flirting with Trotskyism in the 1930s, gravitated after the war to the ideas of utopian socialist and romantic feminist Charles Fourier; Édith Thomas, after breaking with the PCF, retained leftist leanings. Sartre was unusual in drawing back towards Moscow in the 1950s, making his peace with the PCF, and falling out irreparably with Camus who remained steadfastly non-aligned.

All of these movements exerted significant influence through the 1950s and beyond, contributing to the milieu in which Aury lived and worked, and providing the intellectual context for *Story of O*. And Aury was no mere passive recipient of others' ideas. She was, as an editor, translator and writer, a player in her own right, and her novel was simultaneously responsive to Existentialism, a contribution to Feminine Humanism, and deeply implicated in the Surrealist world. She and Paulhan were both identifiable as Humanists, and in their own way placeable on the Third Way spectrum, although as *résistants* they had been Free French rather than left, and one suspects never lost sympathy for de Gaulle (who had also, after a fashion, been searching for a 'Third Way' – see p. 133).

Along with Humanism and sympathy for a Third Way, another point of convergence for Existentialism, Feminine Humanism and Surrealism was in the importance they attached to the erotic in human life, particularly in its darker aspects, and the spirit of high priest of this *érotisme noir*, the Marquis de Sade, in one way or another hovered over them all. Located precisely at this point of convergence, *O* was uniquely situated to stand as one of the touchstones of Parisian literary culture in the post-war period.

In these next four chapters we shall discuss *O* in relation to firstly, *érotisme noir* and Sade; secondly, Existentialism and Feminine Humanism; and finally, and above all, to Surrealism and mysticism. We make no claim to the final word on any of these relationships. Drawing on a range of sources, while making a few observations of our own, this can only be a sketch-map of territory that will invite further and more detailed research by others in the future.

## *ÉROTISME NOIR* AND THE MARQUIS DE SADE

During the Occupation, a taste for *érotisme noir* developed in Resistance circles. According to Jean-Jacques Pauvert, who as a sixteen year old courier in 1942 was making the acquaintance at Gallimard of Jean Paulhan and Albert Camus, there was a continuous circulation of quotes among the *résistants*[2] from forbidden writers, including Lautréamont, Breton and the Marquis de Sade. Trading black humour and other illicit material is common practice among people labouring under pressure, providing cohesion and an outlet for the stresses they are under, and among the *résistants* this was amplified – the circulation of transgressive extracts being in itself an act of subversion, bonding them in secret pacts of trust, while the very nature of the material articulated the sublime thrill that danger, clandestine organisation and camaraderie inspired. Moreover, in struggling to cope with the trauma of defeat and Occupation, Sade's probing of the darker depths of the psyche could provide insight into the times, including the psychodynamics of the weird dance between Nazi brutality and Vichy/collaborationist submission, while granting the *résistants* a sense of psychological power over collaborating compatriots whose complicity in their own humiliation revealed masochistic urges they could not comprehend.

Immediately after the war, a 'cult' of Sade developed in Paris – and not for the first time. In the mid-19th century Baudelaire had been drawn to Sade as a prophet of vice, writers like Flaubert looked to him, as did the Decadents and Symbolists a little later. In the early 1900s Guillaume Apollinaire re-launched Sade for the new century. Poet and pivotal figure in the Parisian arts demimonde (where he fostered the careers of, among others, Picasso, Matisse, de Chirico, Duchamp, Picabia and Ernst)[3], Apollinaire also applied himself to cataloguing the books in L'Enfer (Hell), the collection of 'forbidden' books in the Bibliothèque Nationale (taking the opportunity to pen a couple of lurid romps of his own [4]). Here he discovered the Marquis and high-lighted him in 1909 as 'the freest spirit that ever existed'[5].

A few years later the trauma of the First World War spawned a string of radical movements including Dada in Zurich (1916), Bolshevism in Russia (1917) and Surrealism in Paris (1924). All these movements repudiated the nationalism, religious piety and 'morality' of a world that had destroyed a whole generation of youth in the trenches, and Sade, the pioneer of such rebellion, became the hero of the avant-garde in Paris. In particular he became 'one of the patron saints of the surrealist movement'[6], exerting his influence over Breton and his group, as well as dissident surrealists like Bataille, and fellow-travellers like Jean Paulhan[7], all of whom adopted Sade as trail-blazing standard bearer against moral hypocrisy.

**Sade in his Time – Literature:** Donatien Alphonse François, Marquis de Sade (1760-1816) 'the most unread major writer in western literature'[8], is most notorious for his four 'black novels' (all composed between 1785 and 1797), in which he articulated a philosophy that issued a fundamental challenge to all prevailing morality – cataloguing sexual deviation in the encyclopaedic *The 120 Days of Sodom* (*Les Cent Vingt Journées de Sodome*)[9], recounting the contrasting adventures of two sisters, the victimised virtuous innocent *Justine* and the triumphantly wicked libertine *Juliette*[10], in-between time portraying the corruption of a very willing young girl in *The Philosophy of the Boudoir* (*La Philosophie dans le Boudoir*)[11].

Sade is often seen as a one-off (making it easier to dismiss him as a madman, pervert, satanist or whatever), but in the build up to and detonation of the French Revolution (1789-94), he was in many ways a man of his times. In England one contemporary, William Blake, critiqued pious hypocrisy in his *Songs of Innocence and of Experience* (1794) and preached complete liberation (including sexual freedom) to free us from the 'mind forg'ed manacles'[12] that entrap us, even siding with the satanic sympathies he detected in *Paradise Lost* (1667) by his hero the Puritan poet John Milton[13]. Other English contemporaries created some of the greatest masterpieces of Gothic: Ann Radcliffe in *The Mysteries of Udolpho* (1794) and other novels [14] perfected the 'Female' Gothic dynamic of the suffering heroine, her beautiful love for a sweet if rather dopey 'hero', and her sublime fascination for a demonic but mesmerising anti-hero; Matthew Lewis' *The Monk* (1796) provided the template for the sensationalism and sadism of 'Male' Gothic. Discussing Radcliffe and Lewis, Sade observed that Gothic 'became the essential fruit of the revolutionary upheavals which the whole of Europe felt' [15] [providing a clue on how he would like his own novels to be read.] The most direct parallel to Sade however was his French contemporary Choderlos de Laclos, whose *Dangerous Liaisons* (*Les Liaisons Dangereuses*, 1782) portrayed an aristocracy corrupt, rapacious and debauched yet nonetheless amusing and intriguing [16]. Laclos' aristocrats, bored with their luxurious but purposeless lives, entertain themselves with games of sexual conquest, their victims being predominantly respectable but slightly lower status women, for whom the readers' sympathies are skilfully wrong-footed by the author's deft use of irony and black comedy – Cécile, for example, teenage 'victim' of Valmont, being in Aury's eyes deserving of no sympathy whatever, due to her complete 'lack of character' [17]. As for Sade's pious and hapless Justine, her naive faith in human goodness, coupled with a profound lack of gumption, wit or even basic common sense renders her endlessly gullible and forever bewildered by her relentless misfortunes, and makes her ultimately an almost comical figure [18]. She is eventually hit by a thunderbolt, even Nature finding her too tiresome to put up with. Justine's libertine sister Juliette is however clearly anticipated by Madame de Merteuil, the accomplished female predator in *Dangerous Liaisons*, about whom Aury was to write in 1950 (see p. 262).

Much of the ground here had been laid earlier in the 18th century. England had provided a string of memorable female characters in anarchic bawdy comedies by Daniel Defoe, John Cleland and Henry Fielding [19], along with more sensitive and sympathetic works by such as Samuel Richardson [20] – all of which Sade devoured. In France, 'pornographic' literature was being written by Enlightenment *philosophes* like Diderot, Voltaire [whose *Candide* (1759) to an extent paved the way for *Justine* [21]] and others, all of whom also wrote books on science and political liberty. These three genres of pornography, science and politics were all regarded as 'philosophical', challenging the authority of conservative morality, religious dogma and royal power [22].

All of the writers mentioned above questioned established values and scorned hypocrisy, some offering direct challenges to the legitimacy of religious and social authority, some even openly siding with radical political impulse – Laclos and Sade both played roles in the early stages of the French Revolution, and Blake and Radcliffe were sympathetic to it [23]. An important part of this challenge to authority was the championing of erotic liberation, including an emphasis on the existence and legitimacy of the sexual drive in women. Interestingly, this commonly expressed itself in sado-masochistic terms. The role of cruelty in enhancing sexual excitement was well understood. Some books provided sadistic titillation for the reader at the spectacle of suffering women – here of course Sade is implicated, along with Laclos and 'Monk' Lewis (and perhaps Richardson, of whom Sade was well aware that we grieve for Clarissa when she is raped, but if she wasn't we wouldn't read the book in the first place). Such literature might imply an exclusively male readership ogling at tortured women, but this would be wide of the mark. The novel as a literary form had a particular appeal for women readers, and writers like Richardson and Laclos were enormously popular with female audiences. Ann Radcliffe, a woman writing for women, presented a particularly interesting case. One of the very best-selling authors of her day, rivalling or even outdoing the sales of Walter Scott or Byron, Radcliffe's works appealed very largely to women, whose husbands and fathers would as often as not rather see her books in the fireplace. Her novels regularly subject her central female protagonist to terrifying and often violent ordeals, including threats of rape and murder, which allowed her female readers the luxury of any combination of reaction – sadistic voyeurism, emotive empathy, sexual excitement, masochistic identification and/or whatever other response took their fancy – safe in the knowledge they were reading a fiction provided for their pleasure [24]. The fluidity of response is significant. For women whose deeper erotic natures were denied or suppressed by social propriety, Gothic permitted an outlet, a release for their pent-up *jouissance*, revealing a subtle grasp of the psychological truth that the respectable, socially aware and moral self who inhabits polite society is not the same self as the one who gallops off into the sexually charged landscape provided by the Gothic novel. This understanding took a surer hold in French literary culture [25], and Sade certainly grasped it – one implication of his statement 'Every man wants to be a tyrant when he fornicates' [26] is that when he is not fornicating (admittedly a rare enough event in Sade's novels) he may be something else. Identity is contingent on what we are doing, where we are and our level of arousal. As we noted in chapter II, for Aury, 'Nothing is more fallacious and shifting than an identity' [27].

**Sade in his Time – Politics:** Sade also had his predecessors in political thought. Most obvious was Thomas Hobbes in his *Leviathan* (1651), best known for his description of human existence in Nature as a 'war of all against all', where life was 'nasty, brutish and short', and his conclusion that we need strong central authority to protect us from ourselves. Equally important, in a back-handed way, was Jean-Jacques Rousseau, who in a string of writings – most notably *The Social Contract* (*Du contrat social*, 1762) articulated the new philosophy that came to be known as 'Romanticism', which was among other things a direct repudiation of Hobbes. Sade didn't in fact agree with either, but it was out of their tussle that he shaped his politics, in the context of the French Revolution which from 1793 took a sharp turn towards Terror as the mantra of 'Liberty, Equality, Fraternity' was sidelined by another imperative, the juggernaut of 'Virtue'.

Rousseau had flatly rejected the standard story of his time that the Enlightenment was the apex of history, the efflorescence of reason, prosperity and progress. For him, it was nothing of the sort, being instead a brutal, materialistic and spiritually shallow carnival of inhumanity – after all, one of the most profitable commodities of the nascent capitalism so beloved of the Enlightenment was in human beings kidnapped en masse from West Africa. Effectively restating the Garden of Eden story, Rousseau proposed that God and Nature are benign, and as the children of Nature we are essentially benign and virtuous as well; however, with our sense of 'reason' we created private property, which led to civilisation, whereby we managed to kick ourselves out of the lap of Nature into a corrupt, selfish, money-grubbing hell of our own making. What exactly we can do about this was not altogether clear, but Rousseau retained some faith that innate virtue could still be found in those (he thought) closest to Nature – rural people, the uneducated, children, women (gender equality wasn't his strong suit), and even (to a lesser extent) those men who heeded their hearts and feelings rather than their heads and bank balances. He did not believe that we could turn back the clock to regain the harmony with Nature he imagined we once enjoyed, but he did allow himself the dream of small communities where the shared feelings of the people could coalesce into a collective 'general will', that could be embodied in a virtuous leader who spoke for all. Romanticism has left a complex legacy: fuelling critiques of capitalism, imperialism and slavery; feeding utopian visions of a 'return to Nature'; elevating natural simplicity and emotional 'truth' above education and reason; patronising women as childlike, less intellectual but morally superior to men, and opening the door to 'populist', even fascist politics. Much of the very best and the very worst of modern culture derives from Romanticism.

Sade provided a 'comprehensive satiric critique of Rousseau' [28], turning him on his head, but with a twist. For Sade, there is no God, and the basic principle of Nature is predation, where the strong devour the weak. As children of Nature, predation is central to our natures as well. So far, so Hobbesian, but whereas Hobbes called on the power of centralised 'civilised' government to save us from our nature, Sade saw 'civilisation' as making everything worse. It is civilisation that has invented the pernicious idea of 'Virtue', and all the greatest horrors – war, religious persecution, torture, execution and so on – are all committed in the name of this warped ideal. Sade understood, through a glass darkly, that thwarting our natural desires for sexual violence with morality and virtue does not silence these desires, but renders them pathological and even more destructive. The defining test case was of course working its way through while he was writing – the populist rampages of the later stages of the French Revolution, with Maximilien Robespierre (who saw himself a devotee of Rousseau) presenting himself and his cronies on the Committee for Public Safety as spokesmen for the will of 'the people'. The innate 'Virtue' of the masses, concentrated in Robespierre as embodiment of the Rousseauan 'general will', sanctioned the executions of tens of thousands in the Terror of 1793-94, the guillotine providing the most popular spectacle for the mob. And Sade recognised that the blood-lust of the Terror was the expression of natural violent urges amplified and distorted by the repressions of Virtue, blurting out in mass homicidal madness. By 1818 French utopian socialist Charles Fourier was attributing to Sade the idea that if natural passions are 'suffocated' they re-emerge in more 'malignant' form [29] (in turn Fourier was to influence Marx's idea of 'alienation', Freud on 'repression', and surrealist erotic liberation).

'Virtue' became Sade's bête noir. For Sade, the 'natural' life of predation, sexual plunder and murder was far preferable – crime was nowhere near as destructive as Virtue. In his view, murder committed out of passion or desire was no more culpable than a river bursting its banks, but the organised slaughters of war, persecution and cold-blooded state-sanctioned executions [30] – murders committed out of 'national pride', 'God's will', 'the good of society' or any other pious flummery – were completely beyond justification and utterly contemptible. And Sade put his neck where his mouth was – as a revolutionary judge his refusal to send his quota to the guillotine led to his own arrest and death sentence – a fate he escaped through pure fluke, as Robespierre was overthrown the night before Sade was due for the chop [31].

**The Freud Connection:** In the 1920s, just as the Surrealists were picking up on Sade, another of their heroes, Sigmund Freud, the most insightful of all the theorists of *érotisme noir*, was himself responding to the First World War by recasting his own theory in a Sadean mode. As early as 1905 Freud had discussed three main defence mechanisms for dealing with disturbing or threatening urges and desires [32]. *Repression,* which attempts to push dangerous material into the unconscious, where it festers and haunts us – the 'return of the repressed' manifesting itself in symptoms of hysteria. *Paranoia*, which deploys syllogistic disavowals to reverse our own unacceptable urges into forms that can then be attributed to others, leading us to blame them for our own darker feelings, creating irrational fear and hostility [33]. And *perversion*, where threatening urges or desires are recognised and acted out cathartically as erotic play, or sublimated into artistic or literary fantasy [34]. For Freud, perversion is the opposite of neurosis [35], and the only one of the three not to inevitably carry psychologically or socially damaging pathological baggage – although of course in erotic play, both (all?) sides must want to tango.

If recognising perversion as the legitimate expression of the pleasure principle is the essence of the 'Sadean morality' [36], Freud was already getting close to it, but in the 1920s he drew closer still, reconstructing his theory around two main sets of drives emerging from the Id – the sexual drives (Eros), and the death drives (*Todestreib,* better known as Thanatos, although Freud did not use that term) [37]. Ordinarily Eros manifests itself in the desire for life, sex and pleasure, the death drives in aggression and hostility towards the self and others. But they rarely act in isolation from one another, usually they are in some kind of inter-action – sometimes in direct competition, other times co-operating in self-preservation – the death drives may ultimately desire death, but can join forces with Eros to protect you from meeting it too soon. They can also engage in other complex entanglements, including the sexualising of aggression, externally and/or internally, and even giving rise to the truly 'erotic'. Freud was very aware of the German Romantic idea of the 'liebestod' (love-death), and of Shakespeare , whom he regarded as 'the great psychologist' [38], and knew of the 'complicity between sex and death.. well known in Renaissance texts' [39]. For Harold Bloom, 'the sexual becomes erotic when crossed by the shadow of death' (a discovery he attributed to Shakespeare in *Romeo and Juliet* ) [40].

The energy of the death drives is also invested in the Superego (conscience and ego-ideal) [41]. This serves the valuable function of muzzling uncontrolled aggression from the death drives, and regulating the pleasure principle of Eros into socially acceptable channels, but an over-powerful Superego can be harshly punitive to the individual Ego, inculcating a sense of worthlessness, and imposing psychological pressures conducive to hysteria and paranoia. Given that we are not so much herd animals as horde animals, our psychic lives are contagious [42]. We can pool our hysterias and paranoias, and can invest political leaders with the power of a collective Superego, licensing them to direct our self-hatred onto scapegoats, and all hell can break out. This was the story of 1914, and, as Freud suspected and the rest of the world was soon to discover, a story preparing to repeat itself in an even more horrifying way. Like Plato's metaphorical chariot, Freud saw each of us as an arena where passions (Eros and the death drives, all emanating from the Id), reason (the Ego), and morality (the Superego) all struggle, and understood that dynamic stale-mate was the best outcome – no psychic structure should domi-nate. As a result Freud could share Sade's deep suspicion of the triumph of the Superego – where Rousseauan leaders embody the 'will of the people' into some cultish ideology of collective paranoia or hysteria ('Virtue', racial purity, the perfect society, the culmination of History, 'God's Will', whatever), and create inhuman nightmares. He did not however share Sade's belief that the unbridled release of passionate drives was preferable. For Freud, the existence of destructive and self-destructive urges needs to be recognised and understood in order to offset the very real damage these urges can do [43]. And it is here that, along with the catharsis of 'perversion', the sublimation of our drives – into creative work, imaginative play and love (all of which combine in literature and the arts) – plays its role [44]. In her interview with Deforges, Pauline Réage stated her belief that there is in us 'a need for violence and cruelty', an 'abomination' that needs to be exposed, and that 'this is what literature is largely for, to bring to light this... abomination' [45].

**Sade in Post-War Paris – the Context:** In Paris after the Second World War, Sade found his cachet again, and a deluge of writings about him flooded out. Paulhan's *The Marquis de Sade and his Accomplice* was first published in 1945; Georges Bataille's *Evil in Platonism and Sadism,* Pierre Klossowski's *Sade My Neighbour* and Maurice Nadeau's *Exploration of Sade* followed in 1947. That same year Pauvert began his project to publish all the works of the Marquis, and in the catalogue of the *Surrealism in 1947* Surrealist exhibition, Sade was praised for having 'painted the night through which we are living' [46]. Maurice Blanchot's *Lautréamont and Sade* and Gilbert Lely's *D.A.F. de Sade* appeared in 1948, with *The Accursed Share* (Bataille again) in 1949. Maurice Heine's biography was published in 1950 (the year *O* was probably begun), and in 1951 (the year *O* was completed), Albert Camus' *The Rebel* and Simone de Beauvoir's essay 'Must We Burn Sade?' were released. Lely's multivolume *Life of the Marquis de Sade* came out between 1952 and 1957. Two years after *O*'s publication, Pauvert was in the dock on an obscenity charge, defended once more by the doughty Maître Maurice Garçon, an adventure that was written up and published by Pauvert as *L'Affaire Sade* in 1957 [47]. That same year Bataille was at it again with his *Literature and Evil* and *Eroticism* [48].

This was to some extent a continuation of the clandestine fraternity of *résistant* intellectuals and writers forged during the Occupation [49], but this fraternity was not perpetuating itself out of nostalgia. It found itself constituting a new *résistance* to the dark side of the Liberation, recognising the need to challenge the savage reprisals of the *épurations*, but that in order to do so, that violence needed to be understood. One did not need to be Freud to see that the public humiliation and head-shaving of women collaborators was a symbolic rape perpetrated by men, who felt emasculated by another symbolic 'rape', that of invasion and Occupation, and struggling to reassert their potency [50]. In this, women who had endured the privations of Occupation took part, venting their rage on those who had 'opened up' to the invader. The *épurations* also re-enacted the dynamic of the Revolutionary Terror and its 'tyranny of Virtue', populist politics forging an alliance between the enraged mob and revolutionary ideologues who claimed the moral high ground for persecution – with Aragon as the 'Robespierre of the Liberation' [51]. Some resonance of this can be found in *O* [52], to some degree perhaps an allegory of Occupation and *épuration,* with the rapes and tortures, the use of the word 'confession' (a term used by both Nazi and Resistance interrogators), and the humiliation of O paraded nude at the soirée of the 'Commandant' (itself an interesting term in this context). In her interview with Deforges (1975), Réage spoke of humiliation as the 'most profound form of destruction' [53], and admitted to the fascination that humiliation, torture and death held: 'We were showing, just after the Liberation, photos of women massacred by the Germans. They passed from hand to hand. No one refused to look at them' [54].

At the same time news of the sheer scale of Nazi atrocities in the death camps was starting to become known. The genocide of six million Jews in the Shoah ('Catastrophe'), by a regime that carried out mass murder with the connivance and even support of populations of ordinary people, threw down the gauntlet to the post-war thinkers, challenging them to try to explain how this could have happened in the 20th century. Such a task was not going to be easy: even the re-labelling of the Shoah as 'The Holocaust' (which, precisely defined, is a sacrifice by burning for religious purposes) represents a misjudgement that reveals the difficulty of getting any kind of purchase on something so horrendous.

**The Challenge I – Humanity's Inhumanity:** The writers and thinkers of Paris took up the gauntlet. As the élite of Paris culture, the city that historically laid claim to the literary high ground of the western world, it was the responsibility of the Paris literati to face up to this ultimate example of humanity's capacity for inhumanity. Not just to face up to it, but to face it down – to reinforce the military victory over fascism with a crushing cultural victory, to expose Nazism for the barbarism and betrayal that it was. And this required tackling the hardest questions: how could a 'civilised' culture – that of Goethe and Beethoven – commit such atrocity, and how could so many people across Europe, including in France, have co-operated with it?

Some took a Marxist line that fascism and Nazism were historically contingent, the last ditch defence of capitalism against the threat of proletarian uprising unleashed by the Russian Revolution of 1917. This had explanatory power (even Hitler believed capitalism and Nazism had common cause – remaining baffled by the U.S.A.'s alliance with the Soviets to the end), but did not square well with the case presented by Koestler and Kravchenko and others that the Soviet Union was also guilty of colossal crimes. For some, recognising the scale of Communist evil – gulags, deportations, mass shootings and organised famines costing millions of lives – was too much to ask, and many French intellectuals (including Aragon and Merleau-Ponty, and by the 1950s, Éluard and Sartre) rallied to defend the U.S.S.R. against such 'slanders' [55].

For others the real lesson of the 1930s and '40s was that atrocity on a monstrous scale could be found across the political spectrum – not just the Nazis and Stalinists, but religious authorities, and imperial powers, including France and Britain in their colonies, and even so-called liberal democracies – after all it was the U.S.A. that had detonated atomic bombs over Hiroshima and Nagasaki in August 1945, incinerating 120,000 civilians in two instants.

The idea that inhumanity might actually be a human trait drew Parisian writers and intellectuals back to Sade, to consider what he had to teach about the darkness of the human soul. One lesson was that each of us contains a multiplicity of selves, a Sadean understanding shared by the Gothic writers and formalised by France's leading depth psychologist Pierre Janet (a contemporary of Freud's, whose ideas French psychoanalysts commonly mingled with those of Freud). This idea was taken up by the Parisian intelligentsia, many of whom, including Paulhan, had found themselves having to behave in ambiguous ways during the war, putting on masks and showing different faces to different people, grooming enemies for tactical advantage, even in some cases finding they were forming 'friendships' with them (see chapter III). It seemed possible that the ability of people with family lives, ethical codes, even charitable leanings, to collaborate in genocide was a dark mirroring of how *résistants*, through necessity, had adopted different personae for different purposes [56]. Recognition that there are circumstances when even otherwise 'good' people could do evil, and that all of us have inner ambiguities and different selves, undermined Communist claims to Olympian heights of moral rectitude in their promotion of the *épurations*, exposing their Bad Faith in scapegoating others to deflect attention from their own moral ambivalences and failings.

**The Challenge II – The Danger of Sade:** But turning to Sade to throw light on the times raised awkward questions – one being the disturbing resemblance between the châteaux of Sade's novels, where arbitrary and murderous power was wielded without justice or accountability, and the Nazi death camps and Stalinist gulags. This raised the ugly possibility that Sade did not just foresee the horrors of the 20th century, he was also in a sense implicated in bringing them into being.

Raymond Queneau in 1945 was among the first to articulate this, suggesting that the world of torture and murder 'imagined by Sade and willed by his characters (and why not by Sade himself?) was a hallucinatory precursor of the world ruled by the Gestapo...' [57]. This idea struck a chord with some and has its adherents today (despite the obvious rejoinder that Sade's cruelties were sexual, while the Nazis suppressed expressions of the erotic in the arts as 'decadent' [58]). Many of the Paris literati resisted the idea of Sade's culpability, their books from the 1940s and 50s providing testament to this.

Some, like Paulhan, accepted that Sade presented moral danger but that this was a good thing, providing an inoculation that challenged and strengthened the morality of the reader. Others, like Klossowski (1947) and Blanchot (1949) read Sade as responding to the shock of the death of God – a view Beauvoir (1951) regarded with scepticism [59]. For Camus (1951), Sade was exploring the implications of total freedom, and its manifestation in 'totalitarian societies' [60] (a point Paulhan raised in his Preface, p. xxii). For still others, Sade posed a recognition that the 'Rationalism' of the Enlightenment project was itself a path to monstrosity.

In the final analysis however, they were able to find Sade not guilty of the charge of complicity – his opposition to the death penalty had been sincere (he had after all almost lost his own head over it), and they could agree with Bataille (1947) that Sade would have condemned the mass murder machines and their ideological justifications with as much vitriol as he had damned the Terror. After all, the excuses given by the Nazis and Stalinists for their brutalities – saving humanity from 'racial pollution' or fulfilling the imperatives of historical 'progress' to create utopia – were merely updates of Robespierre's 'Virtue', nothing more than alibis for tyranny and mass murder. [One might also point out that Sade's unerring ability to be imprisoned by every government he lived under – the Ancien Régime, the Revolution, and Napoleon

– strongly suggests that if he had entered a Nazi or Soviet camp, it would have been as a prisoner, not a commandant.]

**The Challenge III – The Role of Erotic Expression:** But post-war Parisian literary circles did not just respond to Sade as political or moral critic, they also responded to his sexualisation of cruelty, releasing the transgressive and *jouissant* power of erotic energy. It was this sexual cruelty that fuelled the *érotisme noir* to be found in Hans Bellmer and other surrealists, along with Pauline Réage, Marguerite Duras and others, and which has been condemned as a failure of nerve, a refusal to face the true horror of Nazi atrocity, trivialising it instead into something manageable – mere eroticism, titillating and tawdry [61]. Such condemnation, however, arises from a failure to understand how people cope with oppression and trauma. On the one hand eroticism is an expression of individual imagination, of inner desires resisting regimentation and rejecting authoritarian dogma – 'the last refuge of liberty' [62]. On the other it provides cathartic release – as for example with French surrealist Valentine Penrose (née Hugo) going into 'horrifying detail' of 'explicit sexual violence' towards women in her biography of *Erzébet Bàthory, The Bloody Countess* (1962) as a 'means of exorcizing the anguish and horror of the war years by writing it out in symbolic form' [63].

The condemnation is misplaced in other ways as well. Marguerite Duras' husband, Robert Antelme, after a year in a concentration camp, wrote of the yawning gap that emerged between experience of the camps and the ability of language to express it. The idea that there was a crisis of expression after the war was articulated in different ways: for Frankfurt School theorist Theodor Adorno it was an ethical issue: 'to write poetry after Auschwitz is barbaric' [64]. But the limitations of language itself had been addressed by Sartre in *Nausea* (1938), and despair over these limitations was already to be found in the work of Artaud and post-war 'Absurdist' writers, but for Breton despair was a luxury we could not allow ourselves, something to be repudiated and transcended in the search for marvellous [65]. [By 1956 Breton was rejecting the whole panoply of pessimism and 'miserabi-lism', banality, realism, existentialism and dull Marxism, in favour of 'exaltation' [66] where words achieve independence – having ceased their play and flirtation, they make love]. Paulhan had addressed the imperative of making language work communica-tively in his major work *The Flowers of Tarbes* (1941) (see chapter III), his views being shared soon after by the Existentialists. Sartre had come around to the view of distrusting the incommunicable as 'the source of all violence'; for Albert Camus 'We live in terror because persuasion is no longer possible', 'Every ambiguity, every misunderstanding, leads to death; clear language and simple words are the only salvation from it' [67]. A case can be made that the very attempt to find a vocabulary to articulate inhumanity is itself a prophylactic against it.

*Érotisme noir* provided such a vocabulary, and not an arbi-trary one. Delving into the depths of human sexuality could provide insights into the sickness at the heart of fascism, and to provide arms and armaments against it. Here, both Sade and Freud could be mined for their perceptions (the former by a wide range of thinkers, the latter particularly by surrealists). A psycho-analysis of fascism reveals a dynamic of failure to handle 'unacceptable' urges which then manifested as collective hysteria and hostile paranoia at horrendous human cost. As Jacqueline Rose put it 'Psychoanalysis brings to light everything we don't want to think about. If you can acknowledge the complexities in your own heart, then you're not going to look for scapegoats' [68]. From this point of view, articulating the sado-masochistic sexual desires that are widespread, even perhaps integral to our nature, not only provides catharsis and exorcism, but offers a repudiation of the psychopathology that spawned Nazism.

Just as Sade acknowledged the darkness in human desire and the truth of cruel pleasure, while rejecting the mechanisation of death in the French Revolution's Terror, so post-war French writers sought to re-humanise the transgressiveness of desire, recognising that the real horror lay not so much in the pleasure of cruelty, but in the *alienation* of that pleasure by ideology and technology into the mass destruction of 20th century war with its gas chambers, carpet-bombing and nuclear weapons. The first step, then, was to recognise our own demonic urges, as Picasso had done in his 'Minotaur' series in the 1930s, to say, as Shakespeare's Prospero does, speaking of Caliban in the final scene of *The Tempest* (Act V, scene i), 'This thing of darkness I/ Acknowledge mine'.

Further, to re-eroticise cruelty and transform it into art was the necessary next step to offset our plunging into another of our self-manufactured hells. Breton and the Surrealists were fully aware that in Sade's imagination lay a liberation beyond the limitations of everyday life. This understanding gained support from both Albert Camus in *The Rebel* (*L'Homme revolté,* 1951) and Simone de Beauvoir in 'Must We Burn Sade?' ('Faut-il brûler Sade?', 1951). For Camus, Sade's cruelty only triumphs 'in a dream', his killings taking place 'in his imagination'; what the world could not give him 'was provided for him by dreams and by creative activity', rendering him 'the perfect man of letters' [69]. Beauvoir, who had been reading Sade in 1949 [70] and, like many other Parisian intellectuals recognised he 'deserve(d) to be hailed as a great moralist' [71], took a similar line. Sade embraced his darkest desires, but his brilliance lay in the fact that 'he chose the imaginary' [72], recognising the superiority of literature over mere reality, being free to 'perpetuate on paper' the most murderous antics that in the flesh would leave the question, 'But what would the tyrant actually do with this *inert object*, a corpse?' [73]. 'It was by means of his imagination that he escaped from space, time, prison, the police, the void of absence, opaque presences, the conflicts of existence, death, life and all contradictions' [74]; and noting Sade's insight that it is much better to express sexual and violent passion as fiction than to enact it in real life cheering around the guillotine, Beauvoir could conclude 'It was not murder that fulfilled Sade's erotic nature, it was literature' [75]. As A. Jodorowsky put it, 'the crimes I commit in my mind are the crimes I don't commit in

Reality... Man always carries out that which he doesn't imagine [76].

For many of the Paris intelligentsia, Sade provided the template for repudiating Terror, acknowledging the darkness in every soul (permitting nobody the inhuman absolutism of any pinnacle of moralistic certitude), channelling it into sexuality, then into literature. Such dark literature has the distinct advantage of leaving considerably fewer bodies lying around, but, mysteriously, seems to incense the sanctimonious guardians of morality far more than actual war, exploitation and massacre [77].

Eroticism doesn't shoulder all the burden however – humour also has a worthy track-record as a cultural antidote to the horrors of history – particularly in alliance with the sexual, in its bawdy and lewd manifestations. Shoah survivor Aharon Appelfeld noted how he and fellow survivors could only talk about their experiences after the war through 'grotesque comic performances' [78], and something that Sade's critics (and some of his supporters) commonly overlook is that Sade comes from a tradition of provocative and outrageous comedy. Sade's works descend from a line that includes *The Thousand and One Nights*, Boccaccio, Chaucer, Rabelais, Jacobean drama (as much black comedy as 'tragedy'), much of which comes during or just after periods of turmoil – plagues, religious wars and so on – not to mention the libertine writings of Voltaire, Diderot and the rest of the French *philosophes*, Restif de la Bretonne and many others. Instead of spluttering outrage over Sade, many of the post-war French writers took a different tack: for Paulhan, '*Justine* reads, or should be read, like a fairy tale' [79], while for Bataille, 'Nothing would be more pointless than literally taking Sade seriously' [80].

For Freud (1930), the very purpose of art is to be a privileged space in which to express that which is threatening to social life – rendering the idea of policing and censoring art as 'immoral' or 'pornographic' completely wrong-headed. This view was developed by, amongst others, Herbert Marcuse in his *Politics and Eros* (1955) that art has the power to liberate us from repression by the Reality Principle, and by Paulhan with his insistence that literature and life are separate realms. *Story of O* presents a defining case study.

**O and Sade:** Just as Beauvoir and Camus were drawing their conclusions on Sade, Pauline Réage was writing her novel, in which 'the most obvious reference is to Sade' [81], especially as reinterpreted by her friends and colleagues among the Liberation Paris literati. She makes use of his 'sexual theatre' of servants, fires and floggings [82], echoes of his châteaux being readily discernible in the enclosed spaces and private autarchies in which O finds herself – Roissy, Sir Stephen's apartment and Samois [83] – and Paulhan made an explicit connection between O and Sade in his preface: 'Few are the men who have not dreamed of possessing a Justine. But as best I know no woman so far has dreamed of being Justine' (p. xxv). Aury, however, denied any direct influence from Sade. In 'A Girl' (1969) she suggested any resemblance was fortuitous – 'So it was that Sade's castles, discovered long after I had silently built my own, never surprised me...' (pp. 15-16), and in 1994 told St Jorre that she did not read Sade until after she wrote O, although she knew of Paulhan's interest in him. [In this account she first encountered Sade through his *120 Days of Sodom,* finding the first fifty pages good and the rest unreadable [84]]. True to form however, Aury gave an alternative account in her 1975 interview with Deforges that she had read Sade when she was 30, that is, thirteen or fourteen years before writing O [85].

Either way, O is without doubt haunted by Sade, although with some differences. O is more focused, avoiding the rambling repetitiveness of Sade, and avoids the orgiastic free-for-alls, retaining some role for the couple [86] (a legacy of the romance rather than Sadean 'pornography'). There is also more psychological interiority than is found in Sade, with O having a consciousness and depth of character way beyond anything attained by the 'ninnies in Sade's tales' [87]. Nevertheless O does owe much to Sade, her character representing a blend of the self-sacrificing and submissive Justine, victim of relentless anal penetration, whippings, branding and mutilation, and the assertive and self-sufficient

Juliette, who rejects the domestic and maternal role of women ascribed by society, refuses monogamy and hetero-normality, violates all taboos and voyages to the wilder shores of sexual gratification. As a blend of the two, O can be the victim at Roissy, accomplice in Sir Stephen's and Anne-Marie's treatment of her, predator towards Jacqueline, and sadist to Yvonne at Samois. Every one of her urges receive gratification.

O remains *the* classic of post-war Parisian *érotisme noir*. Susan Sontag (1967) placed *O* in the French literary tradition from Sade through Lautréamont and Bataille where an alternative understanding of sexuality is articulated. The standard perception of sexuality, which Sontag describes as 'liberal' and attributes to Rousseau and Freud, sees sex as natural and beautiful, wholesome and healthy, and only turning perverse if its energy and natural outlets are blocked by social or moral restrictions (Sontag is right to include early Freud here, but not the Freud of the 1920s and 30s). In contrast, the tradition espoused by Sade and his followers, including Réage, understands that the obscene is primary to human nature, that sex is a demonic power, incorporating violence and the urge for death, the orgasm being akin to an 'epileptic fit... beyond good and evil, beyond sanity' [88]. Bedell (2004) concurred, 'In the end, the most instructive aspect of the book is that is demonstrates the demoniacal nature of sexuality in any or all of us. This quiet, learned woman understood the power of sex. She knew that desire can ignite compulsions to commit sudden, arbitrary violence and induce a yearning for voluptuous, annihilating death' [89]. In 'A Girl', Réage wrote '... Sade made me understand that we are all jailers, and all in prison, in that there is always someone within us whom we enchain, whom we imprison, whom we silence. By a curious kind of reverse shock, it can happen that prison itself can open the gates to freedom' [90]. This quiet, learned woman also knew the wisdom of liberating this enchained inner self in literature, not as neurosis, paranoia or violence. As Aury understood, 'it is not the people who read Sade who made the concentration camps.

Those were the people who had never read Sade' [91].

***L'Affaire Sade:*** As we saw in chapter I, *Story of O* sailed close to the legal wind through the late 1950s without ever coming to court, but the thunderstorm threatening *O* during these years actually broke over Pauvert in 1956, not in regard to *O*, but to his publications of Sade [92]. Since 1947 Pauvert had been engaged on a project to publish all of Sade's works (which he managed to do by 1972, with prefaces by a star cast of Parisian literati, including Paulhan and Aury, Blanchot and others, many with surrealist connections, like Bataille, Lely, Mandiargues and Klossowski). However, in December 1956 Pauvert's project was brought to an abrupt halt when the Commission de Livre, who had been on his case since 1954, finally moved to close him down and charge him with 'crimes against morality' [93] over publishing 'descriptions of scenes of orgies, the most repugnant cruelties, and the most varied perversions' [94]. This precipitated the celebrated *Affaire Sade* which brought to a climax the whole debate over Sade that had been rumbling on since Liberation.

The case came to trial in January 1957, with Pauvert ably defended by Maître Maurice Garçon. Formidable as ever, Garçon's case was to stress the *literary* nature of Sade's work, arguing that any threat posed by literature to society is a threat that society benefits from facing. He also cited freedom of speech (enshrined by the constitution since 1791), and (using an argument favoured by Sade) pointed out the ever-changing nature of the moral landscape, such that establishment pontificating on social issues always managed to be seriously out of date. Pauvert argued for the international importance of Sade, that transgression was one of the essential functions of literature, 'the essence of poetry' (a view derived from Mandiargues and other surrealists), while taking care to reassure the court that any 'threat' from Sade was ameliorated by his private edition being available only to a literate and cultured minority.

In addition, four witnesses for the defence were called to testify. André Breton provided his testimony by letter. His description of Sade in 1924 as 'Surrealist in sadism' had demonstrated both his admiration for him, and his awareness that Sade was not to be taken as a 'realist', and in his letter he insisted on the inspirational insights of Sade, placing him in an honourable tradition of French writers from Baudelaire to Apollinaire who had faced prohibition, and condemned the censorship of ideas as equivalent to the censorship of liberty itself. Publishing Sade would, he averred, contribute to the 'intellectual radiance' of France (a point well made in the context of France reasserting its literary eminence after the war – a mission supported by conservatives as well as progressives, including members of the prosecution and jury). Jean Cocteau also provided a letter, in which he spoke for Sade's importance culturally and as a voice of freedom, 'a philosopher, and in his own way, a moraliser'.

Georges Bataille appeared in person, agreeing on Sade's importance as a philosopher, who, despite the horror and obscenity, had a moral significance, exposing the effects of unreason, and the revelation of the sacred in the profane (whether mysterious pronouncements like this actually helped matters is a moot point; we shall discuss Bataille's ideas further in chapter IX). Also putting in a personal appearance, Jean Paulhan lent his voice to the idea of Sade as a moral thinker – reiterating his view that the danger Sade posed for readers was a moral one, which strengthens them and makes them think, which is after all what literature is for [95].

Ultimately the defence rested on the independence of the literary world from any direct cause and effect relationship with the 'real' world, except as presenting moral challenges which inoculate the readers and strengthen their own moral sinews (a view explicitly endorsed by Aury in her interview with Deforges [96]).

As it happened, the defence failed. The prosecution's case that Sade posed a danger of creating an appetite for and inspiring sexual violence carried the day, and on January 10th 1957 the verdict was given that the books seized from Pauvert were to be destroyed and Pauvert was to pay 200,000 FFr [= approx. $ 570 at the time [97]]. Nothing daunted, Pauvert decided to appeal, provocatively publishing two more volumes of Sade within a few weeks, along with an account of the trial – *L'Affaire Sade* – later that year. Perhaps unexpectedly, the appeal paid off. On March 12th 1958 the court decided that Pauvert's private subscription-only edition did provide sufficient safe-guard for publishing Sade, so Pauvert evaded the fine, but the Brigade mondaine were given extra powers to vet literature before publication, to 'protect' the youth of France.

---

[1] 'L'Humanisme feminin' was a term coined by Édith Thomas for an unpublished work written 1947-9, translated as 'Feminine Humanism' (Kaufmann 1998) or 'Humanist Feminism' (Mahon 2020).

[2] Mahon 2020, p. 126, 134

[3] See Francis Steegmuller: *Apollinaire: Poet Among the Painters* (1963) Penguin 1973

[4] *Les Onze Milles Verges* (*The 11,000 Rods/Whips/Blows;* NB 'verge' also means 'penis' – of an erect variety – and is a near homonym of 'vierge' = virgin) and *Les Exploits (Memoires) d'un jeune don Juan* – both 1907. This was incidentally the year of Picasso's *Demoiselles d'Avignon*, which Apollinaire championed, effectively launching Picasso's career.

[5] *L'Œuvre du marquis de Sade* : Collection des classiques galantes, 'Les maîtres de l'amour', 1909, cited in Neil Cox 'When the Surrealists Were Right', in *Surrealism, Desire Unbound*, Jane Mundy (ed.) Tate Publishing/ Princeton University Press, 2001,  p.248

[6] Sontag 1967 p. 97

[7] He published notes on << *Les Infortunes de la vertu* du Marquis de Sade >> in September 1930 in the *NRF*. David 2006 p. 43

[8] Camille Paglia 1990 *Sexual Personae* Penguin p. 2

[9] Written in the Bastille from 1785 – 1789, the manuscript was lost for decades, resurfacing in the 19th century and finally being published in 1904 – just in time to inspire Apollinaire.

[10] *Justine* first appeared in 1787 as *Les Infortunes de la vertu*, then in 1791 in expanded form as *Justine, ou les Malheurs de la vertu* ('infortunes' and 'malheurs' both usually translate as 'misfortunes', although 'malheurs' is perhaps better as 'woes'). The companion volume was published as *Histoire de Juliette, ou les prospérités du vice* in 1796. In 1797 both were combined in a greatly expanded edition – *La Nouvelle Justine, ou les malheurs de la vertu, suivie de l'histoire de Juliette, sa soeur.*

[11] Published 1795, the title has also been translated as *The Bedroom*

*Philosophers* and other variants.

[12]  Blake 'London' in *Songs of Experience* 1794

[13]  Blake suggested of Milton 'he was a true Poet, and of the Devil's party without knowing it' *The Marriage of Heaven and Hell* c. 1793.

[14]  Five novels written between 1789 and 1797, including *The Romance of the Forest* (1791) and *The Italian* (1797)

[15]  Sade: *L'Idée sur les Romans* (1800) Octave Uzane press 1878 p. 32

[16]  Interestingly, in his *L'Idée sur les Romans* (1800), Sade refers to a comprehensive range of his influences, but makes no mention of Laclos, suggesting a hint of jealousy perhaps?

[17]  Cited in Deforges 1975 p. 203

[18]  Sontag 1967 p. 100-101. 'Justine' figures are a stock in trade in comedy – e.g. Mañuel in *Fawlty Towers* (BBC 1975/79), and Baldrick in *Blackadder* (BBC 1983-89) – in both cases safely masculinised to appease late 20th century sensibilities.

[19]  Defoe: *Moll Flanders* (1722); Cleland: *Fanny Hill* and Fielding: *Tom Jones* (both 1749)

[20]  E.g. *Clarissa* (1748)

[21]  Sontag 1967 p. 100

[22]  Robert Darnton *The Forbidden Best-Sellers of Pre-Revolutionary France* Fontana 1997

[23]  Robert Miles: *Ann Radcliffe, The Great Enchantress* Manchester University Press 1995

[24]  See Reese Saxment *Writing Desire*, Black Scat Books 2024

[25]  Sontag 1967 pp. 104-5

[26]  Cited Beauvoir 'Must We Burn Sade?' (1951-2) in Paul Dinnage (ed.) *The Marquis de Sade* John Calder 1962 p. 16

[27]  'A Girl' 1969 p. 14

[28]  Paglia 1990 p. 2

[29]  cited in *The Utopian Vision of Charles Fourier* ed. Jonathan Beecher and Richard Bienvenu ; Jonathan Cape 1972, p. 353

[30]  'We may kill but we may not judge' Sade cited in Beauvoir 1951 p. 79.

[31]  The view taken by Gilbert Lely: *Vie de Marquis de Sade* vol 2 Gallimard 1957 p. 417 and Donald Thomas *The Marquis de Sade* BCA 1992 p 220. Maurice Lever *Marquis de Sade: A Biography* (1991) Harper Collins 1993 pp. 465-468 suggests somebody in authority had been bribed to 'lose' Sade in the overcrowded prison. Neil Schaeffer *The Marquis de Sade* (1999) Picador 2001 p. 450 records an open verdict.

[32]  Freud 'Three Essays on Sexuality' 1905 in Penguin Freud Library Vol 7 *On Sexuality* 1979; For an excellent and accessible general account of Freud's psychology, see Raymond E. Fancher *Psychoanalytic Psychology*, Norton, 1973.

[33]  Attempts to deny homosexual desire are frequently implicated in paranoia. Denying that 'I love him' may lead to reversal into 'I hate him', which may then reverse again into 'He hates me', leading to a delusion of persecution. The *Othello* syndrome is a variant on this: 'I love him'

is denied into 'I don't love him' and then reversed again into 'She loves him', which in the Shakespeare play led to the murder of an innocent woman. The solution of course is to acknowledge and accept the desire.

[34] Freud 1905 p. 80 note 1.

[35] 'The neuroses are, so to say, the negative of the perversions' ibid. p. 80

[36] Gloria Feman Orenstein: *The Theater of the Marvelous – Surrealism and the Contemporary Stage* New York University Press, 1975, p. 227

[37] Freud: 'Beyond the Pleasure Principle' 1920; Freud's word *trieb* is commonly translated as 'instinct', but 'drive' is more accurate – drives being open-ended, true instincts committing the organism to stereotyped behaviours.

[38] Letter to Lytton Strachey 25 December 1928, cited in *Sigmund Freud*, ed. Ernst & Lucie Freud (1978), Norton 1985 p. 249

[39] Lloyd Davis 'Death Marked Love, Desire and Presence in Romeo and Juliet', in *Romeo and Juliet, New Casebooks*, ed. R.S. White, Palgrave 2001, p. 31.

[40] Harold Bloom, in Burton Raffel (ed.) *Romeo and Juliet*, Yale University Press, 2004

[41] Freud 'The Ego and the Id' 1923

[42] Freud: 'Group Psychology and the Ego' 1921

[43] See for example his correspondence with Einstein, published as 'Why War?' by the League of Nations, 1933

[44] Freud: 'Civilisation and its Discontents' 1930; Fancher 1973 pp. 227-8

[45] Cited in Deforges 1975 p. 192

[46] Maurice Nadeau, cited in Neil Matheson 'The Surrealist Novel and the Gothic' in *A History of the Surrealist Novel* ed. Anna Watz Cambridge University Press 2023, p. 121

[47] Pauvert (ed.) *L'Affaire Sade: Compte-rendu exact du procès intenté par le Ministère public* Editions Pauvert 1957

[48] Paulhan: First published as 'Le Marquis de Sade et sa accomplice', *La Table Ronde* 1945; subsequently as 'Marquis de Sade et sa complice', preface to *Les Infortunes de la Vertu*, Les Editions du Point du Jour, 1946; and *Le Marquis de Sade et sa complice: ou, Les Revanches de la pudeur* Éditions Lilac' 1951 (see David 2020 p. 45; Mahon 2020 p. 132); Bataille: Talk given May 1947, published as 'Sade et la Morale', Cahiers du Collège Philosophique vol 3, 1947, (in *Must We Burn Sade?* Ed. Deepak Narang Sawhney, Humanity Books 1999); Klossowski: *Sade mon prochain*, Éditions de Seuil 1947, (Northwestern University Press 1991); Nadeau: *Exploration de Sade* in Sade *Œuvres* 9-58 (La Jeune Parque, coll. 'Le Cheval Parlant') 1947; Blanchot: *Lautréamont et Sade* (*Les Temps Modernes* 1948); Lely: *D.A.F. de Sade* Seglers 1948; Bataille: *La Part maudite* Editions de Minuit 1949; Heine: *Le Marquis de Sade* Gallimard 1950; Camus: *L'Homme Revolté* Gallimard 1951 (Penguin 1953); Beauvoir: *Faut-il brûler Sade?* In *Les Temps Modernes*,

Dec 1951 and Jan 1952, (in *The Marquis de Sade*, ed. Paul Dinnage, John Calder 1962); Levy: *Vie du Marquis de Sade avec un examination de ses ouvrages* Gallimard 1952-57; Garçon: *L'Affaire Sade* Pauvert 1957; Bataille: *La Littérature et le Mal* Gallimard 1957 (Marion Boyars 1973); *L'Erotisme* Minuit 1957 (Marion Boyars 1987)

[49] David 2006 p. 44

[50] See for example, Marie-Antoinette Morat cited in Mahon 2020 p. 155, #156

[51] Anthony Beevor and Artemis Cooper *Paris After the Liberation 1944-49* (1994) p. 158, cited in Hussey 2007 p. 387

[52] Mahon 2020 pp 154– 155

[53] Deforges 1975 p. 36

[54] Cited in Deforges 1975 p. 187

[55] The Soviet suppression of the Hungarian uprising in 1956 made such apologetics increasingly implausible, leaving some of the more rudderless French intellectuals to gravitate to Maoism. It was not until the 1990s that the French intelligentsia really woke up to the horrors of Communism. See for example: *Le Livre noir du communisme: Crimes, terreur, répression* ed. Stéphane Coutois, Robert Lafont 1997/ *The Black Book of Communism* Harvard University Press 1999.

[56] The question of conformity and obedience has remained a live one, being a major area in social psychology research for decades after. See Solomon Asch 'Effects of group pressure on the modification and distortion of judgements' (1951), Stanley Milgram 'Behavioral study of obedience' (1963), Philip Zimbardo 'A study of prisoners and guards in a simulated prison' Haney, C., Banks, W.C. & Zimbardo P.G.(1973) etc.

[57] 'Lectures pour un front' published in *Batons, chiffres et lettres* Gallimard 1965, Cited in Deepak Narang Sawhney (ed,) *Must We Burn Sade?* Humanity Books, 1999 p. 258

[58] Black 1999

[59] Beauvoir 1951 p. 55

[60] Albert Camus *L'Homme révolté* (1951/ *The Rebel* (1953), Penguin 1974 p. 43

[61] See for example Nancy Hutton *Erotic Literature in Post-War France* (Raritan: A Quarterly Review; 1992 Summer; 12(1): 29-45.)

[62] David 2006 p. 359

[63] Whitney Chadwick *The Militant Muse, Love, War and the Women of Surrealism* Thames & Hudson 2017/ 2021 p. 227

[64] Theodor Adorno 'Culture, Criticism and Society' in *Prisms* (1949) , cited Michael Rothenberg *Traumatic Realism: The Demands of Holocaust Representation* University of Minnesota Press 2000.

[65] *Les Vases Communicants / Communicating Vessels* 1932

[66] 'Sus au miserabilism!' *Combat* March 1956, cited Durozoi 1997/2002 p. 559

[67] Sartre 1947; Camus: *Neither Victims nor Executioners* Combat autumn 1946; World Without War Publications, 1972, p. 21; Camus 1951 p. 247

[68] cited in Parul Sehgal 'How the Writer and Critic Jacqueline Rose Put the World on a Couch'; *New Yorker*, 14 August 2023

[69] Camus 1951 p. 42-43

[70] Perrine Coudurier: *Sade, les femmes et le féminisme dans les années 1950* Itinéraires 2013-2 / 2014 #1

[71] Beauvoir 1951 p. 55

[72] Ibid p. 18

[73] Ibid p. 42

[74] Ibid p. 46

[75] Ibid p. 46

[76] Guzix: The Drama Review p. 76 cited in Orenstein 1975 p. 200

[77] Réage and Deforges discuss this – for example 'Selling guns is not considered a bad thing, but selling obscene books that may arouse people, that is entirely shocking' Deforges 1975 p. 71

[78] Devorah Baum *The Jewish Joke* Profile Books 2017 p. 46

[79] Preface to *Justine*, cited in Cordurier 2014 # 23

[80] Georges Bataille: *La Littérature et la mal* (1957)/ *Literature and Evil* 1990 Marion Boyars. For Bataille, laughter was a powerful force for disruption and subversion.

[81] Sontag 1967 p. 96

[82] Ibid pp. 97-98

[83] Silverman 1984

[84] St Jorre 1995 p. 215

[85] Deforges 1975 p. 124

[86] Sontag 1967 p. 99

[87] Ibid p. 100

[88] Ibid pp. 103, 104

[89] Bedell 2004

[90] Réage 'A Girl' 1969 p. 16

[91] Cited in Deforges 1975 p. 193

[92] See Mahon 2020 pp. 126-133 for full coverage. Unless otherwise stated, what follows here is from Mahon's excellent account.

[93] Wyngaarde 2017 p. 214

[94] Mahon 2020 p. 128, citing Pauvert (ed.) *L'Affaire Sade* 1957 p. 9

[95] Paulhan's defence was published as ' Sade, Paulhan et le President' in *L 'Express* of 4 January 1957, and in *L'Affaire Sade*, published by Pauvert the same year (David 2006 p. 43)

[96] Deforges 1975 p. 193

[97] In today's terms approx $5715/ € 5255

# VII:  O and the Philosophies of Liberation II – Existentialism and Feminine Humanism

## EXISTENTIALISM

For Existentialism to take centre-stage in post-war Paris was not fortuitous. Sartre was an effective strategist and publicist, his review *Les Temps Modernes* was a focal point in the Paris literary world, and he was author of defining texts of French Existentialism. Moreover he was skilful at distancing his movement from psychoanalysis and Surrealism, both of which he saw as rivals dating from pre-war days, and ripe to be supplanted. But he and his circle did not dream up Existentialism out of thin air, it was a philosophy with an ancestry, drawing on the phenomenological method of Edmund Husserl, and with two 19th century philosophers providing its 'ethical origins' [1]. One of these was Søren Kierkegaard (1813-1855), who repudiated the big-systems philosophies of Hegel and Kant on the grounds that neither of them are of any help whatever to real people facing real problems in real life. Although a Christian, he felt the full angst of the human condition, adrift and forlorn in a universe where God does not speak, and where we find ourselves totally responsible for the meaning we find in our lives. The other main founder of Existentialist ethics was Friedrich Nietzsche.

**Friedrich Nietzsche (1844-1900):** Occupying a historic place between Sade and Freud, and with (some) resemblance to both, Nietzsche, like Kierkegaard, also repudiated the big philosophical systems popular in the German-speaking world at the time, to focus on human beings struggling with the human condition. Like Sade and Freud he was an atheist, going beyond Kierkegaard's anxious recognition that God may as well not exist by insisting 'God is dead... And we have killed him' [2], and concluding that this throws us into a world of complete freedom and total responsibility. Prefiguring Freud that we are powered by conflicting urges, Nietzsche postulated a struggle between two drives, the rational conscious Apollonian and the wildly passionate Dionysian. Unlike Sade and Freud, however, his theory was rigidly gendered. It is specifically men who have to contend with these drives as they face the fundamental challenge of life, to choose between two possible paths. One path is the exercise of the Will to Power over one's self, accepting complete responsibility and self-reliance. This is a harsh road of heroism and suffering, but one that entitles the individual to be a law unto themself, granting them the right to all the power and pleasures of being one of the élite of 'supermen' (*übermenschen*). The other path is the one more commonly taken, to bottle out, to refuse the responsibility of taking control of one's life and exercising the Will to Power, preferring instead to hide in the comforts and false reassurances of the lazy, cowardly world of the 'herd' (*untermenschen*). And if a man chooses to be one of the *untermenschen,* he has no right to complain if he is subjugated by the *übermenschen* [3]. Men are what they make of themselves – for them, the self is contingent on existential decisions. Women, in Nietzsche's view, did not face this choice, they were *untermenschen* whether they liked it or not. Humiliation at the hands of the redoubtable Lou Andreas-Salomé in 1882 (she rejected his marriage proposal and ran off with his best friend) put Nietzsche in a misogynistic sulk for the rest of his life, and his best-known work, *Thus Spoke Zarathustra* (*Also Sprach Zarathustra* 1883-85) contained a section 'Of Old and Young Women' replete with comments like 'Man should be trained for war and woman for the recreation of the warrior: all else is folly' [4].

Like Sade, Nietzsche had been celebrated in Paris in the late 19th century, and there was a vogue for him among Parisian intellectuals from the 1920s – Bataille translated him in 1926, Sartre began a Nietzschean novel in 1927 (which never saw the light of day), and Thierry Maulnier in 1935 extolled the need to 'restore to philosophy the taste for blood' [5].

However, Nietzsche had the misfortune to have been survived by a sister, Elisabeth, who became an enthusiastic admirer of Hitler, and who had the opportunity to edit and distort her brother's work to produce a body of ideas that could be incorporated into the Nazi mythos of a racialised *übermenschen*, the 'Aryan Master-race'. Hitler (no intellectual, and certainly no philosopher) was duly impressed, and declared Nietzsche his guiding spirit. Since then there has been no shortage of people across the political spectrum willing to claim or blame Nietzsche as a proto-Nazi [6]. Others realised that, like Sade, Nietzsche needed to be rescued from others' stupidity, and Bataille in the 1940s rallied to the cause with a series of books [7]. In fact it is clear from his contempt for German nationalism and sincere loathing of anti-Semitism (he fell out with his erstwhile friend Richard Wagner over the latter's hatred of Jews) that Nietzsche would have had little time for Hitler and Nazism, but the taint of proto-fascism is less easy to expunge. His misogyny and admiration for war (another point where he differed from Sade and Freud) fed into Marinetti's 'Futurist Manifesto' (1909) and thence into Mussolini's rantings. However, it was not Nietzsche's social and political views but his writings on psychology and philosophy that interested French literary figures: for Bataille, it was the ecstatic and orgiastic Dionysian drive, for Sartre, the existential life choices we face. Unexpectedly perhaps, female writers like Beauvoir (and Réage) found value in Nietzsche once his irrational road-block against women was bulldozed.

**Jean-Paul Sartre (1905-1980)**: In his *Being and Nothingness* (*L'Être et le Néant*, 1943), Sartre discussed the nature of freedom, which he saw as arising when a person moves from the inert state of *Être-en-soi* (*Being-in-oneself*) to active condition of *Être-pour-soi* (*Being-for-oneself*). Attaining the condition of Being-for-itself, the individual becomes a Subject (Agent, Self) [8], and is immediately faced with the existence of others who are Subjects in their own right. This plunges the free Subject into the dynamics of inter-personal relationships, and these Sartre saw in terms of a power struggle in which each person strives to be free, to be their own Subject, but can only do this by reducing the other to the status of an object. The principal means of objectifying the other is through looking – where the Subject imposes their gaze on the other to make them into a thing to be looked at. The problem is that the other person is trying to do the same, and there-in lies the struggle for mastery [9]. Sartre was drawing on Sade's world of dominance and submission, Hegel's 'master-slave dialectic' and Nietzsche's Will to Power over one's self and others, but there may be a more direct debt to Simone de Beauvoir, who was exploring these issues in her novel *L'Invitée* (*She Came to Stay*), published in 1943 but available to Sartre in draft form in early 1940, before he started his magnum opus [10].

There is no way out from this endless struggle for mastery. All relationships are of this nature – even love is basically a means of taking possession of the other and reducing them to dependency, while the experience of being made an object is shameful and alienating. Being an object is to be abject – and most of us live in constant fear of this. Moreover, as Hegel had pointed out, mastery is self-defeating – the 'master' seeks to be recognised as the dominating Subject by the 'slave', but by being dominated the 'slave' loses their subjectivity, and their capacity to provide any meaningful validation of the status and power of the 'master'. Neither is satisfied, both are alienated in the relationship, and this alienated state is the human condition – as explored in the post-war period by 'Absurdist' playwrights like Beckett and Pinter [and firmly rejected by Breton as pessimistic 'miserabilism'[11]].

In some relationships, rather than a power struggle between two would-be Subjects, an apparently more harmonious set-up would seem to be possible if one person takes a submissive, masochistic role, accepting the dependency their partner wishes to reduce them to, embracing the shame of objectification by willingly becoming an object of the Subject's desire. But this masochistic accommodation, and embracing of shame is in fact 'absolute alienation', a stratagem condemned to failure, because no-one can ever truly become an object. Moreover, the sadist/master is dependent as well, reliant on their submissive partner to validate them a true Subject, which, as in all manifestations of the 'master-slave' dialectic, starts to give the 'slave' power over the 'master'. And so it goes on – an endless struggle.

So sadism and masochism both fail, but alienation and grappling for power remains the order of the day, and we can do nothing to resolve it. What we can do, however, is to face up to it, and live Authentically. This means squaring up to the anguish (angst) of our Freedom, and casting aside any illusions, including religion and ideology, that provide us with spurious comfort by masking the true nature of our relationships, and in so doing conceal the reality of how easily we mistreat others. Among these illusions Sartre includes 'romantic love' as an alibi for control and exploitation, enabling both partners to turn a blind eye to the damage they are doing to each other. Like Sade, then, Sartre sees our commitment to freedom as essential to the realisation of our humanness, but inevitably selfish, rendering our relationships fundamentally sadistic. The moral imperative is for us to fully acknowledge this, and repudiate every denial of our freedom, every attempt to escape from our responsibility for our own lives, every manifestation of 'bad faith' (*mauvais fois*), which is always at the very least hypocritical and dishonest, and often enough the route to man-made hell. This is what it is to live the Authentic life. Beauvoir summarised it succinctly in 1949: 'along with the ethical urge of each individual to affirm his subjective existence, there is also the temptation to forego liberty and become a thing... This is an inauspicious road, for he who takes it.. henceforth becomes the creature of another's will... But it is an easy road: on it one avoids the strain involved in undertaking the authentic existence' [12].

The grimness of the Existentialist world view is at first sight hard to square with its fashionable popularity with the jazz-fuelled youth culture of post-war Paris, but its licensing of sex without strings, with predation as the name of the game, and all demands for fidelity, commitment and so on being merely so much romantic 'bad faith', goes a long way towards explaining its appeal – not just to men but to 'liberated' women as well. On a deeper level, Existentialism struck a powerful chord by addressing what many saw as the very root of the horror of the war – not the evil of the few, but the connivance of the many, those who failed to face up to the challenge of freedom and taking control of their own lives, those who submitted to the governance of others, collaborating, even providing their bodies as weapons of war, adopting the Inauthenticity of buying into 'bad faith' ('I have no choice'; 'I must do as the government/police tell me', 'There is no point resisting' etc.). It was Nazism and collaboration that Sartre was targeting primarily, but submission to any doctrine was in his sights, including Stalinism (in the late 1940s at least) [13].

**O and Existentialism**: Aury may have gained familiarity with Nietzsche off her own bat, or through Maulnier's interest in him in the 1930s; either way, in her interview with Deforges (1975) she made some distinctly Nietzschean comments about life – 'Living is exciting, living is cruel and exhausting...' and about the power of war 'the laying bare of the human condition', liberating us from our daily cares and even mental problems, 'No more worries about money, family, situation. A brand new destiny that tears you away from your first destiny. Life is black and white... only one thing matters. With war comes a new deal. And you live anew because you are going to die' [14]. For Romana Byrne (2012) [15], *Story of O* is itself imbued with Nietzschean philosophy, depicting the Dionysian urge to embrace suffering and death as sublime experiences, simultaneously ecstatic and aesthetic, with both pain and pleasure being expressions of a 'lust of cruelty' that is itself a manifestation of the Will to Power. O herself displays a 'talent for suffering' that is certainly masochistic, but is more an 'ecstatic liberation' than anything pathological. Byrne's reading poses a direct challenge to feminist perspectives dominant in the Anglophone world since the 1970s (see chapter X) that attack *O* for its gender politics, accusing it of submitting to patriarchal inequality and 'disempowering' women. For Byrne, the power relations in *O* do not express patriarchal power but Nietzschean aesthetics, where the active principle is coded 'masculine' and the passive 'feminine', without either being aligned clearly with actual gender – hence in *O* Anne-Marie can adopt a 'masculine' role, and René a 'feminine' one. Moreover, the energy of the Dionysian has a destabilising effect that is apparent in *O*. The narrative is dream-like, the story-line uncertain, with two alternative beginnings, and two (and later three) endings. Identities are destabilised as well – Byrne sees individual subjectivities dissolving into a mystical unity, the primordial one-ness that we achieve in orgiastic collective ecstasy when the Dionysian takes hold. We touched on this instability of identity earlier (chapter V), discussing René, Sir Stephen (and the Commander?) as aspects of the same character, the permeability of René's and O's selves, and O's 'name' indicating an absence of subjectivity. When O looks in the mirror what she sees is herself as a reflection of all other women, who have become interchangeable with her – and through the novel she engages progressively with the 'emptying out of herself' [16], until by the end her subjectivity is completely absent.

Other commentators have discussed *O* in Sartrean terms – as exposing romantic 'love' as in the end merely the appropriation of the liberty of the 'other', rendering all resolutions impossible except that of willed death [17], or as confirming the existential view that, in the real world, the master-slave dialectic cannot succeed [18]. The master, by removing the subjectivity of the slave, no longer has anyone to validate their own subjectivity as master; while the slave, unable to attain their desire to be recognised by their loved one as a subject or agent, is punished and lost in isolation and aloneness. The sado-masochistic power relation cannot lead to any kind of transcendence or resolution, only abandonment and death. D.R. Koukal (2001) discusses *O* as a consideration of the power of looking and being looked-at, although this is gendered in *O* in a way that it is not in Sartre. At Roissy, the women are clearly instructed never to look at the men, but to accept their role as objects to be looked at (becoming *body-for-other* rather than *body-for-itself* in Sartre's terminology). O gives up her previous nature as a Cartesian subject, and takes the masochist's role of wanting, not to fascinate and control but to be fascinated and controlled, to become the object of others' desire, a body existing for others to know. Blindfolds restrict her capacity to look, and her body is made into a spectacle for others, who govern her clothing and her posture, and inflict marks upon her with the whip [Sir Stephen and men at Roissy do this, René merely observes]. By becoming an object of men's gaze and cruelty, O embraces a dispossession of herself, and by the end has become completely depersonalised, an object, which would seem to fully vindicate the observation that *O* 'is an allegory, chilling in its implications, of the human alienation to which we cling' [19].

These conclusions are, however, questionable. There are ambiguities in *O*. The protagonist we discover is both sadist and masochist – she is a hunter, but finds a greater pleasure in submission, putting her predatory capacities in the service of others [an interesting parallel with Katherina in Shakespeare's *The Taming of the Shrew* (c. 1593), who becomes Petruchio's falcon, obedient yet potent, and certainly no slavish beast (Act V, scene i)]. Moreover, she asserts herself even with René and Sir Stephen, capturing their freedom by becoming their object of fascination (p. 118), and asserting a powerful gaze of her own. In a neat joke on Sartre's example of a waiter whose role becomes his identity when he realises he is being observed at his job [20], in *O* the waiter notices Sir Stephen has become a statue under O's gaze, and does not refresh his glass [21]. Deforges raises the possibility that 'subjecting' someone to your gaze both allows you to see them as you wish them to be, but simultaneously also enlivens them, giving them an opportunity to take on a new existence that is as much their own as your imagining of them – 'from the time you look attentively, they really start to exist', the person being observed 'feels alive because he is seen' [22].

Certainly in the novel O relinquishes her freedom, something Aury emphasised in her interview with Deforges, admitting to the desire to be freed from herself [23], and again later stating that she sought 'total dispossession of self and non-being' for O [24]. Paulhan's preface threw a different light on this, demonstrating an even more explicit awareness of Existentialism by repudiating its cult of freedom outright. For Paulhan, freedom does indeed always seek subordination of others: 'the only freedoms that we really appreciate are those which cast other people into... (a)... state of servitude', moreover, the 'all-consuming passion for freedom... never fails to lead to conflicts and wars that are no less consuming' [25] [This is something Camus noticed, drawing on his reading of Sade as a philosopher of freedom that cruelty is the logic of pure freedom: 'one is always free at someone else's expense' [26]]. Against this Paulhan postulated what he found in O, the total surrender known to 'lovers and mystics', submitting to the will of another, shedding all self-consideration with joy and dignity [27]. Paulhan's reading of *O* as a mystical text takes us beyond the 'human condition' where Existentialism leaves us imprisoned, and suggests it is less an allegory of alienation than a route *out* of alienation. We shall return to this idea in the next chapter.

## FEMININE HUMANISM

Like most voices at the time, Existentialism spoke of the human condition in generalised terms, but by the 1940s a new focus on gender was beginning to articulate itself in Paris. Women had finally obtained the vote in France in 1944, and in their first election voted strongly for the same conservative political and religious forces that had traditionally kept them subordinate. This raised the question whether obtaining rights for women was possibly not enough, and that women needed also to be liberated from the traditional roles and expectations that still limited them. This was the task adopted by Feminine Humanism, which 'viewed femininity as a social construct underlined by an oppressive set of practices and prevailing attitudes, notably marriage, motherhood, the Christian doctrine of sin' [28], and sought to liberate women from this 'femininity'. Feminine Humanism found its voice in the late 1940s with Simone de Beauvoir's *The Second Sex* (*Le Deuxième Sexe,* 1949) and Édith Thomas' *Feminine Humanism* (*L'Humanisme féminin),* written from 1947 to 1949 but never published, although providing a useful collective name for the movement. Although coming from a different theoretical angle, Marie Bonaparte's psychoanalytic study *On Woman's Sexuality* (*De la Sexualité de la Femme,* 1949) shared the common cause sufficiently to be included as a Feminine Humanist text.

**Psychoanalysis:** Emerging from the work of Sigmund Freud from the 1890s, Psychoanalysis played a pioneering role in engaging with women's issues in the 20th century. This was done in terms of psychological theory, establishing the view that gender arises as the result of developmental and social processes;

it was also done in professional terms, opening its doors to women practitioners and theorists at an early stage, so that by the 1920s many of the most significant psychoanalysts were women.

Freud placed the Oedipus complex at the heart of the psycho-analysis of gender development in the 1890s, working out the male version quite early [29], while the female version was only fleshed out later in dialogue with women theorists (including Lou Andreas-Salomé, Karen Horney, Hélène Deutsch and Melanie Klein) [30]. These dialogues, often quite convoluted, produced a view of the psychic development of the female as considerably more complicated than the male, involving two love objects (mother and father), a whole spaghetti of desires, identifications, rivalries, hostilities, fears, anxieties and guilt, and two genital sex organs (clitoris and vagina) providing different kinds of pleasure. The upshot is that the girl's Oedipus complex is generally too tangled to fully resolve, leading to a whole gamut of complicated and contradictory childhood feelings and fantasies retaining currency into adulthood. These include oral, anal and phallic sexuality, 'active' clitoral and 'passive' vaginal pleasure, desire for both sexes, ambiguous love and resentment towards the mother and a whole mélange of feelings towards the father. Deutsch saw the act of becoming a mother as a manoeuvre in dealing with female oedipal tangles [31] – giving rise to speculation that by so doing she can level the playing field with both her own mother (sidelining her as past her sell-by date), and with her father and men in general (by doing what no man can do). Not everyone was convinced.

For Melanie Klein (1928, 1932) [32], partition from the mother is a process in which birth is merely the first step, with the child's fear of re-absorption into the mother's body prompting the oedipal 'flight to the father' in early childhood. For the boy, this is a clear trajectory, to separate from the mother as an individual, and as a gender ('I am not my mother, and am not like her either'), the danger being that residual fear of female power may lead him to emotional coldness and hostility to the female. The girl has the trickier task of differentiating herself from her mother as an individual while still retaining the gender identification with her, which adds an additional complication to the oedipal imbroglio. The idea that many women remain in 'symbiosis' with their mothers, failing to differentiate fully and remaining entangled in a maternal net that compromises their individuality, was an issue in later feminism [33]. Such women retain a bisexual orientation and a willingness to submit to male power to liberate them from that matriarchal enmeshment, which implicates both sexes in female subordination [34]. Joan Riviere in her 'Womanliness as Masquerade' (1929) used the theory of the female Oedipus complex to explore the psycho-dynamic of the 'independent' woman, noting how different generations of aspirational women adopted different stratagems to manage matters. Among the previous generation, the 'New Woman' was in fashion, with her 'masculine' persona, bobbed hair and plus-fours, repudiating femininity (along with domesticity and motherhood, and often heterosexuality) and issuing a direct challenge to the patriarchal set-up. By the 1920s Riviere suggested that intellectual or high-achieving women were tending to reject this confrontational imitation of men in favour of a display of 'femininity' as a masquerade. This provided them with a disguise to mask unresolved resentment and guilt toward their mothers, and to conceal their competitive wishes towards men, so as to allay their anxiety and hostility, and win their approval and reassurance, both personal and professional [35].

Freud's most shocking claim had been that women are just as libidinal as men, but that society (deploying moral and religious dogmas) in seeking to police the libido of both sexes, is particularly repressive to the female – all but denying the very existence of female sexuality, at enormous cost to the psychological well-being of women. Most women analysts became advocates for the sexual liberation of women – the first step being the recognition that this sexuality exists, and has a range, complexity and richness that challenges the pieties of social propriety and 'morality'. Marie Bonaparte was one of the strongest advocates for women's sexual liberation and since the 1920s had been speaking openly about the subject (and was, not surprisingly, a favourite of the Surrealists [36]). In 1949 Bonaparte argued that society repressed female sexuality by restricting it to its 'natural' biological function of reproduction, trapping women into domesticity as wives and mothers, with a sex life restricted to the service of pregnancy. In her view, the liberation of women from social repression required the liberation of their sexuality from this strait-jacketing. For Bonaparte, women needed to experience and express their erotic capacities to the full, in particular their active clitoral sexuality (commonly associated in psychoanalytic theory with lesbianism). Sexual liberation was not only good in itself, it also released female libidinal energy for more progressive and creative ends personally, socially and politically.

**O and Psychoanalysis:** *Story of O* readily lends itself to be interpreted in terms of psychoanalysis – being in itself almost a Freudian case-study [37]. O exemplifies Marie Bonaparte's idea of an independent woman, with a successful career, free from both 'biological' repression of her sexuality and social repression into the domestic role, being neither wife nor mother, her sexual behaviour being quite unrelated to reproduction. Her libido is thoroughly liberated – she is experienced with both sexes, with active clitoral, even predatory, sexuality with women, and willing to submit to passive vaginal (not to mention anal) sexuality with men. Behind this, O can be seen to be working through complicated oedipal feelings. As we saw on p. 169, Aury readily admitted that Sir Stephen was a father figure, and that much of the pleasure O experiences in the assignations with Sir Stephen around Paris is in being mistaken for his niece or daughter (*O*, p. 169). O's feelings to Sir Stephen are suitably complicated, as befits an oedipal relationship. She feels love and respect for him, along with sexual desire and submission (perhaps displaced from her off-stage 'real' father?), but also a recognition of a similarity that prompts both identification and competition. O is after all, as we observed above, a hunter as well – she takes Jacqueline (and potentially Natalie) as prey, and demonstrates her strength defending René against Jacqueline. But in keeping with Riviere's view, she adopts masquerade to disguise this competitiveness and allay the men's anxieties, adopting increasingly 'hyper-feminine (and) submissive' clothing and masochistic behaviour to mask her 'latent desire to dominate' [38], offering her hunting skills in service to her master, trapping the young couple at the Commander's soirée [39], and donning a mask that simultaneously (and paradoxically) both conceals and highlights her predatory nature. Sir Stephen meanwhile displays the emotional withdrawal and need to dominate women characteristic of a man sensitive to the 'danger' of absorption into female emotional entanglement [40]. This echoes Klein's theory, and raises the question whether O's voluntary submission to his erotic domination is part of her struggle to differentiate herself as an individual (and if so, how successful she is). With Jacqueline, it is O who plays the liberating 'masculine' role, rescuing her from enmeshment in her suffocating matriarchal net, and winning her sexual submission. Anne-Marie clearly plays a parental role alongside Sir Stephen. She is his confederate (symbolic 'wife'?) and is 'mother-superior' of the quasi-convent of Samois, and is, after him, O's most significant 'educator'. Again, complicated oedipal material (reflecting O's sexual feelings for her off-stage 'real' mother?) is acted out indirectly, deflecting these feelings into sexual submission to a mother-substitute.

Literally the most striking feature of O's sexual experience with both 'parental' figures is the physical cruelty that accompanies it – both of them punish her ferociously, Anne-Marie even mutilating and branding her – and O is willing to not merely accept this, but to glory in it. This raises the question of masochism. Influenced by the testimony of his daughter Anna, backed by Hélène Deutsch, Lou Andreas-Salomé, Marie Bonaparte and others, Freud discussed masochism as available to both sexes, but having a particular resonance with female psychology [41]. The idea here is that a girl's unresolved oedipal desires for her father can be turned inwards, transforming guilty love for the father (and concomitant resentment of the mother) into painful guilt-free pleasure, being beaten serving as the 'meeting place between a sense of guilt and sexual love'[42]. Some women theorists made the relationship between masochism and femininity more intimate, with pleasure and pain entwined in the woman's experience of her body, impaled in sex and torn open in childbirth – this latter an experience both agonising and delirious – 'an orgy of masochistic pleasure'[43]. Parallels between O and psychoanalytic theories of female masochism are clearly evident[44], O even being cited as the 'paradigmatic literary text for female masochism'[45]. The role of women hurting O, with Anne-Marie branding and mutilating her, and Norah whipping her, are consistent with 'wicked' mother figures who it has been suggested often feature in the fantasies of masochistic women[46].

The question of masochism naturally raises the question of control. A surface reading sees Sir Stephen and the other men dominating the women, and O subordinated to masculine desire and will (René is an ambiguous case here, and Anne-Marie is a dominatrix, although only over women). However, Anna Freud, like her father, insisted that in a sado-masochistic relationship, it is the masochist who calls the shots[47] – saying, not 'I am tormented', but 'I direct my torment'[48]. For Aury, this was true of her novel, asking (as we saw in chapter II) whether O is the victim of Sir Stephen and René, or whether she uses them 'to obtain the fulfillment of her dream', whether 'secretly' it is her 'requirement that governs them', so that 'She wins, in the end...'[49]. To St Jorre (1994), Aury insisted that O was in control throughout, and always free to refuse what was done to her. This has been questioned[50]. Sir Stephen is careful to ask her permission at every point, but the men at Roissy certainly do not – although that does not rule out the possibility that O's unspoken desires are being gratified, and while she is being put through the most stringent regime of training by the men, this is in a context of an exploration of her own sexual inclinations that is already underway, and may be interpreted as emancipatory. Some have argued that O is very much the 'author' of the narrative, engaged in a system of sexual exchange, her submission being a technique of control, with the marks on her body, rather than being imposed, inscribed and encoded by male power [51], in fact being a corporeal stratagem she adopts to guide what is very much her story [52].

In the novel, O experiences all aspects of the Freudian libido – touching, looking and hurting (all of which can be experienced actively or passively). With touching and looking, O prefers to be active, recalling her past experiences with women where she initiated the kisses and caresses, and accepted 'the gift' of a woman being naked for her gaze, without allowing herself to be seen unclothed by her (*O* pp. 98-100). Her relationship with pain is initially passive endurance and enjoyment, but is later introduced to the active experience of it, the 'terrible feeling of pleasure' in whipping another girl (*O* p. 162). O's active libido again raises the question of her control over proceedings, and this resonates intriguingly with the role played by another woman called 'O' – the 'Anna O' of the founding case-study of psycho-analysis (1895) [53]. 'Anna' was a patient of Freud's older colleague Joseph Breuer, and it was she who nudged Breuer towards the therapeutic practice of a 'talking cure' which was to evolve into psychoanalysis. This parallel raises the suggestion that O, like 'Anna', while ostensibly the passive recipient of her 'treatment', is in fact the driving force behind a new discourse on feminine sexuality and psychic development.

Of course, O is a character in a novel, and as such does not actually have psychoanalytic depth – but Dominique Aury did, and, through the novel, psychoanalysis can perhaps offer insights into the author – although we must be careful here not to over-readily identify Aury with O, or to underestimate the artifice that has gone into creating *O* as a novel. Still, if we can allow ourselves a few minutes of speculation, a little arm-chair psychoanalysis of Aury might throw up some inter-esting possibilities. She seems to fit well with Bonaparte's and

Riviere's depictions of the independent, liberated woman. A successful member of the Paris literary intelligentsia (wearing the mask of 'Dominique Aury'), she divorced an abusive husband and never married again (although never shirking her responsibilities towards her son). She also expressed her sexuality independently of reproductive function and did so in a wide variety of ways – bisexuality, predation, submission, some would say promiscuity, fantasies (of prostitution among other things [54]), her choice of reading matter, and writing *Story of O* (which she did behind another mask – 'Pauline Réage'). Some prefer to see Réage as having no more control over the novel than O had over the story, stressing her obedience to Paulhan over developing the text and allowing it to be published [55], but others insist that she was very much in control, willingly complying with the wishes of her chosen accomplice to achieve ends she herself desired [56]. For Adrienne M. Angelo (2007), *O* was written 'to please and titillate, but also to shock and ensnare, her lover Paulhan'.

We can also trace a complicated oedipal trajectory in Aury's life. In chapter III we discussed how Aury (as Anne Desclos) seems to have rebelled against her father (unresolved feelings of rivalry and hostility, and guilty erotic desire?), and formed a union with her mother (taking her name after her divorce). One wonders if this might have compromised her ability to differentiate from her mother, as Kleinian theory might suggest. In 1941 we suggested she was re-orientating her life – rejecting the right-wing circles of her rebellious youth for the Resistance, and approaching Paulhan, which we speculated might be a sign of reconnecting with her father. In her later life Aury drew parallels between Auguste and Paulhan, and expressed nothing but adoration for both of them, while giving a sour account of relations with her mother. Perhaps we can see Aury finally managing her 'flight to the father', with the aid of Paulhan, to successfully liberate her from maternal entrapment. Unresolved oedipal feelings towards her father were perhaps handled by this conflation of Auguste with Paulhan, her literary 'fathers'. Any fugitive hostility could be allayed by identifying with and impressing them – following them into the life of literature, and thrilling them both with her own admirable career among the Paris intelligentsia and the writing of *O* [57]. Left-over erotic desire for Auguste could be transferred to guiltless love for father-figure Paulhan, and fantasies of the guilt-free painful love of masochistic punishment, while unresolved hostilities to her loved-but-then-repudiated mother may have been assuaged in fantasises of O being punished by mother-figure Anne-Marie (who, as we have seen, is also identifiable with Édith Thomas, another woman for whom Aury felt mixed love and guilt).

The role of fantasy is important, and appreciating it is one of the advantages psychoanalysis has over Existentialism, whose commitment to the 'Real' limits its grasp of the range of possible resolutions to psychological dilemmas. Whereas Existential accounts see all relationships as power-struggles ending in failure and alienation, psychoanalysis understands that, as with wish-fulfilment in dream [58], revealing and articulating desires in fantasy, including (even especially) 'forbidden' ones, provides a way of coping with tensions and frustrations that would otherwise lead to hysteria. Female masochistic fantasy, for example, is a way of addressing tensions arising from women faced with an enticing but frustrating world they want to simultaneously accept and reject, such fantasy being an ambiguous and aesthetically satisfying means of critiquing gendered power relations, and by no means a mere surrender to a patriarchally ascribed 'feminine' role [59]. In keeping with Freud's theory of shell-shock, if femininity is itself the product of 'culturally induced trauma', then the masochistic or Gothic fantasies that endlessly replay traumatic experiences may really be indications of a desire for mastery over them [60]. Effectively then, masochism becomes a stratagem for women in particular to manage their experience of the world, a way to turn powerlessness into power [61], transforming their experience into fantasy, and then finding ways to express it, as Anna Freud recommended [62], and Pauline Réage actually did.

But fantasy, play and literature can be more than simply coping mechanisms, they can also provide potent means for gratifying desire, uncovering and expressing the whole range of female sexual passions in the liberation of women and the enrichment of their lives [63]. Sado-masochistic relationships may be doomed to fail in the real world of Existentialism, but as sexual theatre they have greater potential [64], and *O* may be seen as such a 'performance' [65]. For Benjamin (1983), referring to *O*, 'however disturbing or perverse their form, the impulses to erotic violence and submission express deep yearnings for self-hood and transcendence... Putting aside moral judgment, let us take this fantasy as fantasy' [66], a view Kaufmann (1998) endorses: 'Distinguishing between a fantasy and the desire for its enactment can be crucial... The fantasy of a desire is not the same as the desire for that fantasy to become realized. In Dominique Aury's words, alluding to *O* in conversation, "Fantasies are unliveable, but they help in living"' [67].

**Simone de Beauvoir:** In 1949, the same year as Bonaparte's paper, Simone de Beauvoir's ground-breaking book *The Second Sex* was published. Here she pushed beyond the focus of previous women's rights movements on sex, reproduction, the vote and so on, into a consideration of the experience of what it is to be a woman in the post-war world.

Her starting point was the recognition that world-wide, and throughout much of history, women have been kept in a subordinate position, as the second sex. In Book I Facts and Myths, Part I 'Destiny', Beauvoir looked at biology, psycho-analysis and Marxism, finding none of them could explain (or justify) this subordination. In Part II, 'History', she traced its origin to the establishment of patriarchy, which she associated with the advent of private property (echoing Rousseau).

Her conclusion was that the question is not so much about the position of women as about the *positioning* of women, and here she deployed an Existentialist model, that as man established himself as owner and controller of resources, so woman was positioned in relation to him: 'She is defined and differentiated with reference to man and not he with reference to her; she is the incidental, the inessential as opposed to the essential. He is the Subject, he is the Absolute – she is the Other' [68]. Woman is subordinated so as not to pose a danger to man's Subjectivity [69], and is deployed as a resource to fulfil roles for him, to provide him with what he lacks. This involved the construction of myths of womanhood – and in Part III, 'Dreams, Fears, Idols', Beauvoir examined some of these myths of femininity as found in five male writers, including D.H. Lawrence, André Breton, and Stendhal. Beauvoir depicted them all constructing woman as providing man with some redemptive link to the realm of Nature, or the poetic, or even the supernatural – becoming 'the privileged Other, through whom the subject fulfils himself: one of the measures of man, his counterbalance, his salvation, his adventure, his happiness' [70]. [For Beauvoir, Breton was not very different from the other writers – positioning woman as *femme-enfant*, muse, enchantress, channel to the Marvellous and so on – much like any other romantic poet [71]]. The 'privilege' of this Otherness however comes at a price – it relies on the woman accepting the condition of 'immanence' (Being-in-oneself/ Être-en-soi) and foregoing her aspiration for independent 'transcendence' (Being-for-oneself/ Être-pour-soi), so as not to pose a threat to the male Subject – for if she does she becomes monstrous: 'a praying mantis, an ogress' [72] ('bunny-boiler' anyone?). The complicating factor, arising from the power of myth, is that woman is commonly complicit in this – the 'privilege' of Otherness can be beguiling, and she can collaborate in the dialectic that subordinates her, finding herself 'well pleased with her role as the Other' [73].

In Book II Woman's Life Today, Beauvoir engaged in an analysis of women in contemporary society, her account overlapping much more with psychoanalysis than is often credited – some of the most cited sources in *The Second Sex* are psychoanalysts, notably Hélène Deutsch. Part IV, 'The Formative Years', begins with the most striking quote from the whole book – 'One is not born, but rather becomes, a woman' [74] – and goes on to trace the upbringing and socialisation of woman from childhood through to adolescence, sexual initiation and establishment of sexual orientation. In Part V, 'Situation', Beauvoir looked at women's roles, how marriage and motherhood make her a passive instrument, how careers can trap a woman into a feminine role in a man's world (echoes of Joan Riviere), how the prostitute can turn her 'otherness' to material advantage, and so on.

Part VI, 'Justifications', surveys what goes on in woman's inner being as she negotiates with her positioning, how 'the imprisoned woman' seeks to 'transform her prison into a heaven of glory, her servitude into sovereign liberty' [75]. First, how 'The Narcissist' becomes her own object (which carries with it the danger of frigidity), and then how 'The Woman in Love' and 'The Mystic' both buy into the promise of love. For Beauvoir: 'Love has been assigned to the woman as her supreme vocation, and when she directs it towards a man, she is seeking God in him…'. If for some reason that doesn't work for her, she 'may choose to adore divinity in the person of God Himself' [76]. [The short section on 'The Mystic' (which we shall look at briefly in the next chapter) functions as an adjunct to the principal section on 'The Woman in Love', whose experience is quasi-mystical anyway]. In 'Justifications', Beauvoir described the woman's experience of love as quite different from that of the man, making grand generalisations about gender that can seem a little startling to contemporary readers. For Beauvoir, woman, as the 'second sex', buys fully into the romantic myth: love for her is a state of complete absorption, submission and possession. In Beauvoir's view, 'Love is the whole thing for women'[77], and she cites as 'well said' Byron's lines in *Don Juan*, 'Man's love is of a man's life a thing apart, / 'Tis woman's whole existence'[78]. She also quotes Nietzsche: 'woman wishes to be taken... she demands, therefore, someone to take her, someone who does not give himself, who does not abandon himself, but who wishes, on the contrary, to enrich his ego through love... The woman gives herself, the man adds to himself by taking her'[79], and French poet Cécile Sauvage: 'Woman must forget her own personality when she is in love... A woman is non-existent without a master'[80]. Beauvoir concurs (her only cavil being with Sauvage over her claim that this is 'a law of nature', when for Beauvoir it is the product of woman's situation). For Beavoir, woman is positioned to see man as superior, and she embraces engulfment in love, enslavement to her beloved, taking him as her god, her salvation. Foregoing her desire for 'transcendence' (Being-for-oneself) as an independent individual, she seeks transcendence through unity with her beloved. She 'gives up *her* transcendence, subordinating it to that of the essential other' (my italics), dreaming of 'transcending her being towards one of these superior beings, of amalgamating herself with the sovereign subject'[81]. Her 'deepest desire is to remain under the domination of the man, who is protection and virility'[82], and 'She chooses to desire her enslavement so ardently that it will seem to her the expression of her liberty', 'since she is anyway doomed to dependence, she will prefer to serve a god rather than obey tyrants – parents, husband or protector'[83] (echoing the Kleinian account of the trajectory of the girl in her struggle towards differentiation – see above, pp. 241-242).

From the start Beauvoir's account of women's love carries with it the flavour of the mystical – piety and the erotic echo one another. 'Love becomes for her a religion', and woman wants to 'lose herself in the other', 'she offers him incense, she bows down', and, like the Virgin Mary visited by the Holy Spirit, 'abandon becomes sacred ecstasy. When she receives her beloved, woman is dwelt in, visited...' [84]. She engages in 'total immersion in love – worship, self annihilation', for 'love requires abandonment – annihilated, she becomes one with the whole, her ego is abolished' [85]. But this abandon, this self-annihilation brings a reward: she, by finding 'favour in his sight feels herself transformed into a priceless treasure', for 'this dream of annihilation is in fact an avid will to exist' [86].

Beauvoir realises how much this sounds like an admission of female masochism, and recognises that if this abandon and self-annihilation is accompanied by self-disgust or the desire to take vengeance on or harm herself [87], then a line can be crossed. She attempts to demarcate this line by distinguishing between the impetus to transcend through ecstatic union with the beloved, and the urge to submit to being made an object [88] (although others have questioned this distinction [89]). But Beauvoir is aware that the ecstasy of union does not preclude the delight in pain – although she argues that what 'exalts' the woman who likes to be beaten 'is not the idea of her beaten and enslaved person, it is rather the strength and authority, the supremacy of the male, on whom she is dependent', relishing the intoxicating joy of being subject, even prey, to the free action of an independent sovereign being. Again, there are rewards – her body is transformed: 'through humiliation and suffering she transforms it into a glory. Given over to her lover as a thing for this pleasure, she becomes a temple, an idol', 'Her body is no longer an object: it is a hymn, a flame' [90]. Moreover, this self-abandonment and self-annihilation permits identification with the beloved (the Kleinian 'flight to the father' being played out?); as Beauvoir points out, the cry of every woman in love is to be one with the beloved (citing Cathy in *Wuthering Heights*), for after all, 'one wearies of living always in the same skin'.

But of course the dialectical wheel of power-struggle turns, and this state of ecstatic bliss cannot last. 'Her joy is to serve him – but he must gratefully recognise the service: the gift becomes a demand in accordance with the usual dialectic of devotion', her willing slavery carries demands: he must always be available to her, he must exist for her, not in himself. 'She makes herself a slave in order to enchain him', she burdens him, 'her tyranny is insatiable', 'she is a jailer' [91]. The great paradox of love is that he becomes her prisoner, and as 'a captive, the god is shorn of his divinity' [92]. For man is not a god, and, once enchained, he cannot sustain the illusion that he is, and when a god falls he does not revert to being a man, he becomes a fraud – 'they would not seem to be dwarfs if they had not been asked to be giants' [93] [Paulhan's imagining of O's words to her master, 'You should never have agreed to be a god for me if you were afraid of assuming the duties of a god' provides an interesting echo [94]]. So in the end, the woman's immersion in love fails. She 'abandons herself to love first of all to save herself; but the paradox of idolatrous love is that in trying to save herself she denies herself utterly in the end' [95], and in so doing she dethrones her 'god' as well, and mutual misery results. As Beauvoir concludes: 'the innumerable martyrs to love bear witness against the injustice of a fate that offers a sterile hell as ultimate salvation' [96]. The path of the Mystic has no better outcome. However, 'one day it will be possible for woman to love not in her weakness but in her strength... not to abase but to assert herself – that day love will become a source of life and not of danger' [97], although Beauvoir acknowledges another possibility, that 'if two lovers sink together into absolute passion, all their liberty is degraded into immanence – death is the only solution' [98].

In Part VII, 'Towards Liberation', Beauvoir concluded her work by providing the outline of her solution to this tragic mess – the emergence of the Independent Woman. This woman goes out to work to gain economic independence and some control over her destiny; all to the better if she can become a writer or an intellectual to enable her to explore 'death, life and suffering'[99], but above all she will not seek any individual salvation, whether through narcissism, love or mysticism, but will engage in collective action to overcome economic obstacles and achieve a socialist transformation of society. Only in this way can women liberate themselves from Otherness and the subordinate status of being the second sex.

The power of Beauvoir's writing and the dazzling cascade of insights she reveals are undeniable, and her book has rightly been hailed as one of the foundation stones of modern feminism. But it is a troubled text as well, with her writing and her message to some degree at odds. Beauvoir's account of 'The Woman in Love' is vivid, vibrant and charged, and it is easy to see personal experience adding colour and depth, but also adding Authenticity – an important word in the Existentialist vocabulary. In 1947 Beauvoir had commenced a passionate and fulfilling love affair with American writer Nelson Algren, and at the same time she was witnessing (with some satisfaction) the disintegration of the relationship between Sartre and American broadcaster Dolorès Vanetti due to the latter's 'serious demands' on him[100]. This may have informed Beauvoir's account of 'the usual dialectic of devotion' working its way through, with perhaps her own experience of disenchantment with Sartre adding to the mix. However, it is notable that in comparison with the verve and vim of her writing about the woman in love, when Beauvoir turns to outline the 'solutions' to the predicament of woman, her writing loses its power and conviction and becomes tepid and bloodless[101].

Predictably, *The Second Sex* came under ('very violent!'[102]) fire from  the usual conservative suspects – the Communist Party (for whom it was 'another trivial catalogue of female complaints intended to distract people from genuine class struggle'[103]), the Catholic Church (who put it on the Vatican black-list, along with Sartre's works), along with François Mauriac and the rest of the same crowd who were to attack

*Story of O* a few years later. So far so predictable, but Albert Camus also joined in the chorus of disapproval, having taken offence at what he considered to be an 'assault on masculinity' [104]. Ironically, more recent critics have taken Beauvoir to task for not doing what the Communists accused her of doing, in that she 'did not envision a strategy for women's struggles,' concluding instead that 'socialism would suffice to resolve all women's problems. For her, the feminist fight was not a specific fight' [105].

Interestingly, despite the significant influence of Beauvoir on Sartre's thought and her contribution to Existentialist philosophy [106], to the end of her life Beauvoir never hinted for a moment that she was ever anything but 'the second sex' to Sartre's intellectual leadership. The conclusion that she took comfort, even pleasure, in her subordinate position to Sartre (in the public eye at least) is hard to avoid. For some, this represents a failure on her part, and she has been taken to task for being unable to overcome 'phallo-centered representations' and 'a masculine perspective on women' [107]. Her response was 'Well, I just don't give a damn ... I'm sorry to disappoint all the feminists, but you can say it's too bad so many of them live only in theory instead of in real life' [108]. Beauvoir may have had other reasons for not adopting values fashionable today.

**Beauvoir and Aury** [109]: Dominique Aury and Simone de Beauvoir had a friendly acquaintance. Beauvoir referred in her memoirs to convivial discussions with Aury and Paulhan at *Les Temps Modernes* editorial meetings [110], Aury interviewed Beauvoir in 1945 [111], and reviewed *The Second Sex* in 1950 in an article 'The Face of the Medusa' ('Le Visage de Méduse') [112]. Here she praised the courage of Beauvoir as a writer, to assault 'the gravest of all taboos', a woman exposing herself to reveal and challenge the injustice of women's relegation to the second sex, and speaking openly, 'in clear language', on matters intimate and sexual. For Aury, 'that is why Simone de

Beauvoir's book will go down in history, less due to its content than to its tone of freedom' [113]. Such words would have been equally applicable to *O* a couple of years later.

A common feminist response to *The Second Sex* has been to read it as a critique revealing 'love' to be 'the pivot of women's oppression today', romanticism being a 'cultural tool of male power' [114], but Aury's response seems to have been more complex. The title of Réage's 1969 essay 'A Girl in Love' is a clear echo of Beauvoir's 'The Woman in Love', and *Story of O* reflects the tone, intensity and flavour of the writing in Beauvoir's chapter, along with central themes – O's voluntary enslavement, her engulfment in love, her worship of her beloveds, the wonders of self-abandon and self-annihilation [115], even some of the wording, with O receiving René's ejaculation into her mouth 'as a god is received' (*O* p. 19) echoing Beauvoir [116]. [The obvious kinship between *The Second Sex* and *Story of O* raises a question-mark over Camus' peculiar reaction in 1954, fulminating that no woman could possibly have written such a thing as *O* when he knew full well that Beauvoir had penned *The Second Sex*. Apparently he had been left out of the select circle of those 'in the know' about *O*, but he was no fool and may well have suspected the truth. Perhaps he was offended by the exclusion, or agitated that someone with whom he had once been intimate had written it?].

Several commentators have seen parallels between *O* and Beauvoir's argument. For Brown and Faery (1984) *O* is an analogy of the disastrous life of the married woman, from independence to surrender to death [117]. For Mahon (2020), *O* exemplifies Beauvoir's thesis – the analysis of love, the self-sacrifice, the absolution, the complicity of the woman, amounting to being an 'effort to put into fiction Beauvoir's understanding of the body as sexuate' [118]. Shullenberger (2005) [119] traces the whole dialectic working through – from transcendence, where O submits to her god-like lover, becomes an instrument of his will, and is possessed 'as a god possesses his creation' (*O* p.

19), through to self-abandonment where she loses her sense of self, and is exalted through her suffering and degradation, to the final failure of the cycle as Sir Stephen, having reduced O to total submission, realises he now has a non-person on his hands, one who cannot give him the recognition he demands as a master, and deserts her. Unusually, Shullenberger incorporates *Return to the Château* into this reading, claiming it as the legitimate sequel, and showing O abandoned by Sir Stephen, her transcendence replaced by mere commercial exchange, failing to find recognition for one sub-deity after another, and finally abandoned by Pauline Réage as well.

The authenticity of *Return* as part of Réage's plan for *O* is, as we have seen, highly questionable, but the case that *O* can be read in terms of Beauvoir's philosophy is a powerful one. What is not present however is the exposure of the once-worshipped 'god' as a fraud that Beauvoir talks about. René is dethroned and becomes forlorn, but O does not despise him, rather she still cares for him enough to defend him against Jacqueline's callousness. But as René's status falters, so Sir Stephen, a harsher god, takes over, and he is not dethroned [120]. In 'the most flagrant case of a reversal of the Hegelian dialectic: the slave wants to remain a slave' [121], and man, as O wishes, retains mastery [122]. Equally conspicuous by its absence is Beauvoir's 'solution', the day when 'love will become a source of life and not of danger' [123] [one can almost hear Aury asking what kind of love or life is it without danger?].

*Story of O* does, seemingly, end with O's death. This may be the death that Beauvoir suggested results from the relinquishing of freedom and sinking into immanence (Being-in-oneself) – as implied by the narrator likening her to a thing of 'stone or wax' (*O*, p. 203). But Réage knew that 'one is not free when one is in love' [124], so that does not fully convince. Or it may be an admission by Réage that love can fail through abandonment, something Réage/Aury spoke of many times [125] – 'What is the end of love, if it is not death?', with loss of love as the worst of all fates, 'Death is preferable' [126]. Or it may arise from some altogether more mystical transcendence, something we shall return to in chapter IX.

But if O accepts death as the price for her love, Aury it would seem, found another solution – namely, to accept the protection of a man who would take some of the stress from her, look after her and shield her from (some of) the slings and arrows of outrageous fortune, and perhaps this is something that Beauvoir shared, something that some of her more strident followers did not quite get. Unlike Aury, however, Beauvoir was not following her heart here – she left Algren to return to Paris and the lower-intensity, workable relationship as Sartre's lieutenant. Both Aury and Beauvoir were however to experience the full trauma of abandonment when the men they allowed to protect them died.

In the end Aury and Beauvoir were both aware of the idea that love has a transcendent power – as expressed powerfully by radical anarchist Emma Goldman in 1906: 'A true conception of the relation between the sexes will not admit of conqueror and conquered; it knows of but one great thing: to give of one's self boundlessly, in order to find oneself richer, deeper, better. That alone can fill the emptiness, and transform the tragedy of women's emancipation into joy, limitless joy' [127]. Aury refused to deny her emotional self, preferring to remain in thrall to love – 'the abandonment, the consent, the mystery she grants to the beings she loves, as others grant it to their God' [128]. For Beauvoir (as for Mary Wollstonecraft?) the struggle between head and heart was less easy to resolve.

**Édith Thomas**: Just as the works of Marie Bonaparte and Simone de Beauvoir were being published, so Édith Thomas was finalising a manuscript of her own, composed between 1947-1949, during and just after her affair with Dominique Aury [129]. Comprising an anthology of women writers from the late medieval Christine de Pisan to Simone de Beauvoir, Thomas entitled her work *Feminine Humanism* (*L'Human-*

*isme féminin*) [130], which she presented as a necessary corrective to the masculinist slant of post-war Parisian Humanism, providing her own definition of the movement 'To give to each human being, man or woman, the possibility of developing fully and harmoniously' [131]. The manuscript was due to be published by *Hier et Aujourd'hui* (Yesterday and Today) in 1949, but that year Thomas resigned from the PCF and went public about her reasons, which earned her the ire of the Communist leadership (expressed in startlingly dishonest and brutal terms – see p. 136). Communist leverage over *Hier et Aujourd'hui* was enough for them to cancel publication of *Feminine Humanism* [132].

Thomas does not seem to have attempted to find another publisher for her book, and this invites a little speculation. Kaufmann (1995) described Thomas as Beauvoir's 'shadow sister' [133], and although Thomas had praised *The Second Sex* (describing it as a 'courageous effort of elucidation' [134]), the fact that Beauvoir was published when she was dropped by her publisher (and battered by the PCF to boot) must have been dispiriting at least. In addition, hurt and jealousy in the aftermath of Aury leaving her for Paulhan cannot have been helped by Aury's friendly relations with and enthusiasm for Beauvoir, an acquaintance which Thomas seems not to have shared. Then in late 1950 Aury was telling Thomas of her 'strange enterprise' in writing, which she then withheld for Paulhan's eyes only (see p. 159), which won't have done much to boost Thomas' spirits. Finally in 1951 Beauvoir's Sade essay was published – and if Thomas was shocked by *O* when she finally read it, one can imagine what she thought about 'Must We Burn Sade?'. Did Thomas feel that Feminine Humanism was running away from her, and going off-piste into fields she could not handle, and did this take the wind out of her sails over *L'Humanisme féminin*? And did her experiences with Aury and Beauvoir and their works play a role in cranking her up to explode in Paulhan's face in 1952?

By 1960 however, Thomas was willing to pick up the traces once again, as one of the nine contributors to an illustrated encyclopaedia entitled *Celebrated Women* (*Les Femmes célèbres*). Here Thomas wrote on 'Lovers' and 'Women and Power' [135], and a section on writers and activists including Olympe de Gouges, Mary Wollstonecraft, Flora Tristan, Pauline Roland and Rosa Luxembourg. These she identified as the pioneers of L'Humanisme féminin [136]. Thomas, as we have seen, was a heroic figure in her own right [137], and was fully appreciative of the heroism of the women she wrote about, but she had another side to her as well – a heady taste for the transcendence of total self-sacrifice, something that she and Aury, so different in so many ways, had in common. On June 10th 1944, as Liberation was approaching and the final battle loomed, Thomas wrote a fantasy of ultimate submission to the revolution – four passages, each beginning 'If they said to you...' followed by some mistreatment of her, on the promise that (an unidentified) 'they' would create 'the world you desire', to each of which Thomas responded, 'I would answer, "All right, that's fine".' The final and most extreme of the four passages reads: 'If they said to you: 'You will be put in prison and slandered, and you will die ignominiously in a way that will make everyone believe you were against us, but we will create the world you desire'; I would answer: "All right, that's fine."' [138]. Later, in November 1946, a few days after her seduction by Aury, she made the first notes for what was to become a story of self-annihilation for sapphic love, finally published as 'Le Fin de Gomorrh' ('The End of Gomorrah'), in the collection *Eve et les autres* (*Eve and the Others*) in 1952. In Thomas' story, Lot's wife, (unidentified in The Bible [139], but here named, significantly, 'Édith'), being separated from her lesbian lover 'Deborah' (a thinly disguised 'Dominique'?), refuses to escape from the cursed cities when God's wrath smites them (reputedly for the 'sin' of homosexuality), preferring to take the forbidden look that will turn her into a pillar of salt [140]. It is easy to see in this a fantasy resolution to comfort her after the failure of her real affair with Aury, which, along with her fantasy of sacrifice for the revolution, reveals a passion for complete abandonment of the self.

**Dominique Aury:** The condition and rights of women had been important to Dominique Aury since at least 1944, when she wrote about them for *Femmes Française*, with particular interest in the struggle for the vote in France and the Anglophone world [141], subjects she returned to in 1975 in her interview with Deforges [142]. In 1950 she had praised Beauvoir's *The Second Sex*, but her first significant contribution to Feminine Humanism was her article 'The Revolt of Madame de Merteuil' ('La Révolte de Mme De Merteuil') [143], written in 1950 and published in 1951 (the same year as Beauvoir's 'Must We Burn Sade?', to which it is a kind of sister-text). Here, Aury focused on the female protagonist of Laclos' *Dangerous Liaisons* in a discussion of the situation of women in the 18th century French upper-class games of seduction – the courtesy and the cruelty, the acceptance of libertinism and the complicity of the 'victims' in their own conquest. Aury depicted Merteuil as accepting these rules of engagement, as an adventuress, a strategist, acting on her own behalf rather than that of 'womankind', her revolt being by no means an attempt to overthrow these games or to change the order, but simply to play a winning hand [144]. A controversial text, exploring the political ambiguities of a woman who seizes the chance of 'empowerment', it can be seen in the context of the post-war 'cult' of Sade among the Paris literati. It also made an autobiographical nod to the games she and Paulhan had (and still) played, as well as acting as a curtain-raiser for *O* [145], which she started writing soon after – O being reflected in both Merteuil getting what she wants, and in Mme de Tourval dying when abandoned by the man she loves [146].

*Story of O* was Aury's contribution to the expression of feminine humanist ideas in novel form, as both Beauvoir and

Thomas did (just as the Existentialists – Sartre, Camus, and of course Beauvoir – explored their philosophy through fiction). For Deforges the 'feminist' credentials of *O* were never in doubt: 'It is absolutely a feminist work, empowering to women. For the first time a woman is revealing her sex life, and it is the woman who dominates the situation, her feelings, her responses, her trajectory' [147], a view reiterated by David (2006), for whom Aury 'publicly expresses a feminine truth for the first time', 'the expression of O's sexuality (being) a liberating act, since the respectable (bourgeois) behaviour expected of women is the last bastion of their imprisonment' [148]. Like Thomas, in 1960, Aury contributed to the *Celebrated Women* encyclopaedia, writing the section on 'Women of Letters' ('Les Femmes de lettres'), including those who wrote in the vein of 'L'Humanisme féminin' [149]. She also wrote of another group of women writers, those she called 'Les Inconscientes' ('The Unconscious Ones'), 'who write not because they want to write, but because they are possessed and prisoners: I am referring to women in love and mystics. Saint Theresa and Mariana [Alcoforado], [Saint] Marie Alacoque and Heloïse are sisters. Let us leave them to their gods' [150]. [The reference to 'women in love and mystics' closely echoes the words of Paulhan in his 1954 preface, (p. xxii), and on the evidence of the first sixty pages of *O*, Aury would have been fully within her rights to have included herself here as an *inconsciente*].

As feminine humanists, Aury and Thomas were not completely in step. Thomas saw gender politics much more in terms of women establishing a clear identity as women and struggling for equality as a collective – 'woman belongs to humanity as much as man does and should have all the rights called "the rights of man"' [151]. The need for clear identity mattered to Thomas on a personal level as well – during the war she had, as a member of the Resistance, adopted noms-de-guerre, but after that she steadfastly refused pseudonyms. Aury, by contrast, favoured androgyny, flexibility and shifting selves over gender struggle and identity politics [152], and of course had a distinct penchant for noms-de-plume (although she admired those who did not feel the need for such masks, like Thomas and Deforges [153]). Thomas was aware of this, and in her novel *Jeu d'échecs* (1970) she contrasted the need of Aude (based on herself) for personal coherence and identity, with Claude (based on Aury) for whom such things were of no import [154].

Despite this, both Thomas and Aury shared the fantasy of being dispossessed of the self, submitting to some power – the one to political revolution, the other (via *O*) to love – another kind of revolution [155]. In both cases, these fantasies may be seen as steps towards liberation from other demands for subordination. In Aury's case, religious indoctrination loomed large in her childhood, and nationalist ideology in her young adulthood, after which she renewed herself as *résistant*, then libertine, then 'woman in love'. With Thomas, her almost mystical wish to martyr herself for the revolution came just before relations with the PCF, always ambiguous, started to irretrievably fray. It is tempting to see her fantasy as a move along the way to her rescuing the revolution from the possessive clutches of the Stalinists, a mission shared by many among the Humanists of the Parisian Third Way. In both cases, the fantasises of submission were liberating.

Sade's influence on Feminine Humanism had the apparently contradictory effect of raising awareness of the need for women to be liberated, while at the same time licensing expression of voluntary submission and masochism [156]. These positions may not in the end be incompatible. For Deforges, 'One can be a feminist and take pleasure in being, like O, a sexual object. For who decided to be this object, if not her?' [157], which is consistent with Réage's claim to Deforges that, although never having been a member of any feminist groups, she had 'always been a feminist' [158]. Feminists of other stripes have not always been convinced (as we shall see in chapter

X), but Aury's conclusion in *Celebrated Women* is certainly that of one committed to the liberation of women: 'When, in a hundred years, the encyclopaedia of *Femmes célèbres* will have to be redone (like all encyclopaedias), whatever our errors, however debatable our contribution, we will remain, we of the 1950s, the witnesses to something new and irreversible. We are the anonymous soil. We are barely beginning and we are beginning today. Just wait' [159].

---

[1] Mary Warnock: *Existentialism* Oxford UP 1970

[2] Nietzsche: *The Gay Science* (1882) section 125, trans Walter Kaufmann, Random House 1974

[3] Nietzsche's world view seems to have been adopted wholesale from Homer's *Iliad*, where Achilles is lionised for having chosen the brief, painful, glorious life over the chance of a long, anonymous but happy one, For Nietzsche, Achilles has every right to conquer and dominate lesser mortals.

[4] Nietzsche: (1883-85) trans. R.J. Hollingdale Penguin 1961/1985 p. 91. Other quotes from the same section refer to woman as 'the most dangerous plaything', fundamentally bitter, and to be feared by men who are advised to only approach them armed with a whip.

Lou Andreas-Salomé was quite a character: after dumping Nietzsche she caught the interest of German playwright Frank Wedekind, providing the model for the protagonist of his drama *Lulu* (written 1894), had an affair with poet Rainer Maria Rilke in the late 1890s, and from 1910 was in an intellectual (and possibly amorous) relationship with Freud – becoming a psychoanalyst and making important contributions to the understanding of the psychology of women. *Lulu* was filmed in 1929 as *Pandora's Box* by G.W.Pabst, with Louise Brooks in the starring role.

[5] Mahon 2020 p. 139

[6] For example French moral philosopher Vladimir Jankélévitch in *Le Mal* 1947

[7] Bataille: *L'Expérience Intérieure* (*Inner Experience*, 1943); *Le Coupable* (*Guilty, 1944); Sur Nietzsche* 1945, – all published by Gallimard. See also Surya 2002 pp 93-95

[8] The word 'Subject' can be a bit confusing here as it can mean the active Agent (as opposed to passive object), but also one who is ruled – as in 'subject of the crown'. In Existentialist discourse, it is used in the former sense.

[9] I am indebted in this section to D.R. Koukal : 'Sartre/Réage'

*Mosaic A Journal for the Interdisciplinary Study of Literature*. Winnipeg: vol. 34, issue 3, pp 111-136, September 2001.

[10] See Kate Fullbrook and Edward Fullbrook *Simone de Beauvoir and Jean-Paul Sartre* Basic Books 1994 ch. 5 esp. pp. 100-101

[11] Durozoi 2002 p. 461

[12] Simone de Beauvoir *Le Deuxième Sex* 1949/ *The Second Sex* (1953) Penguin 1972 p. 21

[13] During the 1950s Sartre gravitated towards the PCF, and by 1960 with his *Critique of Dialectical Reason* (*Critique de la raison dialectique*) Existentialism had 'finally succumbed to Marxism' with 'practically none of its own features left' (Mary Warnock: *Existentialism* Oxford UP 1970 p. 131), as Sartre convinced himself that in a classless society all struggles and oppositions between individuals would resolve themselves, and that it would be society, not individuals, who would be free. Later in the 1960s, he managed to become a Maoist.

[14] Deforges 1975 p. 180

[15] Romana Byrne: 'Nietzsche's Aesthetics and Paulie Réage's Story of O' *Papers on Language and Literature* (Spring 2012), vol. 48, issue 2, pp 197-218

[16] Sontag 1967 p. 102

[17] Gordon1971

[18] Jessica Benjamin 1980; Anne Kustritz: 'Painful Pleasures' *Transformative Works and Cultures* 2008

[19] St Jorre 1995 p. 229  citing Peter Fryer *Secrets of the British Museum* Citadel Press 1966

[20] Sartre: *L'Être et le néant* (1943)/ *Being and Nothingness* Methuen 1958 p. 59

[21] *O*, p. 118

[22] Deforges 1975 pp. 56-57

[23] Ibid p. 55

[24] In Rapaport 2004 cited Bethune 2009

[25] Paulhan: Preface p. xii

[26] Camus *Caligula* (1944) – cited in Mahon 2020 p. 158 # 176

[27] Paulhan: Preface xii

[28] Mahon 2020 p. 126

[29] Freud *Three Essays on the Theory of Sexuality* 1905.

[30] Including Andreas-Salome: 'On the Feminine' (1914); Horney: 'The Flight from Womanhood' (1924); Deutsch: 'The Psychoanalysis of Women's Sexual Functions' (1925); Klein: 'Early Stages in the Oedipus Conflict' (1928). Freud's own contributions included: 'The Ego and the Id' (1925), 'Some Psychical Consequences of the Anatomical Differences Between the Sexes' (1925); 'Female Sexuality' (1931) and 'Femininity' (1932).

[31] Deutsch: 'The Psychology of Women in Relation to the Functions of Reproduction' (1924)

[32] Klein 'Early Stages of the Oedipus Complex' (1928), 'The Psycho-analysis of Children' (1932) in *The Writings of Melanie Klein*

Hogarth Press

[33] Nancy Friday: *My Mother, My Self: The Daughter's Search for Identity* Delacorte Press 1977

[34] See Dorothy Dinnerstein *The Mermaid and the Minotaur* Harper Colophon 1977 ; Nancy Choderow *The Reproduction of Mothering* University of California 1978

[35] Lisa Appignanesi and John Forrester: *Freud's Women*, Virago, 1993, pp. 363-364; see also Adrienne M. Angelo : *Histoire(s) de Catherine M.: Echoes of 'O' and the Difference of I in La Vie Sexualle de Catherine M.* Coastal Review, March 2007, Georgia Southern University; Mahon 2020, p. 253, note 148.

[36] They published her translation of Freud's *Question of Lay Analysis* in *La Revolution Surrealiste* in Oct 1927 and discussed her theories of the role of the clitoris in their discussions on sex in 1928 (Mahon 2020 p 156).

[37] Carol Cosman 1974 reads it as 'a voyage into psychic depths which bear an uncanny resemblance to Freud's 'A Child is being Beaten" (1919) ; see also Michelle A. Massé 1992 ch. 4 'Kissing the Rod: The Beaten and *Story of O'*

[38] Angelo 2007

[39] Brown and Faery 1984

[40] Benjamin 1980

[41] Freud: 'A Child is being Beaten' 1919; 'The Economic Problem of Masochism' 1924

[42] Ibid 1919

[43] H. Deutsch (1924) cited Lisa Appignanesi and John Forrester 1993, p. 439. Jill Tweedie attributed the 'stretching fantasy' of being raped or ripped open to a 'psychic rehearsal' or preparation for childbearing in Nancy Friday *My Secret Garden* Quartet 1975 p. 6.

[44] Brown and Faery 1984

[45] Restuccia, E. (1998). 'Conjurings: Mourning and abjection in *Story of O* and return to the chateau'. *Gender & Psychoanalysis,* 3, 123-153. p. 123; Novick, J., & Novick, K. K. (1996). *Critical issues in psychoanalysis: Vol. 3. Fearful symmetry: The development and treatment of sadomasochism.* Northvale, NJ: Jason Aronson p. 62

[46] Hélène Deutsch *The Psychology of Women* 1944, cited in Cosman 1974

[47] Anna Freud: 'Beating Fantasies and Daydreams' 1922; a view supported by Gilles Deleuze: *Masochism: Coldness and Cruelty & Venus in Furs,* Zone 1989, cited in In Deighan 2012

[48] John K. Noyes 1997 *The Mastery of Submission*, cited in Shullenberger 2005; Harvard-educated professional dominatrix 'Jennifer Hunter' endorsed this from practical experience. In her view, most women are sexually submissive, but 'Every good dominant knows that the submissive is really the partner in control. All the submissive woman has to do is relax and enjoy the ride while delicious sexual acts are visited upon her. She is the star of the proceedings. Someone is

ministering to her needs...' cited Maureen Dowd 'She's Fit to be Tied' *New York Times* April 1st 2012.

49  Deforges 1975 p. 205

50  Bethune 2009

51  As Silverman 1984 suggests

52  Angelo 2007

53  Freud and Breuer *Studies on Hysteria* 1895

54  Deforges 1975 pp. 69, 113

55  See Bedell 2004

56  Shullenberger 2005; Réage discussed the importance of the accomplice with Deforges, pp. 105-106

57  Gallus 1997

58  Freud 1900 *The Interpretation of Dreams*

59  Amalia Ziv: 'The Pervert's Progress: An Analysis of 'Story of O' and the Beauty Trilogy' *Feminist Review* No. 46, Spring 1994, pp. 61-75

60  Marie Mulvey Roberts 1994 review of Michelle Massé in *Women's Writing* vol. 1 No 2

61  Deleuze 1989 cited Deighan 2012

62  Anna Freud 1922 'Beating Fantasies and Daydreams'; for her writing is a way for a woman to free herself of repetitive masochistic fantasies – always assuming she wants to be free of them of course. .

63  See for example Anita Phillips *A Taste for Masochism* faber and faber 1998; Nancy Friday 1976; Toni Bentley relishing her experience of Catherine Robbe-Grillet's games: 'An Audience with the Chief Whip', *Sunday Times Magazine*, 1st Feb 2015 (Vanity Fair, Jan 22nd 2014).

64  Sontag 'Fascinating Fascism' 1974 cited in Deighan 2012

65  Angelo 2007

66  'Master and Slave: The Fantasy of Erotic Domination' Benjamin 1983, cited in Kaufmann 1998 p. 901

67  Kaufmann 1998 p. 902

68  Beauvoir 1949 p. 16

69  Rosemary Tong *Feminist Thought* (1989) Routledge 1992 p. 205

70  Beauvoir 1949 p. 278

71  Ibid pp. 261-268

72  Ibid p. 278.

73  Ibid  p. 21

74  Ibid  p. 295; a view entirely consistent with psychoanalysis. Interestingly, in her 1954 novel *Les Mandarins*, the protagonist, Dr. Anne Dubreulh (commonly seen as a fictionalised portrait of Beauvoir herself), is a psychoanalyst.

75  Ibid p.  639

76  Ibid p. 679

77  Ibid p. 653

78  Ibid p. 652 citing Byron *Don Juan* Canto 1 stanza cxciv

79  Ibid p. 668  citing Nietzsche *The Gay Science*

80  Ibid p. 653 Cécile Sauvage 1883-1927

81  Ibid pp. 661, 653

82  Coudurier 2014 # 7
83  Beauvoir 1949 p. 653
84  Ibid pp. 665, 659
85  Ibid p. 659
86  Ibid pp. 657, 656
87  Ibid p. 662
88  Ibid p. 660
89  Benjamin 1980
90  Ibid pp. 684-5, 659
91  Ibid pp. 669, 665, 666, 665 – the exemplary case of this is probably Jacqueline Roque being both slave and jailer to Picasso – a relationship that began five years after Beauvoir's book, and lasted till Picasso's death in 1973.
92  Ibid p. 665
93  Ibid pp. 664, 666
94  Paulhan Preface p. xxx
95  Beauvoir 1949 p. 730-1
96  Ibid p. 669
97  Ibid p. 679
98  Ibid p. 665
99  Tong 1992 p. 211
100  Fullbrook and Fullbrook 1994 p. 167
101  There is a parallel with Mary Wollstonecraft, whose rational philosophical/political treatise *Vindication of the Rights of Woman* (1792) stands in tension with her novels *Mary, A Fiction* (1788) and *The Wrongs of Woman, or Maria* (unfinished; posthumously published 1797) which valorise the affairs of the heart, and express a deep sensitivity to needs, desires and feelings in the lives of women. See R. Saxment *Writing Desire* (Black Scat Books 2024)
102  Beauvoir 1976 interview in *Simone de Beauvoir Today: Conversations 1972-82* Chatto and Windus/Hogarth 1984 cited , Mahon 2020 p. 253 #175
103  Tong 1992 p. 214
104  Ibid p. 214
105  Gisèle Halimi cited in J. Bonnier-Hamon, S. Dupagny and V. Lucas, *Choisir*, no 102, February 2008, in 'La figure féministe la plus importante', *Cahiers de l'Herne*, no 100, 2012 , p. 303. Cited in Coudurier 2014.
106  Fulbrooke and Fulbrooke 1994
107  Cited in Coudurier 2014 # 14
108  Cited in Katie Roiphe 'She works crazy hours...' *Newsweek* 30 April 2012
109  See Mahon 2020 pp. 155-161 for an excellent account of Beauvoir and *O*.
110  *La Force des Choses* (*Force of Circumstances* 1963) Penguin 1968. Cited in Mahon 2020 p. 158.
111  'Qu'est-ce que c'est l'existentialisme?' In *Les Lettres Françaises*

Nov and Dec 1945
[112] In *Contemporains* 2, Dec 1950
[113] cited in Mahon 2020 p. 157
[114] Shulamith Firestone *Dialectic of Sex* 1970, cited in Brown and Faery 1984
[115] Deforges 1975 p. 133
[116] Beauvoir 1949 p. 659
[117] Brown and Faery 1984
[118] Mahon 2020 p. 160
[119] See also Benjamin 1980, 1988
[120] Unless we do accept *Return* as a rightful part of the saga, in which case his disappearance after Carl's mysterious murder might be taken as a 'dethronement'?
[121] Coudurier 2014 # 8-9
[122] Benjamin 1980,
[123] Beauvoir 1949 p. 679
[124] Cited in Deforges 1975 p. 141; see also Paulhan's Preface
[125] In *O* p. 204; Deforges 1975 p. 135 etc.
[126] In Demornex *Elle* interview, 1974, cited in St Jorre 1995 p. 226
[127] *The Tragedy of Women's Emancipation* (1906), cited in Angela Carter: *The Sadeian Woman*, Virago 1979, p. 151
[128] David 2006 p. 247
[129] I am indebted to Kaufmann 1998 for much of the material in this section.
[130] Thomas preferred this to 'feminism', which she considered to be limited to women's movements of the previous century or so. Beauvoir agreed, associated 'feminism' with a fractiousness she wished to supersede, only describing herself as a 'feminist' in the early '70s. By 1975 Aury was also embracing the word, although keeping her distance from any movement – Deforges 1975 p. 59
[131] Thomas 1949 cited in Kaufmann 1998 p. 889
[132] Kaufmann 1998 p. 889
[133] Kaufmann 'Resistance and Survival – Edith Thomas: Simone de Beauvoir's Shadow Sister' Simone de Beauvoir Studies vol 12, 1995
[134] *L'Humanisme féminin* 314, cited in Mahon 2020 p. 149 #126
[135] 'Les Amoureuses' and 'Les Femmes et le pouvoir' (David 2006 p. 430)
[136] Kaufmann 1998 p. 897
[137] Aury described her to Deforges 1975, p. 184: ' I have a friend of the extreme left, violently 'against the war', whose only happy years were the war years, where she was hungry and cold, and afraid, and risked her life every day. She knew, finally, why she was living. She had an alliance with a whole people of unknown friends, of faithful comrades. Brotherhood of arms is not an empty word. And yet she also risked torture.'
[138] Kaufmann 1998 p. 901
[139] Genesis ch. 19.

140  Kaufmann 1998 p. 894

141  Ibid p. 890

142  Deforges 1975 pp, 62-63

143  *Les Cahiers de la Pleide XII*, spring-summer 1951, Éditions Gallimard in David 2006, p. 63, footnote 168

144  David 2006, pp. 65-70.

145  Kaufmann 1998 p. 897

146  David 2006 p. 70

147  Cited Bedell 2004

148  David 2006 p. 50

149  Kaufmann 1998 p. 898

150  *Les Femmes célèbres* 1960 1:176, cited Kaufmann 1998 p. 898 ; Most of these are mentioned in Beauvoir's 'The Mystic' (1949). Ironically, *Portuguese Letters* (1669) turns out to have been a mirror image of *O*. Just as *O* was attributed to a male writer when in fact it was written by a woman, so *Portuguese Letters* was credited to a woman, Mariana Alcoforado (an attribution Aury accepted) , when it seems in fact to have a hoax by the 'translator', Racine's friend the Comte de Guilleragues [Kaufmann 1998 p. 898]

151  cited Kaufmann 1998 p. 900

152  'A Girl' 1969 p. 14; David 2006, p. 441

153  Deforges 1975 p. 218

154  Kaufmann 1998 p. 900

155  Ibid pp 901, 903

156  Coudurier 2014

157  Ibid #21 citing Deforges *O m'a dit* Pauvert (1975) 1995, foreword p. III)

158  Deforges 1975 pp. 62-63

159  *Les Femmes célèbres* 1960, 1:177; cited Kaufmann 1998 p. 898

# VIII: *O* Among the Surrealists

In the last two chapters we have briefly surveyed *Story of O* in the context of some of the philosophical theories prominent in Liberation Paris – *érotisme noir,* Existentialism and Feminine Humanism. This chapter explores *O*'s relationship with Surrealism, suggesting this is particularly intimate, to the extent of raising the question how far *O* can be seen as a surrealist text. Jean-Jacques Pauvert, who was 'one of the publishers most interested in Surrealism' [1], right from the start signalled a direct link between *O* and Surrealism by commissioning surrealist artist/ photographer Hans Bellmer to provide a lithograph for 200 of the 600 numbered copies of the first edition (see p. 22). Bellmer was an admirer of Bataille and Sade, and was best known for his crime-scene evoking photos of contorted female dolls ('Die puppe'/ 'La Poupée') in the 1930s, and photos of women in explicit poses, working with Nora Mitrani in the 1940s and Unica Zürn in the 1950s, whom he photographed in nude bondage scenes. Bellmer had contributed to Pauvert publications before – providing illustrations for his editions of *Justine* in 1950 (with a foreword by Bataille) and in 1952 for Aragon's *Le Con d'Irène* (preface by Pieyre de Mandiargues). The year *O* was published, Pauvert organised an exhibition of Bellmer's work in Paris [2].

The link with Surrealism was further strengthened by André Breton's acknowledgement of *O,* referencing it in the 1955 surrealist calendar [3], and erstwhile surrealist Raymond Queneau taking part in the award ceremony of the Prix des Deux Magots literary prize to *O* in January 1955. This fuelled the suspicion that the author of *O* was to be found among the surrealists – Mandiargues and Queneau being in the frame – a suspicion by no means dispelled by the enthusiasm of surrealist reviewers lionising the book and giving every impression they regarded it as part of the family.

**The Reviews:** First off the mark was Jean-Louis Bédouin in February 1954 (four months before the novel was published) with his 'Eros and the Death Instinct' [4] (a title directly referencing Freud), describing *O* as a 'dangerous' book about enslavement to love and the 'bright reality of desire', depicting how 'carnal desire' leads to a 'mystical escape from spiritual and social dogma' [5] – following the lead set by Paulhan in his 1954 preface. This angle was supported by two major reviews in 1955, which to Pauvert's delight were 'actual articles to welcome (*O*'s) publication' [6], written by heavy-weights of the surrealist world, Georges Bataille and André Pieyre de Mandiargues.

George Bataille was already familiar with Dominique Aury's work, having enthusiastically reviewed her 1949 translation of Hogg's *Confessions of a Justified Sinner* [7], from which he drew inspiration in his 1950 novel *L'Abbé C.* Whether or not he knew Aury was behind 'Pauline Réage' and responsible for *O* (one suspects he probably did – not much got past Bataille), in May 1955 in 'The Paradox of Eroticism' ('Le paradoxe de l'érotisme', published by Paulhan in the *NNRF*) [8], he thrilled to the 'violent revelation' of *O*'s publication, and celebrated it as 'shameful' and 'magnificent' [9]. For Bataille, 'The eroticism in *Story of O* is also the impossibility of eroticism. Accepting eroticism is also accepting the impossible, I would even say, it is made of the *desire* for the impossible. The paradox of O is that of the visionary who *died of not dying*, of the martyr whose executioner is the accomplice of the victim. This book transcends its very own text, to the extent that, on its own, it tears itself apart, inasmuch as it turns the fascination of eroticism into the greater fascination of the impossible' [10]. [We shall return to Bataille and what he means by the 'impossible' in the next chapter].

The following month Pieyre de Mandiargues' review of *O* appeared in *Critique* [11], which chimed in so well with Paulhan's

1954 preface to raise the suspicion that it was composed in cahoots with him. Like Paulhan, Mandiargues (second only to Paulhan as person of interest in the suspected authorship case) praised this 'dangerous' novel, by someone who is a 'great novelist' and 'most assuredly a woman', whom he happily conflates with her character [12]. He also played along with Paulhan's suggestion that part of the novel 'may have been suppressed' (see chapter II). Hinting he knew Pauline Réage (casually dropping the comment that she 'has a good knowledge of English'), he comes over as more than half in love with her – 'Proud Réage... In the midst of her glowing tale, she has a way of involving herself, of slipping... into the skin of her heroine' at the most extreme moments, effectively sharing in O's 'tragic flowering' through slavery, humiliation, prostitution, torture and final death (at her own request). But, again like Paulhan, he repudiated any role for the mere pathology of masochism – emphasising O's 'ardour' as she is 'transfigured by a current that comes from the soul and not the body', a 'complete spiritual transformation... an ascesis', proving this is 'not, strictly speaking, an erotic book', for the mind 'ruthlessly dominates' the flesh, making it instead 'one which we should not hesitate to categorize as a mystic work'. Mandiargues concluded with a paragraph fantasising about women wearing the Roissy ring that identifies them as available to any man who understands the insignia, and asking 'shall we be able to tell which one is Pauline Réage?', admitting 'Probably not', but declaring his conviction that Baudelaire and the Portuguese Nun are there to welcome her into 'that small circle of blessed and accursed creatures which constitutes the only aristocracy which one can consider today with any degree of respect' (an aristocracy to which he and Paulhan doubtless considered themselves members [13]).

A year later, Nora Mitrani, surrealist writer (and partner to Hans Bellmer in the late 1940s), took a different tack in a pair of essays for *Le Surréalisme, Même* [14] in 1956 and '57. Mitrani was not interested in any mystical readings of *O* – her interpretation was a forthright version of Joan Riviere's theory of masquerade and Beauvoir's liberation of women from the imposed roles of wife and mother (see chapter VII). Claiming O as both 'slave' and 'suffragette' of the whip, Mitrani stated 'women still possess a way of proving to themselves that they have ceased to be slaves: that is, in the context of love, the concrete, symbolic and literary use of the whip...', suggesting that although 'Madame d'O, in spite of her degradation, perhaps because of it.... is a happy, fulfilled woman,' she is nevertheless engaging in an act of 'revenge', 'throw(ing) her scandalous way of life back into men's faces,' for 'The woman as object, up to that point consenting, because it is her pleasure, horse-whipped... represents a way of aggression with respect to men....' Mitrani concluded 'One last important thing: in that position, the woman must not forget to remain fundamentally unsubmissive, fiercely protective of what she has not yet obtained: freedom of the mind' [15]. O may be enslaved, Réage most certainly is not.

## SURREALIST INFLUENCES IN AND ON *O*

The kinship the surrealist reviewers clearly felt for *O* is supported by evidence for surrealist influences on the text itself. One influence, that of Leonor Fini, is well known and fully acknowledged [16]. The others we shall explore are less well attested and therefore more speculative.

**Leonor Fini:** Accomplished artist and aficionado of the influence of Sade, Fini's penchant for wearing masks – favouring the cat or the owl – to glamorous costume events in Paris in the late 1940s made her a fashion icon. Photographed by André Ostier at various grand balls in 1947 and 1948 – notably in a white owl mask at the Bal des Oiseaux in December 1948, she was celebrated in the press, and in 1951 her friend Pieyre de Mandiargues wrote the text for a collection of Ostier's photos entitled *The Masks of Leonor Fini* [17]. For O to be paraded in an owl mask in the final scene of the novel was no fortuitous coincidence. Mandiargues in his 1955 review drew attention to the Fini connection, and in 'A Girl' Réage admitted 'Nor did I make up – steal, rather, for which I ask her belated pardon, but the theft was committed out of admiration – the Leonor Fini masks' [18]. Fini was acquainted with Aury, whom she once described as 'a timid, mousy woman who always complains I intimidate her' [19] (a not uncommon reaction to Fini), and her involvement with Réage's works did not end with the mask. She *might* have 'featured' as a character in the novel itself (along with Girodias) as a guest at Roissy [20], and was herself in the frame as a suspect for authorship, which Aury noted in a letter to Édith Thomas in August 1954 [21]. She also provided colour lithographs and monochrome drawings for later de-luxe editions of *O* in the 1960s and 70s [22], focussing on the earlier scenes in the novel, when O is a willing victim at Roissy being prepared by the two maids, with highly phallic men in attendance [23], but also including later scenes, including O at the soirée wearing a mask identical to that sported by Fini in 1948. In a 1970 interview Fini described *O* as 'a very good book,' although 'quite a cold' one (which pleased her), 'a book that possesses the virtue of describing things that are painful and strange', including 'elements of female masochism...' [24], before clarifying that *she* was not that way inclined and in fact identified more with the men – the gender(s) of her fantasy victims remaining unspecified. By one account Fini had 'no feminism' in her, and had no time for equality (a word she 'detested'), instead urging woman to find alternative 'glories' within themselves in an androgynous meeting place, 'without this space of divergence, without this space of hostility' between the sexes [25].

**André Breton:** In his 1924 'Manifesto of Surrealism', Breton, while discussing 'the marvellous', allowed himself a flight of fancy in which the seeds of Roissy can be discerned:

'For today I think of a *castle* (*château*) ...; this castle belongs to me. I picture it in a rustic setting, not far from Paris. The outbuildings are too numerous to mention, and, as for the interior, it has been... restored in such a manner as to leave nothing to be desired from the viewpoint of comfort. Automobiles are parked before the door, concealed by the shade of trees. A few of my friends are living here as permanent guests [*Here Breton listed twenty or so names, including Aragon, Éluard, Desnos, Péret, Artaud, Picabia, Duchamp, Picasso – and Jean Paulhan]* and so many others besides, and gorgeous women, I might add. Nothing is too good for these young men, their wishes are, as to wealth, so many commands... the solitude is vast, and we don't often run into one another. And anyway, isn't what matters that we be the maîtres of ourselves, the maîtres of women, and of love too? ... But is (the reader) certain that this castle into which I cordially invite him is an image? What if this castle really existed! My guests are there to prove it does; their whim is the luminous road that leads to it. We really live by our fantasies when we *give free rein to them*' [26]. [I have taken the liberty of keeping the original 'maître' rather than the translators' 'master', which is a perfectly accurate rendition but carries a different flavour – 'master' connoting dominance and control, 'maître' emphasising understanding and expertise, which is, I feel, closer to the meaning here]. The castle has of course been a staple of Gothic fiction since the 18th century, and was to turn up again in Breton's writings. In 'Once Upon a Time to Come' (1930) Breton again ruminated upon a castle, populated by beautiful but untouchable women, and in 1936 he acknowledged that the Gothic castle represented a precise 'point of fixation' for the human psyche, and that the quest was on to find the contemporary equivalent [27]. But the alluring power of the castle was hard to leave behind: in his 'Ode to Charles Fourier' (1942-43) it was a castle that again provided the site for a disciplined masked orgy [28]. Five years later Julien Gracq saw that 'It is rather the idea of an enclosed and separate order, of an exclusive guild, of a phalanstery which tends to be enclosed by some sort of magic wall (the significant idea of 'the castle' lurks in the background) which seems to suggest itself to Breton from the beginning' [29] – a view that provides a bridge between the vision of Breton and that of Réage. In 1950 Breton was to buy a large farm-house in Saint-Cirq-Lapopie, near Cahors, which his biographer described as the castle he had dreamed of in 1924 [30].

In 'A Girl' (1969) Pauline Réage spoke of her own castle fantasy, recounting how early on she realised that rather than build dream castles, 'non-existent but possible, workable,' where 'friends and relatives would be happy together' (a direct reference to Breton's flight of fancy in the 'Manifesto'?), 'one could without fear build and furnish clandestine castles, on the condition that you people them with girls in love, prostituted by love, and triumphant in their chains', which she recognises coincided more closely with Sade's vision [31]. In 1975 she returned to this theme, telling Deforges of her fantasies of underground chambers 'inhabited by girls who are more or less prisoners' (fantasies whose inspiration she attributed to Walter Scott and Ann Radcliffe), their incarceration being 'Not necessarily' for 'the abuse of their bodies' [32].

Better known than the castle/château fantasy in the 'Manifesto' is Breton's focus on automatic writing as the prime technique of surrealist literary creation [33], defining Surrealism 'once and for all' as 'Psychic automatism in its pure state, by which one proposes to express – verbally, by means of the written word, or in any other manner – the actual functioning of thought. Dictated by thought, in the absence of any control exercised by reason, exempt from any aesthetic or moral concern' [34]. Breton was drawing on his experience as a medic in the First World War where he had become interested in the speech of shell-shocked soldiers, along with the interest of depth psychology in discovering ways for the unconscious mind to express its traumas or desires. Hypnosis was the traditional method. In addition French psychologist Pierre Janet used automatic writing (derived from the practice of 'mediums', although without any messages-from-the-other-side spiritualist baggage). Freud favoured free association on dreams. Breton explored them all.

Here the significance of Réage's descriptions of the writing of O becomes clear. As we saw in chapter II, she told Régine Deforges 'The first sixty pages flowed automatically. Afterwards I tried to build a story, but the first sixty pages came by themselves', going on to describe these pages as 'literally a copy of (her) phantasms,' 'transcribing a dream' [35] [a view consistent with Paulhan in his deposition to the vice squad that any 'danger' posed by *O* lay in 'the endless dreaming it seems to be immersed in' [36]]. To St Jorre, Aury said "The first sixty pages flowed out of me... They wrote themselves. Why was it like that? Probably because I had been dreaming..." [37] (see p. 67). Her account of *O*'s roots in 'oft-repeated reveries, just before falling asleep, in which the purest and wildest love always sanctioned, or rather demanded, the most frightful surrender' [38], echoes Breton's account of the creative state, and corresponds to his goal of 'the resolution of these two states, dream and reality, into a kind of absolute reality, a *surreality*' [39]. The dream-fuelled 'hallucinatory, erotic intensity' of the writing of *O* [40] is however confined to the first part, 'The Lovers of Roissy' [41]. As Aury admitted, *O* is in two parts, 'One is authentic, if you like, given, and the other is invented, thought through, constructed' [42]. The writing of the first sixty pages of *O* can certainly be seen in surrealist terms – as automatic writing emerging from erotic fantasy on the borders of dream and conscious awareness, the very location of Breton's surreality – and Aury's description of it as 'authentic' and 'given' indicates strongly that this is how she saw it.

In addition, Aury was responsive to Breton's idea of *L'Amour fou* (*Mad Love*, 1937), the trance state of being immersed in love or art. Such intoxication was of course stock in trade to the Romantics, whom Breton in the 'Second Manifesto of Surrealism' (1930) had recognised as ancestral to Surrealism – Romanticism being a movement which, despite its much earlier origins, was still a vibrant and creative force, and 'a being who is only beginning to make his desire known through us' (i.e. Surrealism) [43]. Romanticism was itself indebted to Shakespeare, whose *Romeo and Juliet* (c. 1594) and *A Midsummer Night's Dream* (c. 1595) are both hymns to *l'amour fou*, the tragedy of the one being countered by the 'marvellous' resolution of the latter. In the first 'Manifesto'

(1924), Breton had acknowledged Shakespeare as one of the ancestral poets who 'could pass for surrealists' [44], and we should not be at all surprised that Aury, whose love of Shakespeare we have commented on (see pp 82, 86), to have been receptive to his ideas. In 1935 Anne Desclos' correspondence with Maulnier was deploying the vocabulary of suffering and sacrifice, and in 1937 (the year of Breton's *L'Amour fou*) her letters revealed her to be in the grip of a 'cult of love', of 'abandonment, consent, the mystery she grants to the beings she loves, as others grant it to God' [45]. *L'amour fou* provides the very subject matter of *O*, which comes close to incarnating Breton's sacred exhortation of: 'Love, the only love there is, carnal love, I adore. I have never stopped loving your venomous shadow, your deadly shadow. A day will come when man will recognise you as his sole maître, and honour you even in those mysterious perversions that you surround yourself with' [46].

**Three Novels:** The year 1928 attained notoriety for the number of sexually explicit books published – including Louis Aragon's *Le Con d'Irène*, Pierre Jean Jouve's *Hécate*, along with Raschilde's *Why I am not a Feminist*, and posthumous publications of Pierre Louÿs – to the extent that it precipitated a crackdown on 'immorality' [47]. Three books in particular from that year seem to have left their mark on *O*.

**I: *Nadja*:** Nine years before *L'Amour fou*, Breton had made a preliminary exploration of the territory in *Nadja*, published by Gallimard, exploring 'the tension between mental and physical love, freedom and dependency, emotional liberation and bondage' [48]. Echoes of *Nadja* can be detected in *O*. Both books celebrate 'convulsive beauty', both depict the transformation of the female protagonist under the power of her male lover – in *Nadja* Breton writes '...suddenly she surrenders, closes her eyes for good, offers me her lips... Now she tells me of my power over her, of my faculty for making her think and do whatever I desire, perhaps more than I think I desire' [49] – words that could have come from Sir Stephen's private journal. O's willing submission in love leads her to loss of ego, even identity, and her ultimate disappearance into her love; in *Nadja*, the protagonist tells Breton 'If you desired it, for you I would be nothing, or merely a footprint' [50], and, failing to win love she ends up rejected, abandoned and mad, as in the epilogue to Réage's novel, O, abandoned, wishes to die.

*Nadja* begins 'Who am I?', a question that to the narrator amounts to 'knowing whom I "haunt"' [51]; in *O* the questions are transposed as '"Who is she," they were saying, "who does she belong to?" "You if you like" he replied'' (*O* p. 202). Breton's articulation in *Nadja* of the goal of psychoanalysis as 'the expulsion of man from himself' (a view that understandably mystified Freud when he told him) [52], destabilises identity, drawing on the one hand on Rimbaud's *'J'EST un autre'* (literally 'I IS another') and leading on the other to Aury's acceptance of the slipperiness of identity, saying of 'Pauline Réage' that she is someone who 'is the obscure part of another me: from one self to another the fragments slip away and rejoin, constantly back and forth, or rather escape. I no longer distinguish who is who, or at least I don't make out the difference clearly enough for my liking' [53]. Nadja's name is also suggestive, the protagonist having chosen the name 'because in Russian it's the beginning of the word hope, and because it's only the beginning' [54], similarly, O's name has also been considered as signifying a beginning – as in 'ouvert/ open' [55] (see p. 174).

**II: *Story of the Eye*:** George Bataille's *Histoire de l'Oeil,* first published accompanied by eight André Masson lithographs, and reissued in 1940 with six Bellmer engravings, also resonates with *O.* The title of Réage's novel is obviously a homage to Bataille's, and both books create a dreamscape ambience and take the reader on a highly eroticised sado-masochistic roller-coaster, although Bataille's adventure is a much wilder hunt than Réage's. Describing it as 'the most accomplished artistically of all the pornographic prose fictions I've read', Sontag (1967) places it with Sade and *O* **as a text** where sex is recognised as demonic, beyond morality or even sanity [56]. Shades of *l'amour fou* again. The story line of Bataille's novella follows the sexual rampage of a pair of fifteen-year olds – an unnamed boy narrator and his insatiably sexually-driven companion, Simone – with their fetishistic obsessions for eggs and urine, Simone's penchant for inserting bulls' testicles and priests' eyeballs in her sex, and a trail of bodies (a woman cyclist, a teenage girl, a prostitute trampled by pigs, a bullfighter in the ring, and a throttled priest whose eye provides Simone with her vaginal kicks). There is little resemblance to *O* in terms of narrative structure, but there is correspondence between the characters – the rather masochistic narrator is echoed in René, the precocious Simone in Natalie (also fifteen), and Bataille's Sir Edmund, the wealthy Englishman who mentors the teenage tearaways, very clearly in Sir Stephen.

**III: *Belle de Jour:*** This book, by Joseph Kessel, was also published by Gallimard and has a closer entanglement with the saga of *O*. *Belle de Jour* follows one Séverine (a feminised version of the name of the male masochist in Leopold von Sacher-Masoch's *Venus in Furs,* 1870) as she commits herself to a secret career as a prostitute in a brothel, exploring the complexities and contradictions of her desires, her sincere but less-than-scintillating love for her husband, Pierre, and her sexual need for 'supreme animal ecstasy', recognising 'something in her that had to be beaten and subdued, mercilessly defeated' [57]. The novel recounts her addiction, even enslavement to her prostitution, and her journey through submission and humiliation, her desire for martyrdom, and her joy and pride in her degradation, to a rediscovery of a sense of personal strength. When Séverine meets the gangster Marcel, the novel takes on the flavour of a noirish thriller, complete with violent outcome. Joseph Kessel was not himself a surrealist, but *Belle de Jour* is linked with surrealism via Luis Buñuel.

Buñuel made his name in 1929 with his *Un Chien Andalou,* co-written with Salvador Dalí, in which both feature – Dalí as a priest tied to a piano bearing a rotting donkey, Buñuel wielding the razor in the notorious eye-ball slitting opening scene (referencing Bataille's *Histoire de l'Oeil*). In 1967 Buñuel adapted Kessel's novel for the screen in one of his most celebrated films.

His film follows the narrative of the novel closely, but includes fantasy sequences explicitly portraying the masochistic desire for cruelty and humiliation of Séverine (played by Catherine Deneuve) that are not in Kessel. Thematic parallels between Buñuel's *Belle de Jour* and Jaeckin's *Story of O* as art-house erotica have been noted and discussed [58] (see Chapter II), but if Jaeckin was influenced by Buñuel, it is quite possible that Buñuel was himself taking inspiration from Pauline Réage in the fantasy sequences in his film (perhaps representing *O*'s first real influence on screen?). Links between Buñuel's film and *O* may not be provable, but parallels between *Belle de Jour* and the *Return to the Château* are harder to dismiss. Both depict the sexual experiences and inner life of a respectable young woman who works at a high-class brothel with a commanding but protective Madame, and who becomes involved with a criminal who winds up getting shot. Whoever wrote *Return* almost certainly knew *Belle de Jour*, as novel or film or both – and if more detailed analysis flags up specific influence from Buñuel's film, that would fix *Return* as a late 1960s confection.

According to her biographer, Anne Desclos 'discover(ed) contemporary literature... when she was a student' [59], and although it will require further digging to find out for sure, it is reasonable to assume that the significance of 1928 as a turning point in literary liberation would not have been lost on a free-thinking, literate and erotically curious Anne Desclos, just turning 21. It isn't clear how many of the boundary-pushing novels of that year Desclos read, but we might guess several, perhaps many, if not all. Circumstantial evidence from *O* points to those by Breton, Bataille and Kessel all feeding into her imaginings at some point, even if not hot off the press in 1928.

**Longer shots:** In an even more speculative vein, I would like to light-heartedly throw out a few more possibilities of surrealist influences the reader may like to consider. For any of these postulated connections to hold water, Aury must have known about them, but I contend that Aury's levels of cultural awareness, familiarity with the literary and arts worlds and later professional interconnectedness are enough to make this a fairly safe proposition.

**Lee Miller:** The American photographer Lee Miller prefigures O in interesting ways. Having been a highly regarded *Vogue* model, in 1930 Miller had set up her own studio in Paris and went on to become a successful photographer in both the fashion and surrealist worlds (and later an intrepid war reporter). She was in a personal and working relationship with Man Ray from 1929-32, and later married Roland Penrose, engaging in 'exploratory' sexuality with both. Man Ray recounted how in 1930 he and Miller were invited to an apartment where a woman was chained up at the pleasure of the owner, and spent the evening discussing bondage with her. Man Ray wrote: 'Lee Miller told me she had met a man who liked to whip women, it was nothing new for her' [60]. Man Ray also took commissions from fellow-American William Seabrook to photograph women in simulated lesbian sado-masochistic scenarios (including for example *Fetishistic Mise-en-scène for William Seabrook* in 1930 [61]). Seabrook had a habit of trussing up his girlfriend Marjorie Muir Worthington [62], and it might have been she with whom Lee Miller and Man Ray spent their convivial evening chatting about bondage. Some time between 1929 and 1932 Man Ray took a series of photos, entitled *Lee Miller au Collier,* of Miller in a metal collar adorned with rings, designed by Seabrook, with Seabrook himself featured in some frames, caressing or twisting her hair [63]. However, '(t)his apparently blatant display of misogyny is... undermined by the... focus on Miller's subjective experience and her role in staging the scenes' [64], Miller's expression indicating perhaps an anticipation of suffering to come, but no trace of displeasure. Later in the '30s, Roland Penrose gave Miller a set of golden handcuffs that she liked to wear to Surrealist parties [65].

Lee Miller cut quite a dash in Paris, and would have been difficult to miss. More glamorous than Anne Desclos, she shared certain characteristics with her. They were the same age – born in 1907, as was Leonor Fini (and also, coincidentally, Frida Kahlo and Dora Maar, major surrealist artists in their own right); both had a penchant for androgyny – Desclos had been a bit of a tomboy [66] and Miller came 'to embody the "garçonne" or tomboy style' in her clothing [67]; both were attracted to older men [68] and both had deep semi-erotic attachments to their fathers – Desclos' we have discussed, Miller's 'father-complex' was such that she submitted to his camera for nude photos from childhood, through adolescence and into her adulthood [69]. A very plausible picture emerges of Anne Desclos in her early twenties (having just read the novels mentioned above?), noticing this American star in Paris, depicted in a 1931 photograph as the unclothed but veiled *Femme surréaliste* by Man Ray – (perhaps even seeing *Lee Miller au Collier*?) – finding in Miller qualities to admire and perhaps identify with, and drawing on her later in her conception of O – who is of course also a fashion photographer in Paris. [Another minor but pleasing coincidence is that in one of Man Ray's best known paintings, an image of Lee Miller's lips floating across a landscape, is entitled *À l'heure de l'observatoire, les amoureux* (1934), the lower left corner depicting the Paris Observatoire, the landmark that identifies the location of Anne-Marie's home apartment in *O*].

**Max Ernst and his circle:** In the early 1920s Ernst entered a ménage-a-trois with Gala and Paul Éluard, in which it has been suggested that Gala, as well as being the love object of both men, was also effectively the conduit through which Éluard's love and reverence for Ernst flowed, a love-token in the affair between the two men [70], which provides an intriguing parallel with the erotic and emotional dynamics of O, René and Sir Stephen. In the early 1930s Éluard was playing second fiddle to Dalí in a similar ménage with Gala [71].

Ernst's 1940 painting *The Robing of the Bride* (*La Toilette de la Mariée*) is generally understood as a homage to Leonora Carrington, but it may in addition carry a reference to Leonor Fini. Ernst had an affair with Fini in the early 1930s, and they both attended Tristan Tzara's 1936 party where the guests turned up masked but with naked mid-riffs. The image in Ernst's 1940 painting may be a memory of Fini's exotic (un)dress, placed under a dramatic owl head-dress. Réage attributed the owl mask in *O* to Fini's inspiration (see above), which Jaeckin's 1975 film took at face value, the mask in the soirée scene there closely resembling Fini's. In fact the link between O's mask and Fini's might have been Fini's own idea (or possibly Mandiargues') – in Fini's illustration [72] to the 1962 edition, she depicts O in  a mask much like one of her own. However the mask Réage described in *O* – 'the cope of feathers almost completely concealed her shoulders, descending half way down her back and, in front, to the nascent curve of her breasts' (*O* p. 198) – bears little resemblance to Fini's 1948 mask or her 1962 painting of O, or the mask in Jaeckin's film, but does describe very accurately Ernst's painting. The 1969 'confession' that she 'stole' the mask from Fini may just have been another one of Aury's little games.

From 1942 Ernst was in a relationship with Dorothea Tanning that was to last the rest of his life, and in 1949, Tanning wrote *Abyss* (aka *A Chasm*) [73], which in the introduction she described as having been written as a seduction device to keep the interest of an older lover with a notorious roving eye. Again an echo with *O* as a Scheherezade game, as described by Réage in 1975 [74].

**Antonin Artaud**:  Close friend to Paulhan and briefly a member of the surrealist movement (until falling out with Breton over the latter's gravitation to Marxist politics), Artaud went on by the 1930s to flesh out his theory of his Theatre of Cruelty, which he 'created in order to restore to the theatre a passionate and convulsive conception of life, and it is in this sense of violent rigour and extreme condensation of the scenic elements that the cruelty on which it is based must be understood. This cruelty, which will be bloody when necessary but not systematically so, can thus be identified with a kind of severe moral purity which is not afraid to pay life the price it must be paid' [75]; 'Above all, cruelty is lucid, it is a kind of rigid direction, submission to necessity.

No cruelty without consciousness, without a kind of applied consciousness. It is consciousness that gives to the exercise to every action in life its colour of blood, its cruel touch, since it must be understood that to live is always through the death of someone else' [76]. Parallels with Sir Stephen's world view and the epilogue to *O* are fairly plain.

**Raymond Queneau:** An early supporter of *O*, present at the award of Le Prix des Deux Magots to a heavily-disguised 'Pauline Réage' (or a stand-in) in 1955, ex-surrealist Raymond Queneau was on the reading committee of Gallimard, a colleague of Paulhan, and a founder member (along with Ernst, Marcel Duchamp, Eugène Ionesco, Joan Miró and Jacques Prévert) of The College of 'Pataphysics in 1944. In 1960 he co-founded Oulipo (Ouvroir de Littérature Potentielle/ Workshop of Potential Literature) as a subcommittee of the College. Rather than searching out techniques of free expression as the surrealists had done, Oulipo playfully applies constraint, as in restrictive linguistic and literary (or even mathematical) rules, to liberate by forcing heightened creativity [the 'mathematical surrealism' of *Elements of Mathematics* by 'Nicolas Bourbaki' since 1939 being particularly influential here]. Oulipians define themselves as 'rats who must build the labyrinth from which they propose to escape', Queneau explaining that the writer who composes in literary forms structured according to strict, even restrictive classical rules (as Shakespeare does in his sonnets), is 'freer than the poet who writes that which comes into his head and who is the slave of other rules of which he is ignorant' [77]. This perspective echoes Sartre's apparently paradoxical view that 'we were never freer than during the Occupation' [78], and Beauvoir that the willingly enslaved woman converts her prison 'into a heaven of glory, her servitude into sovereign liberty' [79]. It also resonates with the use of bondage and restraint in *O* to heighten erotic desire to a transcendent liberation, and Réage's understanding, through Sade, that 'prison itself can open the gates to freedom' [80]. This offers an interesting parallel to Ouilipo's games, and the fact that Queneau found himself on the list of authorial suspects for *O* raises the possibility that somebody suspected a connection between *O* and Queneau's way of thinking six years before Oulipo was founded.

Finally, the sheer playfulness of the game built around *O* by Aury (and Paulhan and Pauvert) invites comment. Angie David likens it to a 'treasure hunt', which involves not just 'preserving' and 'hiding' the treasures, but 'presenting false leads, abolishing logical sense, and letting chance (*hasard*) decide who finds them' [81]. The privileging of *hasard* in its ability to make things happen is itself a hallmark of Surrealism.

In these last few pages we have left the normal shipping lanes and headed out to the open seas in a bid to get a sense of the range of possible resonances between *O* and the surrealists. Of necessity, this has included much that is circumstantial and speculative, with antecedents, anticipations, family resemblances, suggestive fore-runners and unproven-but-plausible connections unceremoniously shoving demonstrable cause-and-effect sequences to the margins. But then the surrealist world always worked very much on the principles of serendipity, *hasard objectif*, coincidence and hauntings, where things and events exist in cat's cradles of intersecting correspondences rather than arising from chains of causality, so perhaps such a jaunt into the unknown is not wholly unjustified.

However, recognising that at this point the reader might be getting a little sea-sick with fishing in uncharted (and rather choppy) waters, it is only fair to return to more main-stream channels to pin down how familiar Aury really was with Surrealism. We know in the 1930s she was moving in a milieu where Surrealism was seen in a negative way; right-wing nationalists rarely harbour much affection for left-wing internationalism, and her lover (and to an extent mentor) at the time, Thierry Maulnier, thoroughly detested it. We know that in Resistance circles during the war Aury crossed paths with people who were or had been associated with Surrealism, and that during the 1940s her relationship with Jean Paulhan blossomed. And we know that Jean Paulhan had a relationship with Surrealism dating back to its inception, sufficiently intimate to warrant consideration of him as both a facilitator and even a (sometimes disputatious) 'fellow-traveller'.

**Jean Paulhan and Surrealism:** As noted in chapter III, Paulhan had been an admirer of Apollinaire, sharing with him an interest in Sade and *érotisme noir*. By 1918 Paulhan was meeting up with André Breton (who greatly admired his translations of Malagasy poetry [82]) and Louis Aragon at Adrienne Monniers' bookshop in Rue l'Odéon, and on Apollinaire's death in November 1918 Paulhan to some extent stepped into his shoes, introduced Breton to Éluard, and was soon being recognised by these young poets (all ten years or so younger than him) as an *éminence grise* in the Parisian arts and literary scene [83]. These poets gravitated to Dada, and Paulhan participated in the founding of both Breton's *Littérature* (1919) and Éluard's *Proverbs* (1920). [84] However, when Paulhan joined the *NRF* in 1920, tensions began to develop. Dada was suspicious of the literary establishment and sceptical of the authenticity of language itself in their rebellion against the 'culture' that had created the cataclysm of the world war, and in 1920 Éluard bluntly told Paulhan 'I hate the *NRF* and literature and all its subtleties', while making it clear he still felt friendly toward Paulhan himself [85]. Paulhan disliked the misology of Dada, but was happy to publish Breton in the *NRF* in 1921. He lost subscribers by doing so, but he thought that a price worth paying, it being crucial that the *NRF* remain open to the *saugrenu* (the 'off-the-wall'), willingly shedding stuffy and stick-in-the-mud readers as it went (a policy that did not enthuse fellow senior editor Jean Schlumberger) [86]. Paulhan was perhaps drawn to Breton's growing frustration with the limitations of Dada's pranks and provocations, and in 1922 collaborated with him in the proposed 'International Congress for the Determination and Defence of the Modern Spirit', a manoeuvre by Breton to separate his nascent Surrealism from Tristan Tzara's

Dadaism [87]. Later that year Paulhan arranged dodgy identity papers for German painter Max Ernst to live and work in Paris (under the name 'Jean Paris') [88]. Paulhan's reward was to be given central place in Ernst's painting *Au Rendezvous des Amis* (1922) along with Breton, Aragon, Paul and Gala Éluard, Jean (Hans) Arp, Benjamin Péret, Robert Desnos, Giorgio de Chirico, Ernst himself and half a dozen others. This group, depicted as a secret society (complete with arcane hand gestures), was to provide the core membership of the early Surrealist movement.

In 1924, the year of Breton's 'Manifesto of Surrealism' (in which Paulhan is featured as one of the residents in Breton's fantasy proto-Roissy), the *NRF* handled the distribution of Breton's new journal *La Révolution surréaliste* [89] – According to Schlumberger, without Paulhan and the *NRF* Surrealism would not have taken flight at all [90]. Paulhan developed a close relationship with the Sade-saturated surrealist, Antonin Artaud, publishing his works in the *NRF* from 1925, but Artaud was soon having difficulties with Surrealism, mistrusting both the poeticism of Breton and his friends, and also Breton's gravitation towards Marxism. Paulhan's position was eccentric, siding with Artaud over his rejection of political influence in art, while overlooking the latter's hostility to language, and at the same time criticising the surrealists of not having broken sufficiently with Dada's anti-linguistic bias [91].

In 1927 Breton and some of his group joined the Communist Party – a relationship that for Breton had foundered by 1930, ending in divorce by 1933 just as Stalin started to flex his muscles. Breton joining the Party precipitated an unpleasant spat with Artaud, who left the Surrealist group with bad feeling all round. Paulhan's sympathies for Artaud led to a drunken diatribe from Breton which prompted Paulhan to challenge him to a duel [92]. Needless to say, only ink was spilt, no blood. [This ruckus no doubt explains Breton's distortion of the story of his meeting with Éluard in *Nadja* (1928). Breton claimed he was with Picasso at the posthumous opening of an Apollinaire play (late November 1918), when he was approached by a young man who mistook him for a friend who had been killed in the war. 'Naturally, nothing more was said', but a few days later, 'through a mutual friend', Breton began corresponding with a certain Paul Éluard, who turned out to be the young man at the theatre [93]. These details were later confirmed by Aragon, with one difference: Breton had been in the company, not of Picasso, but of Paulhan, who was also the 'mutual friend' who facilitated the correspondence with Éluard].

Relations between Paulhan and Breton remained cool through the '30s, but Paulhan stayed in touch with dissident Surrealists, including Artaud, who, after a stint acting (perhaps best known for his portrayal of Marat in Abel Gance's 1927 film *Napoléon*), began writing tracts on theatre, his *Destiny of the Theatre* and *Manifesto for the Theatre of Cruelty* being published by Paulhan in the *NRF* in 1932. Paulhan and Artaud discussed Sade and the meaning of cruelty, and Paulhan drew on the writers' fund and his own pocket to finance detox programmes for Artaud's opium addiction [94]. In 1937 Paulhan edited Artaud's *Theatre and its Double* for Gallimard (along with Breton's *L'Amour fou,* proving relations had not broken down completely). In 1938-39 he guest-lectured at Bataille's 'College of Sociology' [95].

Paulhan and Breton were in correspondence during the war years, but Paulhan continued to critique what he saw as the Surrealists' negative attitude to language. In his 1941 *Flowers of Tarbes* he positioned Surrealism as a descendant of Romanticism, a view Breton in fact shared (see above p. 280), but to Paulhan Romanticism was guilty of inaugurating the 'Terror' mode of writing, where authors tyrannise their readers with a unique 'vision' (in)articulated through 'rupture' and the distortions of 'reinvented' language (see chapter III), and Surrealism shared this guilt by association [96]. Paulhan's continued conflation of Surrealism with Dada [97] prevented him (for a time at least) from understanding how close he was to Breton, who also in fact repudiated Cartesian privileging of reason in favour of the poetic. Paulhan and Breton both stood firmly against the instrumentalising of language by political doctrines trying to impose 'direct meaning' to create tyranny and 'terror'. Breton was however less committed to clarity and precision, wanting to leave space for automatic writing, dream expression and the irrational – for him, 'Language has been given to man so he may make Surrealist use of it' [98]. By 1947, though, the gap was closing, Paulhan realising that he and Breton both shared the view that 'the sacred has taken refuge in poetry' [99].

Paulhan remained loyal to Artaud. In 1946 he 'managed to have him freed' from Rodez asylum and its regime of electric shock 'treatments' where he had been languishing since 1943 [100]. Paulhan then co-organised a benefit event for him at which Breton delivered his 'Homage to Antonin Artaud', praising him for going further than anyone in Surrealism's 'triple and indivisible aim: transform the world, change life, remake human under-standing from scratch' [101]. When Artaud was found dead of an overdose in 1948 Paulhan hinted at suicide to the authorities, thus saving Artaud from the indignity of a religious funeral of which he had harboured an intense horror. Paulhan then divided the remaining money from the 1946 benefit event among Artaud's neediest friends [102].

Paulhan and Breton maintained regular correspondence, discussing ideas and co-operating on various projects, including the Garry Davies citizen-of-the-world campaign in 1948, lobbying (along with Dominique Aury and others) the Czech Commu-nist government for clemency for Záviš Kalandra in 1950 (see Chapter IV), and supporting Jean Debuffet's Societé de l'Art Brut (Society for Outsider Art). Paulhan helped foster the careers of Jean Fautrier whose art-work was featured in the Surrealism room at the Musée Nationale d'Arte Moderne in 1947. He also fostered Alain Robbe-Grillet, major exponent of the New Novel (Nouveau Roman), who, although criticised in surrealist circles as too acquiescent to apparent 'reality' [103], was read by Breton, the Nouveau Roman being described in the 1960s as Surrealism's 'most recent offspring' [104]. In 1949 Paulhan took Breton on in an editorial role at the *NRF*, and in 1953 rallied to support him in a legal dust-up with officialdom at Saint-Cirq. Paulhan also contributed (along with Bataille and Mandiargues) to Breton's book *L'Art Magique* (1957), and in July 1959 was one of the 28 thinkers and writers (out of 99 asked) to respond to the survey on political engagement for the surrealist publication *Le Quatorze Juillet* [105]. Paulhan and Breton were comrades in arms against vilification by the Communists – Paulhan being the more combative of the two – but they had their differences. Breton and the surrealists condemned de Gaulle's 'usurpation' of power in 1958 [106], and, in the 'Manifesto of the 121', called on French soldiers to refuse to fight in Algeria (see p. 143). Paulhan did not agree on either count.

When Breton died in 1966, Paulhan's obituary in the *NRF* praised his greatness and stated his faith in the future of Surrealism (while hinting that Breton might have become something of a brake on the potential of the movement?) – 'Breton is dead. Everything is beginning again' [107]. In 1968, as the Third Way reached its climax in the Paris Maydays, Paulhan was in hospital. He died later that year, and Louis Aragon, despite all their bitter ructions in the past, wrote a generous obituary to him, stating that 'in truth, Jean Paulhan played a much more important role than anyone says. A whole side of what has made surrealism what it is cannot be explained without this long secret conversation between us and him' [108].

Given Paulhan's deep, if sometimes complicated, involvement with Surrealism from its beginnings, the intimacy of Aury's professional and literary (not to mention personal) relationship with him, combined with her own intellectual and cultural acumen, the idea of Surrealism being in any way unfamiliar territory to her would seem highly unlikely.

## *STORY OF O* AS SURREALIST WORK

With surrealist reviewers embracing *O* so enthusiastically, and evidence both for Aury's familiarity with Surrealism and its influence on her novel, the crunch question arises whether *O* really warrants a place in the surrealist canon – how far can *O* be seen as a truly 'surrealist' text? Direct association between *O* and Surrealism has been made in the past. Susan Sontag (1967) referred to a literary line of descent 'that goes from Sade through Surrealism' to *O* and *The Image* (which we discuss in the next chapter) [109], Janis Pallister (1985) linked *O* with *Return to Roissy* and *The Image* in sharing a 'surrealist tone', the 'characteristics of the surrealist school' being 'all quite discernible' in these books, 'all of which carry their own brand of surrealism' (an observation she did not in fact intend as a compliment) [110], and Anna Watz (2023) refers to Leonor Fini's illustrations for *O* as an example of 'the entanglement between surrealism and the novel form' [111]. The clearest statement however is from Alyce Mahon in *The Marquis de Sade and the Avant Garde* (2020) where she includes a chapter on *O* alongside chapters on surrealist art and performance in her exploration of the influence of Sade on 20th century culture, and refers to 'the case of the modern writer, Dominique Aury, who chose to craft her own modern Sadean heroine named "O" in a 1954 novel Breton would happily claim for surrealism' [112].

In fact this is not as straightforward as it might look. Breton was notoriously outspoken in his condemnation of the novel as an 'inferior category' of writing, which would seem to render the claim of any novel to surrealist status a bit of a forlorn hope. In a diatribe in the 1924 'Manifesto', Breton railed against the 'generous supply of novels' whose commitment to 'observation', 'informative style', relentless 'descriptions', 'clichés' and 'images taken from a stock catalogue' render their 'vacuity' beyond compare [113], reiterating in 1939 'I have a disdainful prejudice against the novel' [114]. This apparent blanket condemnation has however been successfully dissected by J.H. Matthews (1966, 1969), Jacqueline Chénieux-Gendron (1983, 2014) and Anna Watz (2023) who have pointed out that Breton's real target was not the novel per se, but the 'realistic attitude' that had come to dominate novel writing since the 19th century, and which left him 'the only discretionary power... to close the book, which I am careful to do somewhere in the vicinity of the first page' [115]. In fact Breton's view of the possibilities of the novel was more nuanced (in the 'Manifesto' he included prose writers and novelists – Swift, Sade, Chateaubriand, Hugo and Poe – along with Dante, and Shakespeare – in his list of proto-surrealists [116]), but in 1924 the novel in France was not in a glorious state, with some very inferior specimens garnering literary prizes [117].  The full impact of the great modernist turning point of 1922 had yet to be fully felt, and the same year as Breton's 'Manifesto', Jacques Rivière, Paulhan's predecessor as editor of the *NRF*, was commenting that 'we are witnessing a very serious crisis of what literature is...' [118]. Breton's response to this crisis was to condemn the realist novel but also to write some experimental (sort of) novels of his own – *Nadja* (1928), *L'Amour Fou* (1937) and *Arcane 17* (1944) [119]. Other surrealist writers did too – Aragon, Desnos, Leiris and Bataille in the 1920s, and later women surrealists including Leonora Carrington, Leonor Fini and Joyce Mansour.

Given that the surrealist novel is possible, the next question is what would be its distinctive qualities? Breton actually addressed this question in his 'Manifesto', and concluded that there could no more be a formula or 'conventional Surrealist pattern' for the novel than for surrealist painting [120]. The overtly absurd or fantastical was not to be a defining quality of the surreal novel, nor were content, technique, style or any other surface features. Surrealist credentials are to be found rather in atmosphere and mood, an 'instinctive antipathy' towards realism , 'a climate to express the spirit of the surreal', 'the need to explore beyond the known' [121], Breton's own taste being for 'books left ajar, like doors' [122]. These he believed liberate us – 'the provocative emotions aroused by the beauty of these texts' making us 'live poetically according to the myths they bring to life' [123].

Having rejected the possibility of pinning down any defining characteristics of the surrealist novel, Breton then of course went ahead to do precisely that. In the 'Manifesto' he extolled the virtues of the Marvellous: 'Let us not mince words: the marvellous is always beautiful, anything marvellous is beautiful, in fact only the marvellous is beautiful' [124]. Continuing, 'In the realm of literature, only the marvellous is capable of fecundating works which belong to an inferior category such as the novel...', Breton then went on to discuss Matthew Lewis' Gothic classic *The Monk* (1796) as 'admirable proof of this', his novel exercising 'an exalting effect... upon that part of the mind which aspires to leave the earth' [125]. On the following page he launched into his own Gothic fantasy of the proto-Roissy château described above. Other surrealists embraced Gothic as well – for Benjamin Péret, Gothic 'takes the marvellous, trembling with passion, out of the attic to which rationalist thought had relegated it' [126], for Julien Gracq there was a close 'confluence of surrealism and the Gothic novel' [127], both of which take us 'beyond the paltry discrimination of good and evil' [128] into a world of privileged and isolated spaces —like castles— where Desire can take the reins. Along with Gothic, the surrealists also enthusiastically devoured Decadent and Symbolist writers (Lautréamont, Villiers de l'Isle Adam, Huysmans), purveyors of black humour and language games (Swift, Carroll), and pulp fiction (*Fantômas*) [129], but Gothic was always its closest relative. For Matthews (1966), 'Gothic influence coincides with the influence of surrealism' [130], while Wickman (2005) emphasised the effect of 'British gothic' on surrealists like André Breton and René Magritte, the latter finding the Gothic feeling, 'bordering upon terror' providing 'the point of departure for a will to action upon the real, for a transformation of life itself' [131]. When Breton announced in the 'Manifesto' that 'imagination is perhaps on the point of reasserting itself, of reclaiming its rights' [132], Wickman glosses this as 'claiming a gothic heritage', surrealism itself representing a 'recuperation of the British gothic' [133].

If Shakespeare was the god-father of Romanticism, he was equally the god-father of Gothic, with his tortured male protagonists – Brutus, Hamlet, Macbeth – haunted by ghosts as they soliloquise their oedipal angst [134]. Male oedipal concerns fed into

Gothic, but the genre only really took off in the 1790s when Shakespeare devotee Anne Radcliffe shifted the focus on to female oedipal dynamics, with her heroines suffering from, amongst other things, unruly desires for paternal figures, which remains a recurring theme through later Female Gothic [135]. Unsurprisingly, *Story of O*, whose author made no secret of her love for both Shakespeare and Radcliffe, resonates strongly here with convincing Gothic credentials [136]. We can cite among these: the centrality of desire; the suffering heroine (and her complicity in her torments); her 'beautiful' love for a rather feminised lover, and her 'sublime' (quasi-oedipal) love for the more masculine and sadistic older man (ordinarily the object of mixed feelings from the heroine – Coleridge's 'Desire with loathing strangely mixed' [137] – but in *O* it is the Commander who is the recipient of this cocktail – *O* p. 194); We might also cite the location in some not-quite-real and geographically unmoored site for erotic license; the exclusion of everyday life (matters like pregnancy, venereal disease, legal considerations and the practical implications of unexplained absences from work throw no shadow in *O* [138]); and the mystery created around the identity of the heroine (a particular characteristic of 20th century Female Gothic, where heroines' names are commonly incomplete, contested or even absent entirely [139]).

The absence of frontier between Gothic and surrealist literature has long been recognised. Both are typically set in regions at a tangent to or out of kilter with the 'real world', having 'no need for any sort of logic or rational justification for action outside of desire itself' [140]. Both make use of the 'castle' motif – which provide 'the archetypal psychic space, allowing "free rein" to fantasy and the imagination, where the "fantastic" becomes the real... the bastion, site of confinement, excess' [141]. [The prototypes being Elsinore in *Hamlet* (c. 1600) – complete with ghost, murder, guilt, forbidden desire, sadism, suffering women, madness and suicide – and the castles in *Macbeth* (c. 1605), offering a similar menu]. For Breton (1947), 'what makes a work of art a surrealist one is, first and foremost, the spirit in which it was conceived' [142], and for J.H. Matthews (1966), 'When reading surrealist novels we have to adjust to unfamiliar moral attitudes. We have to overcome a feeling of alarm or disturbance released in us by…. the presence of those who are not characters, acting out a strange destiny in a world that is not quite our own' [143]. Readers may decide for themselves how well these observations on surrealist writing apply, not just to Gothic, but also, more particularly, to *Story of O*.

---

[1] Calder 2013 p. 124

[2] Mahon 2020 p. 152, 161

[3] Mahon 2020 p. 150

[4] Bédouin: Eros et l'Instinct de Mort in *Medium, Communication Surréaliste* 2 (Feb. 1954) cited in Mahon 2020, p. 151

[5] Mahon 2020 p. 151 # 137, 138,139

[6] Surya 1992, p. 568, note 14

[7] In *Critique* June 1949, cited in Surya 1992 p. 563

[8] *NNRF* no 29, 1st May 1955

[9] Surya 1992 p. 424

[10] cited David 2006 p. 12 note 8; as always, thanks to Maurice Debonnard with the translation.

[11] 'Histoire d'O' / 'Les Fers le feu la nuit de l'âme' ('The Irons the Fire the Night of the Soul') *Critique* 97, June 1955. Later version in Le Belvédère, © 1958 Éditions Bernard Grasset

[12] all quotes in this paragraph are from Mandiargues in Réage *Story of O*, Ballantine 1983 xv-xx

[13] Silverman 1984

[14] 'Des Chats et des Magnolias' (*LSM* 1 1956) / 'Des Esclaves, des Suffragettes, de Fouet' (*LSM* 3, Autumn 1957). See Mahon 2020 p 152

[15] All quotes are from 'On Slaves, Suffragettes and the Whip' *Le Surréalisme même* no 3 (1957) trans. Myrna Bell Rochester; in Penelope Rosemont ed. *Surrealist Women, An International Anthology*, University of Texas press 1998, pp. 235-236

[16] See Mahon 2020 pp 161– 174 for an excellent account.

[17] *Masques de Leonor Fini* Pub. by La Parade, Editions André Bonne; cited in Webb 2009 p. 166.

[18] Réage 1969 pp 19-20

[19] Webb 2009 p. 234

[20] The opinion of connoisseur of erotica C.J. Schiener ; cited in St Jorre 1995, p. 233. Presumably he meant in *Return* (unless he was referring to

the mysterious 'lost' section?). Pauvert thought Schiener a 'mythomane' (St Jorre 1995 p. 238).

[21] Letter to Édith Thomas 3 August 1954, cited in David p. 432 footnote 97

[22] Notably a 1962 edition for La Compagnie des Bibliophiles, Le Cercle du Livres précieux for which she did 16 full page lithographs. There were other editions, in 1962, 1963, 1968 and 1975. See Webb 2009 pp. 293-4 for more details. It is possible that Pieyres de Mandiargues and/or Lely were instrumental in putting Fini in touch with Pauvert (David 2006 p. 65 note 175).

[23] Mahon 2020 p. 172 sees O struggling with repressing emotions, including rage and desire and the scream, which has her hovering 'between the two roles identified by (Nora) Mitrani: slave and suffragette of the whip', O's face resembling Fini's 1950 painting *Medusa*, and her self portraits in ink.

[24] Marc Perlman: 'Un entretien avec Leonor Fini' *Beaux Arts* 27 June 1970, cited Webb 2009 p, 231

[25] Mahon 2020 pp. 173-174, #227, 228, 229 p. 255 citing Constantin Jelenski *Leonor Fini* Guide de Livre 1968; unpublished text (c. 1972) in Xavier Gauthier *Leonor Fini*, Musée de Poche 1973; A.K. 'Leonor Fini, Un livre, une exposition' *Gazette de Lausanne* 1968.

[26] 'Manifesto of Surrealism', André Breton, 1924; trans Richard Seaver & Helen R. Lane; *Ann Arbor* 1972, pp. 16-18

[27] Breton: 'Limits not Frontiers of Surrealism' in *Surrealism* ed. Herbert Read (1936), Praeger 1971 p. 106 cited in Matthew Wickman 'Terror's Abduction of Experience: A Gothic History' *Yale Journal of Criticism* vol 18, No 1 Spring 2005 pp. 179-206

[28] Polizzotti 2009 p. 477

[29] Julien Graque: – André Breton, Quelques aspects d'un écrivain, *José Corti* 1948 p. 34, cited Matthews 1966 p. 96-97

[30] Polizzotti 2009 p. 512

[31] Réage 1969 p. 15

[32] Deforges 1975 pp. 124-126

[33] Breton 1924 pp. 29-30

[34] Ibid p. 26

[35] Deforges 1975 p. 127

[36] Ref to Paulhan deposition – quoted in Deforges 1975 pp. 8-11

[37] cited in St Jorre 1994, p. 45

[38] interview cited in St Jorre 1995 p. 213/ 215

[39] Breton 1924 p. 14

[40] Bedell 2004

[41] St Jorre 1994, p. 45, Bedell 2004

[42] Deforges 1975 p. 127

[43] Breton 'Second manifeste du surrealism' (1930) in *Manifestes du surrealism*, Folio Essais Gallimard 1962/1979 p. 102

44 Breton 'Manifesto' 1924 (1972) p. 26 – Shakespeare apparently warrants that accolade 'in his better days/ finer moments'. Breton does

not make clear exactly when this might be, but one might reasonably suspect it was when he wrote *A Midsummer Night's Dream*, and the later 'Romances': *Pericles, Cymbeline, A Winter's Tale* and *The Tempest* and (all 1608-1611) – plays where all becomes 'rich and strange' (which Breton glosses as 'the marvellous'). The 'Romances' are perhaps better called the 'Alchemical plays' (Kathleen O'Leary *'The Art of Salvation is but the Art of Memory': Soul-Agency, Remembrance and Expression in Donne and Shakespeare,* PhD thesis, Lancaster University 2007, unpublished).

[45] David 2006 pp. 317, 247

[46] Breton *L'Amour Fou* Gallimard 1937 p. 110

[47] Surya 2002 p. 236. 1938 was also the year of 'Recherches de la sexualité' in *La Révolution surréaliste.*

[48] Chadwick, 1985, p. 34

[49] Breton *Nadja,* (1928) translated Richard Howard, Grove Press 1960 p. 79

[50] Ibid p. 116

[51] Ibid p. 11

[52] Ibid p. 24

[53] Deforges 1975 pp. 219-220

[54] Breton (1928) 1960 p. 66

[55] Benjamin 1980

[56] Sontag 67 pp. 111, 103

[57] Joseph Kessel: *Belle de Jour* (1928)  Pan 1969 p. 77

[58] Deighan 2012

[59] David 2006 p. 31

[60] Man Ray *Self-Portrait* Boston 1963, p. 192,  cited in Chadwick 1985, p.118

[61]  Audrey Warne: 'Staging Sadomasochism: Images of Bondage in Man Ray's Surrealist Photography, 1929–1932', Online ·Immediations No. 17, Courtauld.ac.uk 2020

[62] Florian Illies *Love in a Time of Hate* Profile Books 2023 p. 189

[63] now in the Pompidou Centre Cabinet de Photographie

[64] Warne 2020

[65] Chadwick 1985 p. 106

[66] Deforges 1975 p. 29

[67] Illies 2023 p. 114

[68] ibid 2023 p. 60

[69] Carolyn Burke *Lee Miller: On Both Sides of the Camera*, Bloomsbury 2006

[70] Sue Roe *In Montparnasse* Fig Tree/ Penguin 2018 p, 118

[71] Illies 2023 p 81-82

[72] La Compagnie des Bibliophiles. Le Cercle du Livre précieux; Webb 2009 p. 293

[73] Published in *Zero: A Quarterly Revue of Literature and Art* Nos 3-4, Autumn 1949-Winter 1950

[74] Deforges 1975 pp. 100-101

[75] 'Theatre of Cruelty' in *Theory of the Modern Stage* ed. Eric Bentley,

Penguin 1968, p. 66

76 Cited in Stephen Barber *Antonin Artaud: Blows and Bombs*, Faber & Faber 1993, p. 52

77 All quotes in this paragraph are from 'Introduction' to *Oulipo: A Primer of Potential Literature*, ed. Warren F. Motte jr (1986) Dalkey Archive Press, 1998, pp. 1-22

78 'La République du silence', *Les Lettres françaises*, 1944, Poirier 2018 p. 61

79 Beauvoir 1949, p. 639

80 Réage 1969 p. 16

81 David 2006, p. 547

82 Polizotti 2009 p. 72

83 Cornick 2008;  François Demont 'Le dadaïsme et surréalism chez paulhan' *Littérature* 2020 4 No. 200 pp 22-38

84 Nadeau 1964, p. 64; Durazoi 2002 p. 3

85 Cornick 2008

86 Ibid 2008

87 Nadeau 1964 p. 71

88 Roe 2018 p. 119

89 Polizotti 2009 p. 201

90 Cornick 2008

91 Demont 2020

92 Polizotti 2009 p. 255

93 Breton (1928) 1960 p. 27

94 Barber 1993 p. 86-87

95 Surya 2002 p. 266

96 Demont 2020

97 Ibid 2020

98 Breton 1924 p.32

99 À demain la poésie', cited in Demont 2020

100 Passeron, 2005, p. 210

101 Breton: 'Hommage à Antonin Artaud' (1946) in *La Clé des champs* (Pauvert 1967) cited Durozoi 2002 p. 460

102 Barber 1993, p 162

103 Philippe Andoin in *La Brèche* 1960 cited in Durozoi 2002 p. 598

104 Sontag 1967 p. 88

105 Durozoi 2002 p. 584

106 Polizzotti 2009 p. 541

107 Mahon 2005 p. 195

108 Adapted from Aragon: 'Le Temps traverse' *Les Lettres Françaises* 16 Oct 1968 , cited Demont 2020; Aragon amplifies his reference to 'a whole side' with 'un grande Pan' – a play on words where 'pan' is a side or a flank, but Pan is the Greek god of all things wild (as always, thanks are due to Maurice Debonnard here).

109 Sontag 1967 p.105

110 Janis Pallister 1985 castigates Surrealism for leaving 'such a legacy of blazon, reification and dismemberment of the female body as

to almost nullify its aesthetic accomplishments': 'The Anti-Castle in the Works of Pauline Reage' *Journal of the Midwest Modern Language Association* vol. 18, no. 2, Autumn 1985 pp 3-13, Loyola University, Chicago

[111] Watz 2023 p. 7 footnote 23

[112] Mahon 2020, p. 123.

[113] Breton 1924 pp. 14, 6-7

[114] *Souvenir de la Mexique,* Minotaur No. 12-13 cited Matthews 1966 p. 1

[115] Breton 1924 pp. 6-7

[116] ibid 1924 pp. 26-27

[117] Armand Hoog 'The Surrealist Novel' *Yale French Studies* 8 (1951) 17-35

[118] 'Questioning the Concept of Literature' *NRF* 1924, cited in Sontag 1967 p. 90

[119] Watz 2023 p. 1

[120] Breton 1924 p. 40

[121] Matthews 1966, p. 2; Matthews J.H. 'Surrealism in the Novel' *Books Abroad* vol. 43 no. 2, Spring, pp. 182-188, University of Oklahoma press, 1969]; Matthews 1966 p. 6

[122] Breton (1928) 1960 p. 18

[123] Chenier-Gendron 2014 p. 726, cited Watz 2023, p. 3; Parallels can be drawn here between Breton and Roland Barthes, who contrasted the prosaic 'readerly' text with the more experimental 'writerly' one, the former providing *plaisir*/ pleasure, the latter *jouissance*/ ecstasy; Watz (2023) citing Barthes' *S/Z* (1970), *Le Plaisir du Texte* (1973).

[124] Breton 1924 p. 14. [Paulhan's deployment of this word to describe women in his Preface to *O* (p. xxxiv) one suspects is a knowing wink to Breton.]

[125] Ibid pp. 14-15

[126] Cited in Matthews 1966 p. 23 note 7.

[127] ibid 1966 p. 95 citing Gracq's *Avis au lecteur*, preface to his novel *Au Château d'Argol* 1938 – a novel Breton admired (Durozoi 2002 p. 518)

[128] cited ibid 1966, p. 10.

[129] Watz 2023 p. 6

[130] Matthews 1966, p. 93

[131] Magritte: 'Lifeline' in *Surrealists on Art*, trans. and ed. Lucy R. Lippard, Prentice-Hall 1970, cited Wickman 2005 p. 185

[132] Breton 1924 p. 10

[133] Wickman 2005 pp. 187, 184.

[134] Brutus, Hamlet and Macbeth all wrestle with anxiety and/or guilt over the killing of a father figure. In each case their female love interest goes mad and does away with herself.

[135] See R.Saxment *Writing Desire* Black Scat 2024

[136] For Michelle A. Massé *In the Name of Love: Women, Masochism, and the Gothic*, Ithaca, Cornell University Press, 1992, p. 107 *O* is 'the most extreme instance... of Gothic pornography'.

[137] Samuel Taylor Coleridge 'The Pains of Sleep' 1803

[138] Shullenberger 2005, citing Zizek 2000. Such prosaic matters are however referred to in *Return* – more weight in the balance against it being Réage's work?

[139] See for example *Rebecca* Daphne du Maurier (1938), *Wide Sargasso Sea* Jean Rhys (1966), *Picnic at Hanging Rock* Joan Lindsay (1967), *The Bloody Chamber* Angela Carter (1979), *The Handmaid's Tale* Margaret Atwood (1985)

[140] Elizabeth Brereton Allen 1998 'Surrealist Novel' in Paul Schellinger (ed.) *Encyclopedia of the Novel*, vol II, Routledge 1998, p 1302, cited Watz 2023 p. 7.

[141] Neil Matheson cited in Watz ed. 2023 p. 123

[142] Cited Polizzotti 2009 p. 493

[143] Matthews 1966 p. 176

# IX: *O*, Surrealism and Mysticism

The relationship between *O* and Surrealism takes on additional dimensions when we consider it in the context of mysticism. As we have seen, from the outset *O* was being discussed in mystical terms, and from its own beginnings thirty years before, Surrealism had been linked with the mystical. In the mid 1920s it was already being noted that 'The idea of any sort of Surrealist revolution [...] aims to create a new form of mysticism' [1]. There is mileage in looking at *O* in this context.

## ANDRÉ BRETON AND THE MYSTICAL

In 1914 Viennese psychoanalyst Herbert Silberer had suggested that Alchemy provided a metaphor for psychological development [2]. This idea didn't catch on in psychoanalytic circles – Freud thought it faintly interesting at best, and Jung dismissed it as 'off the beaten track and rather silly' [3], but painter Max Ernst found it intriguing. In 1922 when Ernst came to Paris and met André Breton and his group, he brought with him his fascination for Alchemy, along with a more comprehensive understanding of Freud [4], both of which were enthusiastically received by the nascent surrealist movement.

In the 1924 'Manifesto of Surrealism' André Breton acclaimed the 'Marvellous' as the key to the 'Beautiful', and in the 1929 'Second Manifesto', pointing out the 'remarkable analogy... between the Surrealist efforts and those of the alchemists' (he was particularly enthralled by the work of late medieval alchemist Nicolas Flamel), went on to demand 'the profound, the veritable occultation of surrealism' [5]. The surrealist unification of Alchemy, psychoanalysis and Marxism into an orgasmic vision of human redemption, combined the Chemical Wedding, psychological catharsis and political revolution into one liberating eruption – as Breton put it in the last line of *Nadja*, 'beauty will be CONVULSIVE or it will not be' [6]. Breton never lost his interest in the mystical, and in the 1940s it was centre stage in his thinking again. Having steadfastly opposed fascism and Nazism, he had no intention of submitting to the brave new world that the soon-to-be victorious capitalism and communism promised. Instead he demanded a 'new myth' centred around the erotic, prophesying in 1941 'A new spirit will be born from the present war... As always when socially human life is almost worthless, I think we must learn to read with and look through the eyes of Eros — Eros, who in time to come will have the task of re-establishing that equilibrium briefly broken for the benefit of death' [7]. The following year he was drawing on William James and Novalis in postulating *Les Grands Transparents* (The Great Invisibles/Unseen) who 'exist' (poetically) beyond our senses as focal points of our desires and yearning for the marvellous [8].

***Arcanum 17***: From August to October 1944, inspired by a new love, Elisa Clara, and news of the liberation of Paris, Breton composed his next (and perhaps last) great work, *Arcanum 17*, a 'coda' to the trilogy of *Nadja*, *Communicating Vessels* and *L'Amour fou*, the title referencing the Star, the 17th card of the Major Arcana of the Tarot deck, symbolising 'hope and resurrection' [9]. Drawing on the works of early 19th century utopian socialist Charles Fourier, Breton proselytised the salvation of humanity through a rediscovery of ancient wisdom and myth, in particular the redemptive power of the feminine principle, all of which had been buried for centuries under patriarchal 'civilisation'. The personification of this feminine principle in Breton's new mythology was Melusina, a folkloric faerie woman, usually depicted as akin to a mermaid – half woman, half fish (or serpent) – and claimed as magical ancestor by the Lusignans and other families of medieval French nobility. The most influential version of her story was *Le Roman de Mélusine* by Jean d'Arras (1393) where she is a supernatural being who weds a mortal man and bears him children, but imposes a taboo upon their marriage, that her husband must never spy on her when she is bathing (when she loses full human form and her hybrid body is revealed). Inevitably he violates this taboo, whereupon she turns into a dragon and abandons him. In Breton's mythos, she is the enchanted *femme-enfant*, figure of youth and clairvoyance and love (as found in *Nadja*, where he first mentions her [10]), whose power offers spiritual rescue to mere men. Breton's wish was that one day, 'may we be ruled by the idea of *the salvation of the earth by woman*, of the transcendent vocation of women...', exhorting artists to 'make visible everything that is part of the feminine'... 'The time has come to value the ideas of women at the expense of those of men, whose bankruptcy is coming to pass fairly tumultuously today' [11]. Already an alchemical figure combining different elements, Melusina represents the feminine principle uniting in *conjunctio* with the masculine in the Alchemical Chemical Wedding, from which the Elixir or Philosopher's Stone is born, and an inspiration for a new reverence for woman and a liberation of her sexuality [12].

**Relaunching Surrealism:** Returning to Paris in 1946, Breton was faced with opposition from a range of quarters. Having quit the Communist Party in 1933 and never wavering in his hostility to Stalinism, he was the target of implacable hostility from the PCF, with Louis Aragon, his old colleague and now sworn enemy, as a leading aggressor. In addition, Sartre and the Existentialists, setting themselves up as the fashionable new intellectual/cultural movement in Paris, were strongly motivated to dismiss Surrealism as both out of date and lacking in Resistance credentials. Sartre and the PCF had plenty of problems with each other, but they were united in their desire to dismiss Surrealism as a superficial and irrelevant response to the demands of the times. In this they were ably assisted by Maurice Nadeau whose *History of Surrealism* (1945) celebrated Surrealism as a pre-war movement, but now a dead duck fit only to be stuffed and put in a museum [13]. Paradoxically, all this denigration reminded people about Surrealism and its earlier status and significance, and Breton saw it as his job to put it back on the map as a movement with contemporary consequence and a fruitful future. Here he was supported by old friends like Toyen and Benjamin Péret, some ex-members of La Main à Plume (Jacques Hérold and Victor Brauner), and new recruits like Gérard Legrand and Jean Schuster. Breton's new vision was however divisive. René Magritte, in concert with a grouping calling themselves the Revolutionary Surrealists (which included other ex-members of La Main à Plume, Noël Arnaud and Christian Dotrement, along with Tristan Tzara, Raymond Queneau, Asger Jorn and others), criticised Breton's prioritising of Eros and poetry as a retreat from political engagement into occult obscurantism and esotericism [14]. In fact Breton had not abandoned left-wing politics – he co-authored a pro-Vietnamese independence pamphlet 'Liberty is a Vietnamese Word' in 1947 [15], but he took a firm stance against art and literature as servants of propaganda, and that same year he attacked both the PCF and Sartre on this score, and cut off contact with political organisations [16]. Around the same time, Catholic philosopher Michel Carrouges, who was acquainted with Breton, put the case that Breton and Georges Bataille, by adopting mystical vocabularies (albeit in very different registers), were admitting a need for God in their lives, and were in fact gravitating back towards the Christian fold [17]. In 1948 Jean Schuster roundly rejected this attempt to co-opt surrealist mysticism to religion, and in 1951 when Carrouges had another go at claiming a rapprochement between Catholic spirituality and Surrealism, a sympathiser with Revolutionary Surrealism,

Henri Pastoureau, vigorously retaliated, and was shocked to find Breton unwilling to support either side. Pastoureau denounced Breton as a back-slider, the resulting ruckus went public in the press, and the upshot was that Breton cut ties with both Pastoureau and Carrouges.

**'The Politics of Eros':** Despite the dramas, Breton's new vision won through, guiding a plethora of new publications and periodicals [18] (notably *Le Surréalisme, même* 1956-59, edited by Breton and published by Pauvert), and the major exhibitions of surrealist art in the post-war period – 'Eros qua subversive force' ran through its history, and was now 'pervading post-war Surrealism and shaping landmark exhibitions' [19]. For Alyce Mahon (2005), Breton had not abandoned politics at all, rather he was creating a new one, a 'Politics of Eros', which she described as the best way 'to understanding post-war surrealism, its subversive intent and vital role in the culture of the period' – a radical politics which 'embraced the power of the Id', articulating the 'sexual, erotic body and its uncanny power', presenting the female body as an object of desire, a route to the marvellous, and redemptive in its role as 'the path and space for revolt' against the masculinist brutalism that passes for 'civilisation' [20]. Crucially though, the Politics of Eros was always in Breton's view a profoundly mystical politics.

The first major surrealist exhibition in Paris after the war was entitled *Surrealism in 1947*, alternatively named *Les Grands Transparents* after Jacques Hérold's iconic sculpture, which centred around a series of pagan altars dedicated to creatures or objects 'susceptible to being endowed with mythic life' [21]. With contributions from, amongst others, Duchamp, Ernst, Toyen, Brauner, Joan Miró, Yves Tanguy, Wilfredo Lam and Roberto Matta (and a guest appearance from Juliette Greco in one of the installations), it celebrated magic and the uncanny and presented Surrealism as 'an initiation, through poetry, through art' [22]. It received mixed reviews, with much of the press finding it tired and treading old ground, while the PCF and Sartre (predictably) found it bourgeois and frivolous, but it attracted sizeable crowds and served as a promising re-launch for Surrealism.

Through the 1950s Breton continued to propagate his message of erotic mysticism. In 1952 he was identifying Desire as the 'vital source of all our thinking' and refocusing the mission of Surrealism as doing 'its utmost to dispel the taboos which militate against the fullest treatment of the sexual domain, not to say the sexual domain in its entirety, including the perversions...' [23]. In 1954 he was enthusing about the dynamic symbolism of Celtic art (something that had attracted Aury since childhood), extolling its superiority to the surface perfection of classical Graeco-Roman art, and citing it alongside Oceanic and Native American objects as ancestral to Magic Art [24]. This distinction between symbolic art and the merely 'retinal' (an idea explored by Duchamp) informed Breton's and Legrand's study into *L'Art magique* (1957), which traced the history of art as a vehicle for the magical [25], discussed magic as a quest for analogies and correspondences, placing Symbolism and Surrealism as inheritors of this long tradition, and featured contributions from surrealists like Magritte, Péret, Carrington, Mandiargues and Gracq; dissident surrealists including Bataille and Klossowski; and other luminaries like André Malraux, Martin Heidegger, Claude Lévi-Strauss and Jean Paulhan.

One contributor was Joyce Mansour, brilliant young Egyptian-Jewish poet, rumoured to exist on oysters, hot water and cigars, who had joined the surrealists in 1954 and became Breton's close companion for the next decade, and his 'last great love' (almost certainly platonic, he was twice her age, they were both married, and Breton for one valued marital fidelity). Mansour was a highly erotically aware individual (we shall discuss her work below), comfortable with extremes of sexual explicitness in art and literature – for example, she and Breton admired the work of Pierre Molinier which they encountered in 1956, although most of the rest of the group found him a bit much [26]. Inspiration from the relationship with

Joyce Mansour helped energise the next major exhibition of surrealist art – the 1959 *Exposition InteRnatiOnale du Surréalisme (EROS)* which celebrated the erotic in its most Sadean and fetishistic extremes. Organised by Breton and Duchamp, it featured contributions from Miró, Giacometti, Man Ray, Matta, Tanguy, Bellmer (with his dislocated 'Poupée' and images of Unica Zorn in bondage) and others, including Americans Robert Rauschenberg and Jasper Johns. Its launch was marked by Jean Benoît's performance piece in the tradition of Artaud's Theatre of Cruelty to celebrate the 140th anniversary of the death of the Marquis de Sade, 'Execution of the Testament of Sade', conducted at Joyce Mansour's apartment, with Bédouin, Mitrani, Toyen and Schuster in attendance, which culminated in Benoît branding the word 'Sade' on his chest with a red-hot iron – a move an over-excited Matta repeated on himself. The *EROS* exhibition featured the work of a larger than usual number of women artists, including Mansour, Mimi Parent, Dorothea Tanning, Toyen and Meret Oppenheim (with her 'Cannibal Feast'). Nobody could accuse this exhibition of being stale, and the press was suitably shocked [27], the creative participation of women in such a carnival of 'pornography' provoking the loudest howls of moralistic outrage.

The catalogue for this exhibition featured postcards of works by Dalí and Gorky, written contributions from Mandiargues and Paz, and a paean of praise from Breton for Desire and Love as providing a more nourishing universe than the depressing 'real' world of Cold War and the prevailing climate of sanctimonious narrow-minded moralism [28]. Breton hailed eroticism as 'the only art worthy of man and of space, the only one capable of leading him further than the stars,' 'mankind's greatest mystery', the 'highest common factor' in Surrealist art since the beginning [29], and praised Georges Bataille for his understanding that eroticism 'is that which, in the conscience of man, calls his being into question' [30]. *Story of O* received a name-check in the catalogue as well, Nora Mitrani citing O's ambiguity in being obedient sex slave to

Sir Stephen yet rebelliously refusing his command to masturbate, concluding that *O* was a step towards female emancipation, but not the final word [31].

## WOMEN'S EROTICA IN THE 1950s

Dominique Aury seems to have had a sensitivity to the kind of 'occultation' Breton had talked about. In her *Lectures pour tous* in 1958, she discussed 'literary landfalls', the uncanny moments when reading, when we encounter a passage imbued inexplicably with deep meaning and resonance. For her, 'books are full of summonses', arising from some mysterious interplay between author, reader and language itself, summonses that speak when readers make themselves vulnerable to the text [32] – a perception in keeping with Rimbaud's 'alchimie du verbe' ('Alchemy of the word/verb'), cited approvingly by Breton in his 1930 'Second Manifesto'.

More strikingly, *Story of O* can be clearly seen as a contribution to the Politics of Eros, and Dominique Aury played a role in fostering women's erotic writing – a genre where mystical considerations were never far away. In *L'Arche* in the mid 1940s Dominique Aury had been noting the beginnings of a new approach in depicting the sexuality of women. Lauding Colette as the founding spirit, from her early works in the 1920s to her latest, *Gigi* (1944), Aury also praised new writers, like Violette Leduc whose first novel *L'Asphyxie* came out in 1946, and whose lesbian love story *Thérèse et Isabelle* was censored by Gallimard the same year *O* was published [33]. The milieu of women's erotica emerged alongside Breton's mysticism of the erotic, but the first steps were tentative, and here *Story of O* was significant as a flagship and trail-blazer for the new genre.

***L'Image*** (1954): Interviewed in the 1990s when she was in her sixties, author Catherine Robbe-Grillet recalled the impact of *O* on her, then a 24 year old named Catherine Rstakian: '*Histoire d'O* had an influence on me. It was a beautiful book, that, at the time, made a great sensation. It has been 40 years, you have to imagine what it was like 40 years ago. It was a book that inspired you to dream, extraordinarily well written, it relied on the imagination in such a way that at the beginning of *Histoire d'O*, you are led to believe such a fantasy may or may not have actually happened. Or perhaps it was the result of an amorous imagination, which was in fact the case' [34]. *O* did not however just inspire her to dream, it also inspired her to write her own erotic classic, the novella *L'Image* (*The Image*), published under the name 'Jean de Berg' by Éditions de Minuit (where her lover Alain Robbe-Grillet had been a major player since 1954). *L'Image* recounts the story of the fascination of the narrator, a young man named Jean de Berg, for the sophisticated Claire, a photographer who has in her service a girl, Anne, whom she ritually punishes and uses as a go-between with Jean, until, after tantalising Jean with her photos, Claire finally gives herself to him.

There is a crucial difference between the two texts in that *L'Image* leads to fulfillment in a way that *O* does not. For Sontag (1967), pornography 'as a literary form' permits two narrative patterns, one 'equivalent to tragedy' where the 'erotic subject-victim heads inexorably towards death', the other, more akin to 'comedy', where the protagonist achieves 'union with the uniquely desired sexual partner' in 'terminal gratification' [35]. But the similarities are more striking. For Sontag, both books are examples of pornography 'belonging to literature' [36], and Pallister (1985) places them together (along with *Return to Roissy*) as 'carry(ing) their own brand of surrealism'. Claire, like O, is a professional photographer, and in both novels mirror reflections and photographic images are significant (the title of the Robbe-Grillet novella is a bit of a give-away here). In *O*, our heroine takes a series of more or less fetishistic pictures of Jacqueline, which Sir Stephen peruses to evaluate the model as a potential recruit for Roissy, while in *L'Image*, Claire has photos of Anne, and of herself, to present to Jean to signal availability. Arising from these games with imagery and reflection, both novels deploy an uncanny doubling effect: Anne is not so much Claire's submissive and envoy as her 'image' or 'projection' [37], the novel being seen as 'a deeply symbolic tale about the battle for integration between a woman's own disparate selves—mistress and slave—an eroticized allegory of one of feminism's central psychological dilemmas' [38]. *L'Image* even nods to *O* in specific details: when Claire tells Jean of Anne 'She belongs to me' (p. 11) [39], there is a direct echo in both speech and characters' names of an incident in *O*, where Anne-Marie tells O, concerning one of the girls at Samois, 'Claire belongs to me' (*O* p. 163).

The novella was prefaced by a short introduction (under the name 'Pauline Réage') which merits some consideration. It identifies 'Jean de Berg' as a woman, as the novella 'strongly embodies a female viewpoint' (p. 3), and goes on to flag up the rules of the erotic game of dominance and submission, as men 'in their innocence' assume they are taking the lead, and 'intellectual women' play along by insisting that women are now free and equal and no longer oppressed, and so all seems reciprocal. But the truth is the man 'is the master, without a doubt: but only if his lover allows him to be', and the preface cites the Hegelian dialectic of the master and slave (as Paulhan cited in his preface to *O*) to prove that 'Even when in chains, on her knees and pleading for mercy, it is the woman who is in charge... And she knows it. Her power increases in proportion to her apparent abasement' (all of which echoes psychoanalytic readings of the power of the masochist, see chapter VII). The scene can only be played out with her agreement, for the apparent slave 'is in fact an all-powerful goddess', and the man is her priest, whose 'function is... to perform the rituals of which she is the sacred object' (p. 4), expressions which echo the vocabulary commonly used by Sade. The mystical-religious dimension is stressed – the 'motifs of the book' are 'hieratic', ritualistic, 'churchlike' as well as fetishistic, and the photographs 'can be seen as religious images, a new series of Stations of the Cross'. The preface goes on to insist there are in fact only two characters in the novella – the man and the woman. Claire and Anne are in effect aspects of one person –

'one who submits, the other who inflicts' – this 'bizarre dual nature of womankind' revealing the deepest mystery, that 'a woman, like a man, can worship only that same dichotomous body, in turn caressed and beaten, loved and abused, subjected to every humiliation, but all her own.' Both man and woman are supplicants to her, the 'goddess', 'But she is also the divine object of worship, her continued sacrifices are made to herself. She experiences a double pleasure, unknowable to the man, as she contemplates the subtle game of mirrors in which she sees herself endlessly violated and reborn' (p.4).

The preface's insistence that the name 'Jean de Berg' masked a female writer (a little joke on the widespread, and mistaken, suspicion that 'Pauline Réage' was really a man?) was quite readily accepted. *Publishers Weekly* pointed out sufficient similarity between the writing in *L'Image* and *Histoire d'O* to raise the question whether they were from the same hand [40], but the finger pointed to Catherine Rstakian early on (Sontag was pretty sure she knew who had written it by 1967, although she didn't give the suspect's name [41]). However, Patsy Southgate, who translated *L'Image* for Grove Press in 1966, was of the opinion that the novella was a collaboration between Catherine and her soon-to-be husband Alain Robbe-Grillet. Alain was a pioneer of the 'Nouveau Roman', practitioners of which included Nathalie Sarraute and Marguerite Duras – all of whom were published by Éditions de Minuit, where Robbe-Grillet was literary advisor. In 1956 Minuit published Robbe-Grillet's manifesto for this new movement, 'Pour un nouveau roman', in which (like Breton in 1924) he rejected the conventions of the 'realist' novel – coherent character, clear story-line and ideological or moral content (as favoured by the communists and conservatives) – in favour of a recognition that form and content are inseparable, and the adoption of the technique of providing description of surface detail from which the reader has to construct motive and plot. For Robbe-Grillet, politics and literature were separate, literature being a sacred space where the writer was autonomous [42]. The consonance of Robbe-Grillet's views with those of his mentor Jean Paulhan is clear, and both echo Roland Barthes' distinction between 'readerly' and 'writerly' texts [43]. We have noted Breton's interest in reading him, and Sontag saw the Nouveau Roman as an offshoot of Surrealism [44]. It is also tempting to see *L'Image* itself, with its mysterious narrative that the reader (along with the narrator) has to work out, as an example of the Nouveau Roman.

As for the preface, although the attribution to 'Pauline Réage' is accepted in some quarters, Dominique Aury denied that she had any hand in it – she and Pauvert both suspected Alan Robbe-Grillet was responsible, signing it 'Pauline Réage' as a joke [45] (and no doubt also a canny move to boost sales).

Other comparisons between *L'Image* and *O* can be made. Both got into hot water with the authorities but only *L'Image* was actually banned, although Minuit's redoubtable director, Jérôme Lindon, steadfastly denying any knowledge of the author's identity, kept on printing [46]. In both cases a film version was released in 1975 [47]. By this time Alain Robbe-Grillet had moved into film making, where in an interesting parallel with the Nouveau Roman, the 'Nouvelle Vague' ('New Wave') in French cinema had been developing since 1954. That year François Truffaut's essay 'A Certain Tendency in French Cinema' was published in *Cahiers du Cinéma*, launching the idea of 'auteur' director – which by the end of the '50s included Truffaut himself, Jean-Luc Godard, Alain Resnais and others [48]. Robbe-Grillet became an auteur in his own right, with films like *Trans-Europ-Express* (1966) and *Successive Slidings of Pleasure* (*Glissements progressifs du plaisir* 1974) although he is best known for his screenplay for Resnais' *L'Année Dernière à Marienbad* (*Last Year in Marienbad*, 1961). For some reason he resisted the temptation to make a film of his wife's novella.

In contrast to Dominique Aury's reticence, Catherine Robbe-Grillet has been open to interviewers about her own experiences and predilections, recounting how Alain introduced her to SM, telling her 'I have particular tastes, I like to tie women up and hurt them, and have them obey me,' to which she listened 'as though I had always been destined for this' [49]. She and Alain married in 1957, the year after *L'Image* was published (she was 27, he 35). They had an open marriage, Alain heterosexual, Catherine bi–, and finding it exciting when Alain told her about his extra-marital escapades. In 1958 he presented her with a *Contrat de Prostitution Conjugale,* which stated: 'Her presence being solely to gratify the husband's vices, he shall treat her accordingly, with relentless harshness and brutality... On the appointed day, at precisely the designated time, his wife shall present herself at the rendez-vous, dressed strictly according to instructions ... she shall kneel immediately before her husband, eyes lowered, hands behind her back. ... These postures will nearly always be humiliating. They may be accompanied by chains or any manner of restraint ... during the infliction of torture, or merely to emphasize the condition of slavery.... She shall be relentlessly slapped, bitten etc.; her flesh—preferably in the most sensitive areas—shall be rent by fingernails; finally, she shall be beaten repeatedly during each session, on any part of the body chosen by the husband, with a leather whip...' [50]. Catherine did not sign it, not because she had any objection to anything there, 'There's nothing there that scares me... It wasn't the content I objected to – I knew I wasn't risking my life. It's a very beautiful text, not like the contract in *Fifty Shades*... I didn't sign it because I didn't want to express my consent. I preferred to be constrained' [51]. She did however accept the payment for the sessions Alain decreed.

Recognising that 'A sexual woman is obsessed with sex, and when one is obsessed, one is necessarily a slave,' Catherine understood that submission arises from need – in any sexual power game, 'The one whose need is the greatest is the submissive' [52]. She also provided an explanation for her tastes that may throw light on Aury: 'The Catholic religion in which I was raised is impregnated with the glory of pain and martyrdom. One is saved by pain and martyrdom. I was immersed in these stories because in the Catholic religion, with all its representations, the friezes of the saints are nearly always erotic. They are in pain but at the same time ecstatic. The faces of the saints are always like that. For me there is the same connection with eroticism and – I didn't call it sado-masochism at the time, for me it wasn't that, but I was ready to understand those ideas' [53].

In 1973, at the request of a young male friend, she started to practise as a dominatrix, conducting 'ceremonies' with her *petit clan* of female initiates, staging erotic theatre with themselves as the audience. Her 1985 book *Cérémonies de Femmes* (*Rites of Women*) reinforced her central place in French erotic culture, and in 2005 one of her 'clan', Beverly Charpentier, wrote to her: ' Madame, you have asked nothing of me; it is, therefore, of my own free will that I offer to you allegiance, obedience and loyalty. I swear to serve you faithfully in all things great and small, to obey your orders, carry out your wishes, whatever they may be. I commend to you everything I possess, material, intellectual and physical that you may dispose of what I have as you see fit. I swear to dedicate myself to you, to remain by your side as long as you choose, as your attendant, servant, defender; to support and protect you, whatever the circumstances, in every way possible, even should it cost me my life' [54]. Catherine accepted her pledge. Alain died in 2008, relieved to know that Catherine had someone to care for her after he was gone. Ten years later Catherine and Beverly were married. At the time of writing Catherine Robbe-Grillet still seems to be cheerfully in business at the age of 93.

***Les Gisants satisfaits* (1958):** A leading exponent of the Politics of Eros in 1950s literature was Joyce Mansour. Influenced by Sade, Sacher-Masoch and Lautréamont, Mansour deployed sadism, sensuality, eroticism and 'outrageous humour' [55] in her literary career, which began in 1953 with the poetry collections *Cris* (*Screams*), depicting 'cruel, violent passionate imagery of sex and death' [56]. *Cris* was reviewed by Jean-Louis Bédouin: 'There is nothing here that does not well up from the most obscure depths of the being, in which life and death, anguish and desire, pleasure and suffering fuse in one devouring reality, which devours itself through the object of its covetousness... It is essential that in the days of pin-ups and cover-girls, in the days of inculcated ignorance of true human necessities, a woman should recall in this way that love is a tragic experience, a vital one: like hunger and femininity, a formidable power, capable of violence and of cruelty, although dispensing tenderness and joy' [57]. Soon after, Mansour joined the surrealist group and became particularly close to Breton. As a surrealist, she was, according to J.H. Matthews (1966) 'no mere feminist. Her eroticism is a declaration of war, accompanied by a plea for liberty which surrealism views as essential to the progress of the individual, against the interdictions society invokes'. Mansour's second collection, *Déchirures* (*Tearings* [58]) was published by Minuit in 1955, and was followed by the prose work *Jules César* (1955) and *Le Perroquet* (*The Parrot*), published in *Le Surréalisme, même* in 1956. This last was an early version of *Marie, ou l'honneur de servir* (*Marie, or the honour of serving*) which saw the light of day in 1958 as the first part of her novel *Les Gisants satisfaits* (*The Sated Recumbents*), published by Pauvert.

According to Matthews, 'her inspiration is unmistakably sadistic' [59] and this novel 'is a work of social and moral subversion, thanks to its unbridled assertion of the supreme importance of desire', and 'lucid acceptance of something that respectability cannot entertain, but which takes on meaning as the very image of *something else*'. This idea of the 'something else' connects us to the quasi-mystical 'numinous' quality sought by Gothic writer Anne Radcliffe in her works (the Gothic nature of Mansour's novel being emphasised in Watz 2023 p. 134). Mansour's work recounts the story of a young woman, Marie, whose contempt for 'normality' is such that she sexually seduces and tortures her sister, and agrees to live with and serve a man on the understanding that one day he will kill her. This grants her 'a freedom inaccessible with the bounds of everyday existence, as Marie turns hopefully to an imposed fate', and she partakes in games of pursuit where 'She, gagged, quivering, her sex swollen like an over-ripe pear, howled with joy and pain' (ibid).

Soon after Marie has second thoughts and escapes, but having done so, decides 'I was foolish to run away'... 'I have squandered the ecstasy which was my rightful share; henceforth life will be without spice' [60]... 'I am bored... without the murderer life has lost its smell'. Realising that her body is 'satisfied' when 'bruised and injured, it crawls beneath the hurtful thongs of the whip', she returns to her killer, allowing him to slash her belly, and, 'unable to flee the punishment she approved' she falls 'prey to the hunter she has chosen', who is to her 'the king, the aristocrat of strength', finally submitting to him stabbing her through her vagina and finishing her off. But 'In the end, the triumph is hers, not the murderer's. Marie will pursue her activity after her death,' her 'deliberate, lucid rejection of normality and her pursuit of desire' even as far as her death, 'the complete accomplishment of desire', is 'one of the most remarkable assertions of freedom made in the name of surrealism'. Like many surrealist novels, there is little in the way of psychological realism, characters instead, with their 'vitality which surrealism recognises as authentic', personify 'the need to pursue individual desire to its ultimate consequences' [61]. In Mansour, as in Gothic literature, vampire stories, *Wuthering Heights* and so on, love is *amour fou* of a particularly sublime, demonic and fatal kind. It may be taken as an example of what Kathryn Conley calls 'anamorphic love' – anamorphism being common in surrealist art and literature, where something appears distorted, contradictory, even perverted, but becomes clearly resolved when seen from a particular angle, a love that delivers Marie eventually as a 'sacrificial object' in a story replete with religious imagery. [62]

The family kinship between Joyce Mansour's *Les Gisants satisfaits* and *O* is self-evident, and the possibility of direct influence is not to be discounted. Mansour worked with, among others, Hans

Bellmer, whose photography, in the words of his one-time partner Nora Mitrani, created 'images of convulsive eroticism' – a phrase applicable to Mansour's writing (Matthews 1962) like Mansour's writing, evokes the convulsive beauty of the erotic, and who expressed his belief in the need to develop new desires — an idea going back to Rimbaud's dictum: 'Love must be reinvented'. And Bellmer of course was acquainted with *O* from its publication, having provided the art-work for the first edition. More research will need to be done, but later in this chapter we shall raise the question of two-way traffic between *O* and Bataille. Mansour's familiarity with *O* is worth exploring, as is the establishment of more precise co-ordinates locating Réage's novel alongside Joyce Mansour and *L'Image* in the post-war surrealist Politics of Eros.

**Emmanuelle (1959)**: The other classic erotic text of the 1950s commonly linked to *Story of O* is *Emmanuelle*, their association strengthened by providing the inspiration for the first two films of Just Jaeckin – *Emmanuelle*, starring Sylvia Kristel, in 1974, *Histoire d'O* the following year. The novel *Emmanuelle* was published anonymously and clandestinely in 1959 by Eric Losfeld, and, as with *O*, there was discussion over the author's gender [63]. A female author was indicated by the focus on the protagonist's experience and active sexuality, and the expression of some rhetoric of female liberation, while metaphors of phallic power abounding in the instruction given by her male mentor suggested otherwise. In 1967 a re-publication gave the author as Emmanuelle Arsan but the consensus of opinion attributes the book to her husband, French diplomat Marayat Rollet-Andriane. Although this rules out *Emmanuelle* as example of women's erotica, which is the principal interest of this section, it still warrants some discussion in the context of *O*.

There are resemblances. The story focuses on the experiences of a young woman, Emmanuelle, who has a regular partner (her husband Jean), and meets an older man (an Italian called Mario), who mentors her in matters erotic. Emmanuelle makes love to women as well as men (notably an American woman called Bee – a name that is effectively a single letter, like 'O'), and there is a sexually precocious but untouched teenager, the 13 year-old Marie-Anne (whose name is the reverse of the mistress of Samois in *O*). Réage's novel is even directly referenced on one occasion – a 'blasé little female dog' being petted by an unnamed woman by the pool is named 'O' (*Emmanuelle* p. 24) [64], which ought to alert us to the likelihood that *Emmanuelle* is by no means an admiring homage to *Story of O*.

The differences between the books are certainly more striking. *Emmanuelle* is set in an exotic location – Bangkok – among hedonistic ex-patriots who indulge in plentiful, free and easy sex. In direct contrast with *O*, sex here is described in explicit physical detail, and there is a conspicuous absence of ritual, dominance and submission, bondage or punishment. Emmanuelle is, at 19, younger than O, and, unlike O, fond of masturbation. The gamine, Marie-Anne, is the centre of the network, introducing Emmanuelle to both Bee and Mario, unlike Natalie in *O* who is an outsider trying to get a look in. Homoeroticism is even more pronounced, the heroine, although in practice bi-sexual, insists she is a lesbian (p. 174); Mario is by repute more interested in men than women (p. 118) and literally does have sex with Emmanuelle through another man's body (p. 209) – a relationship that remains on a metaphorical level between O, Sir Stephen and René. Finally, Mario's tutoring of Emmanuelle on the significance of the erotic amounts to page upon page of pontificating – even Emmanuelle thinks he is 'a bit of a windbag' (p. 116) – making Sir Stephen sound the epitome of succinctness and brevity. This heavy-handedness extends to the book itself, every chapter being laden with erudite literary epigrams, just to remind the reader that this is Literature with a capital 'L'.

More importantly, in philosophical terms, *Emmanuelle* stands in actual opposition to *O* [65]. Whereas *O* has a mystical flavour, entwining love, suffering and even death, *Emmanuelle* will have none of this. The doctrine Mario expounds is fundamentally rationalist. He rejects religion as the source of conventions and taboos that suppress the healthy sexual drive, and presents eroticism as 'the victory of reason over myth... a morality... a science... Its laws are based on reason, not on credulity... on confidence instead of fear... and on a taste for life, rather than a mystique of death'. And 'because it helps to desanctify sex, it's an instrument of mental and social health' (p. 136), Eros being the antithesis and even the 'cure' for Thanatos. Despite his claim that 'Eroticism is not the product of decadence, but a progress' (p. 136), he does take a step beyond scientistic logic, and in so doing reiterates a reheated 19th century Decadence. He despises nature (p. 143) and insists that, beyond the physical, the  pleasure of the erotic arises from the transgression and violation of the very sanctions and taboos the novel ostensibly disclaims – for example, 'making love with a boy is erotic insofar as it's against nature' (p. 204).

*Emmanuelle* stands against *O*, and has little resonance with Surrealism, given its repudiation of the mystical and the poetic, and its simplistic grasp of Eros and Thanatos and obliviousness to the richness of their erotic cross-fertilisation. Despite this, both Breton and Mandiargues were both sufficiently taken by *Emmanuelle*'s condemnation of religious doctrine and gospel of sexual freedom to celebrate it, the former on the front pages of *Arts* magazine, the latter in the *NRF,* acclaiming its 'optimistic' and liberating flavour [66].

Later, in 1964, Breton was to respond to the rising culture of 'free love' with an insistence on the superiority of erotic ritual over mere rampant sex: 'The irresistible pressure of Freud's ideas has led to an increasing measure of agreement today that sexuality drives the world... Systematic sexual education can only be meaningful if it leaves intact the incentive towards "sublimation" and finds the means of transcending the lure of "forbidden fruit". The only possible approach is that of initiation, with the whole aura of sacredness – outside of all religions of course – that the word implies, an initiation providing the impulse for that spirit of quest which the ideal constitution of each human couple demands. *This is the price of love'* [67].

This would put Breton some distance from *Emmanuelle*, and closer to the qualities of *O*, with its mystical resonances and recognition of the importance of Sir Stephen's fondness 'for habits and rites' (*O* p. 73).

## *STORY OF O* AND THE MYSTICAL

From the start *Story of O* has been claimed as a mystical text, by Paulhan, the surrealist reviewers Bédouin, Bataille and Mandiargues, and later interviewers like St Jorre, for whom 'Religious references abound and the story is permeated with mystical and sacrificial imagery' [68]. Some have interpreted this as literally mystification, the imposition of a safe reading on *O* by male commentators embarrassed by the sexuality and trying to put a spin on it by veiling it in occult trappings [69] – after all, the earliest translation expurgated the novel, and Austryn Wainhouse admitted his unease with it [70]. Others take the mystical interpretation as a legitimate reading of Aury's intent [71]. Dominique Aury's tastes in literature had always leant toward the mystical – Shakespeare, John Donne and Abbé Fénelon were particular favourites of hers, all of whom addressed the relationship between spiritual and sexual love. In Shakespeare's *Romeo and Juliet* the protagonists deploy the language of pilgrimage and religious devotion in their first declaration of erotic love [72]; John Donne's writings are noted for their 'dramatic and extreme imagery, combining the erotic and the sacred' [73]; and in an article in 1958 Aury identified the essential teaching of Abbé François de Fénelon as 'profane love and sacred love are the same love, or should be...' [74].

In her chapter on 'The Mystic', Beauvoir (1949) discussed mystical love, confirming the identity of the religious and the sexual – 'divine' love being human love 'reaching out towards the transcendent, an absolute' [75]. For her, mysticism was gendered, being very much a female vocation. Women comprised 85% of the people recognised by the Church as bearing stigmata [76], encountering the mystical by abandoning themselves 'to the joys of the heavenly nuptials' in greater numbers and deeper passion than men [77]. Beauvoir depicted women's divine love physically embodied, and this physical embodiment of divine love was commonly accompanied by suffering. In traditional Roman Catholic teaching, pain is an inescapable fact of life, a test from God, and a means of overcoming sin through demonstrating one's faith in God, the doctrine of 'dolorisme' referring to an understanding that seeking pain through one's own free will is a sign of true faith [78]. Various 'Lives of Saints' demonstrate this, and Aury, writing of Fénelon, pointed out: 'Those who are tortured for their truth, what do they find in their sufferings, even in the midst of their groans and their tears, if not the same atrocious happiness that Fénelon wishes for his followers when they suffer?', linking this once again to the unity of profane and sacred love[79]. John Donne encapsulated themes of suffering, along with imprisonment and rape (all of significance in Aury's writings) in his 'Holy Sonnets' (XIV, c. 1610) where he called on the Almighty to 'Batter my heart.../ imprison me, for I/ Except you enthral me, shall never be free,/ Nor ever chaste, except you ravish me'. For Beauvoir, with her emphasis on women, 'most female mystics don't just abandon themselves passively to God, they apply themselves actively to self-annihilation by the destruction of their flesh' [80], stigmata demonstrating 'the mysterious alchemy that glorifies the flesh, since they are in the very presence of divine love, in the form of a bloody anguish' [81]. As an example of a female mystic possessed in divine ecstasy, where sacred and profane love coalesce in a climax of sexual sensuality, spiritual transcendence and holy agony, few can match St. Teresa of Avila's account of her encounter with a 'cherub': 'I saw in his hand a long spear of gold, and at the iron's point there seemed to be a little fire. He appeared to be thrusting it at times into my heart, and to pierce my very entrails; when he drew it out, he seemed to draw them out also, and to leave me all on fire with a great love of God. The pain was so great, that it made me moan; and yet so surpassing was the sweetness of this excessive pain, that I could not wish to be rid of it. The soul is satisfied now with nothing less than God. The pain is not bodily, but spiritual; though the body has its share in it, even a large one...' [82]. For Beauvoir this account 'justified' Bernini's sculpture of *St Teresa in Ecstasy* (1647-52) [83], 'swooning in an excess of supreme voluptuousness' [84], (a tour-de-force Bernini was to repeat with the *Blessed Ludovica Albertoni* in 1674).

Sacred suffering is a way-station on the road to martyrdom. For surrealist poet Octavio Paz, 'O is a saint and saints have a tendency towards martyrdom' [85], a view with which Bonnie Shullenberger (2005) concurred, that O is indeed a martyr, suffering abuse and making no effort to escape, overcome with the submission of a visionary mystic, permitting purgation, encountering miracles, touched by grace, an accomplice in her own suffering and finally death [86]. Martyrdom can be physical self-sacrifice for one's faith – Christians facing lions in the Roman arenas, Reformation and Counter-Reformation burnings and so on, but on a mystical plane, it is more about annihilation of the self in utter devotion, to God, love, or (in the case of Édith Thomas) the revolution. Aury saw this as the key to Fénelon: 'The pure love in which Fénelon in the exact sense of the word annihilated himself is the single discourse of his "spiritual writings"' [87], a view she reinforced in interview with Deforges (1975), that devotional and erotic love are both driven by the pursuit of absolute love, which entails the exalted desire for self-annihilation [88]. This echoed the vocabulary of Paulhan, for whom *O*, as a mystical text, was 'the confession of a lover. It is a book of devotion' [89], and his emphasis on the sublime bliss of surrender and self-sacrifice, well known to 'lovers and mystics' [90], which was itself echoed by Aury in her contribution to *Celebrated Women* (see p. 263). [Aury's claim that Paulhan's sole editing suggestion was to excise the word 'sacrificial' from *O* may not have been an 'in-joke' (see p. 68) [91] so much as the removal of an overly revealing word (assuming Aury isn't just pulling our leg again)].

Mystical annihilation of the ego in devotion was discussed in the last chapter in the context of Beauvoir's account of 'The Woman in Love'. With regard to O, Sontag (1967) sees her as an adept, willing to undergo any sacrifice in order to be initiated into the mystery of the loss of her self, the transcendence of her personality, an 'ascent through degradation', until she attains her ultimate [92], while for Jean Anderson (2018), *O* is very much in the tradition of the Christian ascetics, with their desire for self-annihilation and self-realisation [93]. The obliteration of O's identity in her love and the suffering that enhances love is the central theme in the novel. Her very name, the vowel 'O', references orifices and rings and cuffs, but also the exclamation of pleasure, ecstasy, submission (perhaps the shock of some readers?), symbolising zero but also Unity, O's quest being, not so much the suppression of identity, but the search for non-identity in complete mystical surrender of subjectivity to achieve the ego-less eternal [94]. Although Aury resisted interpretations of the name O, especially anything 'to do with erotic symbolism or the shape of the female sex' [95], she confirmed in her 1974 interview for *Elle* the significance of 'a quest for the absolute... a feeling of abandon... total dispossession of the self' in 'true passion', passion being 'a serious matter' (see chapter II) [96].

*Story of O* has been hailed as 'pornographic mysticism' [97], and as 'erotic mysticism', in the tradition of Fénelon, uniting profane and sacred love [98]. Sontag (1967) noted parallels with religious writing in pornography, including Genet and *O* – sexual obsession in literature aiming to arouse just as religious obsession in other texts aims to convert. For Sontag, *O* is replete with rituals and ordeals, testing the faith of the initiate into an ascetic spiritual discipline, as she experiences 'internal prostration' and sacred submission, listening 'as though a god and not he had spoken to her', and losing her freedom while gaining 'the right to participate in what is described as virtually a sacrificial rite' [99]. For Kenneth Anderson (1999), O is a pilgrim seeking the virtue to be found in religious hierarchy that the modern world has done away with [100].

In Jessica Benjamin's view, (1983), sexual eroticism is the descendent of religious eroticism, effectively becoming a new religion, with sado-masochistic practice taking on sacred significance, gratifying the same urges for suffering, abjection, annihilation and (seemingly paradoxically) recognition, emerging in BDSM ritual as it once did in the ecstasies of the saints [101]. Shullenberger (2005) is quite explicit – 'spirituality in a world where God is dead expresses itself as SM', which is the mystico-religious practice of our times, as much concerned with redemption as any religion, 'the word made flesh' – and O is the classic scripture.

It is through this idea of the mystical annihilation of the ego in ecstatic unity with the beloved that the otherwise alarming preoccupation with death in O and Réage's subsequent pronouncements can be understood. In the epilogue O asks to die, to which Sir Stephen gives his consent, and Réage elaborated on this in her 1970s interviews – telling Deforges 'Women want to be possessed, possessed completely, until death. What one seeks is to be killed... What does the believer seek but to lose herself in God. It seems to me the height of ecstasy to have oneself killed by someone one loves. I cannot think otherwise', and, when asked by Deforges 'whether you would have gone much further than me if you had been given the chance. If at each step you had been asked to take another one? Until death, like O?', Réage replied: 'Isn't this the supreme temptation?' [102]. O's trajectory through the novel is a 'fantasy of surrender', 'a step towards destruction, towards annihilation' [103], her dream being 'her destruction, her death' [104]. For David (2006) 'O finds in torture, in obedience, and in death, the ultimate absolution. In the erotic story, death is always close to pleasure...' [105], yet, as St Jorre (1994) points out, 'paradoxically, she has never been calmer and happier in her life. She is on the brink of the ultimate self-sacrifice and she experiences a feeling of total absolution' [106].

The vocabulary of words and ideas Réage uses reveals O to be on a search for religion without God, an intrepid explorer of the unity of sacred and profane love, the embodiment of erotic devotion in suffering, self-sacrifice, martyrdom and annihilation of the self, to a death that is the ecstatic climax of life itself. This makes *O* a sacred text of the erotic mysticism adored by the surrealists, and takes us particularly into the realms that occupied dissident surrealist Georges Bataille and his circle.

## GEORGES BATAILLE

Rival star to Breton in the surrealist cosmos, Georges Bataille provided an alternate focus around which a number of luminaries gathered.

Exempted from service in the First World War due to ill health, Bataille spent a year at a seminary before repudiating religion for Nietzsche and throwing himself into a life of debauchery, drugs and excess. Retaining a fascination for martyrdom and mortification, he linked his sexual urges to the over-excitable end of Church teaching that sex is sin, woman's body 'a bag of excrement' [107] and so on. Two events in his twenties shocked and thrilled him. In Spain he saw a bullfighter gored through the eye (reminding him of the horror of watching his incontinent and syphilitic father's blind eyes rolling in his head), an event which was to inspire a scene in his *Story of the Eye*. Then in 1925 he saw photographs taken in China in 1905, of the 'Death by a Thousand Cuts' [108], where he convinced himself he could see spiritual and sexual exaltation alongside the agony on the victim's face as his body was 'ravished' by the blades that sliced him apart. In Bataille's mind, religious ecstasy, eroticism, cruelty and death remained inextricably linked.

During the 1920s Bataille hovered on the fringes of the Surrealist movement. Agreeing with Breton on the need to discard the infantilism of Dada, he was nonetheless critical (and jealous) of Breton's popularity and influence, and set about providing an alternative centre for dissident surrealists – attracting Michel Leiris, André Masson and Joan Miró (some of whom retained links with Breton as well). Bataille admired Artaud as the 'black, disintegrating side of Breton', and contrasted Breton's pursuit of the Marvellous with his own pursuit of the Monstrous. For Bataille, there was nothing revolutionary about escapism into the 'marvellous' [109]. While both valued the erotic and the transgression of mainstream morality, Bataille saw Breton's 'amour fou' and belief in the power of poetry to sublimate life and reality into a *sur-réalité* as merely romantic, superficial and safe. By contrast his own approach delved down into a deeper 'reality' (a *sous-réalité* perhaps?) to be found in 'base materialism', the realm of excess and 'limit experiences' – paroxysmal encounters between pain and pleasure [110] – traumatic experience rather than poetic alchemy. He dismissed Breton's view of Sade as a liberated mind as light-weight, sanitised and hypocritical, and accused him of failing to face up to the full horror and disgust in Sade's world of anal sexuality and coprophilia. It was in the eroticisation of the repellent that Bataille found authenticity (although not everyone sees Bataille and Breton as so very far apart [111]).

Bataille's *Story of the Eye* was published in 1928, and the following year he launched his journal *Documents*, which over the next two years explored 'base materialism', celebrated the blood and sacrifice of Aztec religion, rejected poeticism and alchemical escapism, extolled the role of violent destruction in the creative process, and attracted interest from Giacommetti, Picasso and newcomer Salvador Dalí. Bataille reviewed Dalí's painting *Le Jeu Lugubre* (*The Dismal Game*) and praised the artist's 'bestial hilarity' [112]. Dalí and Buñuel had made a grand entrance into the surrealist world with their film *Un Chien Andalou* that year, and Dalí was already presenting himself as the theorist of paranoia (which he saw as a deliriously creative re-interpretation of reality) and disgust (the mask for what we truly desire), attracting the attention of the young psychoanalyst Jacques Lacan (whom we shall meet again in the next chapter) [113].

Disgust was a crucial emotional reaction in Bataille's world view – for him (as for Dalí and Lacan), putrefaction and viscosity provoke both revulsion and morbid attraction in us, which links to our psychological ambivalence towards death. Later he was to clarify: 'The sexual channels are also the body's sewers; we think of them as shameful and connect the anal orifice to them. St Augustine was at pains to insist on the obscenity of the organs and functions of reproduction. "Inter faeces et urinam nascimur", he said – "we are born between faeces and urine"' [114]. For Bataille, taboo substances, those of filth and degeneration, like urine and faeces and blood, are repugnant but at the same time attractive. This creates space for sexually exciting transgression and for religious self-mortification – as in the 'mad rage' with which Beauvoir's female mystics embraced the disgusting to make their bodies abject (St Angela of Foligno drinking the water in which she had bathed the feet of lepers — chewy bits and all; Marie Alacoque licking up the vomit of patients, and so on [115]). For Sade, the pleasure of fornication lay in its 'horror, vileness, the frightful', for Bataille, 'to enjoy to the utmost the ecstasy in which we lose ourselves in orgasm, we must always know what the borderline is: it is horror. [...] there is no form of repugnance that does not have an affinity with desire' [116]. At the root of all this lies the 'obscene', that always tends towards 'the gratifications of death, succeeding and surpassing those of eros' [117]. Bataille was laying the basis for an appreciation of the Abject, which fed through Lacan to Julia Kristeva (see chapter X).

In 1930 things between Bataille and Breton came to a head, each publishing vitriolic attacks on the other – Breton in the 'Second Manifesto', Bataille in 'Un Cadavre' ('A Corpse') – with Robert Desnos, Jacques Prévert, Queneau and Leiris all backing his nihilistic damnation of Breton's redemptive surrealist dream as poetic fraud, with Breton as more priestly policeman than artist, and unable to comprehend the 'excremental force' of the true Sadean vision [118]. Breton's reply was 'M. Bataille likes flies. Not we' [119].

In 1933 Bataille articulated, in *The Notion of Expenditure*, the central tenets of his world-view. As Nietzsche had his Apollonian and Dionysian, and Freud his Ego and Id, so Bataille distinguished Productive and Non-productive expenditure. Productive expenditure is rational, commercial, utilitarian, prudent, the discourse of both capitalism and Marxism – issues of work, pay, productivity, value, profit, distribution (fair or otherwise). Non-productive expenditure is to be found in sacrifice, ritual, cults, potlatch extravagance, spectacle and war – it is about catastrophe, waste, excess, destruction and loss, violence, intoxication, ecstasy and horror and wild laughter.

'Civilisation' presents itself as Enlightenment, favouring the Productive and trying to control the Non-productive – harnessing some of its energy into sport (in some societies, hunting and bullfighting), controlled drinking and gambling, sanitised religion and so on, and suppressing its wilder forms with disgust, morality, religion, and prohibition. But the urge for the Non-productive is coming from a place deep within us, and is not so amenable to being governed [120]. Our underlying hatred of the Productive is profound, and the Non-productive finds outlets in insanity, crime, dream, perversion, revolution and war, and behind the curtains of bourgeois respectability in domestic violence, adultery, incest, alcoholism and so on – all of them wasteful, destructive, often deliriously so. For Bataille, 'our only real pleasure is to squander our resources for no purpose, just as if a wound was bleeding away inside of us: we always want to be sure of the uselessness or ruinousness of our extravagance' [121]. It is the urge for the Non-productive that gives rise to our sense of the Sacred, and for Bataille, it is the demand for and the lure of the Sacred that fuels our deepest and most fundamental drives. One way or another it will find expression [122].

The 1930s saw a degree of rapprochement between Bataille and Breton. The most important surrealist journal of the decade, *Minotaure* (founded 1933, with its iconic first front cover by Picasso), published contributions from both Breton's and Bataille's groups (little by Bataille himself, although the name 'Minotaure' was probably his), and showed a greater resemblance to *Documents* than to Breton's 1920s reviews. In 1935 Breton and Bataille managed to co-operate (briefly) on an anti-fascist journal *Contra-Attaque* — although Bataille's sensitivity to the aroma of the 'Sacred' in the dynamic roots of fascism struck Breton as highly suspect, leading him to accuse Bataille of 'sur-fascism'. [Dalí had already been hauled over the coals by Breton for 'the Glorification of Hitlerian Fascism' and was finally expelled from the surrealist movement in 1939]. But in 1937 Breton and Bataille were again joining arms to petition Stalin against the Moscow show trials.

Between 1928 and 1934 Bataille was married to Sylvia Maklès, an actress who starred in Jean Renoir's 1936 film, *Partie de Campagne* (in which Bataille had a cameo role as a priest), and who from 1938 was the life partner of Jacques Lacan. As his marriage to Sylvia was nearing its end, Bataille had an affair with Dora Maar, who by 1935 was with Picasso, initiating him into the mysteries of the Sacred and the exploration of his darker side. This he symbolised in his art as the Minotaur, representation of sexual and destructive urges and desires – his Caliban, which he came to acknowledge as his own. In 1935 Bataille (with Masson) launched a new journal, *Acéphale,* (from Greek 'Headless') which took particular interest in Nietzsche and the Dionysian, and pioneered the rescuing of Nietzsche from the clutches of Nazism. Behind the journal lurked a secret society of the same name, presided over by Bataille and his new lover, Colette Peignot, with whom he practised extreme sexual games (including, allegedly, asphyxiation and violence), and who wrote masochistic poetry under the name 'Laure'. The core obsession of Acéphale was human sacrifice as the foundation for a new religion that would re-establish a Sacred alternative to fascism and Stalinism [123]. As priestess of this new religion, Laure was honoured by Leiris as the 'saint of the abyss' [124]. There was (apparently) some plan to actually carry this sacrifice out, with Bataille it would seem as willing victim, in keeping with Baudelaire's dictim 'That a sacrifice should be perfect there should be joy and consent on the part of the victim' [125], but Bataille's idea was that the guilt of the sacrifice should bind the survivors in an indissoluble fraternity of shared anguish. In the end, however, it was Laure who died, of TB in 1938, aged 35. This to an extent fulfilled Acéphale's obsession, and the society and journal closed soon after [126]. Bataille's College of Sociology, contemporary with Ácephale, provided a more measured and academic approach, attracting as attendees or contributors Walter Benjamin, Theodor Adorno and Max Horkheimer from the Frankfurt School, Klossowski and Jean Paulhan.

During the war, Bataille sat it out, neither collaborating nor resisting. Typically perhaps, he found the war and Nazism both despicable and oddly exciting in their expression of Non-productive economics, but his ambivalence put him in bad odour with many of his contemporaries. By 1941 Maurice Blanchot had joined the Bataille circle [127], and soon after Bataille was responding to Sartre's distinction between 'bad faith' and 'authenticity', with his own terminology of the 'possible' and the 'impossible', revealing a profound pessimism about the human condition.

But by denying himself poetry, Bataille was unable to

permit himself the poetic mysticism that enabled Breton to recreate the Sacred as the Marvellous [128], leaving him tied to a fundamentally religious world-view. Sartre noticed this, suspecting in the early 1940s that Bataille represented a case of Bad Faith, remaining a guilty Christian at heart, in need of divine grace, but, unable to forgive God his absence, falling into despair [129]. [Michel Carrouges' insistence that Bataille (and Breton) were in fact on their way back to God was fuelled by a similar perception (see above, p. 308). In fact it is hard not to see a 'God-shaped hole' in Bataille, (and perhaps in Sartre too?)].

After the war, Bataille launched the journal *Critique* with Blanchot and Raymond Aron, which, less savage than *Documents* and less deranged than *Acéphale*, was much more successful, and is still going today. In 1947 *The Accursed Share* provided an account of mankind's fall due to the establishment of the 'productive economy' of private property and work (a view that oddly echoed Rousseau), and he made a kind of peace with Breton, describing himself as 'surrealism's old enemy from within' (admitting he saw himself as part of their world) [130].

In 1957 two of his best known books appeared simultaneously. In *La Littérature et le Mal* (*Literature and Evil*) Bataille challenged Sartre's view of literature 'as the instrument of moral action', insisting that literature 'is guilty and should admit itself so', exploring the 'clash of the sacred and the profane' where 'Hell releases its liberating energies, the stink of public urinals inspires creativity and the cruel innocence of childhood teaches us its lessons' [131], but through the knowledge of good and evil expressed in literature, we can attain a higher morality. In *L'Érotisme* (*Eroticism*) he pulled together various strands of his thinking, on taboos, death, transgression, war, murder, sacrifice, religion, the erotic, Sade, mysticism and sensuality and so on.

***Story of O* and Bataille:** The relationship between *O* and

Bataille is complex and intriguing, and deserving of much closer analysis than I can provide here. Certainly Aury was familiar enough with Bataille's *Story of the Eye* to pay homage to it in the title of her own novel (see p. 282), and her location of Anne-Marie's domain at Samois, the small settlement where Bataille lived in 1944, is an interesting detail. Themes in *O* parallel Bataille – Aury having learned from Fénelon about the 'atrocious happiness' of those who suffer torture 'for their truth' [132] (see above, p. 325), and a fascination for disgust is present in O's abjection, her relentless anal penetration by Sir Stephen, and her encounter with the repulsive figure of the Commander whose grotesque size 'so overwhelmed O that she wasn't sure whether she wanted to run away or, on the contrary, have him throw her down and crush her' (*O* p. 194). In her interview with Deforges (1975), the 'Death by a Thousand Cuts' photographs were discussed, and Réage spoke of the human 'need for violence and cruelty' [133].

In addition, *Story of O* displays an absorption in 'the sacred' in sexuality, aligning itself with Bataille's replacement of traditional 'theology of agony' with a new 'erotics of agony' [134], and with the annihilation of the self in the 'Non-productive expenditure' of erotic self sacrifice where death and bliss unite [135], O's trajectory being that of a (redemptive?) human sacrifice in a mystic-sexual cult. For Sontag (1967), Bataille's great realisation was that 'what pornography is really about, ultimately, isn't sex but death' [136], (even that 'sex is death by other means' [137]), and that the 'death bound' O 'takes the same line as Bataille' [138], recognising that 'the urge towards love, pushed to its limit, is an urge towards death' [139], all of which provides the context for Réage's views on the desire to be possessed to death, and the ecstasy of dying at the hands of the loved one (see above) [140].

The deployment of masks by Réage (and Leonor Fini) is consistent with an essay written for *Documents* in 1930 by Bataille's long-term colleague Michel Leiris [141]. This essay,

'The "Capuut Mortem" or the Alchemist's Wife', accompanied photographs taken by William Seabrook of a woman he called 'Justine' in bondage and apparent ecstasy [142]. Part of Seabrook's and Justine's interest here lay in the use of masks (which they co-designed), bondage, sado-masochistic practice and pushing the body to its limits of endurance to impose sensory deprivation on her, heightening her extra-sensory perception and generate 'mystical visions' [143]. Leiris was especially interested in the role of the mask as erotically fetishising the female body as a parallel to the religious usage of sacred objects, both exemplifying a kind of magical thought. The person is simultaneously fetishised and depersonalised, transformed from the previously identifiable person into a foreign object of desire, the extremity of the psycho-physical experience overcoming conscious restriction and control to release unconscious desire, as found also in Man Ray's images of women in bondage or masochistic pose (like *Gloved Figure*, 1930). For Fini, her mask permitted her an 'Otherness' [144], in *O*, the owl-mask both depersonalises, even dehumanises her to the point that she becomes a fetish object – perhaps made of stone or wax, even 'a creature from another world', but also disguises her power as a predator (see p. 244).

Bataille's review of *O* in 1955 has been discussed in chapter VIII, his mysterious claim that *O* expresses the 'impossibility of eroticism' amounting to an expression of admiration for its utter authenticity. He continued to enthuse about *O* as he wrote his own final erotic novels in 1954-55 [145], returning to the theme of Eros and death in the opening line of his *L'Érotisme* (1957), 'Eroticism, it may be said, is assenting to life up to the point of death' [146], a rather precise description of the controversial epilogue to *O*. (and possibly evidence of some influence from *O*? [147]).

The liaison between *O* and the writings of Bataille and others in his circle is close, but in the end, Réage would only go so far. On the subject of disgust, for example, she did not follow Bataille to the end of the line. The tasteful avoidance of anything truly stomach-churning suggests that in the end she was closer to Breton's erotic than Bataille's obscene, and would be with Breton, stepping back from Bataille's taste for flies and the fly-blown.

**The Enigma of Death**: On the subject of death, *O* also diverged from Bataille. For him,  death really was death – even in a paroxysm of ecstatic rapture, death was still The End. But in literary culture, the relation between death and love was more metaphorical. By the late Renaissance, the terms 'little death' and 'la petite mort' were gaining currency. Precise meanings could vary, but erotic connections were always there [148]. In French, love and death are near homophones – 'l'amour' and 'la mort' - and Shakespeare makes sport of this. In *Antony and Cleopatra* (c. 1606), when Antony says they must leave Egypt for Rome, Enobarbus launches on an extended riff - 'Why then we kill all our women... Under a compelling occasion, let women die... Cleopatra catching but the least noise of this, dies instantly. I have seen her die twenty times upon a far poorer moment: I do think there is mettle in death, which commits some loving act upon her, she hath such a celerity in dying' (Act I scene ii).

In the mystical and occult worlds, Death is often a symbolic transformation rather than literal extinction. In the Tarot, for example, the 'Death' card (XIII) stands for change, in which one stage comes to an end and a new one begins. Shakespeare, who can be placed as a major figure in the Occult Renaissance [149], depicts uncanny resurrections in his later 'Romances' or Alchemical plays – in *Pericles*, a woman is raised from the dead, and in *The Winter's Tale*, a statue of a woman is brought back to life. Similar events occur in surrealist literature. In Robert Desnos' *Liberty or Love!* (1927), the heroine Louise Lame is killed off, but the narrator concludes 'Louise Lame's hearse can pursue its way through Paris without accident. I shall not salute it as it passes. I have an appointment tomorrow with Louise Lame and nothing can stop me from keeping it. She will come, pale perhaps under a crown of clematis, but real and submissive to my will'. As is explained, 'Desnos can afford to dispense with his heroine in this brutal fashion because, as he explains and then later confirms by resurrecting (her), he does not believe in material death, but prefers to live in eternity' [150]. Michel Leiris, in his alchemical *Aurora* (1927-28), has his heroine ripped apart copulating with a pyramid (as you do), but resurrected to carry on with the story [151], and the suicide of Clara in Elena Garro's play *The Lady on her Balcony* (1958) is not to be taken at face value. Death in a surrealist drama 'does not necessarily signify a tragic ending. Clara has chosen to merge with the ultimate point at which life and death meet – *le point suprême* in the vast expanse of infinite time...' [152], echoing Breton's avowed aim to reach the point where all apparent oppositions, including life and death, are resolved. 'Everything tends to make us believe that there exists a certain point of the mind at which life and death, the real and the imagined, past and future, the communicable and the incommunicable, high and low, cease to be perceived as contradictions' [153].

Earlier we considered *Story of O* as a novel of two parts – noting a change in pace and tack in the later chapters after the intense erotic fantasy of 'The Lovers of Roissy' (see p. 160). The reading taken in this chapter would support this view, at the same time emphasising that the automatic writing of the 'first sixty pages' and the subsequent mystical trajectory of O towards a 'death' (that may be something other than literal), unifies both parts of the novel in their relationship to the world of Surrealism.

---

[1] Passeron, 2005, p. 64 citing Maurice Nadeau

[2] Herbert Silberer: *Problems of Mysticism and its Symbols* 1914

[3] Cited in M.E. Warlick: *Max Ernst and Alchemy* University of Texas Press 2001, p. 229 note 62. Later Jung changed his mind on this. Reinventing himself as benign mystical guru after his unfortunate dalliance with the Nazis, Jung co-opted Silberer's theory as his own in his 1944 *Psychology and Alchemy*. Breton's circle, aware of Jung's far-right history, were not taken in by him, although many others have been.

[4] Psychology and psychiatry constituted part of Ernst's liberal arts

studies at the University of Bonn before the First World War [Ulrich Bischoff *Max Ernst*, Taschen 2005 p. 8], and, being a native German-speaker, he was able to read Freud in the original, unlike the surrealists who had who had to rely on whatever they could find in French translation.

[5] Breton 'Second Manifesto of Surrealism' (1930) in *Manifestoes of Surrealism* trans. Richard Seaver and Helen R. Lane, Ann Arbor 1972, pp. 173, 178

[6] Breton *Nadja* 1928 (1960) p. 160

[7] 'Interview with André Breton' *View* 1941 cited Mahon 2005 p. 65

[8] 'Prolegomena' 1942, cited Polizzotti 2009 p. 457

[9] Polizzotti 2009 p. 471 ; *Arcanum 17* was published in New York April 1945, and in Paris June 1947 by Éditions du Sagittaire

[10] Breton *Nadja* 1928 (1960) p. 106

[11] *Arcanum 17*, 1944; citations in Polizzotti 2009 pp. 472-474; Mahon 2005 pp. 117-118

[12] In 1948 Robert Graves in his meditation on poetic wisdom, *The White Goddess*, presented a similar vision, welcomed as liberating by many post-war women surrealists, like Leonora Carrington.

[13] cited in Durozoi 2002 p. 441-2

[14] ibid p. 460; Dotrement and Jorn were later in CoBrA; subsequently Jorn moved on to Guy Debord's Situationists

[15] Ibid p. 462

[16] 'Rupture Inaugurale' (1947) ibid p. 463

[17] The Carrouges saga is recounted in Durozoi 2002 pp. 748 note 66, 492, 515-516

[18] J.H.Matthews 'Literary Surrealism in France since 1945 ' *Books Abroad* Fall 1962: 36, 4

[19] Neil Matheson cited in Watz 2023 p. 122

[20] Mahon 2005 pp. 15-16

[21] Polizotti 2009 p. 493; Durozoi 2002 p. 466

[22] Durozoi 2002 p. 472

[23] Breton 1952 *Entretiens*

[24] see Durozoi 2002 p. 554

[25] Polizzotti 2009 p. 537

[26] The material on Mansour is from Polizzotti 2009 pp. 531, 547

[27] Durozoi 2002 p. 591

[28] Ibid p. 587

[29] Breton: EROS catalogue 1959, see Polizzotti 2009 p. 546

[30] Durozoi 2002 p. 591

[31] Mitrani: *Une Solitude Enchantée*; cited Mahon 2020, p. 152-153

[32] Young 2013

[33] 'Le masque de Bonheur' *L'Arche*, no. 10, Oct 1945; note on *L'Asphyxie, L'Arche*, no. 22, Dec 1946; cited in David p. 54 footnote 139, 138.

[34] Gallus 1997

[35] Sontag 1967 p. 105

[36] Ibid p. 84

37  Ibid p. 110

38  Toni Bentley 'An Audience with the Chief Whip', *Sunday Times Magazine*, 1st Feb 2015 ('The Thin End of the Whip' *Vanity Fair*, Jan 22nd 2014).

39  The translation I am using is by Peter Darvill-Evans, Nexus, 1992

40  Pallister 1985

41  Sontag 1967 p. 96

42  'Modernisation and Avant-gardes', Michael Kelly et al., in Forbes and Kelly 1995 pp 165-166

43  Barthes: *Le Plaisir de texte*, Seuil, 1973

44  Sontag 1967 p. 88

45  St Jorre, 1995, pp. 233, 236, 238

46  Bentley 2015

47  Jaeckin's *Story of O*, and Radley Metzinger's *L'Image* (aka *The Punishment of Anne*.)

48  Also Agnès Varda, Éric Rohmer, Claude Chabrol, Jacques Rivette, and Jacques Demy

49  In Gallus 1997

50  Bentley 2015

51  'Lashings of Marital Secrets' – John Follain, *ST* 11 November 2012

52  Bentley 2015

53  In Gallus 1997

54  Bentley 2015

55  Jacques Brunius, 9 Feb. 1960, BBC 3rd programme *In Defence of Surrealism*; cited in Matthews 1966, p. 125

56  Polizzotti 2009, p. 531

57  *Médium, Communication surréaliste*, Nouvelle serie No. 3, May 1954, p.42 cited Matthews 1966, p. 137; unless otherwise stated, subsequent quotes are from Matthews 1966 pp. 137-138, 10-11

58  'Déchirures' is a strong word in French, carrying connotations of painful separation - not necessarily violent but such imagery seems appropriate here (thanks as always to Maurice Debonnard for his linguistic sagacity).

59  Matthews 1962

60  The subsequent quotes from Joyce Mansour *Les Gisants satisfaits* (Pauvert 1958) pp. 61, 63, 73, 125, 129, cited in Matthews 1966 pp. 126-129, 133

61  Matthews 1966 pp. 139, 132, 129, 137

62  Kathryn Conley: 'Anamorphic Love: The Surrealist Poetry of Desire' in *Desire Unbound* ed. Jennifer Mundy, Princeton University Press/ Tate Publishing Ltd., 2001

63  John Phillips '"O Really!": Pauline Réage's *Histoire d'O*' ch. 4 of *Forbidden Fictions: Pornography and Censorship in Twentieth-Century French Literature*, Pluto Press, 1999

64  the translation I am using is by Lowell Bair, Harper Perennial, 2009

65  Phillips 1999

66  Ibid

67  Breton *Surrealism and Painting* 1964, quoted in Mundy 2001 p.49. Ironically Aury was much more sympathique to free sex – see Deforges 1975 p. 96

68  St Jorre 1995 p. 210

69  Cosgrove 1974; Massé 1992 found the 'mystical' reading inauthentic as well.

70  St Jorre 1995 p. 220

71  Including Benjamin 1983; Bonnie Shullenberger 'Much Affliction and Anguish of Heart : '*Story of O*' and Spirituality' *Massachusetts Review* vol. 46, no. 2 (Summer 2005).

72  Act 1 scene v

73  Andrew Hadfield: *John Donne In the Shadow of Religion* Reaktion Books 2021 p. 23. See also John Carey *John Donne, Life, Mind and Art* faber and faber 1981;  O'Leary 2007, unpublished.

74  Cited in Kaufmann 1998 p. 897.

75  Beauvoir 1949 p. 680

76  Ibid p. 686: the figures she gives are 321 people in total, of whom 47 were men

77  Ibid p. 679

78  Shullenberger 2005

79  Cited in Kaufmann 1998 p. 897

80  Beauvoir 1949 p. 684

81  Ibid p. 686

82  *Life of St Teresa of Jesus* (XXXIX.17) (pub 1611) – trans David Lewis, Cosimo Classics 2006

83  Cornaro Chapel, Santa Maria della Vittoria, Roma

84  Beauvoir 1949 p. 682

85  Cited Shullenberger 2005

86  Ibid 2005

87  Mahon 2020 pp. 20,  140

88  Deforges 1975 p. 209.

89  Cited Shullenberger 2005

90  Paulhan 1954 preface xxii

91  interview 1994, cited in St Jorre 1995 p. 215, cited in Bedell 2004

92  Sontag 1967 pp. 101-102

93  Jean Anderson 2018 'Sixty Years On: The (Transatlantic) Scandal of Submissive Agency and the Afterlife of O'. *Contemporary French and Francophone Studies* Vol. 22, No. 1, 104–111

94  Phillips 1999

95  1994 interview with St Jorre 1995, cited p. 228

96  I think that in all true passion, there is a quest for the absolute that can only be attained through a feeling of abandon, of total dispossession of the self... Passion is a serious matter.' Interview with Pauline Réage, by Demornex 1974 , cited in St Jorre 1995 p. 227

97  Kaufmann 1998

98  Rutledge 2017

[99] Sontag 1967 p. 113

[100] Kenneth Anderson: 'The Erotics of Virtue' *Los Angeles Times Book Review* 20 June 1999

[101] Jessica Benjamin: 1983 'Master and Slave: Fantasy in Erotic Domination' in Snitow, Stansell & Thompson ed. *Power and Desire*, Monthly Review Press

[102] Deforges 1975 pp. 133-134, 111-112

[103] cited in Brown and Faerie 1984

[104] Deforges 1975 p. 205

[105] David 2006 p. 30:

[106] St Jorre 1995 p. 210

[107] The genteel observation of tenth century St. Odo of Cluny

[108] Timothy Brook, Jérôme Bourgnon, Gregory Blue 2008 *Death by a Thousand Cuts* Harvard University Press which dismisses Bataille's *Les Larmes d'Éros* (*The Tears of Eros*, 1961) as 'an obnoxious work executed in bad taste' (cited in review by Julian Ward THES 8 May 2008)

[109] Wickman 2005

[110] Hutton 1992

[111] Michael Székely 2005 'Text, Trembling: Bataille, Breton and surrealist eroticism' *Textual Practice* 19(1)

[112] cited in Charles Harrison/ Paul Wood *Art in Theory 1900-1990* pp. 476-478

[113] Dalí's essay 'L'Ane pourri' ('The Stinking Ass') – a title that references a scene in *Un Chien Andalou* – was published in 1930 in *Le Surréalisme au service de la Révolution*.

[114] Bataille *Eroticism* (1957) Marion Boyars 1987 pp 57-58

[115] Beauvoir 1949 p. 685

[116] Cited in Phillips 1999

[117] Sontag 1967 p. 106

[118] Surya pp. 135-138

[119] Breton 1930

[120] Michel Leiris in his *Mysticism and Erotica* refers to 'the intense desire that all men have to overthrow limitations', cited in Mundy *Desire Unbound* ch 10 p. 270

[121] Bataille 1957 p. 170

[122] See Marcus *Lipstick Traces* faber & faber (1989) 2001

[123] Hussey 2006

[124] A term that carries echoes of Aleister Crowley's terminology in his 1913 *Book of Lies*.

[125] Baudelaire: 'My Heart Laid Bare' XLIII

[126] Surya 2002; David 2006 pp. 345-346

[127] Blanchot was to become Bataille's intellectual partner for twenty years, a celebrated (if reclusive) philosopher of language and literature, wrestling, like Paulhan, with the issue of original thought and the conventions of language, and insisting, again like Paulhan, that the principal allegiance of a writer is to writing, not politics (in direct opposition Sartre's view of the 'committed writer'). See Blanchot: *How*

*is Literature Possible?* 1941. Years later Bernard-Henry Lévy (1991, p. 319) found him harbouring an 'immeasurable remorse' for his anti-Semitic slurs of the 1930s.

[128] Here Breton was in accord with Claude Lévi-Strauss that the human mind works metaphorically and diachronically, and is effectively innately poetic (*The Savage Mind*, 1962) , and Freud on the symbolic nature of dream (*The Interpretation of Dreams*, 1899)

[129] Amy Hollywood 1996 'Bataille and Mysticism: A "Dazzling Dissolution"' *Diacritics* Vol 26 , No 2, *Georges Bataille: An Occasion for Misunderstanding* (summer) finds Bataille's mystical thinking owing much to Christianity, for example in his 1944 *Le Coupable* (*Guilty*)

[130] Surya 1992 pp. 407-414

[131] Bataille *Literature and Evil* 1957 (1990), back cover notes.

[132] Cited in Kaufmann 1988 p. 897

[133] Deforges 1975 pp. 186, 191

[134] Sontag 1967 p. 107

[135] Surya 1992

[136] Sontag 1967 p. 106

[137] Benjamin 1980

[138] Sontag 1967, p. 106

[139] Bataille *Eroticism* 1957 (1987) p. 42.

[140] Deforges 1975 pp. 133-134

[141] Warne 2020

[142] 'Le 'Capuut Mortem' ou la femme de l'alchimiste.' in Georges Bataille and Michel Leiris, *Documents: Doctrines, Archéologie, Beaux-Arts, Ethnographie* (Paris: Jean-Michel Place, 1991), 461-466.

[143] Seabrook's 1940 book *Witchcraft: Its Power in the World Today* elaborated on this.

[144] Armand Lanoux *Leonor Fini, la sourciere du merveilleux* in Le Jardin des Arts 14 (Dec 1955) cited in Mahon 2020 p, 254 note 213.

[145] *La Mère, Charlotte d'Ingerville, Sainte* – all 1954-55 (Surya 1992

[146] Bataille 1957 (1987) p. 11

[147] Byrne 2012 suspects not, attributing similarities to both have read Nietzsche

[148] Only during the 19th century did 'the little death'/ 'la petite mort' become more or less exclusively a euphemism for orgasm, both in literature (e.g Balzac) and depth psychology.

[149] Frances Yates *The Occult Philosophy in the Elizabethan Age* Routledge 1979

[150] Desnos *La Liberté ou l'amour!* (1927) p, 63, cited Matthews. 1966 p. 71

[151] Leiris: *Aurora* (1927-28, pub. 1946) cited Matthews 1966 p. 117

[152] *La Señora en su Balcón,* Orenstein 1975, cited Matthews 1966 p. 117

[153] Breton 'Second Manifesto' 1930 (1972), p. 123

# X:  Changing Horizons: O Goes International

## SURREALISM – ENDINGS AND BEGINNINGS

By the 1960s Breton was conscious of new cultural developments arising, and was attentive to those offering some kind of dialogue with Surrealism. He wasn't much excited by the cerebral games of Absurdism, the Nouveau Roman and structuralist/ semiological New Criticism, although he did read Alain Robbe-Grillet, Nathalie Sarraute and Roland Barthes, but Guy Debord's Situationist International (SI, founded 1957) and Philippe Sollers' periodical *Tel Quel* (*As It Is*, established 1960) were of more interest. Both Debord and Sollers revealed their oedipal attitudes to 'father' Breton as they vied for his attention – the one wanting to outrage and impress him with neo-Dadaist provocations, the other adopting him as a role-model and wanting to recruit him as a contributor [1].

In 1965, the exhibition *L'Écart Absolu* (*Total Deviation* [2]), the last one Breton presided over, presented contributions from, among others, Toyen, Leonora  Carrington, Robert Benayoun and Mimi Parent and archive works by Duchamp, Ernst and de Chirico. Joyce Mansour wrote about it, Leonor Fini provided a star turn among the attending crowds, and the exhibition featured another performance piece by Jean Benoît – this time as the 'Necrophiliac' Sergeant Bertrand [3]. *L'Écart Absolu* amounted to a thoroughgoing attack on the forces of alienation – capitalism, commodification, commercialism, technocracy, advertising, economics, religion and sport – the whole 'brain-deadening world of house-hold appliances, computers and astronautics' [4] – everything that hollowed out human life and paralysed Desire into mere consumerism. Again promoting the marvellous, imagination and the erotic, Breton and his group were once more drawing on Charles Fourier's writings, along with Herbert Marcuse [5], and articulating ideas that anticipated some of those in Guy Debord's 1967 Situationist classic *La Société du spectacle* (*The Society of the Spectacle*).

Breton died in September 1966, aged 70. Jean Schuster stepped into his shoes, but immediately the question arose, posed by Mandiargues and taken up by others: Did Surrealism have a future after Breton? [6]. Initially the reply seemed to be in the affirmative. A new periodical, *L'Archimbras*, was launched in April 1967, and was quickly in action rallying surrealist support for the uprisings of 1968. The Prague Spring with its promise of 'socialism with a human face', provided a brief moment of hope and freedom in Communist-controlled Czechoslovakia, warmly endorsed across the spectrum by Czech dissidents, surrealists, and Alexander Dubček's progressive government, before Soviet tanks suppressed it in August. In the Paris Maydays, a student uprising took to the streets, infused with the Situationist spirit, with rioting, barricades and surrealist-inspired graffiti – 'Be Realistic, Demand the Impossible', 'Take Your Dreams for Reality', 'It is Forbidden to Forbid', 'Beneath the cobblestones, the beach', and, rather touchingly, 'André Breton has missed his party'. Unions mobilised, a general strike was called, and de Gaulle's presidency wobbled momentarily, but when he took the gamble to reassert himself, the revolutionary moment fizzled out. Nonetheless the Paris Maydays turned out to be the acid test for Schuster and his circle – now surrealism was out there in the streets, was there really any further need for a specific group or leadership? [7].

Jean Schuster's answer was 'No', and in February 1969 he announced that the time of 'historical' surrealism was now being superseded by a new age of 'eternal' surrealism, an 'ontological component of the human spirit' [8], and declared the Paris group disbanded. Two months later de Gaulle finally resigned – the Maydays had been an acid test for him as well. Despite his dissolution of the Paris surrealist group, Schuster went on to set up a new review, *Coupure*, with Gérard Legrand, Nora Mitrani and Annie LeBrun. Meanwhile Joyce Mansour, Jean-Louis Bédouin and Jean Benoît, denying Schuster's right to speak for the movement or to pull the plug on it, launched their own *Bulletin de liaison surréaliste*. Neither publication lasted long – the first closed in 1972 (incidentally the year Debord closed the Situationist International), and the second in 1976 [9]. The sixties and seventies also saw the passing of many of the old guard: Bataille (1962), Tzara (1963), Magritte (1967), Duchamp (1968), Picasso (1973), Bellmer (1975), Ernst, Man Ray, Queneau (1976), and Lee Miller (1977), all of which reinforced the idea that Surrealism had reached a turning point, if not an actual end.

But Surrealism has a habit of surviving its last rites – it refused to lie down after Nadeau read its obituary in 1945; in 1966, the year Breton died, Penelope and Franklin Rosemont launched a vibrant group in Chicago; and the more informed of the recent commentators, while acknowledging the late 60s/early 70s as the ending of an important epoch, have insisted the surrealist volcano is far from extinct [10].

## STORY OF O – THE AMERICAN CONNECTION

In March 1966, a year after *L'Écart Absolu*, and a few months before Breton died, a new translation of *Story of O* was published by Grove Press in New York, and *O* went fully international. Jean-Jacques Pauvert had sold the U.S. rights to the novel to Barney Rosset of Grove in 1963, who thought 'It was a great book, with great sexuality' [11]. Like Pauvert and Girodias, Rosset was motivated by a mix of 'daring, idealism and financial drive' [12], with a real sense of mission, explaining that for him, 'obscenity can be political... when I had really understood that we would take out four pages ads in *The Times* saying "Sex and Politics"' [13]. The new edition was translated by 'Sabine d'Estrée' (a name as obviously pseudonymous as 'Pauline Réage'), who provided a 'Translator's Note', and the volume contained 'A Note on *Story of O*' by Pieyre de Mandiargues (a translation of a 1958 version of his 1955 review [14]) and the Jean Paulhan preface, under the more accurate title 'Happiness in Slavery'. In keeping with the 1962 Pauvert edition (and subsequent French publications), the postscript contained the two alternate endings to the novel. Susan Sontag had been asked to write a prefatory article, but she could not pull it together in time – which worried Grove that the book would be 'misconstrued' without it [15]. Sontag's piece eventually surfaced as 'The Pornographic Imagination' (1967) which we discuss below.

The publication was not plain sailing however (as if anything to do with *O* ever was). Maurice Girodias, under the impression that he owned the English language rights, felt aggrieved at being side-lined by the new Grove Press deal and sought legal counsel. Unfortunately for him, he owned no such rights, and having already violated his initial agreement with Pauvert with his unauthorised second edition in 1957, *Wisdom of the Lash*, he didn't have much of a leg to stand on [16]. That did not stop him peddling his edition in the U.S., and then, faced with bankruptcy, from trying to sue Pauvert in 1969 [17]. The case did not get anywhere, but Girodias did not walk away empty-handed. As it happened, neither Pauvert nor Rosset had been able to find a U.K. publisher willing to handle *O*, so in 1970 Pauvert (with Aury's agreement) gave the contract to, of all people, Maurice Girodias [18]. The Olympia/ Wainhouse translation has been the standard one in the U.K. since then (and the source of U.S. pirate editions [19]), with the Paulhan preface reinstated, under the rather wide-of-the-mark title 'A Slave's Revolt', and retaining the single sentence epilogue.

**'Sabine d'Estrée':** The Paulhan preface and the Mandiargues review have been discussed earlier (in chapters V and VIII respectively), but the Sabine d'Estrée 'Translator's Note' was original to the Grove publication. Here the history of this 'most curious – and mysterious' novel was recounted, its publication by Pauvert, the enigma of the authorship, whose name was 'completely unknown in French literary circles, where everyone knows everyone'. D'Estrée went on to say the novel was respected by the critics, 'who none the less clearly did not know what to make of this latter-day, female Sade' (p. ix), the Paulhan preface being 'sympathetic' but 'hardly help(ing) to clarify any mystery surrounding the work'. D'Estrée continued with an account of the growing scandal after the Prix des Deux Magots, the involvement of the police, not in an official investigation, but to question Paulhan and Pauvert, before they were called off, possibly by the intervention of a 'high government official, but this remains unsubstantiated'. The mystery of the author's identity was emphasised, along with the reasonable point that it would matter to the public if 'Pauline Réage' turned out to be the cover for a famous writer, or an unknown, or a 'literary hack merely seeking notoriety' (p. x). D'Estrée reported on correspondence with Réage (although they never met), and her delight that Réage approved her translation as superior to the earlier one (which d'Estrée described as more of an adaptation, replete with inaccuracies, omissions, commissions, paraphrases, and insensitivity to the original) [20]. This d'Estrée put down to the earlier translation being done by a man, who wrote as though he was 'in fact embarrassed by the work', suffering specifically from a '*male* embarrassment' (p. xi). Accepting Paulhan's lead that the writer of *O* was indeed a woman, d'Estrée went on to say '*Story of O*, written by a woman, demands a woman translator, one who will humble herself before the work and be satisfied to merely render it, as faithfully as possible, without interpretation or unnecessary elaboration,' for 'Faced with a work such as *O*, male pride, male superiority – no matter how liberal the man, however much he tries to suppress them – will, I am certain, somehow intrude,' so d'Estrée, 'like O' has 'tried to humble (her)self, to remain as faithful as possible... to the intent and style of the author' (while attempting 'to stop short of slavishness'). D'Estrée went on, '*Story of O* is the work of an original writer, who has dared to present us with certain truths... rarely found in literature.' Some will disagree with or dislike what she has done, 'but Pauline Réage has done what all good artists aim for... to arouse us from the lethargy of our set ways and routine lives, to prick us into consciousness, provoke a reaction (...positive or negative...) within us; in short, to make us think. That in itself is a rare enough occurrence so that we should be grateful indeed when we have the good fortune to encounter it' (p. xii). She then cited Paulhan's speculation that Réage left space for a sequel, but 'to date, no sequel has been forthcoming' – the only additional text by Réage since *O* being the preface to *L'Image* in 1956. 'Since then, she has not been heard from again'. But d'Estrée thought this was to the good, as we must face the novel 'uncluttered by any outside considerations', 'For beyond the more or less general consensus that the author is a woman, nothing is certain about the work.' 'Like O before her judges, the work stands naked and alone' (p. xiii). [This 'Translator's Note', reprinted without update in subsequent Grove and Ballantine editions for decades after, became a voice frozen in time, unaffected by subsequent developments – the 1969 'sequel', the attribution of *L'Image's* introduction to Alain Robbe-Grillet, the interviews and 1990s revelations about the author of *O*].

It was evident from the start that 'Sabine d'Estrée' was a pseudonym, and the question immediately arose 'who was s/he?'. In 1994, flying high after his revelation that Pauline Réage was Dominique Aury, John de St Jorre was on the case. Sabine's name had by then turned up again as translator of, among other things, the 1971 Grove edition of *Return to the Château preceded by A Girl in Love* [21]. The breakthrough came when St Jorre found correspondence about *O* between 'Sabine Destré' and Richard Seaver in the Grove Press archive in the University of Syracuse Special Collections. We briefly met Seaver on p. 72, as publisher, editor and translator, and a figure of real status in the literary world – probably best known for his work with Samuel Beckett. Beckett, although English-speaking, wrote many of his major works, including *En attendant Godot* (*Waiting for Godot*, 1953) in French, and then needed assistance translating them into English. Seaver was the man for the job, and it was Seaver's work that brought Beckett to the attention of the Anglophone world.

St Jorre noted that Sabine d'Estrée had only ever worked for Richard Seaver, following him to Viking Press after he left Grove (where she translated Deforges' *O m'a dit*), and (following a tip-off from James Cameron), that Seaver's wife was named Jeanette Sabine [22]. St Jorre's conclusion was that the real face behind 'Sabine d'Estrée' was in fact Richard Seaver himself (with Jeanette possibly playing a role – perhaps in writing the 'Sabine Destré' half of the archive correspondence, unless Seaver was simply writing to himself [23]). Seaver of course denied all this, claiming the real 'Sabine' lived in France and that he had taken an oath of secrecy over her identity.

The identification of 'Sabine' with Seaver is widely accepted [24], but it does produce a couple of interesting knock-on effects. One is that Sabine's insistence 'she' was better placed to translate *O* because 'she' was a woman proves the Americans to be just as capable of jokes and hoaxes as the Paris lot. Another is that Seaver's suggestion to St Jorre that 'Sabine' had been a contributor to the composition of *Story of O* (see p. 72), would amount to a claim that Seaver himself had a hand in writing it. Whether St Jorre or Pauvert realised what Seaver was implying, neither had any time for multiple authorship hypotheses.

Probably inevitably, Dominique Aury had a couple of false trails of her own to lay. One was that the translator of *O* might have also translated the memoirs of General de Gaulle in the 1950s. The de Gaulle translation was known to be the work of American poet Richard Howard, and he was in fact a very plausible candidate, having an impressive track record with a range of French writers, including Baudelaire, Breton (*Nadja,* 1960, for Grove Press), Nadeau, Beauvoir, Camus, Sartre, Barthes and Alain Robbe-Grillet. Howard however flatly denied any hand in *O* or any knowledge of Sabine. But then Aury, always quick on the draw with a red herring, also hinted to St Jorre that 'Sabine d'Estrée' was in fact Catherine Robbe-Grillet [25]. It seems as though everyone was out to pull St Jorre's leg over the Grove Press translation. And the matter still won't seem to rest. Only a few years ago the idea was mooted that the veracity of the Grove translation might be due to 'Sabine d'Estrée' actually being a mask for Pauline Réage/ Dominique Aury herself (– or at least that Aury's hand contributed to the 'Translator's Note' [26]). Readers will just have to draw their own conclusions.

**The Press:** The North American reaction to the New York publication of *O* was lively. There was speculation about the gender of the author, but it was generally accepted that 'Pauline Réage' was a woman [27], and there was widespread interest in what she had to say, fuelled by the media which gave *O* plentiful coverage. Some of that coverage was less than enthusiastic – for the Chicago *American* (March 13th 1966) it was 'garbage', while on March 20th *The Washington Star* and *Book Week* both reached for culinary metaphors – the one finding it as exciting as 'a chicken dinner at the PTA', the other claiming it 'reads like a recipe'. In *The Nation* (October 3rd) it was suggested *O* was 'the vengeful fantasy of some neglected maiden lady...' [28]. The suspicion that some reviewers were affronted to see the male world of sexually explicit writing colonised so brazenly by a woman is hard to avoid. A couple of years later a *New York Times* columnist dismissed it as 'unarguably the dullest db ('dirty book') ever written, it set pornography back fifty years', and the reviewer for the Toronto *Telegram* claimed to have burned his copy of this 'work of surpassing pornographic degeneracy' [29].

Some reviews took other tacks – on April 14th Pearl Chang suggested *O* could be read as a kind of parody of the life trajectory of every house-wife, from independence through enslavement to disappearance [30]. Overall however, the general tone of reviews of the U.S. edition of *O* was approving, even admiring, and extracts from several were reprinted as endorsements in subsequent Grove/ Ballantine editions. Some emphasised the importance of *O* in political terms. Eliot Fremont-Smith for example, in 'The Uses of Pornography' (*The New York Times*, 2ⁿᵈ March 1966), hailed it as a break-through for freedom of speech so decisive that it might have fatally torpedoed the ship of literary censorship, so that 'pornography as a concept may soon disappear'. [This article was later republished under the title 'Censorship Went Out With *O*' [31]]. Others read *O* in mystical or psychological terms, intentionally or not echoing Beauvoir on the intimacy between women and mysticism, and Hélène Deutsch and Marie Bonaparte on femininity. These included *Playboy*, which admired the book's 'redeeming art', and described it as serving a 'mystic rather than an erotic purpose' [32], and an anonymous *Newsweek* review (21 March 1966) which saw the text as illustrating how 'traditional feminine passivity becomes a craving for total sexual submission, even a hunger for torture, suffering and humiliation in the service of love', acclaiming this 'ironic fable of unfreedom, a mystic document that transcends the pornographic and even the erotic... What lifts this fascinating book above mere perversity is its movement toward the transcendence of the self through the gift of the self. That the gift is so horrifying, outraging cherished beliefs in the sanctity of the body and in personal freedom is precisely the tale's source of effectiveness... To give the body, to allow it to be ravaged, exploited and totally possessed can be an act of consequence, if it is done with love for the sake of love' [33].

Particularly influential was Columbia University Professor Albert Goldman's essay in *The New York Times Book Review* (23 March 1966). Goldman recognised Pauline Réage as 'a more dangerous writer than the Marquis de Sade' because 'art is more persuasive than propaganda', interpreting the text as 'a rare instance of pornography sublimated into purest art'. Going on to praise it for revealing 'the dark and repulsive practices and emotions that the better self rejects as improbable or evil', he described the author 'drawing us irresistibly into her private world through the magnetism of her own selfless absorption in it. Like some exquisitely balanced, undulating instrument, she carefully inscribes the cruel shocks inflicted on her heroine's refined sensibility – and we believe' [34]. Following Mandiargues in confirming *O*'s mystical significance, he hailed it as a 'spiritual history of a saint and martyr', 'a perversion of the Christian mystery of exaltation through debasement, of the extremity of suffering transformed into an ultimate victory over the limitations of being'. Moreover it spoke a psychological 'truth', revealing the 'total realisation of the potential of femaleness', exhibiting 'exaggerated feminine submissiveness' and observing that 'the more O is brutalized, the more feminine she becomes—the more open, obedient and willing to offer herself' [35]. Soon after, a review in *Choice* (July 1966) reinforced the view that *O* was 'a significant work of literature. It is quite obviously written from a woman's point of view. O's desire to realise herself completely through a kind of masochistic acceptance of her lover's personality which imposes itself on her through sadistic means leads to a final fusion through physical love that is an apotheosis of female sexuality' [36].

These endorsements, praising *O* for reaching out to the sacred through 'profane' love, for fatally weakening 'pornography' as a concept in literary or moral censorship, and for its profound insights into 'true femininity', were to provoke and fuel a virulently hostile conservative back-lash that followed on soon after [37].

**Susan Sontag:** Various literary luminaries had rallied to *O* – for J.G Ballard 'Here all kinds of terrors await us, but ... Touched by the magic of love, everything is transformed. *Story of O* is a deeply moral homily', while Harold Pinter approved it as 'A remarkable piece of work', for Brian Aldiss it made 'pornography (if that is what it is) an art,' and Grahame Greene had it as 'A rare thing, a pornographic book, well written and without a trace of obscenity' [38]. But the first serious engagement in the English language with *O* as literature was by Susan Sontag, whose 1967 article 'The Pornographic Imagination' [39] was the final fruit of the preface she did not manage to finish for Rosset two years earlier.

Sontag's main thesis here was to broaden out our understanding of 'pornography', to liberate it from being discussed in exclusively social, moral, legal or psychopathological terms, as something to be judged and dealt with (censored, licensed, whatever) – the sort of debate that had dominated, for example, in *L'Affaire Sade* (see pp. 223-225). Sontag wished to raise another question, the possibility of pornography as legitimate art or literature. Readily admitting that precious few titles do qualify as such, she singled out five texts as true examples of pornographic literature: Pierre Louÿs' *Trois filles de leur Mère* (1926), Bataille's *Histoire de l'Oeil* and *Madame Edwarda*, and *Story of O* and *L'Image*. It was Bataille and *O* who were of greatest interest to her. But making the case that 'pornographic literature' could even exist as a legitimate category was a tough one – in part because the literary establishment remained locked in to the assumption that 'proper' literature was 'realist', failing even in the 1960s to take on board non-realist alternatives, including literatures of the imagination like *Ulysses*, surrealism and erotica – which aim for 'disorientation and psychic dislocation' (echoing Breton's view in the 1920s, see p. 296).

For Sontag, Bataille's realisation that pornography is not about sex but about death  indicates the route O was to follow, on her 'death bound' psychic 'journey', as 'step by step she becomes more what she is, a process identified with the emptying out of herself. In the vision of the world presented by *Story of O*, the highest good is the transcendence of personality. The plot's movement is not horizontal, but a kind of ascent through degradation... to reach the perfection of becoming an object'  – O finally achieving the 'otherness' of becoming 'a creature from some other world'. O is in fact an 'adept', 'whatever the cost in pain and fear, she is grateful for the opportunity to be initiated into a mystery, that mystery is the loss of the self'.

Sontag noted that from Sade via the surrealists to *O*, the French literary canon recognised the 'demonic' power of sexuality to take us 'beyond good and evil, beyond sanity', in 'breaking through the limits of consciousness' – recognising the gap between our social and moral existence and our erotic being. So far so Freudian, but Sontag also acknowledged that religion was, after sex, 'the second oldest resource which human beings have available to them for blowing their minds', both routes to the delirious obliteration of the self. This led her to emphasise the devout solemnity of *O*, with its religious metaphors of invocation and exorcism, sacramental rites, salvation through servitude and *O*'s 'need to believe'.

Recognising she was sailing close to the mystical here, Sontag made a point of critiquing Mandiargues for, having rejected the psychiatric terminology of 'masochism', then replacing it with a religious vocabulary and going on to claim *O* as mystical rather than erotic. Sontag was sceptical. For her *O* really was an erotic book, and she insisted on the legitimacy, authenticity and 'total imagination' of those outside of the norms – the artist, the eroto-maniac, the revolutionist and the madman – to defy the reductive labels and straitjacketing categorisations of either psychiatry or religion. Artaud's refusal of sanity, and Bataille's challenge to any art-lover 'to love a canvas as much as a fetishist loves a shoe' [40] hover in the background here. Should we wish to, we can perhaps take the liberty of reminding ourselves that psychiatry does not own 'masochism' any more than religion owns the 'mystical', enabling us to accept Sontag's validation of *O*'s erotic credentials while at the same time retaining the concepts of masochism and the mystical, freed from spurious claims of ownership by psychiatry or religion.

Sontag's essay argued strongly for *Story of O* to be taken seriously as literature, in a 'pornographic' genre that also needs to be taken seriously as an art form. Pornography can be shocking, even revolting, but for Sontag the 'dialectic of outrage' is part of what art and literature are for, and if we close the shutters against anything that challenges our world-view, then we should ask ourselves what else we would be shutting out along with the 'pornography'. Her case threw down the gauntlet to a conservative literary establishment – the same establishment Barney Rosset sought to shake out of its narrow-minded torpor. To rephrase

Réage's point about those who have not read Sade posing greater danger than those who have [41], Sontag and Rosset, in keeping with Pauvert and his defenders in *L'Affaire Sade* (pp. 215-217), understood that those who can interrogate their values do much less harm to others than those whose values are dogmatic reflexes posturing as moral certainties. It is a question of cultural literacy, and Sontag forcefully condemned the 'bone-deep denigration of the range and seriousness of sexual experience that still rules this culture' [42], the wilful ignorance that closes off any chance of understanding the artistic and cultural significance of erotica. Texts like *O* demand, not to be morally caged, pathologised or otherwise explained away, but to be faced head-on, so they can transport us to territories rich and strange, even if disturbing.

## THE FLOWERING OF *JOUISSANCE* IN THE 1970s

The Grove paperback edition of *Story of O* was published in 1967, just in time for the Summer of Love, and sales took off over the following years, aided by the release of the 1975 film. *O*'s success internationally coincided with the 'sexual revolution' of the 1960s and '70s – part of this being the relaxation of licensing laws in Europe and the U.S.A. (see p. 56) which fuelled a burgeoning 'porn' industry and an explosion in sexually explicit cinema. More interestingly, the 1970s saw female writers, artists, intellectuals and activists seizing control of the expression and celebration of women's sexuality. Some of these women were surrealists, many were not, but all contributed to bringing a liberating feminist dimension to the Politics of Eros.

A brief, highly subjective, admittedly Eurocentric, by-no-means-comprehensive but roughly chronological survey flags up a few high-lights (please feel free to add your own): the exploration of love and longing and loss by North American singer-songwriters – notably Joni Mitchell in *Blue* (1970) [43]; Germaine Greer's revolutionary *The Female Eunuch* (1970); Jeanne Aeply's novel *Eros Zéro* (1972) and Erica Jong's *Fear of*

*Flying* (1973); Pina Bausch becoming artistic director at Tanz-theatre Wuppertal in 1973, and her production of *Frühlingsopfer* (*The Rite of Spring,* 1975) that brought world attention to the ecstatic power of her choreography; Nancy Friday's ground-breaking anthologies of the range of women's sexual fantasies, *My Secret Garden* (1973) and *Forbidden Flowers* (1975), rescuing fantasy as a realm distinct from reality, and unafraid to face the darkest imaginings; Carolee Schneemann's performance pieces *Up to and Including her Limits* (1973-76), taking 'action painting' to a (literally) new level, and *Interior Scroll* (1975), reading a text extracted from her vagina – symbolically giving her vulva a voice; Hannah Wilkes' body-art photography including *S.O.S. Starifica-tion Object Series* (1974-5); the performance pieces by Marina Abramović – including *Rhythm 0* (1974), 'an essay in submission' where her avowed acceptance of any action of spectators on her was such that 'she would not have resisted rape or murder' [44], and *The Lips of Thomas* (1975) where having whipped herself and razored a star-shape in her belly, she lay naked on a cross of ice blocks until the audience intervened; Régine Deforges' *O m'a dit,* her 1975 interview with Pauline Réage, occupying a pivotal place in the decade and this story; Merlin Stone's *The Paradise Papers* (1976) [45], reinterpreting archaeological evidence to hypothe-sise on Neolithic goddess-worship and matriarchy; Anne Rice's influential gender– and sexuality-exploratory *Interview with the Vampire* (1976); Dorothy Dinnerstein's *The Mermaid and the Minotaur* (1976, a title oddly evoking both Breton's amphibious Melusina and Picasso's savage yet vulnerable alter-ego), posi-tioning the pre-Oedipal mother as 'the sum of all sensual, mental, polymorphous erotic life' in the unconscious [46]; Eva Švankmaje-rovà's paintings *Bed* and *Menstruation* (1976); Penny Slinger's photo-collage collections, including *Hear What I Say* (1977) and *Mountain Ecstasy* (1978) – 'a unique combination of the erotic and the mystical' [47]; Francesca Woodman's ethereal photographic self-portraiture, including *On Being an Angel* #1 (1977); Linder's punk photomontages; Nancy Chodorow's *The Reproduction of*

*Mothering* (1978), which along with Dinnerstein's book, updates psychoanalytic exploration of gender, and the particular complexities of female development; Régine Deforges' lesbian schoolgirl memoir *The Stolen Notebook* (1978) [48], directly inspired by Dominique Aury's achievement with *O*; Ellen Moers' pioneering essay on 'The Female Gothic' (1978) [49], finding in *Wuthering Heights* and *Goblin Market* recollections of the wildness and savagery of childhood sexuality; Kate Bush's uncanny rendition of her uncanny song named for Emily Brontë's masterpiece (1978); Maria Marcus' unflinching exploration of what it is to be both political feminist and sexual masochist in *A Taste for Pain: On Masochism and Sexuality* (1978), complete with discussion of *Story of O* [50]; Pat Califia and Gayle Rubin's lesbian-feminist BDSM group 'Samois' (named after Anne-Marie's fiefdom in *O*), established in California in 1978; Kathy Ackers' 'post-punk porn' novel *Blood and Guts in High School* (1978 [51]); Judy Chicago's installation *Dinner Party* (1979) – 'widely regarded as the first epic feminist art-work' [52]; and two 1979 books by Angela Carter – her idiosyncratically feminist appreciation of the legacy of Sade in *The Sadeian Woman*, with its 'Polemical Preface: Pornography in the Service of Women', and her psychoanalytic/ surrealist revisiting of folk tales in *The Bloody Chamber*, where her young heroines leave the path through the forest to explore the Dark Continent [53].

Despite the range and variety of these works, most of them lend themselves to being discussed in terms of a small cluster of concepts – *jouissance* (ecstasy/ rapture), *écriture féminine*, 'writing the body', the pre-oedipal 'semiotic' and the 'Abject'. These ideas were coined or brought into focus in the writings of a highly influential group of women thinkers making their names in Paris in the 1970s – Julia Kristeva, Luce Irigaray and Hélène Cixous – who have come to be known collectively in the Anglophone world as the 'French feminists'.

**'French Feminism':** Paris retaining its position as capital of the Politics of Eros in the decade(s) after the death of Breton owed much to the writings of Kristeva, Irigaray and Cixous (all of whom are still with us at the time of writing). They did not work closely together, so did not constitute a group as such, but there is enough family resemblance in their thought to give them a sense of collective identity.

To provide some historical context: in the aftermath of the Paris Maydays, a new generation of feminists in France organised, setting up the Mouvement de Libération des Femmes (MLF) in 1970, reinforced by the support of older activists, notably Simone de Beauvoir, who announced in 1972 'I have become truly a feminist' [54]. Naturally there were varying viewpoints among the MLF members, with some linking women's liberation to class struggle, others considering women as constituting an oppressed class in themselves. But there was widespread agreement on a number of points: that women suffered oppression; that political and material progress needed to be made; that achieving equality with men within the existing system was not enough, and that patriarchal society itself required radical change.

In 1972 however a new group burst on the scene, led by Antoinette Fouque, which called itself 'Psychanalyse et Politique' or 'Psych et Po', and which struck out in a radically different direction. Well-organised, and well-resourced [55], Psych et Po set up their own publishing house (Édition de femmes), reviews and bookshops ('des femmes'), and by 1979 they had taken over and even trademarked the name 'Mouvement de Libération des Femmes' for themselves, much to the chagrin of other feminists. Beauvoir (1984) described them as 'anti-feminist', promoting a doctrine of 'neo-femininity', replacing the mainstream feminist view of women as *oppressed* with a more psychoanalytic idea of women as *repressed* – side-stepping head-on struggle against patriarchal inequality in favour of urging women to explore, discover and express the deepest well-springs of their nature, celebrating 'women's cycles, rhythms and bodily fluids' [56]. For Psych et Po, the 1968 revolution had failed because the proletariat had become absorbed into bourgeois society, and no longer presented the revolutionary challenge to capitalism that it had (supposedly) done in the past. This created space for a new revolutionary force, and this, Psych et Po believed, was to be found in women. Not in feminist power-struggle within the existing or a modified social/political/economic framework, but in finding a voice for the feminine, a new language to articulate female erotic desire and *jouissance* – to generate new meanings and unleash new powers to challenge the structures of signification embodied in the system, and to break that system wide open.

Kristeva, Irigaray and Cixous all had connections with Psych et Po in the 1970s, and the thinking and writing of all three shows a consistency with its core ideas. Psyche et Po's skill in promoting itself meant that by the late 1970s Anglophone commentators, excited by new ideas from France, were seeing Psych et Po as the very essence of French feminism, with Kristeva, Irigaray and Cixous as the core of Psych et Po. By 1980, this iconic trio had become identified as 'the French Feminists' [57], and the term stuck, ill-fitting though it is for several reasons. There are plenty of feminists in France who do not share their views [58]; Kristeva and Cixous (along with Psych et Po itself) do not describe themselves as 'feminist' [59]; moreover, with Kristeva being Bulgarian and Irigaray Belgian the use of the word 'French' is a bit of a stretch (Cixous, from a German-Jewish background in Algeria, is the least anomalous on this point). Using 'Psych et Po' as an alternative collective label is possible, but not an ideal one, as it distorts the picture by eclipsing other members, and implying that all three had been heavily involved with the group (which is true only of Cixous). Other terms have been tried, for example 'post-modern feminism' and 'poststructuralist theoretical feminism' [60], but 'French Feminism' has been hard to shift. [For what it's worth, I favour 'Psych et Po'].

Despite all these labelling issues, making connection between these three writers and the Politics of Eros is a firmer bet. Although none of the three would describe themselves as 'surrealist' *per se*, parallels and interconnections with the world of surrealist thought are strong.

**The Influence of Jacques Lacan:** The most direct link with Surrealism was through psychoanalyst Jacques Lacan, whose theory 'provides Psych et Po with a conceptual framework from which they elaborate a theory of the feminine' [61]. Kristeva, Irigaray and Cixous were all influenced by Lacan, and although by the 1970s they were all carving out their own paths, their world-views remained substantially Lacanian, and Kristeva and Irigarary remained practising analysts. As we saw in the last chapter (p. 331), Lacan was in the 1930s and 40s well-connected with the Paris cultural élite. He knew the Sartre/Beauvoir set, but it was with the dissident surrealist world he was most intimately involved, with close links to Bataille, Dalí, Leiris and Queneau. In addition he was Picasso's physician, tried his hand at treating Artaud, and supervised Dora Maar's mental health issues, committing her to hospital and acting as her therapist. His psychoanalytic theory, as it developed, retained a consistency with dissident surrealism.

Lacan's take on Freud's 1920s tripartite division of the psyche into Id, Ego and Superego, was a theory of three 'orders' – the Real, the Imaginary and the Symbolic [62]. The child begins life in the order of the Real, where experiences of *jouissance* prevail – ecstatic, often agonising – experiences that cannot be articulated or even consciously recollected (shades of Bataille's 'limit experiences'). Soon the child goes through the Mirror Phase, where the sight of its reflection as a unified body enchants it into a misperception that its psyche is equally unified, and that it exists as a coherent identity [63]. This leads the child into the order of the Imaginary where it fantasises itself as a self-governing conscious individual in a world of other conscious individuals. Only with the Oedipus Complex, the intrusion of the 'father' with his strictures and commands, does the society – the Symbolic Order – intrude, with its gods and rules, its language, and its patriarchal power – the Law of the Father. The truth of the human condition then is to be intimidated by the commands issuing from the imposing edifice of the Symbolic Order, and haunted by what lies beneath, the unnameable subterranean dynamics lurking in the unconscious – the Real. Most of us try to hide in a comfort zone of the Imaginary, the 'everyday life' which we fondly believe is 'reality', struggling to deny the truth that the Real is perpetually 'decentring' our subjectivity, and rendering the Imaginary merely an escapist fantasy.

Again the kinship with Bataille's world view is evident, but Lacan was if anything more pessimistic. He agreed that the abject energies of our 'sous-réalité' would indeed disrupt the fictitious 'everyday life' we like to believe in and the power-structures that oppress us if they could be articulated. However, for Lacan such articulation is not possible, because that would require language, and language is part and parcel of the machinery of the Symbolic Order. Hence, by definition, the *jouissance* of the Real can never be spoken, and its disruptive potential can never be realised.

What was of particular interest to Psych et Po was Lacan's take on gender. He accepted the psychoanalytic view of gender differences in the trajectory through childhood and experience of the oedipal crisis, leading to the genital focusing of the male libido, while the female's remains more multiple and free-flowing (see p. 241). Lacan explained this in terms of gendered relations with the Symbolic Order. The privileged signifier of the Symbolic Order is the phallus (as enshrined in all indicators of power, from towers and steeples to guns, blades and missiles), permitting a (highly anxious) degree of identification by the boy, and hence his incorporation into the oedipal system. His psyche is inscribed, and his erotic energy is genitally focused – captured, limited and controllable – promising him acceptance as one of the Fathers, sharing in their power, and accessing the 'rational' thought and language the Symbolic Order privileges. This phallic identification is not available to the girl, and she becomes a split subject, part-subordinated and part-excluded from the Symbolic Order. Her psyche is less inscribed by the 'logic' and 'rationality' of the system, thus her eroticism is not genitally focused or fixed, and remains free-flowing, excessive and *jouissant*. If her erotic desires could be articulated, they would unleash a tsunami of meanings way beyond anything the Symbolic Order could handle. But of course, in Lacan's view, there is no language by which this can find articulation. As such, female *jouissance* can never manifest as the disruptive force it could be, and is condemned to remain inexpressible, flowing through the realm of the Real where raw encounters with pleasure and pain can be experienced, but remaining forever outside the capacity of the conscious mind to recall, or of language to express. Female desire, which like all desire (in Lacan's world) originates in a sense of lacking something, must remain frustrated. [This lack, from which all desire originates, is denominated by Lacan (interestingly enough), as 'O' [64]].

**Psych et Po:** This is where Psych et Po broke ranks with Lacan. For them, the suppression and exclusion of women from the Symbolic Order – their 'Otherness' – puts them, by virtue of their much greater intimacy with their *jouissance*, in a position of extraordinary potential leverage and power. And it will be possible to find, or create, new languages to express this *jouissance*, and unleash its radical power to undermine the edifice of significations that constitutes the Symbolic Order – 'femininity escapes symbolic structuration, but is capable of subverting it' [65].

For Psych et Po, this quest to find new languages to articulate *jouissance* and deploy it as a revolutionary weapon against the Symbolic Order, reveals mainstream feminism to be profoundly wrong-headed. To struggle for equality within the Symbolic Order is to struggle for acceptance into the system of capitalism, imperialism, racism, misogyny, homophobia and all the other manifestations of oppression and repression, which is not only politically pointless, but can only be achieved by women abandoning what makes them distinct to slot in alongside the men incorporated into the system. Hence Psych et Po valorise 'femininity' and the 'feminine', while taking a dim view of the word 'feminist' (perhaps revealing an intellectual ancestry in Feminine Humanism?). Rather than rearrange the proverbial deckchairs on the Titanic, it is a higher imperative to discover/ create the languages by which feminine *jouissance* can be articulated, by which the feminine can be brought into existence, to fracture the Symbolic Order and liberate both (all?) sexes [66].

Julia Kristeva is the most frequently referenced member of the three names we are considering, joining *Tel Quel* in 1966 (just after Jeanne Aeply left), and soon after marrying its founder and editor Philippe Sollers. In Kristeva's theory [see for example, *Powers of Horror* (*Pouvoirs d'horreur*, 1980)], the infant is born into the pre-oedipal feminine realm, the 'Semiotic', in sensual symbiosis with the maternal body in a state of fluid exchange and 'poetic' pre-Symbolic rhythmic acoustics. As the infant develops into becoming a speaking subject, so this symbiosis is broken and the maternal body is pushed away, and the child begins entry into the Symbolic Order of rigidity, clarity, orderliness, masculine control, with its own language of logic and fixed meanings. The Symbolic identifies and asserts itself through separating itself from the Semiotic, rendering anything reminiscent of the Semiotic, including the maternal body and the fluids that mediate the symbiosis as *Abject*. Anything that defies the boundaries or divisions of the Symbolic Order are made abject – not just substances (blood, urine, vomit, faeces, mucus), but also states (disease, decomposition), people (the mad, perverts, criminals) and actions (murder, incest, necrophilia, cannibalism) [67]. The Abject in all its manifestations generates a sense of horror and dread, and is rejected, expelled as defiling and disgusting, excluded and made Other. Among the excluded are women, still linked to the pre-oedipal maternal semiotic, abject in the fluidity and leakiness of their bodies, and like other rejected groups, facing denial of their agency and validity. They can hear the pulsating rhythms of the poetic that threatens continually to break through into Symbolic discourse, and retain a dark attraction for the Abject, that which 'stirs the ghost of the maternal body'. For Kristeva, the very Otherness of women, their abjection, their exclusion from full membership of the Symbolic Order, gives them leverage to challenge the system that marginalises them, and provides them with revolutionary power. The resonances in Kristeva's work with Melanie Klein, Bataille, Dalí, Artaud, Debuffet's 'Outsider Art' and of course Sade are clearly evident.

Luce Irigaray in her *This Sex Which is Not One* (*Ce Sexe qui n'en est pas un*, 1977), emphasised the multiplicity of female sexuality: '*Woman has sex organs just about everywhere. She experiences pleasure almost everywhere.... the geography of her pleasure is much more diversified, more multiple in its differences, more complex, more subtle, than is imagined...*' [68], and postulated the entwined lubricated lips of the vagina as a dynamic symbol of female sexuality to pit against the static and arid erection of the male phallus (an echo of Man Ray's 1934 painting *À l'heure de l'observatoire, les amoureux*?). This underlies the plurality of femininity itself, in contrast to the rigid unity of masculine 'identity'.

Hélène Cixous championed an alternative way of writing, *l'écriture féminine*, wild, musical and spontaneous, as a challenge to the dominance of the patriarchal authority of logical, commanding *littérature*, where all signifiers march in disciplined rhythm to dictate meaning to the reader. For Cixous, the joyous and receptive openness and embracing of otherness of *l'écriture féminine* expresses the plurality and fluidity of the feminine self and its commitment to an economy of giving [69], and stands in stark opposition to the stasis, fear and rejection of otherness characteristic of *littérature*. She recognised both sexes could have access to both modes, and acclaimed Joyce and Genet as exemplary writers of *l'écriture féminine* while still seeing it as writing from a feminine subject position, enabled by women's more direct access to the oceanic *jouissance* of their bodies, providing them with a source of expression for their erotic writing, their *sexts*. In 'The Laugh of the Medusa' ('Le Rire de la méduse' 1975) [70], a luminous prose-poem that is both an illustration of and a call to arms for *l'écriture féminine*, she extolled the power of female desire. Repudiating Lacan's view of the root of desire, she riposted 'What's a desire originating from a lack? A pretty meagre desire', insisting instead that woman's 'libido is cosmic, just as her unconscious is world-wide', and that her own 'desires have invented new desires, my body knows unheard-of songs'. Urging women to overcome the shyness she suspected almost all had felt in their early days, creating their own secret worlds of fantasy, and trying to write their desires, before giving up in embarrassment, she reassured them that 'beauty will no longer be forbidden', exhorting woman to write, 'because this is the invention of a new insurgent writing which, when the moment of her liberation has come, will allow her to carry out the indispensible ruptures and transformations in her history'. 'Women must write through their bodies, they must invent the impregnable language that will wreck partitions, classes, and rhetorics, regulations and codes...', and their bodies must not be silenced, for 'Censor the body and you censor breath and speech at the same time', and acknowledging the complicity of many women in silencing themselves or others, she adopts an uncompromising tone – 'We must kill the false woman who is preventing the live one from breathing'. In the end, Cixous was upbeat: 'Almost everything is yet to be written by women about femininity: about their sexuality', but now was the time, for women to 'go into the forest', to explore the 'Dark Continent', and she called on her readers to 'Write your self. Your body must be heard  Only then will the immense resources of the unconscious spring forth'. Again Bataille hovers in the background, with the power of laughter to shatter restrictive systems of meaning, and the value of non-productive economics – the generosity of potlatch taking precedence over the commercial exchange of capitalist transaction.

**Matters Arising:** The works of Kristeva and her colleagues have generated libraries of discussion over the last decades. Here we can do little more than nod briefly at a few points.

Psych et Po's focus on the physical embodiment of femininity and feminine desire throws light on a point we have reached before (chapter VII), of being shepherded by 'masculinist discourses' (Existentialism, Absurdism) towards the conclusion that alienation is inevitable, a conclusion that more 'feminine' approaches resist. The discourses of Psych et Po, on the maternal body, on the feminine's embrace of otherness and on the economy of giving, raise the question whether the very embodiment of feminine psychodynamics, motivation and desire militates against the lure of the abstract philosophising of alienation and what Breton calls 'miserabilism', opening the door to alternative, more liberating conclusions.

Since its inception [71], psychoanalysis has defined hysteria as unconscious or repressed material, denied access to consciousness awareness or linguistic articulation, finding other ways to express itself, as some kind of symptom (and the inventiveness of hysteria in how it manifests is never to be underestimated [72]). Psych et Po's search for other languages, particularly embodied ones, crosses into the territory of hysteria, something the Psych et Po writers understood and embraced. For Kristeva the natural feminine language of the Semiotic, with its pre-oedipal rhythms and intimacy with the physicality of the maternal body, is indeed hysteric – and hysteria contests the Symbolic Order. For her, women's literature is essentially hysteric. Psychoanalyst Juliet Mitchell concurred, the novel 'has to be the discourse of the hysteric. The woman novelist has to be an hysteric. Hysteria is the woman's simultaneous acceptance and refusal of the organisation of sexuality under patriarchal capitalism. It is simultaneously what a woman can do to be both feminine and to refuse femininity within patriarchal discourse' [73]. This view is consistent with that of the surrealists in 1928, who acclaimed hysteria as 'the greatest poetic discovery of the 19th century' and something to be explored and celebrated [74]. Mainstream psychoanalysis takes another view, that hysteria is something to be cured, and that writing is a means to that end [75], a view presented (in direct opposition to Kristeva) by Elaine Showalter that writing – even *écriture féminine* – is after all a way of linguistic expression, and as such can provide the repressed with a voice. Far from being symptomatic of hysteria, it is a way beyond it [76].

All of the three writers we have been considering here took

an interest in the mystical and religious – a 'radical process of re-imaging and re-visioning religious discourse, or, even, of inventing divinity anew' [77]. Irigaray for example follows Beauvoir that 'mysticism is the domain of the feminine: here the unconscious speaks' [78] – St Teresa providing the exemplar of the feminine divine embodied voice – simultaneously immanent and transcendent. For Irigaray, the mystic erases her own identity to mirror the divine and share in that new selfhood, enabling the re-envisioning of 'God' in a feminine mode and rescuing the maternal body from its elision in traditional religion. In the space necessary for spiritual becoming, Irigaray postulates angels as mediating between flesh and spirit, and Mary as mediating between the maternal and the divine. Cixous also writes about divinity, dream and the mystical, the need to write the impossible, and re-reads the story of Eve as exemplifying the 'feminine economy' of opening up to otherness and extremities of pleasure, with Eve taking delight in ingesting the forbidden fruit into her body, even though, or even because, it will lead to loss of the self and death [79]. For Cixous' colleague Catherine Clément, drawing more directly on Bataille, the focus is more on the *jouissance* of rapture, the syncope, the space for mysticism, love, creativity and joy, but also seizure and possession and hysteria – by no means a place of innocent pleasure, but encompassing the violent, the macabre, the bloody and the agonising [80].

The Psych et Po triad provide a vocabulary to speak about the women artists and writers of 'The Flowering of *Jouissance*' referred to above, but their work also carry resonances with Dominique Aury/Pauline Réage and her writings. *Story of O* is a narrative of *jouissance* and abjection, and Kristeva's pre-oedipal semiotic is prefigured both in the novel being the 'story of eau' (as Truffaut and Godard had light-heartedly referenced in 1958, see p. 57) – the 'cosmology of the female element' – and in the matriarchies of both Jacqueline's family and more particularly Anne-Marie's realm at Samois [81]. Réage's account to Deforges that 'female pleasure is often more diffuse, distributed wonderfully over the whole body, rather than in the sole explosion of orgasm' (something she saw as more masculine) [82], parallels Irigaray on the richness of female sexuality compared to the more focused and limited male experience (although O refuses the auto-eroticism that runs through Irigaray's writing) [83].

It is however with Cixous that **Aury** is most in tune. While Cixous linked *l'écriture féminine* closely with women, she refused to rigidly gender it, hailing Joyce and Genet as prime exponents, while Aury raised the question with St Jorre (1994), 'Were they male fantasies? That's what everybody says. I've always been reproached for that. All I know is they were honest fantasies – whether they were male or female I couldn't say', and insisted to Kaufmann (1998), 'Everyone has the right to all realms of the imagination' [84] (a view common to many women surrealists, including Leonor Fini). There are further resonances: the title of Cixous' prose-poem echoes that of Aury's 1950 review of Beauvoir's *The Second Sex*, 'The Face of the Medusa' ('Le Visage de Méduse') [85], and Cixous' description of adolescent girls creating their imaginary worlds in secret  is consistent with passages in Réage's interview with Deforges on the writing of her own childhood fantasies [86]. Most intriguing is the resemblance between Cixous' exhortation to women to 'write the body' and Réage's description of the writing of *O* in 'A Girl in Love' – 'The girl was writing the way you speak in the dark to the person you love when you've held back the words of love too long and they flow at last. For the first time in her life, she was writing without hesitation, without stopping, rewriting or discarding; she was writing the way one breathes, the way one dreams' ('A Girl p. 11). The 'spontaneous, gushing writing of *Histoire d'O*'[87] – (or at least the 'first sixty pages' that we have already linked to surrealist 'automatic writing' see p. 280), along with Aury's 1960 writings on 'Les Inconscientes' (see p. 263), not to mention 'A Girl in Love' itself, would seem to be referencing, even providing examples of, *écriture féminine* – sexts – *avant la lettre*. I am not aware of any of the Psych et Po triad making direct reference to *Story of O* (although I stand to be corrected here!), but it would seem highly unlikely that literary scholars of their standing would have been unaware of it. The parallels and echoes may be signs of influence, but it is perhaps more likely that they signify a confluence of thought – both Psych et Po and Aury were fishing in the same rivers of ideas.

## *STORY OF O* AND ANGLOPHONE FEMINISM

Not everybody wanted to join the 1970s *jouissance* party. In the U.S. anxiety had been brewing in the 1960s among conservative and religious groups over the youth counter-culture of the time, with its psychedelic drugs, activism against the Vietnam War, and sexual freedoms. Richard Nixon was elected president in 1968 by the so-called 'moral majority', and the stage was being set for reaction. Emerging 'second wave' feminism (the 'Women's Liberation Movement') found itself pulled in different directions. Very much part of the counter-culture, asserting the rights of women over their bodies and reproduction against an unsympathetic patriarchal establishment, at the same time it encompassed groups of 'radical feminists' who found themselves in agreement with the moral majority's dislike of sexual celebration. The U.S. publication of *Story of O*, compounded by the press hailing it as the death knell for censorship of 'pornography' and the 'true expression' of female sexuality [88] provided these radical feminists with an early focus to get worked up about. The first expression of protest however implicated *O* only tangentially.

In 1968 New York, Valerie Solanas targeted (in a quite literal way) three men whom she accused of 'exploiting' her – Andy Warhol, Maurice Girodias and Barney Rosset. The first two she had met. She had been at Warhol's Factory, had bit-parts in a couple of his films, and had offered him a sexually explicit film script which he had taken and 'mislaid'. She had also approached Girodias (who had an office in New York) with her 'S.C.U.M.' ('Society for Cutting up Men') Manifesto, which he found 'entertaining', giving her an advance and a promise to publish. Deciding the advance was insufficient, and that Warhol and Girodias were in cahoots to steal her work, Solanas went out for 'revenge'. She went first to Girodias' office, but finding he was away at a meeting, proceeded to the Factory where she shot and wounded Warhol and another man. She then took an ice-pick to the Grove Press office looking for Rosset, but left without incident and gave herself up to the police [89]. Warhol's hapless visitor was not seriously hurt, but Warhol was, and he never fully recovered from his injuries. Solanas was diagnosed as paranoid schizophrenic and served 31 months for 'reckless assault with intent to harm' [90]. *Story of O* was not directly cited in the incident, but the targeting of Girodias and Rosset is suggestive – in particular the latter, with whom Solanas had no personal acquaintance, but whose reputation was high-profile at the time, largely because of *O*.

**Radical Feminism and *O*:** Subsequent Radical Feminists shared many of Solanas' views, but adopted less extreme methods, restricting themselves to polemics, pickets, demonstrations and sporadic book-burnings. Various quarries came into their sights: the Miss World contest was flour-bombed in 1970, and *Story of O* became a favourite target. Eschewing the sort of considerations that have distracted us in the last few chapters, radical feminist ideology had no time for the literary sophistries of such as Susan Sontag, and saw literature as in essence elaborate advertising. For them, *O* was simply a parable of gender power, indisputably the product of a depraved male mind, and a particularly pernicious specimen of propaganda for the exploitation of women. Kate Millett (1970), having condemned Freud for linking masochism to female psychology, claimed contemporary society advocated that 'abuse is not only good for women, but the very thing she craved', and that '*The Story of O* is an extreme statement made upon such assumptions' and therefore 'counter-revolutionary' [91]. At the same time Robin Morgan wrote of *O*, 'This is supposed to be by a woman. It sounds more like a man's fantasy' [92], while in 1974 Andrea Dworkin condemned *O* as 'a book of astounding political significance' – misogynistic pornography legitimating the oppression, rape and brutalisation of women, and without doubt the product of a fetid masculine mind: 'The thesis is simple. Woman is cunt, lustful, wanton. She must be punished, tamed, debased. This is as it should be – natural and good. It ends necessarily in her annihilation, which is also natural and good, as well as beautiful, because it fulfils her destiny' [93]. Susan Brownmiller (1975) testified that she 'nearly retched' when she read it, and went on, 'I am vehemently hostile to suggestions that some known, popular sex fantasies attributed to women are indeed the product of a woman's mind, or the product of a healthy woman's mind. I am thinking here of that scurrilous, anonymous pornographic classic 'The Story of O' by 'Pauline Réage', a pseudonym that only men delight in believing masks the name of a real woman' [94]. A little later Nancy K. Miller's conviction that *O* was the product of 'masculine desire attached to a male body' was so incontrovertible that should proof emerge to the contrary she admitted 'I would then have to start all over again' [95]. These radical feminist diatribes against *O* were almost tailor-made to vindicate Sontag on the level of ignorance about sexual experience and erotic art that pervades the culture [96], and their capacity for being wrong about the author's gender (and inaccurate with the book's title) did little to inspire confidence in their polemics. Nonetheless, the anti-porn agenda gained a remarkable degree of traction in feminist circles, with Grove Press as an early target, accused of 'crimes against women', humiliating, degrading and dehumanising them through the publication of sado-masochistic literature [97]. By 1977 French surrealist poet Annie Le Brun was already characterising radical feminism as 'Stalinism in petticoats' [98].

Again some historical context is helpful. In 1972 the women's movement in the U.S., with Betty Friedan and Gloria Steinem in prominent roles, committed itself to Equal Rights Amendment (ERA) to outlaw sexual discrimination. In Washington, the political establishment showed little hostility: the Democrats agreed to support ERA, and the Republicans shrugged. The opposition came instead, not from the patri-archal establishment, but from the conservative women of 'Stop-ERA', launched and led by Mrs. Phyllis Schlafly [99]. This was a 'family values' movement, opposed to feminism, abor-tion rights, gay and lesbian rights and so on, and defending what they considered to be the real rights of women, and the source of their status – to be wives and mothers (the 'Stop' stood for 'Stop Taking Our Privileges'). This galvanised the Republican party to back Schlafly or risk losing conservative women's votes, so they took a stand, and ERA was defeated in 1982. Being trounced by conservative women in a soror-icidal war was a traumatic experience for feminism, which comforted itself with two (not entirely consistent) claims: first, that patriarchy (the real culprit behind it all, of course) had brainwashed the 'Stop-ERA' cohorts into embracing domes-ticity; second, that the struggle had nonetheless 'empow-ered' Schlafly's cohorts as women activists. Ameliorating the trauma could be achieved by forming alliance with Schlafly's supporters in a common cause that united them as women – if such a cause could be found. Anti-pornography was the answer. Both radical feminists and the religious right could rally to this, citing 'pornography' as the principal unmitigated evil, the source of all violence against women – as the influ-ential (although unproven) slogan had it: 'Pornography is the theory, rape is the practice' [100].

**The Politics of Prohibition:** Out of this alliance grew what can be described as a 'Politics of Prohibition'. [This term has been appropriated from the anti-alcohol Temperance Movement of the late 19th– early 20th centuries [101], which, like the anti-porn campaign, was predominantly a women's movement, with strong religious connections, committed to 'morally cleansing' society and strengthening oppressive legislation. Its success in achieving nation-wide prohibition of alcohol in the U.S.A. in 1920 back-fired spectacularly – the alcohol industry, rather than shutting up shop as it was supposed to, went underground and into the hands of bootleggers and gangsters, precipitating a crime wave that led to the repeal of prohibition in 1933]. The politics of prohibition of alcohol has mostly drifted into the political margins, but the politics of prohibition of the sexual has burgeoned since the 1970s, peaking in the 1980s, the decade of conservative resurgence in the U.S. and the U.K. with the governments of Ronald Reagan and Margaret Thatcher respectively. Anxieties over matters sexual ran high in the 1980s, manifesting in a variety of ways, including moral panics about 'Satanic ritual abuse' [102], and hostility towards homosexuality during the AIDS epidemic [103]. In this context, anxieties over pornography were easy to stoke, and Andrea Dworkin's 1981 *Pornography: Men Possessing Women* had a marked impact. By 1983 Dworkin and her colleague Catherine MacKinnon were working with conservative religious groups on commissions to draught new legislation to restrict 'pornography' – contributing to the Reagan-backed Meese Report in 1986. Working alongside evangelical groups committed to depriving women of their basic reproductive rights seemed of surprisingly little concern to them [104]. In 1982 the Barnard Conference on Sexuality was picketed by anti-porn demonstrators who intimidated the organisers and contributors. At the same time, spokespersons for WAVAW (Women Against Violence Against Women) declared all representations of women to be objectifications of their bodies, and all erotica (including Lesbian) to be porn and therefore a threat to be suppressed [105]. By 1986 moves were afoot in the U.K. to ban topless 'page 3 girls' in tabloid newspapers, and the Campaign Against Pornography (CAP) was demanding the removal of 'nudie' magazines from newsagents' top shelves [106]. The new prohibitionism took hold on U.S. campuses – copies of *Story of O* were burned [107], and Angela Carter was 'virtually boycotted' by the 'really hard-line radical feminists' of the Women's Studies department during a stint teaching at the Writers' Institute at New York State University in 1988 [108]. The influence of U.S. radical feminism spread: in the early 1990s Odile Hellier of the Village Voice bookshop in Paris described how she had first read *O* in the

1960s and loved the emancipation of O to enact her fantasies, the mystical flavour and the elegant literary style, before continuing how the 'political correctness' of 'hard-core feminists' has ruined that reading – 'American feminism has left its mark on us, and it is difficult now to view erotica without the feminist spy in us passing judgment' [109].

In fact, more sophisticated feminist critiques of *Story of O* were available. In 1984 Brown and Faery, drawing on Pearl Chang's 1966 review (see above p. 352), suggested that while 'The Lovers of Roissy' had been genuine erotic fantasy, the rest of *O* was a 'sardonic fable' of the story of marriage – a parody of the ideal of wedded perfection venerated in Mrs Schlafly's world. This ideal had been propagated by Marabel Morgan in her best selling evangelical Christian 'self-help' manual *The Total Woman* (1973), which advocated total female surrender as the road to marital bliss. Reading *O* in this way would place it somewhere near Ira Levin's *Stepford Wives* (1972) as a spoof on domestic 'perfection'. The idea of *O* as parody has proved a popular reading in some circles [110]. This is sometimes attributed to Sontag, who did in fact consider parodic elements in *O*, before concluding they were not of major importance. For her, *O* was a text of deeply serious intent [111]. However, the subtlety of critiques like that of Brown and Faery were swimming against the tide in a decade where dogmatic simplicity and shrill condemnation were in fashion.

Nonetheless, through the 1980s resistance was brewing, and voices accusing the radical feminists of actually being anti-feminist were being heard. In 1979 Carter had identified the 'holy terror' of the erotic as 'the source of all opposition to the emancipation of women' [112], while Margaret Atwood in her novel *The Handmaid's Tale* (1985) pointed out how 'Gilead' had emerged from a strange connivance between porn-burning radical feminism and fundamentalist religion [113]. Meanwhile others insisted that while women were entitled to safety from attack and abuse, 'we don't want that safety at the cost of challenge, risk, exploration and pleasure'[114]. Meanwhile the Feminist Anti-Censorship Task-force (FACT) succeeded in blocking Dworkin-MacKinnon initiatives, making the case that the pornography-violence link was unproven, and that the anti-porn campaign was a red herring, diverting attention from real feminist issues while bolstering the government and right wing/ anti-feminist elements against freedom of speech and women's rights[115]. By the end of the 1980s there were hints that the tide might be turning.

**Sea-Change:** In the U.K. in 1989, Feminists Against Censorship (FAC) was launched, and quickly scored a success deflecting the NCCL (National Council for Civil Liberties) from supporting the prohibitionist lobby. The FAC manifesto *Pornography and Feminism: The Case Against Censorship* (1991) and other allied texts made the case that 'pornography' is a complex genre that serves multiple purposes – challenging sexual mores and hypocrisy, and foregrounding desires, adventure and pleasure for women as well as men. Moreover, the anti-porn campaign was an alliance of conservative traditionalism, right-wing religion and moralistic leftism that could only benefit reactionary agendas. Feminists who jumped on this band-wagon were neglecting areas of serious work for women's political, social and economic good in pursuit of a vendetta against words and images. The claim that pornography triggered violence was unproven; censorship of sexual materials was hitting gay and lesbian erotica[116] and economically damaging the livelihoods of women in the sex industry. In addition, the anti-porn lobby was infantilising women and was undermining the real feminist struggle for women to take control over their own bodies, sexuality and reproduction (which turned out to be a disturbingly accurate warning)[117].

Some felt that U.S. feminism had gone off the rails in the mid 1970s and needed to be reset[118]. From the point of view of the Politics of Eros, prohibitionist 'radical' feminism was profoundly reactionary, even Victorian. Adopting the 'woman-as-moral-guardian' role was accepting the function of women ascribed by 19th century patriarchy – [particularly in the Anglophone world, (as enshrined in Coventry Patmore's 1858 poem 'The Angel in the House'), unlike the French model where women, since the 17th century, had run salons, taking the role more of cultural guides and enablers than a moral police force [119]]. Moreover, the prohibitionist view of eroticism deliberately ignored a century of depth psychology – as Carol Clover succinctly put it 'If the unconscious were a politically correct place it wouldn't need to be unconscious' [120] – something to which radical feminism remained intransigently oblivious. By bolstering the power of the 'oppressive state apparatus' (i.e. patriarchal law) to suppress sexual expression, radical feminism was, in the vocabulary of Psych et Po, proving itself a loyal servant of the Symbolic Order in the repression of *jouissance.* On her death in 2005, Dworkin was praised by right wing commentators, her husband confirming that she had 'enjoyed the company of conservative writers', having rejected the U.S. liberal left as 'largely full of shit', and deploring the fact that 'so-called mainstream feminism had allied itself there' [121].

Further, the anti-porn lobby was accused of overstating the malevolent content of porn, with mainstream Hollywood films being far more misogynistic than hard-core porn, which was the only genre where a woman could gratify her desire and have pleasurable sex without incurring some dire repercussion – the only genre really enabling 'exploration of women's sexual fantasy and desire' [122]. And insofar there really was deeply unpleasant content in some porn, the solution was not censorship or prohibition, but better quality material. Moreover, this sexual material needs to be 'integrated into the culture' [123] – much as alcohol has been integrated, with fine wines and single malts achieving high status, and champagne the very icon of celebration – the idea being that quality erotica will militate against misogynistic trash just as quality alcohol militates against toxic bootlegged hooch.

Alongside this, more playful retaliations were in evidence – Suzie Bright, Lesbian 'sexually radical feminist' toured with her deliberately provocative 'How to Read a Dirty Movie' show in a sustained attack on the 'sexual illiteracy' and 'erotophobia' she found in society, propagated by women's groups laying claim to progressive credentials [124].

These arguments started to have their effect. In 1993 the Virgin 'Black Lace' imprint of erotica by women for women was launched, and in 1996 Nadine Strossen's *Defending Pornography* [125] identified the 'MacDworkinites' as the enemy against the more enlightened struggle to show that porn and feminism are not fundamentally incompatible. BDSM (Bondage-discipline/ dominance-submission/ sado-masochism) subcultures started to raise their profile and articulate their world view of consensual 'perversion' as sophisticated erotic play, pleasurable and life-enhancing, and by the late '90s women were asserting themselves in the creation of erotica/porn [126].

**Surrealism and *Story of O* in Changing Times:** The 1980s and '90s brought the question of women and Surrealism into sharp focus. In 1985 Whitney Chadwick in her *Women Artists and the Surrealist Movement* performed a much-needed task of turning the spotlight on to the often-overlooked women artists with surrealist links. However, in keeping with the prevailing climate of the 1980s, she adopted the 'women-exploited-by-conspiracies-of-men' angle, arguing that the male surrealists had been to blame for marginalising the women and trapping them in the subordinate roles of *'femme-enfant'* or Muse, a strait-jacket from which they could only escape by repudiating Surrealism. This proved contentious with some, including Leonor Fini (who had little time for feminism), Dorothea Tanning and Meret Oppenheim, who all refused to co-operate in Chadwick's project, disliking being categorised as 'women artists', and/or rejecting the idea that Surrealism was prejudiced towards women [127]. [It is likely Toyen would have taken a similar attitude, but being dead she didn't have much say in the matter]. In fact closer inspection puts the blame for the marginalisation of the women artists at the door, not of the surrealist movement, but of the critic/ gallery/ dealer/ auction house/ art-historian nexus that moved in to colonise it – Dorothea Tanning for one confirmed that Max Ernst did everything he could to draw the attention of critics and dealers to her work, but they were unresponsive [128]. In 1998, Penelope Rosemont, in her *Surrealist Women,* rejected the 'divisive agenda' of separating women artists into a sub-category, insisting that Surrealism was in fact remarkable for its openness to women and their work, and heartily dismissing the 'insidious fiction that surrealism is yet another "Men Only" movement' [129]. In 2020, Penny Slinger in her article 'I am using myself as my muse', stated 'I never felt feminism was about getting the same powers as men, but about having the power of the feminine recognised', simultaneously questioning Whitney Chadwick over 'Muse' being a patriarchal trap for women artists, and lending support to feminisms that take the concept of the 'feminine' seriously [130]. The debate over whether Surrealism was a prison or a liberation for women continues to rumble on [131].

It was of course in the mid 1990s that Dominique Aury allowed herself to be revealed as the author of *O*, which reignited interest in her novel at a time when its claim to be a progressive, even feminist work, and an exemplar of quality erotica, written by a woman for women, could be taken sympathetically (which would have been much harder ten years before). *Story of O* has been generating a sustained stream (if by no means a flood) of articles in academia from the 1970s to the present, much of it (especially in the Anglophone world) concerned with gender politics, some a little judgemental but mostly refreshingly free of polemic. Some writers were hedging their bets about the gender of the author of *O* as late as the early 1990s [132], but on the whole the identity of Réage as Aury was accepted after 1994. Many of these articles have been discussed elsewhere in this book: some were interested in pornography and literature (after Sontag), some in the philosophical (Sade, Hegel, Nietzsche, Sartre and Bataille all being drawn into the conversation), some made comparative analyses of *O* with other texts, including Female Gothic (the study of which also flourished in the 1990s), but a recurring focus of interest has been in exploring O's subjectivity and sexuality, usually in a highly nuanced way, often with reference to the mystical and/or psychoanalytic theory.

---

[1] Polizzotti 2009 pp. 539-540

[2] 'Absolute Deviation' Mahon 2005 p. 177; 'The absolute divide' Durozoi 2002 p. 608

[3] Mahon 2005 pp. 187-88; Durozoi 2002 pp 608-632

[4] Polizzotti 2009 p. 553

[5] Durozoi 2002 p. 629

[6] Ibid p. 635

7 Claude Courtot, cited Polizzotti 2009 p. 559.

[8] Durozoi 2002 p. 643

[9] Ibid p. 644

[10] Including Durozoi (2002) who ends his narrative in the early 1970s, and Mahon (2005) who ends hers in 1968. For Will Gompertz, Surrealism's spirit, uniquely, 'has stayed the course' and continues to inspire film, art, and literature. *What are you looking at?* (2012) Penguin 2016 p. 235

[11] Cited St Jorre 1994 p. 48

[12] Amy Wyngaard gives an excellent account of the American publication and reception of *O* in her articles: 'Sade, Reage and Transcending the Obscene' in Mudge, Bradford K.(ed.) *The Cambridge Companion to Erotic Literature.* Cambridge University Press 2017, and 'The End of Pornography: The Story of Story of O' *MLN* Sept; 130(4) 980-997. Johns Hopkins University Press 2015.

[13] Cited in Rapaport 2004

[14] first published in *Le Belvédère*, Paris, in 1958

[15] Wyngaard 2015

[16] Calder 2013, p. 219; St Jorre 1995, p. 221

[17] St Jorre 1995, p. 225

[18] Wyngaard 2015

[19] For example, the Collectors Publications version (California) 1967, entitled *The Story of O* (*sic*).

[20] Sabine's might have over-stated Réage's enthusiasm. Réage's account (to St Jorre 1994 p. 49) was that she had never had any contact with Sabine, and her view of the translation was that it 'seemed to be all right.'

D'Estrée's indictment of the earlier translation was presumably a reference to the first Olympia version in 1954 rather than the (not at all terrible) Wainwright translation of 1957 – although if the 1954 translation was by husband and wife team Baird and Denny Bryant as some allege (Campbell 1994 p. 167 and Calder 2013 p. 128), d'Estrée's claim that its fault lay in it lacking the female touch does stray rather off-target.

[21] Reissued in 1980 by Grove Press as *Story of O Part II, Return to the*

*Château. Preceded by A Girl in Love*
   22   St Jorre 1995 p. 236
   23   Wyngaard 2015
   24   See for example Wyngaard 2015
   25   The whole story is recounted in St Jorre 1994: p. 49-50: 1995 pp. 237-238
   26   Young 2013
   27   'a woman friend of mine said... only a woman could think of things so cruel' John Crowley 'Story of O' *Washington Post* June 18 2000
   28   Wyngaard 2015
   29   *New York Times* Jan 9th 1968; Toronto *Telegram* Sept 8th 1969; cited Wyngaard 2015
   30   Pearl Chang 'O Dear' *New York Review of Books* April 14th 1966
   31   *San Francisco Sunday Examiner and Chronicle* March 20th 1966; Cited in Wyngaard 2015, 2017
   32   Wyngaard 2015
   33   quoted in Wyngaard 2015; Ballantine edition 1973/1982; Brown and Faery 1984
   34   Extracts from Ballantine edition of *Story of O*, 1973, 13th printing 1982
   35   Extracts cited in Brown and Faery 1984; Young 2013; Wyngaard 2015 and 2017
   36   quoted in Ballantine edition 1973/1982
   37   Young 2013
   38   Cited in *Story of O* Corgi 1972; Campbell 1994, p. 170; Ballantine edition 2013; Marilyn Simon 'My Own Private Château' *Quillette* Oct. 18th 2020
   39   In *Styles of Radical Will*, Martin Secker & Warburg 1967; all Sontag quotations in this section are from the reprint in Georges Bataille *The Story of the Eye*, Penguin, 1982 pp 106, 101-102, 104, 112
   40   Bataille 'L'esprit moderne et le jeu des transpositions', *Documents* 1930, quoted in Denis Holler and Loesl Ollman 'The use-value of the Impossible', *October* 60 (1992)
   41   Deforges 1975 p. 193
   42   Sontag 1967/ 1982 p. 114.
   43   Also Carol King, Buffy Saint-Marie, Laura Nyro, Melanie, Carly Simon. Janis Ian, Dory Previn and others.
   44   Nancy Spector: 'Marina Abramović Rhythm 5' *Guggenheim* 1994; Thomas McEvilley: 'Marina Abramović/Ulay, Ulay/ Marina Abramović' cited *Artforum* vol 22, No. 1, Sept. 1983
   45   Virago, published in the U.S. as *When God was a Woman* (Dial Press 1976)
   46   Nancy Joyce Peters 'Women and Surrealism', in Rosemont 1998 *Surrealist Women* p. 463
   47   Introduction to *Penelope Slinger: Hear What I Say* Riflemaker 2012. p. 8
   48   *Le Cahier volé*
   49   In *Literary Women*, Womens' Press

⁵⁰ Tiderne Skifter, Copenhagen 1978, published in English translation by Souvenir Press 1981. For Gloria Steinem, every woman is faced with the stark choice between being a feminist or being a masochist (cited *British Vogue* 4 June 2017) – Marcus explored what it meant to be both.

⁵¹ Back cover note, Picador edition 1984

⁵² Wikipedia 'The Dinner Party'

⁵³ Carter was influenced by Leonora Carrington's stories and the Czech film *Valerie and her Week of Wonders* (Jaromil Jireš 1970), itself based in a 1935 surrealist novella by Vitěsla Nezval. From stories in *The Bloody Chamber*, Carter scripted her 1984 film *The Company of Wolves* (dir. Neil Jordan).

⁵⁴ Beauvoir interview with Alice Schwarzer, *Ms*, July 1972, cited Marks & de Courtivron 1980 p. 150

⁵⁵ With money inherited from the house of Jean Schlumberger (the jewellery designer, not Paulhan's colleague at the *NRF*).

⁵⁶ Beauvoir 'France: Feminism is Alive and Well and in Constant Danger' [in Robin Morgan ed. *Sisterhood is Global* (1984 pp, 233-34)

⁵⁷ As in Marks and de Courtivron *New French Feminisms* (1980); the Signs edition on *French Feminist Theory*, and the Yale French Studies volume on *French Feminisms* (both 1981).

⁵⁸ See for example Christine Delphy, who sees the concept of 'French feminism' as a U.S. fiction. 'The Invention of French Feminism: An Essential Move' Yale French Studies 87, *Another Look, Another Woman* ed. Huffer 1995 Yale University

⁵⁹ Morny Joy, Kathleen O'Grady, Judith L. Poxon, *French Feminists on Religion* Routledge 2002 p. 6

⁶⁰ Rosemary Tong *Feminist Thought* Routledge 1989 p 217/ Mary Klages 'Helen Cixous: The Laugh of the Medusa' Oct 23 2001 – http://www.Colorado.EDU/English/engl2010mk/cixous.;ec.html

⁶¹ Claire Duchen *Feminism in France: From May '68 to Mitterand* Routledge, Keegan & Paul 1986 cited Joy et al 2002 p. 7

⁶² Begining with His 'Rome Discourses' 1953, discussed in Bice Benvenuto and Roger Kennedy *The Works of Jacques Lacan* Free Asociation of Books 1986

⁶³ *L'Image* can be seen as a game with such perceptions and misperceptions

⁶⁴ Phillips 1999

⁶⁵ Silverman 1984

⁶⁶ See for example Toril Moi *Sexual/Textual Politics* (1985) Routledge 2001; Joy et al. 2002 for excellent accounts of Psych et Po.

⁶⁷ Joy et al p. 93-94

⁶⁸ Irigaray *This Sex Which is Not One* (1977) Cornell University Press 1985 p. 28

⁶⁹ Cixous 'Sorties' 1975 cited Marks and de Courtivron 1980 pp. 90-98

⁷⁰ In *L'arc* 1975, in translation in *Signs* summer 1976, and Marks & Courtrivon 1981 pp. 245-264. The subsequent quotes from Cixous are all from here, pp. 262, 259, 246, 250, 256, 248, 255.

[71] Freud and Breuer *Studies on Hysteria* 1895

[72] Elizabeth Bronfen *The Knotted Subject: Hysteria and its Discontents* Princeton University Press 1998

[73] Juliet Mitchell: 'Psychoanalysis: Child Development and Femininity' in *Women, The Longest Revolution* Virago 1984 pp. 289-290

[74] Louis Aragon and André Breton: 'Le Cinquantenaire de l'hysterie (1878-1928)', in *La Révolution surréaliste* No. 11, March 15th 1928, in Durozoi 2002 p. 167

[75] Anna Freud 1922

[76] Elaine Showalter *Hystories* Picador 1997

[77] Joy et al 2002, p. 9

[78] Joy et al. 2002, p. 29; Irigaray has been writing on this since 1974 – see 'le Mystèrique' in *Speculum de l'autre femme*. She was the key-note speaker at the 2005 Liverpool University Conference on 'Woman and the Divine'

[79] Cixous 'Extreme Fidelity' in *Writing Differences*, OUP 1988, cited in Joy et al. 2002 pp. 210-211, 222

[80] Catherine Clément: *Syncope, the Philosophy of Rapture* (1990), University of Minnesota Press 1994; Joy et al 2002, p. 197

[81] Jan B Gordon 1971; Silverman 1984

[82] Réage cited in Deforges 1975 p. 122

[83] Silverman 1984

[84] St Jorre 1994 p. 45; Kaufmann 1998 p. 900; Young 2013

[85] *Contemporains* 2, Dec 1950 cited in Mahon 2020 p. 157, 253 # 173

[86] Cixous 1975 p. 246; Deforges 1975 p. 126

[87] David 2006 p. 28

[88] Brown and Faerie 1984

[89] St Jorre 1995, pp 281-83

[90] Peter Hogan *The Dead Straight Guide to the Velvet Underground*, Red Planet Publishing 2017, pp. 58-59

[91] Millet 1970: *Sexual Politics*, ch. 4: 'The Counter-Revolution' pp. 194-5,

[92] Morgan *Sisterhood is Powerful* 1970 cited in Brown and Faerie 1984

[93] Dworkin 'Woman as Victim: Story of O' Feminist Studies 1974 vol 2, no. 1 pp 107-111/ *Pornography , Woman Hating* II 3, p. 55 , Plume, 1974

[94] Brownmiller *Against our Will* Simon & Schuster 1975

[95] Nancy K. Miller 'The Text's Heroine: A Feminist Critic and her Fictions' (1982) in *Subject to Change: Reading Feminist Writing* Columbia University Press 1988, cited Kaufmann 1998 p. 902

[96] Sontag 1967 p. 114

[97] Wyngaard 2015

[98] Cited in Durozoi 2002 p. 762 note 47

[99] 'How Phyllis Schlafly Derailed the Equal Rights Amendment' *History.com* Lesley Kennedy 19 March 2020

[100] Attributed to Robin Morgan in 1974

[101] For example: Lisa M.F. Anderson *The Politics of Prohibition: American Governance and the Prohibition Party 1869-1933* Cambridge University Press 2013

[102] Triggered by Michelle Smith and Lawrence Pazder *Michelle Remembers* (1980), and reinforced by Ellen Bass and Laura Davis *The Courage to Heal: A Guide for Women Survivors of Sexual Abuse* (1988). Philip Jenkins and Daniel Maier-Katkin 'Satanism: Myth and reality in a contemporary moral panic' *Crime, Law and Social Change* 17 (1) 1992 provide an early paper debunking 'Satanic ritual abuse' as a moral panic. Elaine Showalter's *Hystories* (1997) includes it as an example of modern hysteria.

[103] In the U.K. Section 28 of the Local Government Act 1988 passed by the Conservative government legislated against the 'promotion of homosexuality'.

[104] See Andrew Ross 'The Popularity of Pornography' in *No Respect: Intellectuals and Popular Culture* (Routledge 1989); Lynne Segal Introduction to *Sexuality and the Pornography Debate* Virago 1992; Jerry Barnett *Porn Panic!* Zero Books 2016

[105] Caroline Harris and Jennifer Moore 'Altered Images' *Marxism Today* Nov 1988

[106] Barbara Norden 'Pornography: The Debate Goes On' *Everywoman* Dec 1990-Jan 1991

[107] Bedell 2004; Sallie Baxendale 'The Psychology of O' *The Psychologist* Vol 22 No. 3 March 2009

[108] Carter quoted in Edmund Gordon *The Invention of Angela Carter* Chatto & Windus 2016 p. 385

[109] Cited in St Jorre 1995 pp. 229-230

[110] E.g Carmela Ciuraru 'The Story of the Story of O' *Guernica* 2011

[111] Sontag 1967 p. 98. This conclusion may come as a surprise to a generation accustomed to post-modern 'irony' as the height of sophistication.

[112] Carter *The Sadeian Woman* 1979 p. 150

[113] The protagonist, June, has been renamed 'Offred' (= offered?), denoting her as the possession of Fred, the man who is to impregnate her. All the handmaids are renamed 'Of' whichever man 'owns' them. These men are designated Commanders, and all the handmaids have names beginning 'O'.

[114] *Caught Looking: Feminism, Pornography and Censorship* Caught Looking Inc. (eds) The Real Comet Press, Seattle 1986, cited in Rodgerson and Wilson (eds) 1991

[115] *Pornography and Feminism: The Case Against Censorship* Feminists Against Censorship ed. G. Rodgerson and E, Wilson Lawrence and Wishart 1991

[116] See for example Emma Healey *Lesbian Sex Wars* Virago 1996.

[117] Rodgerson and Wilson 1991; Norden 1990-91; Segal 1992

[118] For example Linda Williams cited in 'The pro-porn feminist' Andrew Billen *The Observer* 4 July 1993

[119] Faith E. Beasley 'Revising Memory: Women's Fictions and Memoirs in 17th Century France' (1990) cited in Ronald W. Tobin, "The Female Canon' *TLS* December 9th 2022

[120] Carol Clover Introduction to *Dirty Looks: Women, Pornography, Power* ed. Pamela Church Gibson & Roma Gibson BFI 1993. Cited in 'Exposed: The X-Rated debate' Cherry Smith *Guardian* July 1993

[121] John Stoltenberg cited in 'Right hails Dworkin sex campaign' Sarah Baxter *Sunday Times* 17 April 2005

[122] Mandy Rose cited in Harris and Moore 1988

[123] Williams in Billen 1993

[124] 'How to Read a Dirty Movie' Chris Willman *Los Angeles Times* Feb 1st 1990

[125] Abacus 1996

[126] See for example 'Bad Girls' Maureen Freely *Independent on Sunday* 14 May 2000; 'Women lead the porn revolution' Tracy McVeigh *The Observer* 6 August 2000

[127] Chadwick (1985) 1991 p.12

[128] Dawn Ades zoom talk April 2021

[129] Rosemont 1998 p. xxx

[130] In *The Debutante* Issue 1, Jan 2020.

[131] See for example the first issue of *The International Journal of Surrealism* Volume 1, Number 1, Fall 2023.

[132] Pallister 1985 insisted *O* was written by a man, or if not a very disturbed woman; In 1991 Marilyn French *The War Against Women* was implying sympathy to the idea that *O* had been written by Malraux.

# Afterword:  Into the 21ˢᵗ Century

By the beginning of the new millennium, women were very
much on the ascendant in the erotica industries [1], but internet
availability of large amounts of overtly sexual imagery was
giving rise to 'raunch culture', which earned the disapproval of
a wide range of individuals – including Catherine MacKinnon.
For it spelled a huge step back – 'post-feminism is really a
return to pre-feminism' [2], while Jean-Jacques Pauvert doubted
if eroticism could survive the tsunami of explicit images
unleashed in the new age of mass media [3]. Not everyone was
willing to throw in the towel, however, and *Story of O* was cited
as the inspiration for novels written by women for women that
sought to keep the erotica wavelength open and broadcasting.

**Women's Erotic Writing in the New Millennium:** *The
Sexual Life of Catherine M. (La Vie Sexuelle de Catherine M.,*
2001)* was a high profile example. Written by Catherine Millet,
editor of *Art Press* in Paris and an admirer of Bataille, *Belle de
Jour* and *Story of O* [4], this was an explicit, libertine and orgiastic roller-coaster, fore-grounding the protagonist's refusal
to refuse sex of any sort with seemingly any man. It was a
best seller in France, hailed by the press, accepted by feminists, although dismissed by some intellectuals as 'commercial' and 'bourgeois' [5], or in the case of Pauvert, ineffectual
as erotica [6]. It sold well in the U.S.A. and continental Europe
as well, although not so much in the U.K. [7]. In contrast with
*O*, Millet's book presented itself as non-fiction, the autobiography of a writer who made no effort to conceal her identity, and was explicit in description and vocabulary, while
eschewing sado-masochism and the mystical. What the two

books had in common was a female protagonist submissive to others' desires by her own will, providing the reader with the challenge of a woman who takes control of her sexuality by voluntarily surrendering it. Adrienne M. Angelo (2007) described *Sexual Life* as 'erotobiography', and noted similarities with *O*. In both, the protagonist lives a double life, a highly sexualised private one, and an arts-media public one (Millet an art editor, O a fashion photographer). Both books function as 'erotic performance', and in both cases authorship and narrative are complicated by 'bifurcated identity'. Millet is ostensibly writing about 'herself', but as in any autobiography, the protagonist is the literary creation of the author, while 'Pauline Réage' concealed an author writing about an all-but-nameless woman who may or may not have been some kind of alter-ego. Moreover, both women were writing in collaboration with a male partner – Millet's husband Jacques Henric providing a 'photographic addendum', *Légendes de Catherine M.*, published four months after the publication of Catherine's book, while Jean Paulhan of course provided the preface to accompany the publication of *O*.

Other novels achieved some prominence: in 2003 *Submission* (*Entre ses mains*) by 'Marthe Blau' followed the lead of *O* more closely with its theme of an unnamed woman subordinating herself to the sexual domination and cruelties of a 'master', echoing O's experience with Sir Stephen through prostitution to the final point of abandonment and emptiness. It even had an author who refused to divulge her real identity, although she revealed her profession as a Parisian lawyer and was willing to be interviewed and even photographed. In 2008 there was Charlotte Roche's German novel, *Wetlands*, with its explicit engagement with the Abject. Neither managed to break over the sea-wall the way Millet's book had done.

Unexpectedly, the crest of the wave came from the U.K., with EL James' *Fifty Shades* trilogy [8], recounting the sado-masochistic affair between ingénue Anastasia Steele and the impossibly wealthy Christian Grey. Originating in 2008 as postings on a *Twilight* fan-fiction website [9], James' trilogy was first published in limited edition in 2011, and republished in 2012 to immediate off-the-scale popularity. Breaking records for sales around the world, it retained a high profile for the rest of the decade, spawning three films between 2015-2018 and three follow-up novels (the story from Christian Grey's perspective) between 2015-2021. With its readership being predominantly female, the trilogy was hailed by some as a feminist victory, an aphrodisiac enhancing women's sex lives [10], a liberation from shame [11], and an act of defiance in the face of those who would restrict women's rights [12]. It also did wonders for the sex-toy and male escort industries [13], and boosted membership of BDSM clubs (who were happy to instruct people on how to get it right – there having been some unease over the practices and equipment depicted in the books) [14].

*Fifty Shades* also stimulated discussions on a range of questions. First, on 'consensual non-consent' (necessary in BDSM practice), which is frequently misinterpreted as oppression of women, a view that (*pace* Sontag) 'illustrates a problem of cultural literacy' [15]. Second, on imagination and real life, clarifying that 'when women talk about rape fantasises they don't actually want to be raped, they want Brad Pitt to climb in through the window' [16]. And third, on why such fantasies retain their popularity. For Fay Weldon, it was Darwinian selection – 'the most powerful man is the one you dream about' [17], while for Katie Roiphe (2012) there is something 'basically liberating about being overcome or overpowered', especially for emancipated women who find equality a strain [18]. This view upset some feminists, who asked 'is this what we went to the barricades for?'. Roiphe's reply was both a challenge to common interpretations of the 1970s feminist slogan 'the personal is political' [19], and an endorsement of Sontag's fundamentally psychoanalytic observation that our social selves and our sexual selves are not the same selves: 'barricades have always been oddly irrelevant to intimate life'... 'it is perhaps inconvenient for feminism that the erotic imagination doesn't submit to politics' [20].

Some accused *Fifty Shades* of setting a dangerous precedent for relationships, eroticising stalking and sexual abuse [21], suggesting the apparent consensual non-consent of being somewhat less consensual than claimed [22]. But the generally 'sex positive' flavour of feminism of the time ensured that criticism generally refrained from 1980s-style calls for banning or burning (although there were a few [23]) – and authoritative voices like Rutgers professor Helen Fisher spoke up to warn off 'keening feminists' and remind everyone 'this is a world of fantasy and play' [24]. Others however found *Fifty Shades* rather conservative, 'hetero-normalising' romance and monogamous marriage [25], reinforcing capitalist submission to money [26], and celebrating individualism, with characters lacking social significance and offering no route to collective emancipation [27]. Some of these points may miss the mark – in the end EL James was quite open that *Fifty Shades* was essentially a love story, with no claim to social significance (beyond the possibility of having therapeutic value – James claiming it helped women overcome experience of real-life abuse [28]).

Anne Rice pointed out that *Fifty Shades*, like its predecessor *Twilight* (and Daphne du Maurier's *Rebecca*, 1938) all descend from *Jane Eyre* [29] – which is true of much Female Gothic, many examples of which (including *Jane Eyre*) revisit traditional tales, notably *Cinderella* and *Bluebeard* [30]. *Fifty Shades* draws on both of these, along with *Beauty and the Beast*, where the behaviour of the 'monster' is explained as a curse that can be cured by love. This enabled James' books to pathologise Christian Grey's predilections as the result of childhood abuse, providing a link with the 'misery memoirs' that enjoyed popularity from the mid 1990s [31], and attracted another cohort of readers who could appreciate the alibi that it was not the SM that truly delighted them, but the redemption of suffering through true love. Other antecedents of *Fifty Shades* are revealing. In the 2002 film *Secretary* [32], the female protagonist, Lee Holloway (portrayed by Maggie Gyllenhaal), submits to the SM demands of her male employer (incidentally also a Mr. Grey, played by James Spader), and ends up marrying him. In *Secretary*, however, the SM games serve the desires of Lee much more than they do Anastasia in *Fifty Shades*, who puts up with them as part of her search for love. And of course it has been noted that *Fifty Shades* 'owes much to *O*' [33], although the differences are more striking. Unlike Ana, O is by no means an inexperienced ingénue, and displays more agency in her story [34]. Moreover, *O* is a much more subversive text – with O's multiple partners, bisexuality and avoidance of wedding bells [35], although her relations with René and then Sir Stephen retain a (rather flexible) hint of 'coupledom'. There is even an apparent nod to the mystical in Ana's periodic encounters with her 'inner goddess', but 'she' seems more like a cartoonish internalisation of the male gaze than anything, policing Ana from within [36]. Although 'EL James' is also a pseudonym, there was little secret about her real identity as Erika Mitchell, and she has been far from interview- or camera-shy. Like Réage, however (and Catherine Millet), James had a male confederate to assist – her husband, an accomplished screenwriter who set her up with a literary agent, had his own novel published later in 2012, and wrote the script for the second film.

Where *Fifty Shades* was most vulnerable to criticism was in the quality department – with the writing, characterisation and dialogue all coming under fire – the whole being dismissed in some quarters as 'mommy porn' [37]. Some of this can be attributed to moralistic and/or feminist hostility that could not denounce the content openly in a liberal-minded climate, so displaced itself into more 'literary' criticism. Some may arise from continued unease over erotica being produced by women – the condescending prejudice being 'if it is by a woman, it must be bad' [38], although it isn't clear how strong this reaction is now. The problem is that *Fifty Shades* made an easy target of itself here, and even some who might have been disposed to think well of it found it wanting badly. For Erica Jong, it was dull and poorly written, and Katie Roiphe found the only really shocking thing about it was the willingness of millions of women readers to put up with such appalling prose. It certainly would not have strengthened Sontag's claim that pornography can be 'literature'. This was the general tone of critical response in France, where 'mommy-porn' translated as '*porn de ménagère*', and *Fifty Shades* was dismissed as mere fluff, 'sado-masochism light... flavourless', lacking the 'philosophy' of the 'heavy-weights of erotic literature' – Sade and *Histoire d'O* – the 'authentic SM of the French' [39]. For *Elle*, it was 'spiced-up Mills and Boon', with 'laughable' sex scenes; for *Le Figaro*, 'the only real surprise is the style, which is far worse even than the disaster one might have expected', predicting the French 'will soon tire of these Barbie Doll orgasms' [40]. Even the managing director of the publishing house admitted 'Everyone says it is not literature, which is true,' but justified it as a new genre, 'a book that is erotic but is also about love' [41]. Despite all, copies flew off the shelves as quickly in France as anywhere else.

**Return of the Politics of Prohibition:** Amber Jamilla Musser began her 2015 article querying the 'lack of feminist backlash against *Fifty Shades*'. She spoke too soon – a new political and cultural weather-front was on its way. In 2016 the right wing gained significant victories in the Anglophone world, with Donald Trump elected president of the U.S.A., while the Brexit referendum took the U.K. out of the European Union, and the Conservative government lurched to the right.

And the lesson of the 1980s remained pertinent, that censoriousness, even when flying 'progressive' colours, flourishes best in right-wing climates.

A new wave of the Politics of Prohibition launched itself off the back of the #MeToo and #Balancetonporc ('Grass-up/ denounce your pig') movements arising from the Harvey Weinstein case. In October 2017 New York papers had reported on the testimony of more than 80 women accusing Weinstein of rape and sexual assault over three decades. Weinstein was arraigned in May 2018, convicted in 2020 and sentenced to 23 years with more convictions and sentences following (although in April 2024 the initial conviction was deemed unsafe and a retrial ordered). The hash-tag movements went viral immediately, and collective action against other male predators abusing their power followed. Within a few weeks, however, anxieties were starting to arise that the entirely justifiable aims of these movements were in danger of 'mission creep', or even being commandeered by pressure groups with authoritarian agendas.

On 7th January 2018 *Le Monde* in Paris published an open letter, signed by 110 French women – writers, journalists, artists, academics, media professionals, actors, psychoanalysts, medical practitioners and so on. Inaccurately described in some quarters as an 'Anti-#MeToo manifesto', it was written by a team of five, including Catherine Robbe-Grillet and Catherine Millet, and signed by, among others, Catherine Deneuve. It began by stating unambiguously 'Rape is a crime', and (alluding to the hash-tag movements and the Weinstein scandal) applauded the 'legitimate awakening about sexual violence' toward women that these movements had achieved, stating unequivocally, 'This was necessary'. Where the Paris letter became controversial was in flagging up the danger of this 'awakening' being 'turned on its head' and leading, not to liberation, but to repression. This repression was taking several forms: a 'witch-hunt', with allegations (some of trivial acts in the distant past, some of dubious veracity) against men automatically deemed 'guilty' once accused; restriction of freedom in the arts (which must include 'the essential freedom to offend'); demonisation of seduction and 'gallantry'; and the sanitising of sexuality (which is 'by nature, offensive and primitive'). More than that, this rising tide of doctrinaire intolerance was dictating to women what their values and tastes should be, and silencing their freedom of thought and speech – 'We are being told what it is proper to say and what we must stay silent about – and the women who refuse to fall into line are considered traitors, accomplices'. In this 'climate of a totalitarian society', there was serious danger of the 'awakening' playing into the hands of 'the enemies of sexual freedom, the religious extremists, the reactionaries and those who believe – in their righteousness and the Victorian moral outlook that goes with it, that women are a species "apart", children... who demand to be protected'. Rejecting the enslavement of women 'to the status of eternal victim', the letter concluded, 'Our freedom is inviolable. And this freedom that we cherish is not without risks and responsibilities' [42]. The letter precipitated a strong reaction, and a few days later in *Libération* Deneuve felt the need to clarify her position, with a reminder that she supported women's rights (having signed Simone de Beauvoir's 'Manifesto of the 343' in April 1971 demanding the right to abortion in France), and took rape very seriously, while clearly restating her opposition to the cultural clampdown being urged by some sectors of the women's movement [43]. Meanwhile, in the U.S., Katie Roiphe echoed the concerns of the Paris letter in an article for *Harper's Magazine* and was rewarded with a storm of social media abuse accusing her of being 'pro-rape', 'human scum', 'a ghoul', 'a bitch' and so on. Roiphe found 'the Stalinist tenor' of this reaction 'shocking', and warned that 'the basic assumption of freedom of speech' was 'imperilled in our culture right now', a view echoed by film critic Kyle Smith that 'The post-Weinstein revolution has reached its "terror" phase' [44].

*Story of O* found itself being dragged into the storm in 2018 when artist Natalie Frank was informed that the planned exhibition of her *O*-inspired paintings in a New York gallery had been cancelled. The reason given by the gallery owner was anxiety that the content 'could act as a trigger for victims of abuse and violence', a decision Frank found 'curious' [presumably by 2018 a warning notice enabling adults to take responsibility for themselves would not provide either visitors or gallery with sufficient safe-guard]. Frank had long been interested in 'women's experience of pleasure and pain', and, regarding *O* as a 'feminist triumph', wanted to explore 'O's experience of pleasure, the way it contorts her body and explodes her sense of self'. But unease over female-authored 'profanity in art' evidently still persisted, prompting one of Frank's colleagues to ask 'Why is it that female desire is something which is so scary?' [45].

In the last few years, as we are all no doubt well aware, the political and cultural climate has become tangled and fractious. New terms and vocabularies have been reaching public awareness: 'culture wars', 'Wokeness', 'cancel culture', 'TERF', 'critical race theory', 'gender critical theory', 'cultural Marxism', 'identity politics' and so on. Each term has its own point of origin on the political spectrum; some are recent coinages, some have a history; some are intended to be descriptive, others derogatory; some are precise, some exaggerated, some chimerical; some are restricted to particular viewpoints, others have gained wider currency; many are contested in meaning. The upshot is factions at loggerheads, ideological bandwagons careening and colliding, passions rising and pressure to silence opponents coming from various directions (creating openings for all sorts of unlikely people to present themselves as 'defenders of free speech'). Everyone can join up the dots to make their own map of what they think is going on, but political bun-fights are not without consequence. Racism and anti-Semitism [46] are on the rise, as are misogyny (and misandry), homo– and other phobias. In a climate of fear, confusion and intolerance, much heat and little light, serious shifts in the landscape have occurred — one particularly disturbing case being the U.S. Supreme Court in 2022 overturning the Roe v. Wade (1973) ruling that had recognised women's legal right to abortion. This set-back has confirmed the predictions of Feminists Against Censorship (and Margaret Atwood) that if misguided 'progressives' form alliances with the religious right and give them credence, only the forces of reaction are going to benefit.

**Resistance:** And *Story of O* has demonstrated its relevance again, this time offering itself as a means of critiquing the cultural and intellectual impoverishment of our times, and reminding us of the possibility of an enriched sense of life that is fading from our current awareness. In 2020, Shakespeare scholar Marilyn Simon described her encounter with *O*, [47] noting its direct visceral effect on her, and how the account of O giving herself for men's use was not a 'picture of masculine sexual fantasises'... 'but a vision of my own'. For her *O* was most definitely the product of a female imagination. She then contrasted the sexual ethics of *O* with the current culture that foregrounds 'self-expression' and individuality, giving rise to identity politics as 'the foundational dogma of progressive ethics', placing the self central to all considerations in a world of claustrophobic individualism and a relentless imperative to self-understanding, judging our own and others' words and thoughts.

Contrary to this, O takes a less austere, introspective and judgemental path, one that is 'more ancient, more dangerous', but also one that retains sensuality, fun, play, risk and sexiness. *O* acknowledges Nature, the body, relationships, giving and devotion in a story that Simon noted for its (perhaps unexpected) 'tenderness, its kindness... its decency'. Simon is well attuned to the mysticism of O, which she sees in pagan terms, a 'story of erotic devotion'... 'a hymn to Eros, the god of love'... who 'like all gods, requires sacrifice. And the very thing O sacrifices is her individuality.' And this is the most transgressive thing about *O* today. More than the 'obscenity' or 'pornography' or the 'degradation' of women, *O* repudiates the ultimate goal of self-actualisation, self-esteem, self-confidence, self-worth and all the rest of the self-regarding obsessiveness that dominates today. Citing Terry Eagleton's *Radical Sacrifice* (2018) Simon sees O as undergoing the passage of consecration from ordinariness to transfiguration, the 'place for transformation' being opened by O's 'action of violent generosity', a sacrifice of her individuality that enables her to flourish, freed from the 'suffocation and shallowness of the self'.

But such is the impoverishment of the contemporary world view, that few can see in *O* anything more than 'abuse', or O as psychologically damaged. They cannot see that surrender can be liberating and beautiful, and Simon pointed out that her students can't even grasp *Romeo and Juliet*, their cynicism about love – which they see as 'sophisticated' – being unshakeable. Worse, in the present climate, literary works cannot be seen as works of imagination: 'One of the tragedies of our modern age is that even imagination must be cross-examined for evidence of moral unorthodoxy. We are constantly self-scrutinising in order to exorcise even our unconscious incorrect thoughts'... which dehumanises us 'by inflicting upon the self a kind of paranoid vigilance', which 'makes the imagination – the very thing that makes us uniquely human – the enemy'. For 'if one must always search out one's own desires in order to correct them, then we are suddenly no longer in Aury's tender world of flesh and fantasy, but rather in Orwell's world of surveillance and paranoia'.

   *Story of O* presents the most fundamental challenge here – illuminating 'the darker aspects of the human mind', showing us that 'human nature is a mystery: opaque to us', and Simon takes inspiration from *O* to cherish mystery and the imagination, and to protect our privacy from inquisitorial interrogation, acknowledging what *O* has done for her in her private world of 'erotic imaginings', deepening her and 'plant(ing) the seeds of private fantasies to be shared and discovered with a lover... a co-conspirator in laughter, the imagination, and sensuality, and in secret touches and in all things forbidden. Things wicked and sweet and brutal and tender. My own private Château.'

   Echoes of those we have met before can be clearly heard in this article – from Jean Paulhan describing the 'decency' of *O* [48], to Sontag's account of the mystical journey of O [49], to psychoanalytic awareness of the unconscious and mysterious. It also resonates closely with Psych et Po that the current cult of 'identity politics', denial of the feminine, and dogmas that sex and gender are 'socially constructed' are in no wise liberating for women – rather they amount to submission to the all-pervading values and defining power of the Symbolic Order. The ultimate triumph of patriarchy.

   *Story of O* has not been alone in standing up against the politics of prohibition. Alyce Mahon (2020) wrote of *O* in a context of Surrealism as legatees of Sade [50], and given that Surrealism first appeared during a period of ideological dogma and censoriousness from both right and left in the 1920s and 30s, it is perhaps appropriate that Surrealism should be reviving again to face similar challenges today. Surrealism never went away, despite Jean Schuster's fiat of 1969, but the last few years have seen a new burst of energy. In 2022 Surrealism was described as 'bounc(ing) back a century after its birth', 'enjoying another golden age with international events and exhibitions... a modern renaissance' [51], including in 2018 the launching of The International Society for the Study of Surrealism, the first issue of its journal appearing in 2023 [52]. Even more encouraging has been the emergence of new collectives, with surrealist groups, some time-honoured, many of them new, flourishing in Paris, Madrid, Stockholm, Canada, the U.S., Brazil, Egypt, the Czech Republic, Portugal, the Netherlands, the U.K. and many other places – 'specialists in revolt' bringing a 'much needed flash of lightning in these dark times' [53].

Several of these groups publish reviews, journals and magazines, and on-line there is a plethora of blogs and so on (of varying quality) on Surrealism and related subjects. In addition there are still a few independent print publishers working away, flying the flag handed on from Pauvert, Rosset and Girodias in keeping challenging literature in print. [Black Scat Books is an exemplar (and not just because it is publishing this book!) [54]. Born on the Fourth of July in 2012 in the San Francisco Bay Area, Black Scat specialises in absurdist fiction, dada, surrealism and 'pataphysics (including classic and more contemporary writers [55]) and, more pertinent to this book, quality erotica, nurturing the legacy of *Story of O*].

We can hope that the current impoverished climate of prohibition and priggishness, of the policing of desire and imagination, of sanctimonious condemnation of the moral failings of the art and literature of the past, is a temporary phase, and that more open-minded and culturally nourishing times are soon to return. Or perhaps we are in for a longer haul, it is hard to tell. Either way, the struggle for Surrealism and the Politics of Eros must keep up the pressure. This book, first published the year of the 70th anniversary of *Story of O*, and the 100th anniversary of the Breton's 'Manifesto', hopefully will do its bit, celebrating *O* as a touchstone for both Surrealism and Eros.

---

1  See for example; 'Women take control of cyber-porn' Cherry Norton at the American Psychological Association conference' *Independent on Sunday* 6 August 2000; 'She's gotta have it' Jessica Berens *The Observer* 10 Sept. 2000; 'A Woman's Touch' Anna Moore *The Observer* 20 July 2003; also Freely 2000 and McVeigh 2000

2  Catherine MacKinnon cited in 'Raunch culture and the end of feminism' Sarah Baxter *The Sunday Times* 7 May 2006

3  Stuart Jeffries 'Body of Evidence' *Guardian* 30th June 2001.

4  Jessica Berens 'The double life of Catherine M' *Observer* 19th May 2002; Jenny Diski 'Hang on to the Doily' *LRB* 25th July 2002

5  Stuart Wavell 'No love please, I'm a sex maniac.' *Sunday Times* 24/8/2003

6  Stuart Jeffries 'Body of Evidence' *Guardian* 30th June 2001.

7  Cristina Odone 'Why so coy about sex?' *Observer* 11 August 2002

8  *Fifty Shades of Grey; Fifty Shades Darker; Fifty Shades Freed*

9  Celebrating Stephanie Meyers' teen Gothic novels, published between 2005-2008

10  Jen Doll 'The Dirty Book That's Changing the Lives of Upper East Side Moms' *The Atlantic Wire* Feb 28th 2012, cited in Amber Jamilla Musser 'BDSM and the Boundaries of Criticism: Feminism and Neoliberalism in *Fifty Shades of Grey* and *The Story of O' Feminist Theory* 16 (2) 2015; 'EL James: Author, 51' *Sunday Times* March 16th 2014.

11  Soraya Chemaly 'Virgins, Bondage, and a Shameful Media Fail.' *Huffington Post* 20 Apr. 2012, cited Wyngaard 2015; Francesca Hornak: 'Put That filth Away!' *Sunday Times* July 1st 2012

12  SB Sarah 'Fifty Shades of Grey: Why is it so Increasingly Popular?' *Smart Bitches Trashy Books* March 2nd 2012, cited Musser 2015; Lollywillowes quoted in Zoe Williams *Guardian Books Blog* July 14th 2012.

13  Martin Amber 'Fifty Shades of Sex Shop', *Sexualities* 16 (8) 2013 cited in Musser 2015; Heber; Conal Urquart 'Women Flock to Sex Shops' *Observer* July 1st 2012.

14  A V Flox 'The Troubling Message in *Fifty Shades of Grey*', *BlogHer* April 23rd 2012, cited in Musser 2015

15  Fowles SM 'The fantasy of acceptable 'non-consent': Why the female sexual submissive scares us (and why she shouldn't' In: Friedman J and Valenti J (eds) *Yes Means Yes: Visions of Female Sexual Power and a World Without Rape.* Berkeley, CA: Seal Press, 2008, cited in Angelika Tsaros 'Consensual Non-Consent: Comparing EL James' *Fifty Shades of Grey* and Pauline Réage's *Story of O'* *Sexualities* 16 (8), 2013

16  Marcelle d'Argy Smith cited in Margaret Driscoll *ST* 22/4/2012; Nancy Friday was flagging this up in 1973; for Anne Rice, 'A woman has the right to pretend she's being raped by a pirate if that's what she

wants to pretend' cited Maureen Dowd 'She's Fit to be Tied' *New York Times* April 1st 2012

[17] Katie Roiphe reports evidence that around a third of women harbour rape fantasies; cited in Margaret Driscoll 'The Modern Girl's Secret Surrender' *Sunday Times* April 22nd 2012.

[18] Jennifer Hunter concurs: 'The book seems to have resonated with so many women because, after a long day of managing employees, making all the decisions and looking after the children, a woman might be exhausted about being in charge and long to surrender control', cited in Dowd 2012.

[19] Originating perhaps as the title of an article by Carol Hanisch in *Notes from the Second Year: Women's Liberation in 1970*, ed. Shulamith Firestone and Anne Koedt, Radical Feminism, 1970

[20] Roiphe: 'She works crazy hours...' *Newsweek* 30 April 2012

[21] Alison Flood 'Fifty Shades of Grey Condemned as "Manual for Sexual Torture"' *Guardian* August 24th 2012 cited in Musser 2015

[22] Musser 2015: Tsaros 2013 is also aware of the danger of 'consent seepage' in texts that seem to be situated in the 'real' rather than a fantasy world.

[23] 'Women's Refuge Boss Slams 50 Shades' *Yahoo News / Press Association* 23rd August 2012 reports a call for *Fifty Shades* to be burned.

[24] Cited Dowd 2012

[25] Tsaros 2013

[26] Andrew O'Hagan 'Travelling Southwards' *LRB* July 19th 2012

[27] Alex Dymock 'Flogging Sexual Transgression: Interrogating the Costs of the "Fifty Shades Effect"' *Sexualities* 16(8) cited Musser 2015

[28] Cited in Tanya Gold 'He's my Fantasy Guy' *Sunday Times* December 9th 2012

[29] cited in Dowd 2012

[30] Since Rice's own *Interview with the Vampire*, the 'humanising' of Gothic monsters has led to a sanitising of the genre into teen romance, and since the 1990s the sadism and cruelty of Female Gothic has largely migrated into female detective fiction (Kathy Reichs, Tess Gerritsen etc.), with heightened intensity.

[31] David Peltzer's *A Child Called It* 1995 being one of the first.

[32] Directed Steven Shainberg

[33] Wyngaard 2015, 2017

[34] Musser 2015

[35] Tsaros 2013

[36] Ibid 2013

[37] Dana Schuster 'Mamma Mia!' *New York Post* Feb 27th 2012 cited Musser 2015

[38] Emily Eakin 'Grey Area: How 'Fifty Shades' Dominated the Market.' *NYRBLOG* 27 July 2012, cited in Wyngaard 2015

[39] Les Inrocks cited in Kim Willsher *Guardian* 16-17/10/12 'Fifty Shades struggles to excite in France, the home of Sade'

[40] Henry Samuel 'Fifty Shades a hit in France – despite critics' *The*

*Telegraph* 19th October 2012
  41  Isabelle Laffont, cited in Willsher 2012
  42  *Le Monde*, 10 Jan 2018. 'Full Translation of French Anti–#MeToo Manifesto Signed by Catherine Deveuve' – Martin J. Kraft/lameufafrange via Instagram/Worldcrunch; see also 'Catherine Deneuve and Others Denounce the #MeToo Movement' Valerie Safranova *New York Times* 9 Jan 2018
  43  *New York Times* 12 Jan 2018; *Hollywood Reporter* 14 Jan 2018
  44  'Twitter feminism is terrifying moderate voices into silence' Josh Glancy *Sunday Times* 11 Feb 2018; Roiphe 'The Other Whisper Network' *Harper's Magazine* March 2018
  45  Material, quotes and citations in this paragraph are from Priscilla Frank: *A Notorious 1950s Erotic Novella Proves Just as Contentious in 2018* [Huffington Post US  25 Aug 2018]
  46  Of course anti-Semitism is a racism, but is often 'overlooked' as such (which is itself anti-Semitic), as discussed by Frederic Raphael *Anti-Semitism* Biteback 2015 and David Baddiel *Jews Don't Count* TLS 2021. Given that 'anti-Semitism' is an imprecise term, since Arabs are also Semitic, it may be better to refer to anti-Jewish bigotry as 'Judeophobia'. 'Islamophobia' is currently widespread on the right, Judeophobia infects both left and right.
  47  Marilyn Simon: 'My Own Private Château – Pauline Réage's "Story of O" Revisited', *Quillette* Oct 18th 2020
  48  Paulhan 'Preface' 1954, p. xxiv
  49  Sontag 1967 p. 102
  50  Over the last decade Stephen Prince has been running an informative website dedicated to *O*: www.storyofoinfo
  51  Kim Willsher 'Surreal: art's weirdest worldview...' *Guardian* 7 March 2022. London for example has hosted a string of major exhibitions: 'Dreamers Awake' in 2017, of women artists influenced by Surrealism from the 1930s to the present (White Cube Gallery, Bermondsey), retrospectives of Dorothea Tanning and Dora Maar in 2019, and the 2022 'Surrealism Beyond Borders' international exhibition (all at Tate Modern).
  52  Edited by Alyce Mahon and Kathryn Conley
  53  'Surrealism lives on...' letter by John Richardson, *The Guardian* 11 March 2022. See also 'Wales and Surrealism – a Short Survey' (John Welson and John Richardson, in *Abraxas* 2019). Continuing with the U.K. as an example, long-established groups in London, Wales, Birmingham and Leeds have been joined by more recent convocations including Surrealerpool (2017), The Debutante (2020) and La Sirena (2021). Surrealism in Wales set up two of the largest international surrealist exhibition/gathering events in the U.K. in recent years: *Surrealist Murmuration* in Aberystwyth in 2017 and *Once Upon a Tomorrow/ Un Tro Yfory* in Hay-on-Wye in 2023.
  54  www.BlackScatBooks.com

[55] Including Sade, Jarry, Éluard, Baudelaire, Brecht, Alphonse Allais, Duchamp; also Terry Southern, Stanislaw Witkiewicz, Derek Pell, Norman Conquest.

# Appendix I: Paulhan's Testimony to Brigade Mondaine Aug 5. 1955[1]

BRIGADE MONDAINE. HEARING OF M. JEAN PAULHAN.
5 August 1955. We, FRIEDRICH... took a statement from M. PAULHAN Jean, man of letters, residing at 5, rue des Arènes, Paris.

WHO STATES: around three years ago, Mme Pauline Réage (a pseudonym) paid me a visit at the Nouvelle Revue Française where I am director and submitted a thick manuscript titled *Histoire d'O*. I receive eight to ten manuscripts a day, but this one struck me immediately, both by its literary quality, and, if I may say so, for a subject so perfectly risqué, by its restraint and decency.

I had the sense I was in the presence of an important work as much for its form as for its tone, pertaining more to the mystical than the erotic, and that could be to our time what the *Lettres de la Religieuse Portuguaise* or *Les Liaisons Dangereuses* were to theirs. That's what I said to Mme Réage when she came back to see me. I added that I would be willing to talk about this book to Gaston Gallimard, and that if Mme Réage managed to have the book published I would endeavour to write a preface.

Gaston Gallimard, after two years of hesitation, declined the book. M.Defez, director of "Deux Rives" first accepted it but then, in the wake of some political matter where he was implicated (the Despuech affair) asked Mme Réage to take it back.

It is then that I presented it to M. Jean-Jacques Pauvert who accepted it enthusiastically and published it at once. In the meantime I had written the promised preface that was published as introduction to the novel. This preface, that highlights the philosophical and mystical sides of the work, found itself somewhat at odds with the contents of the book. M.Pauvert, in agreement with Mme Réage, having removed from the book the whole of the third part where the heroine is faced with her decline without telling me at the time.

I do not know anything about the print run.

I add that Mme Réage, coming from an academic family she was afraid to scandalise, has always refused until now to reveal her real name. This is the first novel she has written.

Moreover I add that I am not the author of the manuscript, nor have I made any corrections to it. This is obvious if you compare my style to that of Mme Réage.

I do not think that this is a book for everyone, any more than *Les Liaisons Dangereuses* or *Les Lettres d'une Religieuse Portugaise*, however, I believe that, if one reads it carefully, it is clearly not in any manner comparable to a pornographic production. If it presents any danger it is rather by the violence of the passion one finds depicted, and by the endless dreaming it seems to be immersed in.

I have no comments to make either on the material circumstances of its publishing or its distribution.

As I told you, Mme Réage does not want her name to be known. I have promised her as I have done with other authors not to reveal her name.

Nonetheless, given that I have the opportunity to see her regularly, I will inform her of the statement I am making now, and in the event she were to decide to make herself known, I would invite her to get in touch with you.

Signed...

---

[1]  cited in Deforges : 1975, pp. 8-11

# Appendix II: Abbreviations

| | |
|---|---|
| BDSM: | Bondage-Discipline/ Dominance- Submission/ Sado-Masochism |
| CNE: | Comité national des écrivains/ National Committee of Writers |
| CNR: | Conseil national de la Résistance/ National Council of the Resistance |
| LRB: | London Review of Books |
| MLF: | Mouvement de libération des femmes/ Womens' Liberation Movement |
| NRF: | Nouvelle Revue Française |
| OAS: | Organisation armée secrète/ Secret Army Organisation |
| PCF: | Parti communiste française/ French Communist Party |
| RDR: | Rassemblement démocratique révolutionnaire/ Democratic Revolutionary Assembly |
| RPF: | Rassemblement du peuple françaises/ Assembly of the French People |
| THES: | Times Higher Education Supplement |
| TLS: | Times Literary Supplement |

# Index

# About the Author

Reese Saxment is a writer and lecturer in psychology, Romanticism and Gothic, art and literature and Surrealism, was a founder member of Surrealerpool and a regular contributor to *'Patastrophe!*. Married to Kathryn and living in the U.K., they are keen Europeans, and drink (probably too much) French wine, especially Burgundies.

# Colophon

This edition was typeset in Utopia, an Adobe Originals text face designed by Robert Slimbach in 1989. It combines the vertical stress and pronounced stroke contrast of eighteenth-century transitional typefaces like Baskerville and Walbaum with contemporary innovations in character shapes and stroke details.

Headers are set in Didot which takes its inspiration from John Baskerville's experimentation with increasing stroke contrast and a more condensed armature.

<u>Editor's Note</u>: The cover and title page of *Story of O* published by Jean-Jacques Pauvert, Paris, 1975, was set in Baskerville. The type was kerned so tightly that only a "hair space" separates the letters. Was this the style back then, or a subtle reflection of the novel's theme?

www.ingramcontent.com/pod-product-compliance
Lightning Source LLC
Chambersburg PA
CBHW031520150726
47990CB00001B/23